Silent Inheritance

A Novel of Repression, Loss and Survival

JESSICA ZHANG

 Iron Bell Press

Silent Inheritance

A Novel of Repression, Loss, and Survival

Copyright © 2025 Jessica Zhang

Originally published in Chinese as 一粟浮沉 (*The Crimson-Eyed Buddha*) © 2017 Jessica Zhang

English edition translated by **Jessica Zhang**
Edited by **Stacy Mosher**
Illustrated by **Jessica Zhang**

Published by **Iron Bell Press**
ISBN: 979-8-9999124-0-4
Printed in the United States of America

This book is dedicated to my father

My deepest gratitude to Stacy Mosher, whose sharp eye
and wise counsel brought clarity and grace to these pages.

Table of Contents

HongGe 1

(1) THE WEDDING 1

(2) THE BABY 5

(3) NO GOOD DEED GOES UNPUNISHED 9

(4) NANNY WU'S PROMISE 14

(5) BUSY NEW YEAR SEASON 18

(6) THE FIRST HINT OF TROUBLE 22

(7) STRANGERS ARRIVE 26

(8) THE RETURN 30

(9) THE LAST SMILE 34

(10) CHAOS 39

(11) THE PUBLIC TRIAL 43

(12) REVENGE 48

(13) ESCAPE 52

Daffodil 57

(14) A FORTUNATE BRIDE 57

(15) LIFE BY THE GREAT BAIYANG LAKE 61

(16) THE JAPANESE ARRIVE 65

(17) A MAN WITH A FUTURE 68

(18) THE WAIT BEGINS 72

(19) FAMINE 76

(20) A JEEP ARRIVES 80

HongGe 84

    (21) A DISPLACED BOY 84

    (22) END OF CHILDHOOD 89

    (23) THE LONER 93

    (24) THE ZEBRA CLUB 98

    (25) YANRUO 104

    (26) LOVE 108

    (27) A BLOOD LETTER 116

    (28) THE FACTORY 122

    (29) THE DEATH OF NANNY WU 127

Daffodil 131

    (30) THE GIRL WITH AN ACCENT 131

    (31) DAQING COMES OF AGE 136

    (32) A BIG FAMILY 140

    (33) MOTHER AND DAUGHTER 145

    (34) DETERMINED 150

    (35) FACTORY GIRLS 154

    (36) THE MOTHER-IN-LAW 159

    (37) FIVE STEAMED BUNS 166

    (38) THE CURLY HEAD 172

    (39) FIRST KISS 178

    (40) COUSIN TROUBLE 184

    (41) HE IS GONE 190

HongGe and Daffodil 195

    (42) THE DUMPLING DINNER 195

    (43) A GIRL RESEMBLING YANRUO 200

(44) THE CULTURAL REVOLUTION 204

(45) A LETTER DROPS 211

(46) ALCOHOL AND CIGARETTES 217

(47) COUSIN LAN 224

(48) THE MONEY INCIDENT 231

(49) NEW PARENTS 240

(50) MAO'S BOOK 245

(51) GRANDMA'S HOUSE 251

(52) FALSE IMPRISONMENT 257

(53) LILY 263

(54) THE CRIMSON EYED BUDDHA 267

Jasmine 272

(55) GOING HOME 272

(56) A SOLITARY GIRL 279

(57) LIFE IN FOUR CORNERS 284

(58) STARTING SCHOOL 289

(59) MOTHER'S WORDS 294

(60) NEW CONFLICT 299

(61) SHE HAD HER FATHER'S EYES 304

(62) LOST HOPE 309

(63) A NEW ERA FOR FOUR CORNERS 316

(64) THE SIGNATURE INCIDENT 321

(65) SCHOOLMATES 327

(66) YUE 332

(67) SUICIDE 338

(68) GRANDMA GOES TO HEAVEN 344

(69) BOOKS AND OPERA 349

(70) A HANDSOME BOY 354

(71) PUPPY LOVE GONE WRONG 360

(72) REFORM TIME................................ 368

(73) REUNION 373

(74) SEEING YANRUO AGAIN 378

(75) TAKING THE SAFE PATH 384

(76) THE LOST PHOTO 390

(77) LAN AND TIGER 395

(78) BACK AT THE GAO COMPOUND 401

(79) CLOSURE................................ 407

(80) FLY HIGH 412

List of Illustrations

THE LAST SMILE...38

SUMMER PALACE...112

GRANDMA LOTUS AND BABY JASMINE.............256

JASMINE'S DEPARTURE FOR AMERICA.............417

HongGe

(1) THE WEDDING

———————— ✦ ————————

It was a January morning in the late 1930s. Dangerously low temperatures gripped the northeastern plains of China. Wolf-Hair Xu sat on a wooden stool, staring at a stack of elegant stationery on the table before him. He had been summoned by the most prominent family in the area, the Gaos, to create calligraphic wedding invitations and posters for their youngest son, Third Young Master. This prestigious job was far better paying than his usual income from writing letters and notes for illiterate villagers.

But Wolf-Hair Xu was feeling more frustrated than ever. Earlier that morning, he had entered the Gao compound and paid his respects to Mistress Gao, the matriarch of the family. Mistress Gao had courteously asked, "Mr. Xu, would you like some breakfast?" Addressed as "Mister" by the honorable Mistress Gao, Wolf-Hair Xu didn't know how to respond, but something made him stand up and say: "Thank you for your kindness, Mistress Gao. I've had breakfast, so I don't need to trouble you." He couldn't believe those words had actually come out of his mouth, and he wanted to slap himself; the fact was that he'd run out of food and had eaten nothing since noon the day before. "Very well," said Mistress Gao, and she instructed a maid, "Serve tea for now and prepare lunch for Mr. Xu later."

Now, with the sun high in the sky, Wolf-Hair Xu's stomach rumbled. He thought miserably, "What's the point of being pretentious? Torturing my stomach to save face!"

Wolf-Hair Xu's real name was Xu Yingju, which meant "academic success," and he actually came from a family of scholars. His parents had died early, leaving him on his own, and the family's wealth was soon exhausted. As the Qing Dynasty transitioned into rule under Manchuria, the imperial exams to qualify for official positions were abolished, depriving Xu for any hope of improving his prospects. Now he had nothing but a run-down one-room flat and a few pieces of worn-out furniture. He never knew where his next meal was coming from. The only thing left that connected him to his cultured upbringing was a set of exquisite writing brushes made out of a rare kind of wolf hair. This heirloom had been his family's treasured possession for generations. When he walked village streets in his worn-out clothes trying to find a writing job to earn some food, some villagers mistook him for a beggar or a thief and would unleash their dogs to chase him away. He'd wave his precious wolf hair writing-brushes while running and shouting, "I'm a scholar! I write for a living!" He would show off his writing brushes to anyone who was willing to take a look, and he'd proudly declare, "Made out of real wolf hair!" That's how, over time, he came to be known as Wolf-Hair Xu.

The calligraphy table was set up in a servant's common room, where servants busily came and went as they carried out their chores. Every time the door opened, Wolf-Hair Xu raised his eyes in hope that his lunch was arriving. At long last, two maids entered the room, each carrying a wooden tray. Without saying anything, they laid on the table a typical Gao household servant lunch: cornmeal congee, steamed buns, thinly sliced pickled radish topped with sesame oil and sesame seeds, and a big bowl of pork with pickled cabbage. Wolf-Hair Xu hadn't seen decent food for a long time, and his hands trembled so much that he could hardly hold the chopsticks. Forgetting the dark ink on his hands, as well as his manners, he grabbed a bun, buried his face in the pork bowl and ate until the veins on his forehead bulged.

In the main dining hall, the Gao women were having lunch as well. Mistress Gao was joined by her two daughters-in-law, First Madam and Second Madam. Mistress Gao asked, "Have the phoenix and the dragon been carved on the wedding bed frame yet?" First Madam replied respectfully as a daughter-in-law should, "Yes, Mother, the dragon and phoenix wedding bed is done, and I believe it's the most magnificent bed in the entire Northeast! The paint is the modern kind from overseas – so shiny! I've made sure that all the other wedding furniture has been done well too." Second Madam also chimed in: "Mother, don't worry. I've also ordered a complete repainting of our Gao compound. We're well prepared for Third Brother's wedding!"

Mistress Gao nodded: "Very well. Although things can't compare to when the Elder Master was alive, our family still has status, and our weddings must be the best of all. When my father-in-law, the Elder Master Gao was alive, he always said the Emperor coming to establish Manchuria would bring prosperity to us in our dear Northeast. Those Japanese have ruined everything. Our good life is no more!" The two Madams simpered, "But look, now it's the New Year and our Third Brother is getting married; what could be better than this! We hear that our future Third Madam is well cultured; she'll bring happiness to our family for sure. Mother, your only concern is how to best enjoy such a blessed life!" Mistress Gao said with a smile: "I have to deal with tailors, carpenters, workers and cooks. Even the rouge flowers worn by the maids have to be chosen by me. The blessing brought by the Crimson Eyed Buddha can be enjoyed by you younger folks."

The Crimson Eyed Buddha was worshiped by many throughout the Northeast. People believed that the Bodhisattva had 33 transformations, one of which was called Yuanguang Buddha. The Yuanguang Buddha first appeared in southern China and also underwent several transformations. The Crimson Eyed Buddha was believed to originate from Yuanguang and had been residing in Northeastern China for centuries. This buddha had blazing crimson eyes, and any place touched by his holy gaze would enjoy abundance, prosperity, justice and new life. The Gao family had worshiped the Crimson Eyed Buddha for many generations. Elder Master Gao once met a jade craftsman who produced an amazing carving of the Crimson Eyed Buddha using an exquisite piece of translucent light green jade. The statuette was the size of a palm and had two bright crimson dots for eyes. Elder Master Gao spent half of his fortune to acquire this rare treasure as his family's heirloom for generations to come. The Gao family's Crimson Eyed Buddha had become a legend. Nobody outside of the Gao family had seen it. Some said it was so big that it took up half a room. Others said it was as small as a child's pinky. Some even said it could change its size at will. The mystery grew and brought the Gao family more widespread awe and respect.

In late January, the third son of the Gao family married Third Madam Meidi in the Gao compound amidst magnificent music and celebrations. Meidi was tall and pretty with fair, delicate skin, large, deep-set eyes and long eyelashes. The chief butler said, "She looks like a girl from a foreigner's family." The chief butler's wife took her pipe out of her mouth: "No matter where she comes from, look at her face and see how long her earlobes are! That's a sign of good fortune!"

Third Madam Li Meidi was from a family of high-level imperial officials. Meidi's grandfather had married a woman from Siberia, so their family had bloodlines from the far north. The name "Meidi" was given to her by her grandfather. It originated from a poem by Liu Yuxi that praised the beauty of the northern plains. Although Meidi grew up in a privileged household and received a superior education, the sad reality was that the Qing Dynasty had ended. Her grandfather and her father had both passed away, and the family had to live off of their inheritance, with no new source of income. When a matchmaker came to the Li residence to introduce the Third Young Master of the Gao family, Meidi's mother was favorably impressed, especially given that the family was graced with the Crimson Eyed Buddha. Observing that the Gao's Third Young Master was kind, handsome and talented, she agreed to give him Meidi's hand in marriage.

Third Madam Meidi deported herself with calmness and modesty in the Gao compound. She paid her respects to Master Gao and Mistress Gao daily as a dutiful daughter-in-law should, and she accompanied her husband, Third Young Master, whenever he was home. When her husband was away, she would spend time with her two sisters-in-law, First Madam and Second Madam. She soon became Mistress Gao's favorite daughter-in-law. The more Mistress Gao looked at Meidi, the more she believed that Meidi had the look of good fortune. The only disappointment for Mistress Gao was that after nearly a year, Meidi was still flat-bellied, with no sign of bearing a son for Third Young Master.

(2) THE BABY

The Gao family's more than 2,000 acres of farmland were rented out to local peasants. In the spring, soybeans, wheat and rice were planted, with the wheat harvested in the summer and soybeans and rice in the fall. Crop processing and rent collection continued all the way until December. Only after sending away the short-term laborers and settling all the accounts could the entire household, from Master Gao and Mistress Gao to the servants, enjoy some rest.

Snowflakes as big as cotton balls had been falling the entire night. The sun finally emerged in the morning, glimmering on the icicles that hung from the roofs. The servants had cleared the walkways in the main courtyard where Master Gao and Mistress Gao lived. Stirring the charcoal in her antique hand-warmer, Mistress Gao looked up and told a maid to invite her three daughters-in-law to come over and play cards. After a while, First Madam and Second Madam both entered the main courtyard and made their way to the front hall. A maid came in and announced, "Third Madam says she's feeling unwell this morning. She skipped breakfast. She's very tired and has a headache. She sends her apologies for not being able to join you."

First Madam said, "The poor woman! Coming from a scholar's family, she's never had to worry about complicated chores like collecting rent and paying workers. She must feel overwhelmed." Mistress Gao called in the chief butler: "Quickly get Dr. Ge to come and see Third Madam!"

Dr. Ge was the chief doctor of Ciji House, a well-respected clinic and pharmacy of traditional Chinese medicine. He always saw patients at Ciji House and rarely made house calls, but when the Gao family palanquin stopped in front of his clinic, he climbed in without hesitation. As the palanquin approached the gate of the Gao compound, one of the bearers tripped on a pile of snow and fell, sending the palanquin toppling to the ground. Everyone yelled: "Dr.

Ge! Dr. Ge! Are you all right? Are you hurt?" Dr. Ge said: "I'm fine. In any case, we're here now and I'll walk the rest of the way."

Just then, that pile of snow moved and a man emerged from it. Everyone was startled and cried out, "Who is that?" The man in the snow pile said with a trembling voice, "Please be kind enough to give me some food." With that he collapsed in the snow again. Dr. Ge rushed over and took his pulse, then told the palanquin bearers, "Bring him in!" The servants carried the man into the doorman's room and brought him some water. Finally he regained consciousness, and his eyes began to focus. The servants turned to Dr. Ge and said, "Doctor, please don't worry. We'll give him food. The Gao family is the most charitable around. We never send anyone away hungry. Please go to the third courtyard. Our Third Madam is feeling unwell!" Hearing this, the man from the snow pile raised his head and said, "Third Madam must be so kind! Third Madam must have good fortune and good health! Third Madam must have lots of sons and a happy life!" Everyone laughed: "He really knows how to take the hint to please people!"

A servant took Dr. Ge to the third courtyard while another servant brought a big bowl of cornmeal congee to the beggar. Like a hungry wolf pouncing on a lamb, the beggar grabbed the bowl and inhaled almost half of the congee instantly. A servant said, "We'll give you another bowl of congee and two buns. Then you can be on your way." The beggar bowed deeply with gratitude.

While the beggar was burying his face in his second bowl of congee, an older maid entered the doorman's room with a pack of cold sliced pork. She said to the beggar with a big smile, "Today is truly a good day. Third Madam isn't sick, she's pregnant! Dr. Ge said you brought good luck with your kind words, so Third Madam wants to give you this meat. You can enjoy it and then be on your way. Remember our Third Madam's grace!"

The beggar had not seen meat in a long time, and he knelt and kowtowed: "I sincerely thank Third Madam! I wish Third Madam and her baby well! Please let Third Madam know my name is Zhao'er. I would like to pay my respects to Third Madam and kowtow to her in person!" The maid didn't think that was a good idea. "There's no need for that. Third Madam's health is very delicate. She cannot see guests." But Zhao'er kept pleading, and other servants also said, "Please grant his wish; maybe he can just kowtow on the veranda." The maid finally said: "All right, just on the veranda. But you mustn't go inside!"

In the third courtyard's guest hall, Third Young Master had ordered the maids to serve tea and pastries for Dr. Ge. He had also ordered the servants to go to the main courtyard to announce the good news to Master Gao and Mistress Gao. Third Madam Meidi was propped up on a day bed surrounded by maids in the master bedchamber. The maids ensured that she was comfortable with embroidered large pillows behind her back and a fluffy blanket lined with embroidered silk covering her lap.

Zhao'er's voice came from the veranda through the window: "Congratulations to Third Young Master and Third Madam! You are so kind, you saved my life! Zhao'er hopes for a chance to work like a horse to serve Third Young Master and Third Madam!"

Third Young Master frowned: "Who let a beggar into my courtyard? He's so loud and disturbing! Give him some food and send him on his way!"

Not wishing to overstep his boundaries, Dr. Ge courteously said, "It's kind of him to express his good wishes on a happy day like this."

A maid entered the guest hall and said, "Excuse me, Third Young Master, Third Madam sent me to say that she thinks this beggar Zhao'er brings good luck. She wonders if he can stay here as a servant. Even if we can't keep him, Third Madam would like him to have lunch in the servants' courtyard and then be on his way when the sun is high in the afternoon."

Third Young Master's face softened: "If that's what Third Madam wants, let him stay."

Meidi then asked Dr. Ge to examine Zhao'er: "He must have frostbite. Please treat him as mercifully as you do all of your patients." Dr. Ge gladly obliged.

The following June, the rolling fields were filled with wheat ready for harvest. One of the most diligent and capable of the field laborers was Zhao'er. Restored to his health in the Gao compound, and his frostbite healed, he was a new person. Beggars came to the Gao compound every day and could not possibly all be taken in; Zhao'er was a lucky one.

During the harvest season, Third Madam Meidi gave birth to a bouncing little boy. The entire Gao household held a formal ceremony to offer thanksgiving to the Crimson Eyed Buddha. In celebration, the Gao compound lit nine rolls of firecrackers representing longevity, and distributed food to the masses for ten days in honor of their new grandson. The compound was piled high with gifts from the villagers: longevity locks, embroidered pouches, baby clothes and good luck charms. Master Gao named the baby himself. As the baby was of Gao family's "Peng" generation, Master Gao named him Gao Penghong. Everyone in the Gao compound called him HongGe, "Ge" being an affectionate way of saying "little boy" or "brother."

(3) NO GOOD DEED GOES UNPUNISHED

—————— ★ ——————

As a little Master in such a prominent household, it was customary in that day and age for HongGe to have a wet nurse, called naima or "milk mother" in Chinese. After all, a woman of Third Madam Meidi's status should not have to endure the cumbersome chore of nursing a baby. Quite a few prospective wet nurses were presented to Meidi, but she rejected them all. She didn't like any wet nurse who was too thin, for fear that the woman would have too little milk to feed her baby or too little strength to hold him. She wanted someone sturdy and strong but with a kind and soft heart. Meidi's due date was imminent, but she had not yet found a satisfactory wet nurse for her baby.

Finally, the chief butler brought in a woman named Wu. Wu had given birth to a boy named Song Zi who had unfortunately died when he was only four days old. The village doctor said that Wu's health was too poor for her to have any more babies, which triggered a crisis at home. Wu's mother-in-law insisted that Wu was a dark witch sent by the forces of evil to destroy the family. She insisted that Wu had caused her baby's death and was now determined to deprive the family of further offspring. At that time, a mother-in-law had absolute authority, and could drive her daughter-in-law out of the house if she found her unsatisfactory. Her son had to obey her and was unable to stand up for his young wife. The mother-in-law had driven Wu out, leaving her homeless and destitute.

Wu came to the Gao compound just as Third Madam Meidi's water broke. Meidi's forehead was beaded with sweat, and maids and midwives were running around in a flurry, but Meidi said through clenched teeth, "Bring her in." Wu entered the room and kowtowed: "Third Madam!" Mysteriously, Meidi felt a wave of calmness and relief as soon as she set eyes on Wu, as if a huge weight was lifted from her shoulders. She knew that Wu would be her baby's wet nurse even without asking her a single question. "Show Nanny Wu to her room!" Meidi ordered a maid. "Tell the kitchen to serve her the most nutritious food but with as little salt as possible, so she can produce more milk. Call in the tailors to make clothes of all seasons for Nanny Wu."

HongGe was a loud baby whose bellows rang throughout the third courtyard. While desperate for sleep, Third Young Master happily said, "Just listen to that volume! This is really my son. He sounds like someone who will do great things!"

HongGe's good looks were more evident when he wasn't crying. Everyone loved his cute little face. He had a handsome little forehead, large eyes and thick eyebrows for a baby, and he had his mother Meidi's beautiful skin. Nanny Wu held HongGe in her arms almost all the time: "You look so much like my Song Zi!" she would murmur when no one was around. While nursing HongGe, she would gently stroke his soft hair and say, "My Song Zi! Mama's Song Zi!" Often she wept.

One morning, Nanny Wu was sitting on the porch holding HongGe when he rubbed his face in her breast and kicked her with his little feet. Nanny Wu laughed, "Is my Song Zi hungry again so soon?" Before the words were out of her mouth, she turned pale with fear: "How could I be so stupid, calling the little master Song Zi in broad daylight?" She nervously glanced around to see if anyone had heard her. A maid happened to be right outside the porch, and she asked, "Who's Song Zi? Why are you calling the little master Song Zi?" Nanny Wu lowered her head: "Song Zi was my son. I called the little master Song Zi by mistake." The maid asked, "Who's feeding your son back home?" Nanny Wu lowered her voice and replied, "My son was unfortunate. He passed away when he was four days old." The maid turned and went into the house.

Now Nanny Wu was really worried – what if the maid told Third Madam? Calling the little master by the name of a dead baby was a serious offense, and she could be in a lot of trouble if not losing her position as wet nurse all together! Nanny Wu was sick with worry when she was summoned by Third Madam. Holding HongGe tightly, she lowered her head as she entered Third Madam's chamber. Third Madam said, "Nanny Wu, please have a seat."

Servants were not supposed to sit in the presence of the masters and madams, so Nanny Wu didn't dare really sit down, and her bottom barely touched the edge of the chair that a maid set out for her. Third Madam said: "I heard about your son. I'm so sorry for your loss. As a mother you must be devastated. HongGe must be the same age as your son. Please take good care of HongGe and feed him well. I'm sure he'll treat you like his own mother when he grows up. Servants aren't allowed to carry out mourning ceremonies in this compound, but I'll have a maid take you out to burn paper money for your son so that he is provided for in the next life. On the first of the month, I'll send you to the temple with some money for a large oil lamp and some incense to burn in the name of your son, to wish him happiness in his next life."

Nanny Wu knelt down in tears: "Third Madam! You're so kind. My son and I will always remember Third Madam's kindness and mercy! Please be assured I will feed, protect and serve little master HongGe with my life. He is my life!"

Third Madam smiled: "Please get up. I knew there was a special bond between you and HongGe the very first time I saw you."

As they were talking, a maid came in and said, "Third Madam, Mr. Xu is here to borrow money. Mistress is feeling unwell today and doesn't want to receive guests. Mistress wishes for Third Madam to take care of it." Meidi straightened her jacket: "I will see him in the guest hall."

Mr. Xu was none other than Wolf-Hair Xu, who had been hired to do calligraphy for Third Young Master and Third Madam's wedding. In recent years he had become destitute from chronic gambling, and had lost his sole possession – his one-room house. He had come to the Gaos to borrow money to build a straw hut to live in, but when winter came, Mistress Gao had bought back his one-room house and given it to him so that he wouldn't perish in the cold. Wolf-Hair Xu had long given up telling people that he was a scholar, and his wolf-hair writing brushes were nowhere to be seen. All he cared about now was gambling, and he kept coming to the Gao household to borrow money. Master Gao and his three sons left all financial matters to Mistress Gao and the three young Madams and didn't concern themselves with things like small loans of money, so they didn't receive Wolf-Hair Xu. Now Mistress Gao was avoiding him, and First and Second Madams wanted nothing to do with him. That left the new young Madam, Meidi.

As Meidi entered the guest hall of the third courtyard, Wolf-Hair Xu shuffled over in his ragged shoes with his big toes showing, and bowed to Meidi: "Good day, Third Madam! You're famous for your goodness, and now your goodness has been rewarded with a son. Congratulations!" Meidi responded: "Please have a seat, Mr. Xu. Thank you for your kind words. How can I help you?"

Wolf-Hair Xu had barely touched the chair when he leaped to his feet: "The Gao household is graced by the Crimson Eyed Buddha and has been my savior. Now I've learned that Third Madam has a son, and Master Gao and Mistress Gao both think so highly of you that they put you in charge of everything. I'm so happy for Third Madam. I'm here to express my congratulations! I was the one who wrote the calligraphy for Third Madam's wedding. Now I hear that Mistress Gao has made Third Madam the decision-maker of the house, so I'm here to pay my respects."

Meidi quietly heard out his nonsense, then sipped her tea and said again, "What can I do for you?" Wolf-Hair Xu hesitated and finally said, "It's getting colder, so I need to borrow money to buy food and firewood and prepare for the winter."

Before he could finish his sentence, Meidi rapped her tea saucer on the table, and Wolf-Hair Xu immediately shut his mouth. Meidi waited for a moment, then said, "Mr. Xu, you know our family has always helped you. But there's an old saying that 'Money can save an emergency but can't solve poverty.' If you don't plug that draining hole of yours, nothing that we give you will make any difference." Wolf-Hair Xu bowed: "The Gao family is famous for their kindness. I know you won't leave me to die."

"I have an idea," Meidi said. "I'll send you home with some food and firewood, ten days' worth at a time, for a total of five times. In those fifty days, you'll resume your writing business. I'll buy you a set of new clothes, writing brushes, ink, paper, a table and a bench. You won't have to pay me back for any of those things, and you'll go back to writing for a living. What do you think?"

Believing he'd gotten his way, Wolf-Hair Xu happily responded, "Third Madam is a Buddha! How can I trouble you so much? It's enough for you to give me the money for everything you just said."

Meidi said, "Please excuse my stubbornness, but I shouldn't give you money. If you agree with my idea, I'll tell the chief butler to give you what I said. If not, I suggest you seek help elsewhere."

Wolf-Hair Xu had no choice but to follow the chief butler and get ten days' worth of food and firewood. The chief butler wanted to send a servant with him to buy writing supplies. Wolf-Hair Xu begged the chief butler again and again to give the money directly to him, but the chief butler refused. Wolf-Hair Xu left the Gao compound full of rage and hatred towards Third Madam and the chief butler: "I swear that one day I'll have the Gao family kneeling in front of me and begging for their lives!"

(4) NANNY WU'S PROMISE

It was another harvest season. The entire Gao household was bustling with chores and business, but the third courtyard was very quiet. Third Madam Meidi had been suffering from severe coughs ever since spring, and she was listless and bedridden. Mistress Gao and Third Young Master both thought Meidi was pregnant again, but Dr. Ge said she was not, and he prescribed medicine to clear her lungs and reduce her cough. But Meidi's cough worsened in April. Her windows and doors had to be tightly closed, as any air coming in from outside would induce terrible coughing spells. In May, Meidi started to cough up blood, and no amount of ginseng or other medicine brought any improvement to her health. The Third Young master led everyone in the third courtyard in praying to the Crimson Eyed Buddha for many days. Now it was June. Meidi's beautiful face was thin and wan, and her eyes were sunken and had lost their shine. Meidi felt her weak body floating in air, as light as a feather. When a gentle wind blew in one direction, she could see her late father; when it blew in another direction, she could see HongGe and Nanny Wu. When she woke up, she knew her time was near.

Third Young Master sat by the bed with his head hanging low and his lips clenched tight as if holding back sobs. He said: "Bring HongGe here! " Nanny Wu hurried to fetch HongGe. He had just learned how to say "Ma," and he climbed onto his mother's bed and called out, "Ma! Ma!" Meidi's tears streamed down her face as she slowly placed HongGe's hand into Third Young Master's large hands. She focused her tearful gaze on her husband and tried in vain to speak. Third Young Master sobbed and said, "Don't worry! Don't worry! Leave HongGe to me! Don't worry!"

Meidi turned her gaze to Nanny Wu and raised her weak hand to point to HongGe. Nanny Wu burst out crying: "Third Madam! I know what you're trying to say! HongGe is my 'milk son'. You want me to take care of HongGe. Please don't worry. I will devote my life to HongGe!"

Meidi's funeral was lavish. According to the Gao family traditions, funerals for Gao women who had given birth to sons should be of a certain caliber. On top of that, Meidi was Mistress Gao's favorite daughter-in-law, and Third Young Master loved her dearly, so Meidi's funeral rites far exceeded the ancestral traditions.

After the funeral, Mistress Gao told her two remaining daughters-in-law: "This is not an auspicious year. Your third brother's wife is gone. Bad luck has afflicted our family ever since the late Elder Master passed away. We should consult a fortune teller and a Feng Shui master. Your Master and I are both getting old. At last we lived to see our three sons all married and all with sons of their own. We felt we could finally face our ancestors after we died, but now we've lost a daughter-in-law and must start looking again. Let's take advice from the wisemen."

Mistress Gao burnt incense in front of the Crimson Eyed Buddha. The best fortune teller and Feng Shui master were asked to the Gao compound. Both of them said that the Gao family was guarded by powerful spirits and should have superb fortunes because they had always been charitable and kind. The only thing they said was that no one in the Gao household was born in the year of the dog. They said that since the Third Young Master was born in the year of the horse, he should marry someone born in the year of the dog.

As the fortune teller and Feng Shui master left, Mistress Gao realized there was a problem. A girl born in the year of the dog would now be twenty years old. Since Third Young Master was now twenty-four, that would be a good match in age, but it was customary for country girls to marry at the age of sixteen or seventeen. Girls almost never married beyond the age of eighteen. Where would she find a twenty-year-old unmarried girl to become the new wife of her third son?

The news spread fast that the Gao family was looking for a new Third Madam and that she had to be born in the year of the dog. Many people talked about it, but no matchmakers came forward. The honorable Third Young Master of the Gao family would normally have many girls to choose from, but the age restriction made it hard to find a match, not only in the nearby villages but also in the surrounding towns.

One crisp autumn morning, Mistress Gao was having tea with her two daughters-in-law when a maid entered the room and said, "Mistress, First Madam, Second Madam, Wolf-Hair Xu is here and wishes to see our Mistress." First Madam sneered, "Coming to us for gambling money again?" Second Madam said, "Or asking for winter money again. He's really a parasite." Mistress said, "Tell him I'm not receiving guests today." The maid disappeared but soon returned: "Mistress, Wolf-Hair Xu says he's here to introduce a girl for Third Young Master, a girl born in the year of the dog."

The late Third Madam Meidi had given Wolf-Hair Xu food and firewood in the hope that he would stop gambling and get back on his feet. But Wolf-Hair Xu sold the all the supplies and continued with his gambling. Just as he'd lost everything and was on the verge of starvation, two people came to his house: his uncle and the uncle's daughter, his cousin Xiulian. The uncle's village had been destroyed by the Japanese and they were forced to flee. Luckily Uncle Xu had some money, and he rented a two-room house next to Wolf-Hair Xu and lived there with his daughter.

Unfortunately, Uncle Xu soon died, leaving Cousin Xiulian on her own. Wolf-Hair Xu robbed Cousin Xiulian of the remaining money in the name of "funeral costs," leaving her destitute. Her sole good fortune was that her father had paid the rent until the end of the year, so at least she had shelter for a few more months. Dr. Ge hired her to work for food as a cook in Ciji House, but she had no idea where her rent was going to come from and where she'd be able to live in the coming year. Wolf-Hair Xu was planning to sell Cousin Xiulian to one of the brothels in town, but his attitude toward her completely changed when he heard that the Gao family was looking for a new Third Madam born in the year of the dog.

"Good day Mistress, Good day Madams!" Wolf-Hair Xu put on his best smile as Mistress Gao offered him a seat and ordered a maid to serve him tea. Wolf-Hair Xu went straight to the point: "I know a family like ours is no match for the Gao family, and we would never presume to marry one of our girls to the honorable Third Young Master. But my cousin was born in the year of the dog, so according to the fortune teller, she'd be a blessing to her husband. My uncle was an educated man from a good family, and if not for the damned

Japanese, they'd have had a really comfortable life. My cousin is beautiful with lots of wisdom and skills. All the villagers admire her! She even has a red birthmark on her right eyelid. That's a sign of blessing from the Crimson Eyed Buddha!"

Mistress Gao's face showed no emotion, and determined to follow their mother-in-law's lead, First Madam and Second Madam also remained silent. After a long while, Mistress Gao said, "This is no small matter. We need to ask Master Gao. We women cannot make such a major decision without asking Master Gao. Then we will give you an answer." Wolf-Hair Xu could tell by the look on Mistress's face that she was not at all interested, and he made a desperate last attempt: "Mistress! I know our family is far beneath the Third Young Master of the Gao family. But Third Young Master needs someone from the year of the dog. What if my cousin could become Third Young Master's concubine?"

It was common back then for rich men to have concubines. A man would marry a wife with high social status, and then take concubines from among society's lower strata. Those girls would become servants for the man's wife while providing for his sexual pleasure. The concubines had no social status, and their children were little more than servants, with very limited rights in the family. Wolf-Hair Xu continued: "Then you can find a Third Madam from a nice family. Once you've solved the problem of finding a girl from the year of the dog, you can look for any girl you want as Third Madam!" Mistress Gao became thoughtful.

But when Master Gao heard of this, he immediately shook his head: "No! We shouldn't take even a concubine from Wolf-Hair Xu's family. Besides, the red birthmark on her eyelid is in conflict with the Crimson Eyed Buddha. Having the traits of the Buddha on one's face is not a good sign." Third Young Master also firmly rejected this idea: "Concubines are a thing of the past. People rarely have concubines nowadays, and taking someone from Wolf-Hair Xu's family will shorten my life!"

At the end of December, Cousin Xiulian faced starvation and homelessness. When the landlord took back the house, she had no place to go, so Wolf-Hair Xu kidnapped her and sold her to a broker for the town brothel.

(5) BUSY NEW YEAR SEASON

A family like the Gaos paid hefty sums to matchmakers, who worked extra hard in return. In January, a matchmaker found a young girl from a few towns over named Guan Lingzhi, who was born in the year of the dog. She had been in mourning for three years after her mother died, so she was still unmarried at the age of twenty. The Guans were the family of a prominent military general from the Qing Eight Flags Royal Army, and their offspring were all trained in Kung Fu and sword fighting, including their youngest daughter, Lingzhi. Master Gao, Mistress Gao and Third Young Master had all seen Lingzhi's photo. She was beautiful and slender, and they all liked her very much. Lingzhi and Third Young Master's astrological charts also matched perfectly. The two families were overjoyed. In March, a grand wedding celebration took place, and the new Third Madam Lingzhi entered the Gao compound.

HongGe was now four years old. He spent all his time with Nanny Wu and was as attached to her as if she were his real mother. He had only vague memories of his birth mother Meidi. Now when he met his stepmother Lingzhi, he was very curious about her and immediately started to play with her. Lingzhi said to Nanny Wu, "Poor HongGe, losing his mother at such a tender age. Please bring him to my room often and I will play with him." Nanny Wu bowed and said, "Third Madam is so kind to HongGe. You are now his mother!" She turned to HongGe and said, "You must always respect and love Third Madam!" HongGe said, "HongGe loves Third Madam." Lingzhi giggled, "Silly boy, you should call me Mother, not Third Madam."

The new Third Madam brought joy and laughter to the Gao compound. She was the center of jokes and tricks when playing cards with Mistress and the two other Madams. She gathered the children from the three courtyards to play hide-and-seek and to teach them Kung Fu. When the children saw her, they all called out, "Third Auntie, Third Auntie," and HongGe in his confusion called her Third

Auntie too. Lingzhi patted him on the head: "You should call me Mother, not Third Auntie." Even the usually serious Third Young Master now walked around the compound humming happy tunes. Mistress gave a sigh of relief: "It really was a good choice to have a daughter-in-law from the year of the dog! Now my only wish is for a new grandson."

Another busy New Year season arrived. As Mistress Gao advanced in age, she gradually withdrew from the family business, leaving everything to her three daughters-in-law. First Madam was responsible for running the Gao household's New Year festivities and the grand ceremonies for paying respects to the Gao ancestors. Second Madam was responsible for distributing salaries and bonuses to all the laborers and servants, directing the tailors in making new clothes for everyone, and running the food center that distributed supplies to the villagers at the New Year. Third Madam Lingzhi was responsible for collecting the annual rent from the hundreds of tenants on the family's land, and for ensuring that all payments, whether in money or goods, were inventoried, stored and recorded.

This year's rent collection was Lingzhi's first public appearance as a new Madam of the Gao family. She sat in the Gao compound's main hall with a delicate tea cup in her hands, two maids standing behind her, and the chief butler sitting to one side with the tenant book open, ready to record the payments. Servant Zhao'er, who had been saved by the late Third Madam Meidi, led a few other servants who stood at the ready to carry goods in and out. Lingzhi asked, "How many tenants are here today?" The chief butler stood up and replied, "Third Madam, today there are nine farmland tenants and five mountain tenants." Lingzhi nodded: "The mountain tenants came from far away and have a long journey home, so let's call them in first."

The Gao family had not only two thousand acres of farmland rented out to many farmers, but also many forested mountains that they rented to hunters and foragers. One of the foragers, nicknamed Li Ginseng, was regarded as a god in the local ginseng industry. Leading a team of ginseng foragers, he was able to find the most valuable wild ginseng that had been maturing underground for decades. It was as if the ginseng roots all knew him and called out to him from their hiding places. Li Ginseng had once been homeless and a troublemaker in the village, with oozing frostbitten skin and wild, menacing eyes. He stole people's chicken, fought people's dogs and squatted in the village temple, where he scared the women and children. Master Gao finally had enough of his mischief and summoned him to the Gao compound to work as a servant. But Li wasn't meant for life in a compound. He ignored the Gao family's rules and fought with everyone he encountered. He was strong and fearless, and no one could control his behavior except Master Gao.

One day Master Gao summoned him and said, "It looks like being confined to a compound doesn't suit you. How about this? I have a mountain up north with nobody living on it. It's a wilderness full of animals and woodland treasures. If you want, I can rent it to you, and I'll waive your rent for three years to get you started. After three years, you'll pay rent just like the other mountain tenants. Would you like that?" Li Ginseng had always dreamed of mountain life and gladly agreed. Three years later, he brought Master Gao a gigantic hundred-year-old ginseng root that was worth far more than its weight in gold.

Now Li Ginseng was a forty-year-old mountain man. He and his eldest son walked into the main hall and bowed down: "Third Madam! Chief Butler!" The chief butler had been beaten up by Li Ginseng many years ago, and the experience remained fresh in his memory, so he responded to Li Ginseng's greeting with an awkward clearing of his throat. Li Ginseng offered an impressive piece of ginseng: "Third Madam, a dozen brothers worked tirelessly for three days to dig this ginseng out of the ground in one piece. This is for Master Gao!" He then produced a gleaming otter fur: "This is for Mistress Gao!" These were two items of great value, and on top of that, he'd brought four deer, four boars and six fox furs. The chief butler converted everything to money based on the market price. It was more than enough to cover Li Ginsengs yearly rent for the mountain.

HongGe ran into the hall, and when he saw the otter fur, he asked, "Mother, what's that?" Lingzhi smiled: "This is an otter fur. It's for Mistress." HongGe said, "I want this otter fur. I will go ask Nana for it!" Everyone laughed. Li Ginseng said, "This little master has a good eye. Otter furs can only be used by people who have a special connection with the hunter. If Mistress gives this to the little master, it means that he and I will have an eternal bond!"

Once all five mountain tenants had paid their rent, Lingzhi ordered the chief butler to record what had been received and then directed Zhao'er and his team to store the animals, furs, ginseng and other mountain products. She asked for a deer to be sent to the kitchen, and for the best cut of venison to be served to Master and Mistress Gao for lunch; the rest should be served to everyone else at dinner. All these chores made the morning seem to pass in an instant. The maids accompanied Lingzhi to an inner room, where they massaged her shoulders, brought her fresh tea and served her lunch. While Lingzhi was eating, HongGe ran into the room: "Mother! Nana gave the otter fur to me so I can have a new fur jacket made!" Lingzhi smiled, "What a lucky boy. You should have a wonderful New Year!"

(6) THE FIRST HINT OF TROUBLE

The farmland tenants were called in after lunch. Although it was Lingzhi's first time as rent collector, things were going smoothly with the help of the chief butler and Zhao'er's team of servants. As money, grain and other goods streamed in, Lingzhi told the servants: "Don't be too strict on the peasants. They've worked hard all year long. It's all right if they're a little short in their payments." Everyone received a gift basket upon paying their rent, a token of appreciation and good wishes for the New Year from their landlord.

After a dozen days of busy work, at long last, only two tenants had yet to pay their rent: Widow Liu and Qiu Erguo. Widow Liu stepped into the hall and kowtowed to Lingzhi: "Third Madam, have mercy! Allow us a few more days to pay, please! My husband passed away in the spring, leaving only me and my young son, who is also unwell. The land has been taken over by weeds. We're really desperate!" Lingzhi stood up, walked over to Widow Liu and raised her from her knees: "Mrs. Liu, please have a seat." Returning to her own seat, Lingzhi said: "I'm new here and haven't yet met all the folks in the village, so I just heard about your family's loss. I'm truly sorry. Let me ask Mistress and I'm sure she will find it acceptable to waive your rent for this year." Lingzhi motioned for a maid to go ask Mistress Gao. The maid came back in a little while and said, "Mistress says she'll accept whatever Third Madam decides. She thinks it is reasonable to waive Widow Liu's rent, and suggests also giving them some money to help them through the coming winter." Lingzhi praised Mistress Gao's mercy and said, "As Mistress wishes, I will waive your rent for this year. Next year, see if your son is healthy enough to work in the fields and then pay what you can. It doesn't have to be the full rent. The year after that, your son will be an adult, and he can decide if he wants to continue renting our land. If he doesn't want to rent it anymore, I can take him in as a servant in the Gao compound, and he will earn a servant's salary." Then Lingzi turned to the chief butler and said, "Make sure Mrs. Liu goes home with enough money to last her and her son until springtime." Overwhelmed, Widow Liu kept kowtowing and murmuring her gratitude.

The last tenant, Qiu Erguo, was a notoriously dishonest and lazy man. Any land he got his hands on became low-yield land within a short period of time, and he came up with countless excuses for every rent collection season. This time, he pretended to be ill and sent his wife to the Gao compound to see Third Madam in his place. When she entered the hall, Qiu's wife didn't bow to Lingzhi but only murmured, "Third Madam." This was the first time Lingzhi had met Qiu's wife, and she was repelled by her disrespectful manner and gaudy attire, but she politely said, "Please have a seat."

Qiu's wife plopped down on a chair and started complaining: "Our family is so poor, we don't even know where our next meal is coming from. We can't compare to your family – such fortune and fame! I hear your jade Crimson Eyed Buddha statue takes up half a room! How valuable it must be! My Goodness! And just look at how lavish your wedding was. Tsk, tsk..... You're not even the first wife of Third Young Master, but the wedding was still so grand!"

Lingzhi frowned: "What are you saying?"

Qiu's wife blurted out, "Please waive our rent too. Our fields were bare this year. The land you rent to us is no good. It produces very little, no matter how hard we work."

Before Lingzhi could reply, the chief butler felt compelled to respond:" Mrs. Qiu, you have to speak factually and with a good conscience. How can you say that land is not good? The tenant before you paid full rent every year and still had enough to live comfortably. When you moved here, you begged us to rent out a piece of land to you. You said you were new at farming so you needed rich soil, and you picked this plot of land yourself. You've never paid full rent on it. Even good land becomes baren in your hands. But you have the nerve to ask for a waiver and claim that the land is not good?"

Qiu's wife leaped to her feet: "You old dog! Why do you bark so loudly before Third Madam has a chance to say anything? You're out of line!" Lingzhi rapped her tea saucer down on the table. Glancing at Third Madam Lingzhi, Zhao'er said to Qiu's wife, "Shut your mouth! Where do you think you are? How dare you be so disrespectful in front of Third Madam!"

Qiu's wife immediately fell silent and sat back down. Finally she said, "The world is changing and the rules of the old society won't hold. Nobody can stop that. My nephew is carrying out land reform in Shangyang, and he's told us that your way of life is called ex..... ex....... p, p...... loita...... That's right, exploitation! It means getting grain and goods without working for it yourself. The new government says that's a crime!"

The chief butler jumped up from his seat again: "You ungrateful old witch! Tenants should pay rent. That's only just and fair!"

"Sit down," Lingzhi said quietly. Everyone stopped talking and sat back down. Lingzhi said, "Mrs. Qiu, I've only been here for a year and haven't met you before. I don't know what happened earlier, but let's just talk about what happens next. Do you still want to rent my land next year, or would you like to return it?"

Qiu's wife said anxiously, "No, I don't want to return it."

"If you don't want to return it, that means you want to rent it. If you rent it, you need to pay rent. Isn't that right?"

Qiu's wife turned her face away: "It was right before, but it may not be right in the future."

Lingzhi laughed: "You seem to be a sensible person. Think about what you just said and whether your words were fair and just. If you have difficulty paying the rent, I'm sure our kind and merciful Mistress will support me in reducing your rent or giving you more time to pay. As fellow villagers, that's something we can do. But telling us straight out that you want to rent our land without paying for it is something else. Excuse my ignorance, but that's something I've never heard of. Please go home and discuss it with your husband. Have him come talk to me next time. Zhao'er, please see her out."

As Zhao'er escorted Qiu's wife out of the hall, she turned her head and yelled, "The Land Reform Team will be here in the spring! You don't believe me now, but just wait and see!"

After Qiu's wife left, Lingzhi asked the chief butler, "What is a Land Reform Team?"

The chief butler said, "I've never heard of such a thing. Could it be a team to reconfigure the land to yield more crops?"

No one in the Gao household realized that immense communist tidal waves were engulfing the entire country. Anyone who owned

land, property or any form of capital was in mortal danger. The social
law and order that had been the backbone of society for thousands of
years would soon collapse into oblivion.

(7) STRANGERS ARRIVE

———————— ✦ ————————

The frozen ground of the great north showed initial signs of thawing. Dripping ice converged into streams that danced through the mountains. When the snow had disappeared to reveal the dark dirt roads, a group of men traveling from afar walked up to the village. Each wore a greenish-yellow hat and matching uniform with two or four pockets on their jackets. They wore odd-looking shoes and walked in a way that the villagers had never seen. And they carried guns!

The villagers thought these strange people would just keep passing through, but instead, they rented a peasant's courtyard and moved in. The next morning, the strangers set out a long table in the busy village threshing yard and served tea to anyone who passed by. Whoever stopped for tea was treated to a warm welcome and conversation: "Uncle, how many people are there in your family? How much land do you manage? Whose land do you rent? How's the yield? Is there enough to provide for the family after paying rent?" "Little brother, how many people are there in your family? How many rooms in your house? Enough for everyone?" "Granny, how many sons do you have? Do they all live on their own? Do you live with any of them? Are you having any difficulties?"

At first, the villagers treated the outsiders with caution. The number of pockets in their uniforms suggested that they were officials, and those scary guns made them look like people to avoid, so the villagers didn't want to tell them anything. But then, the villagers saw that the leader of the group spoke the local dialect, and that the men ate the same food as the peasants and chatted the same way as the peasants, and the questions they asked were things that the peasants cared about. They had the complexion of peasants and even smelled like peasants. Gradually people let their guards down and opened up to them. Before long, the outsiders became very familiar with the villagers and their families.

One day, Qiu Erguo came to the threshing yard, and when he saw the team leader, his eyes lit up and he dashed over: "Nephew? Isn't that my dear nephew Horsie?!" The team leader looked up and laughed, "Uncle! It's so good to see you! Don't call me by my baby name Horsie anymore. We've been liberated by the Communist Party, and I now work for the communist government. My name is now Qiu Jiefang, meaning liberation. I'm here to liberate the poor peasants!"

Qiu Erguo was amazed: "The government? My nephew is an official?"

Qiu Jiefang said, "I'm here to serve the people and start a revolution!"

"Re.... Re... vo... What?" Qiu Erguo mumbled.

Qiu Jiefang's land reform team often asked the villagers, "Who is the largest landowner in this area? How many people do they have in their family? How much land do they have? How many tenants?"

Every time they got the same answer: "Of course it's the Gao family! Who knows how much land they have? They own land as far as the eyes can see! Everyone in this area works for them or rents land from them."

"In their family there are Master and Mistress Gao, three Young Masters and Madams, plus six little kids. They live in the Gao compound. It's so spacious and well-built! The main courtyard is for Master and Mistress Gao. It's as big as this threshing yard. The three other courtyards are huge too, and those are for the three Young Masters. Even the servants' courtyard is better than anything we've seen. To us villagers, their compound is like the emperor's palace!"

"They have cooks from the city to prepare their meals. Every meal is like a banquet. Even dumplings are commonplace. They don't bother with steamed buns and roast pork!"

"They have so many tailors working for them! At New Year's time, they buy up entire shops worth of fabric and silk and have dozens of tailors working day and night to make new clothes."

"I hear their Crimson Eyed Buddha jade statue takes up half a room! How valuable it must be! Can you imagine a piece of jade of that size?!"

People were so busy talking that they didn't notice Qiu Jiefang's furrowing eyebrows. He banged his fist on the table: "Those parasites! They don't work in the fields or hunt in the mountains, but they enjoy the best fruit of other people's labor!"

"But it's all land passed down from their ancestors. Master Gao is the only son, so all of the Gao ancestral land is his. Who can compare to that!"

Someone else said, "The Gao family is very charitable. Every year they hand out food and save many lives!"

"Without the employment provided by the Gao family, all of us would starve to death!"

Qiu Jiefang sighed and said to the other Land Reform Team members, "See the task we have cut out for us? The parasite landlord has exploited them for so many years, and yet they're grateful to the landlord!" Qiu Jiefang's aide, Zhou, asked, "Should we start with posters again?"

In a couple of days, the Land Reform Team put up large posters in the village's gathering places. These posters used illustrations that catered to the illiterate peasants. The first showed several fat and ugly people in fine silk clothes and shiny jewelry sitting at a lavish banquet table topped with mountains of good food. Below them, masses of people in rags labored in the fields. In the foreground, at the entrance to the fields, was a basket of millet and other coarse food for the peasants. The second poster depicted a completely different scenario, with rows and rows of nice houses next to beautiful farmland. In each house, well-dressed peasants gathered around tables topped with dumplings, pork and buns.

As crowds gathered to look at the posters, Qiu Jiefang shouted through a loudspeaker: "Look here! Look at these two ways of life. Which do you want? Which one do the poor peasants want? The landlords haven't spent even an hour in the fields, but they eat fine food, wear fancy clothes and live in huge houses provided to them by your blood and sweat! They are blood-sucking parasites who condemn you to poverty. Not one gram of wheat is the fruit of their labor. Not one pig has been raised by them. Why can't the laborers in the fields eat what they plant? Why is it that people working on pig farms can't enjoy a meal of pork? Wake up, everyone! You aren't supported by the landlords, the landlords are supported by you, by your blood and sweat!"

Someone in the crowd said, "But it's their land. And they're nice about it, too. We should be grateful."

Qiu Jiefang climbed up onto a big rock and yelled, "We'll take the land from them and give it to poor peasants! The farmers should have the land. Land will be distributed according to household size. No more paying rent to the landlords!"

Qiu Erguo's wife slapped her thighs: "That's right! Paying rent every year is such a nuisance. If every family had land and didn't have to pay rent, how great would that be! Don't you all want that?!"

The crowd started buzzing. Wolf-Hair Xu blinked his eyes: "Is the world really changing? Can it be that the Gao family's wealth and prestige are coming to an end?"

(8) THE RETURN

————————————★————————————

After a few days, the Land Reform Team disappeared, and the once busy compound where they had stayed was now empty and quiet. The villagers all said, "What kind of nonsense was that? They bragged about land for everyone and no more rent and now they're gone! It was too good to be true! How could the law and order of thousands of years be changed overnight by a few outsiders? Impossible!"

Widow Liu's son died, and the whole village turned its attention to her family. Poor Widow Liu had already lost her husband the spring before, but luckily the Gao family had waived their rent for the year and had given them money to make it through the winter. The Gaos also paid her son's medical bills. That spring, the Liu family's only son, Liu Tianzhen, had dragged his sickly seventeen-year-old body to the field and worked hard. He said that as the only man left in the Liu family, he would honor the Liu name and not live on charity. Widow Liu did everything she could to stop her son. Dr. Ge at Ciji House also told him, "You need to take time to recover. The Gaos are the kindest people I know. They won't mind if you can't pay the rent." But Liu Tianzhen insisted on planting the spring seeds in the ground: "I won't bring disgrace to the Liu name. The Liu family doesn't take handouts!" While working the fields, he collapsed and never got up again. The doctors at Ciji House tried everything and could not revive him.

Widow Liu fainted with sorrow and exhaustion from crying. Villagers massaged her limbs and sprayed cold water on her face to revive her, but upon waking she wept herself unconscious again. Mistress Gao was very sad about Liu Tianzhen. She gave Widow Liu money for the burial and sent her servant San Wang to help with the funeral arrangements.

San Wang organized the funeral well, and it was proceeding smoothly in accordance with village tradition when Qiu Jiefang and his men appeared out of nowhere and hovered around Widow Liu. Qiu Jiefang asked, "Sister, how did you lose your son?"

Widow Liu's empty eyes suddenly filled with wildness upon hearing the word "son." Raising a trembling hand to point aimlessly before her, she said, "My son, my only child, all I had, sick, coughs, nothing helped, medicine, rest, he wanted to work, worried, debt, rent, waived one year, but next year, how could we pay, the land, the seeds, worked in the field, the rent, the Gaos, nice people, can't keep owing them, Third Madam, waived one year, but what about next year, he worked, he worked in the field until he died, my son, only seventeen, only seventeen!...."

Qiu Jiefang jumped up and shouted to his team behind him, "Comrades! Did you hear?! This poor tenant farmer lost her son. Her son died from hard work! Because the Gaos forced them to pay rent and didn't care if they died trying to pay it! Down with those evil landlords!" The team all raised their fists and shouted, "Down with all evil landlords!"

Only then did the country folks realize that the Land Reform Team had returned with about thirty more men this time, all carrying dark and sinister guns. Their sheer presence overwhelmed the small funeral hut, and when they shouted in unison, they were downright terrifying. The villagers were dumbfounded. Even Widow Liu forgot to cry as she focused her big, empty eyes on them.

The Gaos' servant San Wang, leading the funeral, stepped forward and said, "Thank you all for coming to pay your respects to the deceased. Please have some tea in the courtyard." Qiu Jiefang's assistant Zhou asked, "Who are you?" San Wang replied, "I was sent by Mistress Gao to help with the funeral. I'm a servant of the Gao residence." Zhou said with a nod, "Good, you are one of the exploited, so you belong to the same class as us." San Wang had no idea what Zhou was talking about. He politely said, "You're too kind. I'm not worthy of what you said." Qiu Jiefang was furious: "Not worthy, my ass! You think you're unworthy to be one of us? Do you want to be an evil landlord?!"

Qiu Jiefang stormed into the courtyard and ordered his team, "All of you go door to door. Round up young men from every family and tell them we'll give them land and abolish rent. In three days I want to see an army of new soldiers for our cause! Understand?" The whole team shouted, "Yes, Sir!" Qiu Jiefang then told his assistant Zhou,

"Find anyone you can who has been mistreated by the Gaos. Preferably those who have lost loved ones! Find them within three days – the more the better!" Zhou said, "Yes, Sir!"

Someone was watching all this with fascinated and inquisitive eyes – Wolf-Hair Xu. Like a shark smelling blood, he sensed his once-in-a-lifetime chance: "Excuse me, honorable Mr. Qiu, well, uh, Comrade Qiu. I don't know much, but I can tell that what you're doing is just grand. Do you need help? I can help!"

Looking at his ragged clothes, Qiu Jiefang asked, "Who are you? Do you have any wealth?"

Wolf-Hair Xu replied, "I write for a living. I'm dirt poor with no land. The only thing I have is a leaky old room full of mice!"

Qiu Jie Fang asked, "What do you have to do with the Gaos?"

Wolf-Hair Xu immediately replied, "I hate them! I hate them all!"

Qiu Jiefang patted him on the shoulder: "Great! We need fired-up proletarians like you! In ten days we'll go raid the Gao compound. You can come with us and help record their assets." Unable to believe his ears, Wolf-Hair Xu nodded and bowed repeatedly.

The Land Reform Team moved back into the peasant courtyard where they'd stayed the last time. One day, Qiu Jiefang and his teammates were having a meeting when the front gate opened. Zhou entered, followed by a woman dressed in an eye-popping silk dress and a pair of high heels. Everyone gawked at her and froze. Qiu Jiefang felt his throat going dry and he asked with a raspy voice, "Who's this? Who are you?!"

Zhou said, "Sir, Wolf-Hair Xu told me about this woman. You wanted me to find people who have been wronged by the Gaos, so I found her."

Before Zhou could finish talking, Wolf-Hair Xu cried, "Cousin Xiulian! My poor Cousin Xiulian!" This woman was none other than the cousin Xu had sold to the town brothel!

Without a word, Xiulian walked up to Wolf-Hair Xu and slapped him in the face with all her might: "You bastard from hell! You sold me to the devils. I will haunt you forever after I die!"

Qiu Jiefang shouted, "No hitting! How dare you!"

Xiulian turned to look at Qiu Jiefang, who stood there like an iron tower in his military uniform and with his shiny handgun on his belt.

Without knowing why, Xiulian found herself losing all her power and strength at the sight of Qiu Jiefang, and she collapsed on a bench and started to cry. "Nothing annoys me more than a crying woman!" Qiu Jiefang said, and Xiulian immediately stopped crying.

Zhou said with embarrassment, "Sir, you told me to find people who have been mistreated by the Gaos. Wolf-Hair Xu told me the Gaos made him destitute and tricked him into selling his cousin to the brothel. Now the town is liberated and the brothel has been closed. All of the prostitutes are returning to their home villages, so I brought her back here."

Xiulian leaped to her feet: "How can you believe Wolf-Hair Xu's lies?! His heart is as black as coal!"

"Sit down!" Qiu Jiefang ordered. Xiulian sat, and Qiu Jiefang turned to Wolf-Hair Xu: "What's going on?"

Wolf-Hair Xu cried, "Cousin Xiulian, I'm not the one you want to blame. It's the Gaos! Their Third Young Master wanted you as his concubine and I said no. And they forced me to pay back all the money they'd loaned me. I couldn't come up with that kind of money and I didn't want to force you to become a concubine. Then Third Young Master tricked me into believing that he sent a man to find you a good husband. I didn't know that man was an agent from the brothel. The Gaos tricked me because they wanted revenge for my saying no to them! It was all because of the Gaos!"

"What the hell!" Qiu Jiefang banged on the table: "That evil landlord should be shot dead!"

Xiulian was about to say something but now she was quiet. Qiu Jiefang asked her, "Do you want to be a witness to their crimes and help the exploited become owners of this land?" Xiulian had no idea what he meant, but afraid to say no, she tentatively nodded.

Wolf-Hair Xu was overjoyed: "Dear cousin, you're making the right choice! Once the Gaos are down, we'll all live well!" He then turned to Qiu Jiefang with a pleading smile: "Comrade Qiu, can my cousin stay here as a cook and work for the Land Reform Team so she has a livelihood?"

Qiu Jiefang thought for a moment: "Zhou, get her a set of decent clothes and give her a pair of scissors so she can cut her hair. I don't want anyone looking like a slut in this team!"

(9) THE LAST SMILE

Servant San Wang dashed into the Gao compound and ran straight to the main courtyard and into the front hall. He stopped abruptly in front of Master and Mistress Gao with one hand holding his chest and the other hand pointing outside, gasping to catch his breath. Mistress Gao laughed, "What's the big hurry? Give him a drink of water."

"Master, Mistress, the Land Reform Team is coming tomorrow to lock up the Gao compound and raid our belongings! They all have guns!"

Master and Mistress Gao exchanged glances: "Sounds like bandits from the mountains who like to target rich families. Where did you hear this? Have you seen them?"

San Wang said, "They're staying in our village, in the courtyard next to the northern woods. They have about thirty people all living in that courtyard. Their leader's name is Qiu and they said they'll be coming here to raid us tomorrow!"

Master Gao said, "That's absurd! Bandits living in the village? Announcing their plan to rob us? Don't they always come down from the mountains in the dead of night when nobody expects it, and then ride away into the darkness before the police arrive?"

Mistress Gao said, "We haven't had bandits for a long time, so we sent away most of our guards years ago. What should we do now?"

Master Gao said, "The Gao family has had a strong reputation for many generations. We're charitable and well-respected. If anyone comes to rob us, the villagers won't just stand by and watch it happen." Mistress Gao nodded in agreement.

San Wang said, "That man Qiu is telling everyone that he'll give people the Gao family's land. He says whoever joins them will get more land. A lot of families have sent their sons to join their team these last few days. Now they're all in the threshing yard being trained as soldiers! There's about a hundred of them!"

"That's a rebel upheaval!" Mistress Gao declared. "We have to report this to the officials and ask them to send the police!"

Master Gao thought for a moment and said, "I know the county government has been taken over by the Communists. If we want to report this, we'll need to send someone to the county Communist leaders by nightfall."

San Wang interrupted, "No! Don't do that! Qiu Jiefang and his team are Communists themselves!"

"What? Government bandits?!" Both Master Gao and Mistress Gao were astonished.

Master Gao got up and walked into the courtyard. He called out to the servants: "Zhao'er, Biao'er, Da Wang, Er Wang, the four of you take some men to the villages, the fields and the threshing yard to see what's going on. Ask around to see if anyone is trying to stir up trouble against our family. Report back at lunch time. San Wang, you stay here and check the deadbolts on every door in every courtyard. Make sure they're all secure and in good working order."

After sending away the servants, Master Gao lowered his voice and said to Mistress Gao, "Get our three sons. Put the title certificates for every piece of land, mountain and house we own into a box, then put the box into a big clay pot, along with all of our gold ingots and valuable jewelry. Bury it somewhere hard to find, and bury it deep!. Remember, only you and the three boys – no one else should know. Don't even let a passing fly see you! Understand?!" Mistress Gao nodded and hurried off. But Master Gao called her back: "Don't bury the jade Crimson Eyed Buddha. Give the Buddha to our eldest son and tell him to protect it with his life!"

The servants who came back at lunchtime brought more bad news. Zhao'er said: "Those bastards! They said Widow Liu's son was killed by Third Madam because she forced them to pay rent. And that Wolf-Hair Xu's cousin was forced into prostitution by Third Young Master! If Biao'er hadn't held me back, I'd have stuck a knife into the bellies of those scoundrels!"

Da Wang and Er Wang both said, "They found a bunch of beggars who all said their parents had been driven to suicide by Master and First and Second Young Master, and that was why they became beggars! Those sons of bitches aren't even from here. They don't even speak the local dialect!"

Biao'er said, "That bastard Qiu said these few things were enough to bring death sentences on the Gao family. He's telling everyone that he'll distribute the Gao family's land and money. Everyone is going crazy. They think whatever land they're renting now will become their own. No one is speaking up for the Gao family. Everyone is keeping quiet! These ungrateful bastards!"

Master Gao was deep in thought. After a long while, he said, "Go have lunch, all of you." Then he returned to his chair and sat quietly for a long time. Mistress Gao led her three sons into the hall. They quickly walked up to Master Gao and reported: "It's all buried. Not even a ghost can find it! It's in ……"

"Stop!" Master Gao raised a palm: "Don't tell me where you buried it!" Mistress Gao and her three sons looked at one another in puzzlement. Master Gao focused his gaze on his wife, then on each of his three sons. He said: "Throughout history, every time there's a transfer of power, rich families have to shed wealth for the new power. There's never been an exception. Losing wealth is acceptable as long as we all stay safe. But it looks like they want more than money: They're crying for blood! Otherwise, why would they make up all those stories and take the trouble to find so many people to oppose us?" The three young masters cried out: "Father!"

Master Gao said: "I'm old. My only wish is that when I die I can face the Gao ancestors with peace of mind and honor. I will tell the Communists that I am responsible for any crime they want to accuse us of, and it has nothing to do with any of you. That way we can keep you three safe – you're our three blood lines! If anyone asks where the deeds and gold are, tell them I'm the only one who knows. Tell them I've kept it secret from everyone! Understand? Don't ever tell me where you buried the wealth. Even if they torture me to death, I won't give away our secret because I truly don't know! I can't give it away even if I wanted to!"

The three young men all cried out, "Father! If they dare to touch you, it will have to be over our dead bodies!"

Master Gao shook his head: "How can I face the Gao ancestors if any of you are hurt or killed? Remember, protect our younger generation and preserve the Gao bloodline, no matter what! That's what we must do!"

Mistress Gao cried, "Wealth doesn't matter; if it can save your life, just let it go. The Gao ancestors started with just thirty acres of land. We can do it again. I just want all of us to be safe!"

Master Gao said, "That's pure woman's talk! If they take ten ounces of gold from you, they may let you live. But if they take ten thousand ounces of gold from you, they'll kill off your whole family so you have no offspring to demand it back from their offspring! Revealing our wealth is a death sentence to the whole family, even our little ones!" Mistress Gao collapsed to the ground.

Master Gao said, "Perhaps it's not as bad as I think. Maybe money can take care of it." He told his third son: "They've made up crimes to accuse you of. You need to leave by nightfall. Go to your aunt's house. We'll come for you when the danger has passed."

After making these arrangements, Master Gao said, "I want to see QuanGe, YuGe and HongGe, and also my three granddaughters." Surrounded by their nannies and maids, the three grandsons and three granddaughters of the Gao household walked up to Master Gao. This was a vivid childhood memory of HongGe's. His grandfather wore a black silk hat and a black silk suit and patted each of his grandsons on the head. Then he said to his own three sons, "Each of you has given me only one grandson! Such a disappointment. We need more! More children!" Then he bent down to look at his grandsons again. Back then, sons carried on the family name and were considered the bloodlines of the family, so he naturally focused on his grandsons more than his granddaughters.

HongGe didn't know where he found the courage, but he reached out and tugged on his grandfather's gray beard. Master Gao looked at HongGe and smiled. HongGe remembered for the rest of his life that he was the one who received his grandfather's last smile.

(10) CHAOS

—————————————— ★ ——————————————

At the break of dawn, HongGe was still sleeping in Nanny Wu's bed when Cai Xia, his stepmother Lingzhi's maid, rushed in: "Nanny Wu! Quick, wake up HongGe and take him to the main hall! Third Madam wants him there now!" HongGe leaned half asleep against Nanny Wu as she quickly changed him out of his pajamas. "My sweet baby HongGe, please wake up," Nanny Wu pleaded. "It looks like something bad is going to happen to your family today. Let's go see your mother!" As they approached the main hall of the third courtyard, they heard the servant Zhao'er say, "Lock the gate! Guard Third Madam and HongGe!"

The maid Cai Xia hurriedly took HongGe to Third Madam Lingzhi, who opened her arms and clutched him to her breast. Glancing around in confusion, HongGe asked, "Where is Dad?" Lingzhi looked seriously at HongGe and said, "My dear HongGe, listen to me: If anyone asks you where your dad is, tell them he's visiting a relative. Understand?" Then she turned toward the door: "Zhao'er, what's happening out there?"

Zhao'er reported, "About a hundred people armed with guns and other weapons have surrounded the compound. Master was taken away. Mistress is locked up in a side room in the main courtyard. Those people have just gone through the first and second courtyards, and now they're heading our way!"

Lingzhi asked, "Didn't Master and Mistress give them money?"

"These people seem to want more than money!" Zhao'er said.

All of a sudden, there was an eruption of people yelling and banging on the front gate: "Open up! We want the evil landlord's third son Gao Zhanren! We want the evil debt collector Guan Lingzhi!" "Blood for blood! A life for a life!" "Gao Zhanren! Guan Lingzhi! Come out! Open up!"

Her eyes blazing, Lingzhi said, "Nanny Wu, hold onto HongGe and stay in here. Don't go out, whatever you do. Don't let anything happen to HongGe! Zhao'er, Cai Xia, come with me!"

Lingzhi led Zhao'er, Cai Xia and the other servants into the open courtyard. Watching as the front gate was shaken loose by the crowd outside, Lingzhi straightened her jacket and smoothed her hair. "Open the gate," she ordered.

A gang of armed men burst into the courtyard as soon as the deadbolt was released. Qiu Jiefang was in front, followed by Wolf-Hair Xu. "Stop!" Lingzhi shouted. The crowd came to a halt. It was impossible for anyone to ignore Lingzhi's firm authority, her elegance and her beauty. Her mere presence was enough to halt the crowd.

Qiu Jiefang paused briefly, but quickly recovered: "You must be Guan Lingzhi. You killed Widow Liu's son Liu Tianzhen by extorting rent from them. We represent the people's government and we're here to arrest you! Where is your husband, Gao Zhanren? He forced a woman into prostitution and he's got the blood of others on his hands. We're here to arrest him too!"

Lingzhi sneered, "What evidence do you have?"

Qiu Jiefang circled Third Madam Lingzhi while eyeing her from head to toe: "Why do I need evidence to lock up someone like you? You'd better give us your husband. We may reduce your punishment in return. To tell you the truth, a death sentence for someone so pretty is not something I want …" He reached out and pinched Lingzhi's face. Zhao'er charged at Qiu Jiefang to protect Third Madam Lingzhi, but two soldiers tackled him to the ground. Qiu Jiefang closed in on Lingzhi again. All of a sudden, Lingzhi jumped up and aimed a powerful kung fu kick at Qiu Jiefang's ribs. The Land Reform Team never imagined that this landlord's wife came from a military family and had learned kung fu. They rushed over to tackle her, but Lingzhi injured two more soldiers before Zhou pointed a gun to her head: "One more move and I'll blow your head off!"

Qiu Jiefang struggled to his feet: "How dare you attack a revolutionary official? I've been a Communist Party member since 1936, and you're nothing but the wife of an evil landlord. Are you seeking a quick death?" He turned to the others: "Tie her up and lock her in the cellar!" Wolf-Hair Xu jumped up and helped the soldiers tie up Lingzhi and shoved her into a cellar.

Nanny Wu and HongGe were hiding in a corner of the main hall, but HongGe began crying when he heard the shouting and fighting in the yard. Nanny Wu covered his mouth: "Please don't cry! We can't let anyone hear us!" She had barely spoken these words when several men burst into the main hall: "Gao Zhanren! Show your face!" Upon hearing his father's name being called, HongGe piped up, "My Dad went to visit a relative!" Nanny Wu's heart skipped a beat as she tightened her arms around HongGe.

Qiu Jiefang walked over to them: "Your Dad? You're Gao Zhanren's son?" He asked Nanny Wu, "Who are you?" Nanny Wu said, "I'm his wet nurse. I'm a servant."

"Good!" said Qiu Jiefang, "You're one of us. Lock up Gao Zhanren's son! I'll bet my life that he'll come looking for his son!"

Two soldiers began grabbing at HongGe, who screamed as if he were being murdered. Nanny Wu held onto HongGe with all her might: "Please leave him alone. He's just a six-year-old boy! Leave him alone!" She clutched HongGe tight and pinned him to the ground with her body. Zhao'er, Cai Xia and the other servants, who'd been forced to the ground by the soldiers, all yelled at the top of their lungs, "Leave HongGe alone! Don't touch HongGe!"

Wolf-Hair Xu came up to Qiu Jiefang: "This old witch is trying to protect the landlord's son! Let's lock her up too!" Qiu Jiefang ordered, "Lock both of them up in the side room!" Soldiers dragged HongGe and Nanny Wu into a side room and locked the door.

HongGe cried for a long time but finally fell asleep in Nanny Wu's lap. Then pangs of hunger awakened him; he hadn't had breakfast yet, but no one showed up to give them food, no matter how much Nanny Wu called for help. There was nothing for them to do but just sit there from morning to dusk. Then came the sound of someone trying to pry open the back window. Cai Xia's hushed voice came through the window: "Nanny Wu! HongGe!" Nanny Wu dashed over and shook the window as hard as she could to help Cai Xia crack it open. Cai Xia passed a few steamed buns through the window: "Have something to eat. Don't let anyone see. They didn't lock me up because I'm only a maid. I said what they wanted to hear so they're not watching me anymore. I stole some buns for you. Be patient! Zhao'er and I will try to get you out!"

"And what about Master, Mistress and Third Madam?"

Cai Xia said, "Master, First Young Master and Second Young Master were all chained up and taken heaven knows where. It sounded like they were all going to be put to death! Thank God Third Young Master escaped, but they're out looking for him! Mistress, First Madam and Second Madam are all locked in one room. Third Madam is still locked in the cellar! QuanGe, YuGe and the three little misses are locked up in their own courtyard side rooms with their own wet nurses."

Nanny Wu cried, "Those bastards! What did our Master ever do to them to deserve this!"

Cai Xia said, "There will be a public trial tomorrow. They're forcing everyone in the village to go. It sounds like they will sentence Master, First Young Master and Second Young Master. I heard that even Third Madam will be sentenced! What a disaster!"

HongGe started crying again. Nanny Wu said, "My dear HongGe, don't be afraid. As long as I have breath in my body, I will never let anything happen to you!"

(11) THE PUBLIC TRIAL

The morning peace was broken by soldiers shouting and banging on gongs in the streets: "Gather in the threshing yard! Public trial for evil landlords Gao Liancai and his sons Gao Zhanwen and Gao Zhanwu! Whoever turns up gets land! Whoever stays away gets nothing! Whoever captures the escaped third son Gao Zhanren will be rewarded with two extra acres!"

On one side of the now crowded threshing yard, the soldiers had erected a temporary stage with a row of chairs and a long table. Qiu Jiefang and his men were saluting an important-looking man who sat in the middle of the stage between Qiu Jiefang, Zhou and a few other key members of the Land Reform team. Qiu Jiefang summoned Wolf-Hair Xu and Qiu Erguo to sit with them on stage. He introduced them to the important man: "These are the representatives of the poor peasant class." The man nodded.

With grateful tears streaming down his face, Wolf-Hair Xu said, "Comrade Qiu, you're my savior!" The important man laughed: "You should thank the Communist Party!" Wiping his tears, Wolf-Hair Xu compliantly recited, "Long live the Communist Party!" The important man praised him: " Now here is a promising comrade!"

The public trial began. Drawing himself up to his full height on the stage, Qiu Jiefang shouted through a megaphone, "Bring them up!" Three men bound with thick ropes were pushed onto the stage. Each had a large cardboard sign sticking up behind their backs, stating "EVIL LANDLORD" in bold black ink. As they were forced to bow their heads and kneel at the front of the stage, the crowd realized who these three men were: Master Gao and his two older sons, First Young Master Gao and Second Young Master Gao! The crowd broke into loud gasps and shouting and would not quite down, no matter how much Qiu Jiefang yelled into the megaphone. With a nod from the important man, Zhou pulled out his gun and fired into the sky. Bang! Bang! Bang! The deafening gunshots immediately brought silence to the entire threshing yard. Women covered their children's mouths with their hands to keep them from making a sound.

Qiu Jiefang spoke again into the megaphone: "This is the public trial for guilty and evil landlord Gao Liancai and his sons Gao Zhanwen, Gao Zhanwu and Gao Zhanren! These monsters have exploited the masses and enjoyed the lavish lives of parasites! They have so much blood on their hands! Many people have died because of them, and many more have become beggars because of them! Now is the time! The time for the people to get justice!"

Master Gao raised his head and yelled, "Whatever you want to accuse us of, blame it all on me! I did it all! It has nothing to do with my sons. Let them go!" Qiu Jiefang waved his arm, and a soldier swung a heavy wood pole and beat Master Gao on his back until he collapsed. "Father!" Gao Zhanwen and Gao Zhanwu leaped to their feet and screamed, but more wooden poles landed on their backs until they dropped like their father.

The four women of the Gao household were bound and forced to kneel at the back of the stage to watch the public trial, and upon seeing their men being beaten, they all began screaming and crying. Seizing his opportunity, Wolf-Hair Xu jumped up and ran over to the Gao women, slapping each of them on the face with mighty swings of his arms. Third Madam Lingzhi was slapped more than her mother and sisters-in-law. Qiu Jiefang and the important man both looked approvingly at Wolf-Hair Xu. Third Madam Lingzhi shouted, "Wolf-Hair Xu! You will rot in hell!" Upon seeing the honorable Gaos being humiliated and abused like this, the crowd descended into chaos again. Needing no prompting this time, Zhou fired his gun into the sky three more times. The threshing yard once again fell silent as fear and confusion roamed through the crowd.

Qiu Jiefang continued: "Guan Lingzhi is the third daughter-in-law of the Gaos. She attacked revolutionary officials and the Land Reform team, and she hid her escaped husband. Tenant Liu Tianzhen died because of her. Bring this evil woman to the front!" Two soldiers dragged Lingzhi to the front of the stage.

Qiu Jiefang said: "Dear peasants! Dear class of the exploited! With the backing of the new Communist people's government, you have nothing to fear anymore! We will give you power against the landlords! Whoever has been hurt by the Gaos, whatever they've done to you, now is your time to seek revenge! Come up here! Come up and tell everyone about the crime of the Gaos!"

Nothing but silence came from the crowd. The important man frowned. Qiu Jiefang repeated his words again and again through the loudspeaker, but nobody came up to the stage. He had no choice but to aim commanding looks at his uncle Qiu Erguo and Wolf-Hair Xu. Qiu Erguo hesitantly stood up: "The Gaos have wronged me!" Looking like he'd found gold, Zhou said, "Mr. Qiu, please speak up, don't hold anything back!" Qiu Erguo stepped forward and pointed at the Gaos: "They gave me barren land but their rent is sky high. Even if I break my back I can't get enough crops off their land. Every time my wife goes to beg them to wave our rent, they always have excuses for refusing..." As he finished, Zhou raised his fist: "Down with the evil landlords!" The soldiers and Land Reform Team members raised their fists and echoed in unison: "Down with the evil landlords!" Their cries rang through the fields. Qiu Erguo inconveniently added, "It was just the year before that they waved our rent and gave us money to get through the winter. My wife kowtowed to them in gratitude." Zhou dashed to the front of the stage to stop him: "Mr. Qiu! You must be thirsty from talking so much. Please sit down and have some tea!"

Finding it unbearable that Qiu Erguo was the center of attention, Wolf-Hair Xu jumped up and yelled, "The Gaos have wronged me in countless ways!" Qiu Jiefang said, "Keep talking! And bring his cousin Xu Xiulian up too!" With great elaboration and detail, Wolf-Hair Xu described how terrible the Gaos were, how difficult it was to borrow money from them, and how Third Young Master Gao had forced his cousin Xu Xiulian into prostitution. Upon hearing this, Mistress Gao coughed up blood and fainted.

Qiu Jiefang said, "This evil third son Zhao Zhanren is now on the run, but we'll find him and bring him to justice! Now bring up Widow Liu!"

Paralyzed with fear, Widow Liu had to be propped up by two soldiers. Qiu Jiefang gave her a cup of water and said, "Drink this. Don't worry, just talk. How did the Gaos kill your son?" With big empty eyes and a trembling voice, Widow Liu said to Lingzhi, "Third Madam, you're a good person, but there's nobody left in my family.

I'm the only one left!" She collapsed on the ground in tears. Qiu Jiefang dragged her up by her collar: "What about your son? I want you to talk about your son! Liu Tianzhen!" At the mention of her son, Widow Liu's eyes became wild. She clawed at her clothes and mumbled, "Son, my son! Worked to death, I told him not to work, but he wouldn't listen, he wanted to pay rent, wanted to show respect to Third Madam, so he worked and worked, and he died!"

"Down with the evil landlord!" "Down with debt collector Guan Lingzhi!" Deafening shouts erupted from the soldiers and the Land Reform Team. The crowd was utterly confused.

More and more "witnesses" were called to the stage to testify. Some were jealous of the Gaos. Some were scared or had been bribed by the Land Reform Team. Others vented their frustration at the Gaos for not lending them all the money they asked for. Before long, the Gaos were painted as the worst criminals known to all mankind.

Qiu Jiefang turned to look at the important man, who gave him a nod. Qiu Jiefang then announced: "Evil landlord Gao Liancai along with his sons Gao Zhanwen, Gao Zhanwu and Gao Zhanren have all committed unspeakable crimes! The blood on their hands floods heaven and earth! On behalf of the people's Communist government, I hereby sentence Gao Liancai, Gao Zhanwen, Gao Zhanwu and Gao Zhanren to death with immediate execution!"

Three soldiers pulled out their guns, pointed them at the heads of the Gao men and opened fire. The crowd descended into complete chaos as people screamed and ran for their lives. Prepared to control the situation, Qiu Jiefang had positioned soldiers around the crowd, and the soldiers all began firing their guns into the sky at the same time. The villagers stopped in their tracks, and the silence was filled with the heartrending screams of the Gao women as Mistress Gao died of a heart attack upon witnessing the execution of her husband and two sons.

Qiu Jiefang looked at the important man for further instructions. When the man smiled and nodded, Qiu Jiefang returned to the megaphone: "The evil debt collector Guan Lingzhi also deserves the death sentence! But since her husband is on the run, we'll keep her alive until her husband is found!"

He then announced: "This is the great triumph of the masses! The landlords are gone! The exploited class will now enjoy good lives! Let's gather here again tomorrow to distribute the Gao family's land and money to the masses!" As the crowd began murmuring, Wolf-Hair Xu and Qiu Erguo seized the opportunity to shout, "Long live the Communist Party!" The Land Reform Team and the soldiers all joined in: "Long live the Communist Party!" But the crowd remained silent. Qiu Erguo's wife and the few people on stage who had testified against the Gaos started to join in as well, followed tentatively by some villagers: "Long live the Communist Party!" The important man had a satisfied smile on his face as he stood up and applauded and then shook hands with Qiu Jiefang, Wolf-Hair Xu and Qiu Erguo.

(12) REVENGE

Shadows moved swiftly through the dark night onto the stage in the threshing yard. They were the Gaos' servants, Zhao'er, Da Wang, Er Wang and San Wang, who had come collect the bodies of Master and Mistress Gao and their two sons. Each had grabbed a body, and they were dragging them away when a man jumped out of the woods. The servants began running until they saw that the man was none other than Third Young Master Gao Zhanren.

Tears streaming down his face, Third Young Master knelt before the bodies of his father, mother and brothers and kowtowed. Zhao'er rushed over: "Third Young Master! Didn't you go to your aunt's house?" Third Young Master said, "Men from the Land Reform Team were at my aunt's house looking for me, so I didn't go in. I've been hiding in the woods for two days! My parents! My brothers! They're all dead! I'm going to go kill those bastards!" The servants quickly urged him, "Third Young Master! Please lower your voice! We've snuck out to collect the bodies. You have to run. The world has changed. You have to run away!" Third Young Master asked, "Where are Third Madam and HongGe?" When the servants told him what had happened, he lowered his head in silence. Then he grabbed a shovel from the servants and helped to bury his parents and brothers.

HongGe had cried for a long time and was just falling asleep in Nanny Wu's lap when there was a light knock on the back window. "Who is it?" Nanny Wu asked in a hushed voice. After she asked several times, Third Young Master showed his face. Nanny Wu covered her mouth with both hands to hold back her screams. Third Young Master asked, "Is HongGe here?" Nanny Wu said in a trembling voice, "They're out front looking for you! HongGe is here with me. Don't worry. Take a look at HongGe and then run for your life! Just find a way to stay alive and you'll see HongGe again!"

Third Young Master looked at his sleeping son, then knelt down and kowtowed to Nanny Wu: "Nanny Wu, my family is dying. I just went to see Lingzhi. It looks like she may not live much longer, either.

I'm giving you my HongGe. Please keep him safe. Please preserve this blood line for the Gao family. I, Gao Zhanren, will be forever in your debt. Whether alive or dead, whether in this life or future lives, I'll be in your debt for all eternity!" He kowtowed to Nanny Wu again and again.

Nanny Wu stomped her feet: "Third Young Master! What are you doing? HongGe is my life. I'll never let anyone touch HongGe for as long as I have breath in my body! Don't you worry. Run! Run someplace far away and never come back!" Third Young Master stood up and said, "I have a cousin by the name of Gao Zhanxiang who's a well-known doctor in Beijing. If you go to Beijing Union Hospital and mention his name, everyone knows him. Bring HongGe to him!"

"All right! Now please run!" Nanny Wu pushed Third Young Master away and closed the window.

The sound of gongs echoed through the streets again in the morning. The soldiers shouted: "Gather in the threshing yard to get your land, grain and money! Whoever goes will get some, and if you don't go, you get nothing!" The important man from yesterday was not at the gathering today. Everyone in the village turned up. People felt sorry for the Gaos, but no one wanted to be left out when there was wealth and land to be had.

Zhou announced the names of the villagers one by one, along with how much land, grain and money each person would get, and each person went up to the desk to sign their ownership papers. The land, grain, goods and money were distributed evenly per person, while the Land Reform Team kept the livestock. Furniture, jewelry, paintings, antiques, clothing and household items were all distributed to the village folk as well, and the villagers couldn't believe that they had suddenly gained more than they could have earned in a lifetime. Sympathy for the Gaos was quickly replaced by joy at their newfound fortune, and people began laughing, talking, singing and dancing.

Wolf-Hair Xu, who was sitting on stage, stood up and shouted, "Comrade Qiu! We've distributed their wealth, but what about their women? The women should be distributed to the poor peasants too!" Several men yelled, "Yes! That's right! If the landlords can fuck them, we can fuck them too! Put their names in a hat, and whoever draws their names can have them!"

Upon hearing this, the three Gao madams, kneeling bound on the stage, started crying and cursing at the top of their lungs. Qiu Jiefang shouted, "Shut them up!" Soldiers grabbed handfuls of dirt and pebbles and shoved them into the mouths of the three Gao madams, but the women kept screaming. Qiu Jiefang walked over and kicked them violently: "Shut up, bitches! One more sound from you and I'll have your lower mouths stuffed tight too!" Several men yelled excitedly: "Do it! Do it! Stuff them tight down there!"

A huge explosion erupted in front of the stage as a homemade bomb sent the yelling men flying. Dropping to the ground, Qiu Jiefang avoided the impact. Third Young Master Gao Zhanren leaped from a tree holding a long knife and tried to stab Qiu Jiefang, who rolled off the stage with Gao Zhanren in hot pursuit. As Gao Zhanren's knife stabbed at Qiu Jiefang's back, Zhou pulled out his gun and shot Third Young Master Gao Zhanren in the back.

The crowd scattered in chaos, with everyone running in different directions. Qiu Jiefang ordered the soldiers to surround the threshing yard and fire into the sky to stop people from running away. Then he stood on the stage again and shouted, "Peasants! Don't you see? They want revenge! If we don't kill them off, every one of us can be a target, and all of us might die!"

Wolf-Hair Xu jumped up: "Comrade Qiu! The Gao family has three grandsons! We should kill them too, so they don't grow up and take revenge on us!"

The three Gao Madams fought desperately against the ropes that bound them and finally crawled up to Wolf-Hair Xu and knelt down to beg him. Wolf-Hair Xu froze for a second and then broke into a satisfied smile: "I knew it! I knew that one day it would be you begging me for a change!"

Qiu Jiefang said, "We communists have our policies. We don't kill children." But some peasants who hated the Gaos yelled, "If they have offspring, we won't be able to take their land, money and grain, because they'll grow up and take revenge on us. Our children and grandchildren will spend the rest of their lives sleeping with one eye open! What kind of land reform is this? Let's all return what we just got. Let's all return everything to the Gaos so their grandsons won't kill us someday!"

Qiu Jiefang gritted his teeth: "All right! There's always blood in a revolution! We can't be soft! Yesterday the director said we'd be the role model for the whole province. How can we let up now! Soldiers! Go get the three Gao grandsons!"

The three tied-up Gao madams screamed, kicked, rolled and crawled to stop them, but Qiu Jiefang said, "Take them away!"

Nobody noticed that Zhao'er had quietly left the crowd and snuck away.

(13) ESCAPE

The soldiers who were watching Nanny Wu and HongGe had locked the door securely and gone to the public meeting with the rest of the crowd. Zhao'er went to the back of the room and with a great crashing sound smashed the back window into pieces. HongGe and Nanny Wu both screamed. Zhao'er yelled: "Get out and run! They're coming to kill off the three grandsons to leave no roots behind! You'll die if you don't run now! Third Young Master went for revenge but was shot dead! Now that Qiu bastard is after HongGe!"

Shaking all over, Nanny Wu held the weeping HongGe up to the window: "Don't cry! You can't make a sound! You'll die if you do!" She pushed HongGe through the window, and Zhao'er grabbed HongGe and pulled him out and then helped Nanny Wu to get out too. Carrying HongGe on his back, he started to run, and Nanny Wu summoned all her strength to keep up with him.

"We can't climb over the walls. We can't get out of the compound! You have to hide!" Zhao'er said.

Nanny Wu could already hear people approaching the third courtyard. She whispered to HongGe, "My dear HongGe, please listen to your Nanny Wu – YOU CAN'T CRY TODAY! YOU CAN'T MAKE ANY SOUND! Do you hear me? Otherwise you'll die!" As if understanding the danger, HongGe nodded quietly.

After a few turns, Zhao'er led them to a stack of tree branches waiting to be chopped up into firewood. He quickly broke an opening into the pile and pushed HongGe and Nanny Wu inside: "Don't make any sound! Wait for me!" Then he concealed them with more branches and dashed back to the room where they'd been imprisoned. Just as the soldiers entered the third courtyard looking for HongGe, Zhao'er ran out from the back yelling, "Help! Help! Gao Zhanren got his son out! They've escaped!" The Land Reform Team rushed over to the broken back window: "Son of a bitch! He broke the window!" Then someone said: "Gao Zhanren is dead already. How fast can a woman and child run? They must still be around, let's search the compound!"

"A maid said she saw several people on horses dashing away. Maybe Gao Zhanren had accomplices. We need to find fast horses and chase them!" Zhao'er looked genuinely concerned. A soldier named Chuanzi eyed Zhao'er with suspicion: "The Gaos saved your life. How can we trust you? I bet they're hiding right here in this compound!"

Zhao'er said, "Saving my life, my ass! They just wanted a laborer who could work like a horse. I broke my back for them! But you have a different story, don't you? I remember how every New Year you would kowtow to Mistress Gao and receive all kinds of goodies from her! You're secretly helping them, aren't you? That's why you're delaying us!" Zhao'er then turned to the man leading the soldiers: "Just look at the bomb and the long knife Gao Zhanren used. Doesn't that show he had accomplices? I bet he has allies among our very own soldiers who are trying to slow us down!"

The team leader laughed: "Don't worry!" He pointed to a few soldiers: "You three set the Gao compound on fire. You four round up fast horses and set off on all the major roads. They won't be able to escape or hide!"

A soldier said, "Mr. Qiu said the Gao compound was going to be used as the headquarters for the county government. Can we really burn it down?"

Zhao'er interrupted, "Of course we can burn it down! It's landlord property after all. We can burn it whenever we like!" He then turned to the team leader: "My only concern is the grain storage. The poor peasants were just allotted grain but they haven't come here to claim it yet. There might be an upheaval if the storage is burnt down"

The leader thought for a brief moment and said, "Very well. Search every corner of this compound! And the four of you, get horses and chase them down!" Zhao'er said, "You need insiders to show you where to look. How about if I help you? Cai Xia can help too. We know every nook and cranny of this compound. We even know their secret hiding places!" "Great!" the leader said. "We need more people like you! Get to it! And let's see if we can find that Crimson Eyed Buddha too!"

Cai Xia and Zhao'er quickly exchanged glances and started to lead the search. With their "expert directions" the soldiers found three floor tiles that were removable, and antiques, paintings and jewelry were pulled out of underground storage places. A hidden passage from a bedroom to the outside was also found. As people were searching the hidden passageway, some soldiers came and announced, "We've got YuGe and QuanGe!" The screaming and crying of the two Gao grandsons could be heard even deep inside the hidden passage. Zhao'er and Cai Xia looked mournfully at each other. The team leader said: "Good! Although one kid escaped, we got the other two and found hidden treasures and the hidden passage. Too bad the Crimson Eyed Buddha wasn't found, but we have enough now to report back to Comrade Qiu!"

Deep in the night, Nanny Wu and HongGe heard someone moving branches away from where they were hiding in the wood pile. Zhao'er and Cai Xia helped both of them out and gave them a satchel: "You have to run. QuanGe and YuGe have both been killed, and HongGe is the only boy left among the Gaos!" Cai Xia said, "There's clothing and food in this satchel, and HongGe's otter fur jacket is there too. You can sell it when you need money." Nanny Wu took the satchel and pulled HongGe in front of Zhao'er and Cai Xia: "HongGe, kneel down and kowtow to Zhao'er and Cai Xia! They're your saviors!" HongGe kowtowed with tears streaming down his face, but Zhao'er and Cai Xia stopped him: "Run!"

Zhao'er led them out of the compound through a back door. He told them, "I went into the mountains this afternoon and found Li Ginseng. He still remembers the grace and mercy of Master Gao. He and his men are waiting for you behind the big pagoda tree at the back of the village. Go there and they'll take you away. I can't go far — they're still keeping an eye on me!" He bent down and looked HongGe in the eye: "You have to live on! Live a long life! Your father died trying to get revenge. Don't ever take revenge for anything. Your life is the best revenge. Live on, no matter how hard things get!" He then turned to Nanny Wu: "Nanny Wu, every Gao ancestor since the beginning of time is kowtowing to you from above!" With that, Zhao'er disappeared into the dark night.

Nanny Wu held HongGe's hand and led him to the back of a slope. She gave HongGe some food and told him, "Listen to Nanny, my HongGe! Be very quiet. Stay close to me and run as fast as you can. If anyone tries to grab me, don't you worry about Nanny! You hear me? You have to leave Nanny and run by yourself, all right? Run to the pagoda tree. You'll have a chance to live if you get there! Do you understand me?"

Behind the pagoda tree, a few men were quietly waiting on horses in the dark shadows as the moonlight revealed the silhouette of Nanny Wu and HongGe running towards them. Two men shot out from behind the pagoda tree like bullets. Lifting HongGe and Nanny Wu behind them, they dashed back into the woods. Li Ginseng put HongGe on his own horse. Looking at the otter fur jacket that HongGe was holding, he said, "I always knew you and I were connected!" The sound of horse hooves carried them deep into the mountains.

Nanny Wu and HongGe lived in the mountains for a year with Li Ginseng's family and his men. Gradually, they heard about people from the Gao compound. Zhao'er and Cai Xia, who had risked their lives to help them escape, were now married and they continued to live in the village. Third Madam Lingzhi, HongGe's stepmother, had been unable to bear the torture and rape and had committed suicide. First Madam and Second Madam had been forced to marry two peasants who had drawn their names from a hat. News also came of the three Gao granddaughters, HongGe's three girl cousins. Seven-year-old Cousin Lin had been beaten to death when she scratched and bit the soldiers as they approached her. Four-year-old Cousin Ning had been accidentally trampled by stampeding Reform Team soldiers and had died of head injuries. Three-year-old Cousin Lan, daughter of Second Young Master and Second Madam, had been adopted by the peasant who had forcibly married Second Madam, and who took pity on her. She was the only girl survivor of the Gao descendants and the only Gao child who still had a mother. The Gaos were just a few among the two-and-a-half million landowners who were robbed of their possessions and killed throughout China during the communist land reform.

Li Ginseng wanted to adopt HongGe as his own son and raise him in the mountains, but Nanny Wu didn't agree: "He's the only male survivor of the Gaos. He has to maintain his ancestry! Third Young Master told me he has a cousin in Beijing named Gao Zhanxiang who's a doctor at Union Hospital. I want to take HongGe to him."

Li Ginseng sent one of his men to escort Nanny Wu and HongGe to Beijing, pretending to be part of their family. The man saw them out of the mountains, across the northern plains, into the city and onto a train to Beijing.

Daffodil

(14) A FORTUNATE BRIDE

It was an early autumn morning in the early 1940s in Hebei Province. Crisp morning air carried the smell of reed canary grass by the great Baiyang Lake. The wetlands grass had sprouted milky white feathers that floated on top of lush green stems and leaves. On the road along the great lake, a wedding band and a gold-roofed red wedding palanquin were heading towards Xu Village.

The bride, Lotus, sat inside the palanquin with her head covered by a flowing red veil. A bride might have a hundred thoughts while riding in her wedding palanquin, but Lotus was thinking of just one thing: When could she eat?

Since the day before, Lotus's mother had been telling her: "The bride shouldn't open her mouth on her wedding day until she has reached her husband's house. When she wakes up on her wedding day, she won't talk, nor will she eat or drink anything. She has to keep her mouth shut. If you do that, you'll have many sons. Remember, don't open your mouth until you're in your husband's house!" Lotus laughed and asked her mother, "What if my nose is blocked and I can't breathe unless I open my mouth?" Lotus's mother patted her on her shoulder: "You're getting married tomorrow. Do you really have to be so naughty?"

The night before the wedding, Lotus's mother made eggs, fish with chives and hot pepper, and flatbread, ensuring that Lotus stuffed herself: "This is the last meal from your mother before you leave home. Eat slowly and eat a lot!"

But no matter how full she was the night before, she was hungry this morning. Lotus wanted to lift her veil to see how high the sun was and how long they had traveled, but she remembered her mother's warning: You can't misbehave once married. After all, she was already seventeen years old. She had to be a good bride. The rocking of the palanquin made her want to fall asleep. At long last, Lotus heard the music becoming louder, as well as firecrackers and the sound of people cheering. Realizing that they had arrived at her husband's village, Lotus quickly smoothed her top and her skirt, straightened her veil and sat upright as a proper bride should.

Amidst the sound of firecrackers and cheering, Lotus moved her bound feet and stepped out of the palanquin with the help of the wedding maids. In the olden days of China, it was a social norm for girls to bind their feet at the age of six or seven and go through excruciating pain to achieve the ideal "three-inch golden feet," considered a mark of beauty, delicacy and propriety. By the late 1930s, China had banned this barbaric abuse of girls and women, and Lotus was one of the last victims of this tradition. Her feet were much smaller than normal size and were disproportionate to the rest of her body.

The wedding maids directed Lotus to step over a basin of lit charcoal to symbolize her willingness to accompany her husband through any obstacles in life. She then stepped over the threshold of the front gate, marking her entrance into a new family and separation from the family of her birth. After she took her place next to her groom, they kowtowed to heaven and earth, then to the parents and ancestors, and finally to each other. Kneeling down and getting up three times made Lotus dizzy, but she managed to steal a glance at her groom from under her veil. The bride and groom had not met before today; their marriage had been arranged by their parents. All Lotus could see was a pair of gigantic shoes and the cuff of his wedding trousers.

After the kowtowing, the bride and groom were officially man and wife. Lotus was then led to the wedding chamber. It was customary for the bride to sit on the bed in the wedding chamber with her veil covering her head and wait for the groom, who had to serve the male guests at the banquet. The wedding bed was sprinkled with dates, chestnuts and peanuts, homonyms in Chinese for the phrases "quickly have sons" and "have both daughters and sons." These items were sprinkled on the wedding bed as a good wish, and the bride was supposed to sit among the dates, chestnuts and peanuts for the entire day to absorb the good fortune they brought until her groom came to her.

Female guests were allowed to enter the wedding chamber to see the bride. They crowded into the room and said, "Look at her three-inch golden feet, how pretty!" "She's tall. I bet she's even taller than the groom." "Three-inch golden feet are not in style anymore. Natural feet are much healthier." A group of children suddenly rushed into the room. The older women herded the kids away after stuffing their pockets with candies, nuts and dried fruit.

Soon it was after lunch time, and Lotus was unbearably hungry. When the women guests left the room, Lotus thought about reaching out for some of the peanuts on the bed, and shelling and eating them. But she was afraid that would be improper. As she hesitated, she felt someone putting something in her hand. A man's voice said, "You must be hungry. Please have this." Lotus found a piece of rice cake in her hand! Without hesitation, she lifted her veil just a tiny bit and stuffed the rice cake into her mouth in two big bites. The man laughed: "I'll go get another piece for you."

Lotus couldn't see him through her thick veil, but she heard his footsteps moving towards the door until someone suddenly stopped him. "What are you doing in here? So eager to see your bride? Don't worry, you'll get to see her after all the guests are gone! What's the hurry?"

Lotus realized that the man who'd given her the piece of rice cake was her husband. The other voice drew near to Lotus, and a pair of hands patted her wedding skirt: "What's this? Rice cake crumbs? I had rice cake made for the important occasion of your wedding. The guests haven't even had any, and you're giving it to her! What a great husband you are!" The woman's voice was shrill and sarcastic.

"Mother, she hasn't eaten all day. She must be hungry. That's why I brought her a piece."

"Go serve your guests!" The woman said. The man left.

Lotus heard her mother-in-law walking up to her and froze with nervousness. The mother-in-law stopped for a brief moment, uttered a "Hmm!" and then walked away. Lotus thought about the meal her mother had made for her the night before, and then what unpleasantness a simple piece of rice cake had created in her mother-in-law's house, and she shed tears of sadness. She hated her mother-in-law already! That old woman must be an evil witch!

At long last, all of the guests were gone; the courtyard was quiet and red wedding candles were lit. Lotus continued waiting until she heard footsteps and someone bolting the door. A gentle hand lifted her veil. She lowered her head and caught a glimpse of her husband. She was overjoyed to see that he was handsome, with friendly eyes, a broad forehead and well-shaped lips. She felt lucky to have such a good-looking husband. The groom's name was Xu Yixin. He was a peasant boy who was well-educated and versatile, skilled not only in calligraphy and accounting, but also in fishing and farming. Seeing how pretty Lotus was, Yixin smiled happily. He turned and produced a plateful of rice cake: "You haven't eaten all day. Please have some food. You seem to like rice cake."

The next morning, Yixin and Lotus went together to pay respects to Yixin's parents as a newly wedded couple was supposed to do. Yixin's father said nothing beyond a brief response to their greeting. Yixin's mother, however, said with a sneer, "You've married into our family, and you have to abide by our family rules. It's not like you're a maiden in your own house anymore. You'd better pray that your belly is blessed. Have a son right away. That's the best thing you can do." In those days, a mother-in-law had so much authority and power over her daughter-in-law that Lotus could do nothing but nod.

For many years afterwards, women in the village talked about how fortunate Lotus was. She not only gave birth to a son as she approached her first anniversary, but also gave birth to two more sons over the next two years. The three sons were named Daqing, Erqing and Sanqing. With three grandsons surrounding her, Lotus's mother-in-law finally became friendly to Lotus. Many years later, Lotus would tell her own daughters before their wedding days, "Don't open your mouth on your wedding day, and you'll have sons." But her daughters paid no attention to her.

(15) LIFE BY THE GREAT BAIYANG LAKE

Early in the morning, Yixin skillfully maneuvered his oars to send his boat gliding through the thick morning fog across the great Baiyang Lake. Crossing reed canary grass wetlands and lotus lagoons, he returned home in the afternoon with loads of leaping fish and shrimp, fresh lotus roots, pearl-like lotus seeds and sometimes even eels. When he didn't go to the lake, he spent all day in the fields. Yixin and his father carefully worked their twelve acres of land, pulling out even the smallest weeds. Returning from the fields, Yixin picked wild raspberries and blackberries to bring home to his boys.

Unlike the majority of illiterate peasants, Yixin was an educated man. He could read classical literature and his calligraphy was beautiful. Anyone who needed a letter written or a door poster painted would come to Yixin for help, compensating him with a couple of duck eggs or a bunch of spring onions. During the harvest season, Yixin was especially popular because he of his mastery of accounting and the abacus.

The abacus with its beads and rods had been used for centuries among traders, not only in Asia but even in Europe, and once its calculation rules were mastered, it could perform addition, subtraction, multiplication and division on large numbers at lightning speed, even faster and more accurately than punching the numbers into a modern day calculator. Yixin had first seen someone calculating on an abacus when he was a teenager, and he followed the man around and watched him for days with total fascination. Soon after that, he went to a used book stand and traded a dozen duck eggs that he'd collected by the lake for a book on abacus rules. He then stole his mother's hen to trade for a large abacus. Infuriated at losing the family's source of eggs for a set of stupid wooden beads in a bamboo frame, his mother had thrashed Yixin soundly, but he didn't care – he was too busy figuring out his abacus.

Before long, Yixin could make the abacus dance with calculations on his right hand, after which he spent double the time practicing on his left hand. After a few months, his massive seventeen-column abacus came to life under his ten flying fingers as he carried out two sets of completely unrelated calculations simultaneously on either end of the abacus. His mother was so amazed that she no longer minded the loss of her hen: "These skills will make my son a wealthy man!"

Landlords, merchants and store owners came to Yixin from near and far. In the busy season, Yixin came home every day with money, liquor, chickens, ducks, tofu and pork.

Lotus was now responsible for all of the family's meals. Every morning she made tea, cornmeal congee and Northern Chinese pancakes, about three feet in diameter and paper thin. Carrying the wheaty fragrance of fresh flour, they were seasoned with hot pepper oil, minced garlic in salt water, spring onions and black bean paste. Accompanied by fresh cornmeal congee, a single pancake could satisfy even the biggest appetite. For lunch, Lotus made a gigantic pot of fish soup complemented by chunks of fresh, golden cornbread. When the men returned from the lake or the fields for dinner, Lotus made fried fish, steamed shrimp and soft, fluffy steamed wheat buns. She also picked cucumbers and chives from their garden to make stir fry or cold dishes. Tilapia steamed with lotus roots was a favorite dish of her three boys. Adding a plate of fresh lotus seeds made the ideal dinner. Sometimes, the men brought home tofu, cold cut meat or fried peanuts, which she put on plates and served with liquor to her husband and father-in-law.

Aside from cooking, Lotus was busy taking care of the pig and chickens, making dried fish, pickling vegetables, tending the garden, doing laundry and sewing clothes for the entire family. She was so busy every waking minute that she had no time to play with her three boys. Daqing had to help his mother pick peapods when he was three, and to take care of his younger brothers when he turned five. Erqing followed Daqing around with a runny nose, while Sanqing struggled to move his chubby legs fast enough to keep up with his two elder brothers.

One day, when the three brothers were playing on top of a dam over the lake, Sanqing lost his balance and tumbled headlong into the lake! The terrified Daqing and Erqing began screaming and crying at the top of their lungs, and a nearby boatman dashed over and jumped into the water to pull Sanqing out. But by then, Sanqing had already turned blue and stopped breathing.

Yixin was so overwhelmed with grief that he didn't speak for a month, and Lotus nearly died of sorrow. But her mother-in-law was different; she was sad but accepting: "This is normal in a peasant family. Almost every family has lost a child or two. It's a natural culling. God takes every third child back to Him, and that's as it should be." With Lotus incapacitated, the family descended into chaos, having no one to cook and clean. The mother-in-law complained all day long: "What a weakling! Becoming sick as a dog over the loss of one child? I had four children, and now only Yixin is left, but I'm still as strong as a horse! What are women made of nowadays?" Lotus hated her mother-in-law even more when she heard her say such things: "She is so heartless, even about her own flesh and blood! It's no wonder she's so mean to me!" The more the mother-in-law complained, the sicker Lotus became, until she was completely bedridden.

Yinxin brought home a doctor and begged Lotus, "Please think of Daqing and Erqing. If anything happens to you, they won't have a mother! Please let the doctor see you. You have to get better!" The doctor felt Lotus's pulse – an important diagnostic method in traditional Chinese medicine. He turned to Yixin with a smile: "Your wife is pregnant again. Looks like she's two months along."

The tearful Lotus struggled upright: "Really? It's my Sanqing! My Sanqing has come back to Mama!" The new life gave Lotus hope and strength, and soon she was once again busying herself in the kitchen, the courtyard and the fields. She became quieter and more easygoing, with a steadier and calmer strength.

In the fifth month of the lunar calendar, Lotus went to the lake to do her laundry, staggering along with her enormous belly. The sun shone brightly on the lapping water, the reflection was so bright that it was almost blinding. As Lotus dipped the clothing into the water, the patterned shiny waves seemed to form different shapes. Suddenly,

Lotus saw daffodils in the water. But how could that be? When Lotus pulled the clothes out of the water, the daffodils disappeared, and when she dipped the clothes back into the water, there the daffodils were again! Lotus was puzzled, but then as the baby kicked inside her belly, she suddenly had a revelation: "It's a girl! I should name her Daffodil!"

When the days turned hot and humid, Yinxin and Lotus's first daughter was born, and they named the bouncy little girl Daffodil. The mother-in-law was also very happy and made soft noodles with poached eggs, which she brought to Lotus in the best porcelain bowl she could find: "Eat it while it's hot." Lotus looked at her with gratitude. Maybe she wasn't so bad after all.

Daffodil had beautiful large eyes, a slender face, and a hearty, bellowing voice. Lotus thought to herself, "What charming eyes! She will have many suitors. But her face is too narrow for good fortune. I hope she won't have trouble in her future marriage!"

(16) THE JAPANESE ARRIVE

Having invaded China, the Japanese had now arrived in the region of the great Baiyang Lake, disturbing peaceful rural life. All sorts of rumors kept people awake at night. Some said the Japanese liked to spear the bellies of pregnant women with their bayonets and then pull out their fetuses and throw them around like balls for fun. Some said the Japanese raped any women they could get their hands on, even seven-year-old girls and sixty-year-old grandmas. Some said the Japanese could suck the marrow from your bones just by looking you in the eyes. Some even said the Japanese could walk through walls as if they were transparent or non-existent. Nobody knew what was true or not true, so everyone was sick with fear and worry.

The village head bought a big brass horn and assigned men to take turns watching the road that led to the village. He told them that if they saw anything suspicious, they were to sound the horn so everyone in the village could run into the corn and sorghum fields to hide: "Leave your gold and silver, leave your livestock and belongings; the only thing to take is the lives of everyone in your family!" he warned. "The sorghum and corn are producing well, so as long as we hide there we can survive for a long time!"

Lotus wrapped Daffodil in a big piece of cloth, and tied her tiny body to her own chest. This not only made breastfeeding easier, but also allowed for a speedy escape. If she heard the horn, she could just grab Daqing and Erqing with Daffodil strapped to her chest, and run for their lives. The village women rubbed their faces with black kitchen soot to make themselves look scary and ugly in hopes that the Japanese would not rape them. After hearing about this method, Lotus also daubed thick patches of soot on her face. Daqing and Erqing both cried when they saw their mother's face turn black, but Daffodil just grabbed at her mother's face and then sucked at her little blackened fist.

Yixin returned from the fields so parched that he went straight to the water pot. He was drinking from the dipper when Lotus walked up and asked, "Do you want your lunch now?" When he turned to Lotus, Yixin immediately threw away the water dipper and coughed loudly: "What did you do to your face?" When Lotus told him the whole story, Yinxin said, "Wash it off! It won't work!" and strode out.

The whole village was on high alert, but the horn never sounded. One day at lunch time, a loud, strange mechanical sound came from the distant sky. At first people thought it might be thunder, but it sounded different and came closer and closer as a few bird-like black shapes became bigger and bigger. People realized that these weren't birds at all, but some kind of flying metal giants! People yelled, "The Japs! The Japs!" and ran in all directions.

Lotus was making cornmeal in her yard with Daffodil strapped to her back when she turned and saw a Japanese airplane flying almost as low as her roof. The Japanese pilot turned to look at her the instant the plane passed. Lotus felt her spirit fly out of her skull and she collapsed to the ground, remembering what people had said about the Japanese sucking out your bone marrow just by looking at you. She truly felt as if she'd been sucked dry, but then Daffodil's loud squalling pulled her back to reality. Swinging Daffodil into her arms, she ran like crazy to look for her two sons.

The Japanese didn't bomb the village this time, but all of the villagers were in a panic. More absurd rumors came out of nowhere about the amazing powers of the Japanese, prompting curses from Yixin and his friends: "Those God-damned bastards! Fuck them all the way to their ancestors! You cowards, stop that nonsense. Do they have three heads and six arms? Are they more powerful than the Monkey King? They've invaded our homeland, but all you do is scare our own people. If you're a man, take up arms and fight them to death! Otherwise, go home and shut your mouth!"

One morning, the brass horn sounded at the village entrance. People who were eating breakfast stuck their heads out to see what was going on. Men from the village head's family ran through the village banging on gongs: "Run! The Japs are coming! Run!"

Yixin grabbed one son under each arm. Lotus already had Daffodil strapped to her back, so with her two free hands she grabbed two hens. Yixin's parents also grabbed some chickens and ducks, and then they ran into the sorghum field in the back of the village. The sorghum plants were tall and crowned with flowering heads, creating perfect cover. Everyone found a place to sit, and the women held their children close and told them not to make a sound. They sat there from morning to noon and then to dusk. Everyone was hungry. The sorghum field was across the road from the corn field. A few men went to the edge of the sorghum field, and after making sure that the road was quiet and safe, then they directed each family of villagers to cross the road and hide in the cornfield. Once the whole village was in the corn field, the men joined them. Everyone started eating the corn, which was tender and juicy. Women chewed up corn to feed the babies who didn't yet have teeth. The villagers stayed all night in the corn field, their clothes dampened by the night dew. Although it was only September, a night in a dewy field chilled them all to the bone.

The men lost patience first: "Let's go home! The Japs are gone!" A few young men went to the edge of the sorghum field to look at the village from afar. Everything seemed quiet and normal, but the women all said, "What if the Japs are hiding in wait to ambush us?"

Yixin said, "We're just ordinary peasants. Those bastards have no reason to ambush us. Let's go home!"

Everyone carefully snuck back into the village. Lotus held Daffodil and Yixin held Daqing and Erqing's hands as they slowly opened the front gate to their courtyard. It was completely quiet. Yixin said, "It's all clear. Let's see what food we have left." Lotus hurried into the kitchen and opened the grain cabinet. Ear-piercing screams erupted out of nowhere and filled the whole house! Lotus joined in the screaming, and Daffodil, held tight in her arms, was so frightened that she began to bawl, filling the room with the sound of complete madness. Yixin and his parents rushed in: "What's wrong!"

It turned out that two teenage neighbor girls had not run to the field but had hidden in Lotus's grain cabinet, crouching down and pulling the cabinet door shut from inside. When Lotus opened the cabinet door, they thought that the Japanese had found them and both started to scream. Everyone hugged each other in relief. Yixin said with contempt: "Those damned Japanese! Why couldn't they stay on their own soil! Why do they come here and do evil things! Stop crying, all of you. Many women have been raped and killed by the Japs. You're lucky to be alive!"

(17) A MAN WITH A FUTURE

The Chinese military was recruiting new soldiers every day. Many from the village had enlisted, and Yixin also wanted to go, but his parents begged him not to: "The bullets don't have eyes, they can hurt anyone! We're old and frail. We can't survive if anything happens to you!" Lotus also begged Yixin not to go.

One afternoon, Yixin entered the kitchen holding two roasted pork feet, a rare delicacy during war time. Smiling at her husband and at the delicious fragrance of pork feet, Lotus said, "I'll pour some liquor so you and Father can enjoy the pig feet." Yixin led Lotus to a chair and sat her down. Then he put the pig feet into a bowl and placed the bowl in Lotus's hands and said, "They're for you." Lotus had tears in her eyes. In all the years of her marriage, this was the first time her man had served food to her, and the first time she'd been offered food before everyone else had had their fill. She didn't know what to say.

Yinxin lowered his head and then said, "Erdan, Tiezi and I went to the military station this afternoon and we all signed up. I'm here to say goodbye. I'm leaving in the morning." Lotus dropped the bowl with a crash: "You did what?! You're really joining the army?!"

Yixin picked up the bowl and the pork feet: "I have to fight the Japs. They're on their last legs, and I want to be with the troops who drive them out of China! I want to be part of that! Besides, look at Xu Pingyuan's family. Xu Pingyuan was my childhood friend. We swam together in the lake, we played in the mud together and caught frogs together. He went into the army a few years ago and now he's a captain! He's risen in the world, and I'm still a peasant! Our family has been peasants for generation after generation, and Daqing and Erqing will grow up to be peasants too. Daffodil will grow up to marry a peasant and have the same life as us. I want things to change for our family! I want to give our kids a better life!"

Lotus said anxiously, "But Xu Pingyuan's wife says he 'eats danger for dinner' and almost lost his life several times!"

Yixin replied, "That's called being a man! What good is it to stay home tucked in warm and safe? That's for a baby! I'm wasting my life if I don't at least try to change things." Lotus wept quietly. Yixin looked at her and said, "Erdan and Tiezi are going with me, and the three of us will look out for each other. I'll be very careful. Don't worry, I'll be fine. I'm sorry to burden you with taking care of our parents and children."

Lotus wanted to say: Erdan and Tiezi are both single, but you're married with three kids and two elderly parents! But she held her tongue and wiped her tears: "If you really want to go I can't stop you. But I hear there's the Communist army and the Nationalist army, so which one are you signed up for?" Yixin looked surprised: "God damn it! I forgot to ask! Doesn't matter. We're all Chinese and we're all for driving out the Japs! It's all the same!"

The next morning, Yixin, Erdan and Tiezi showed up at the new military encampment near town. Six new soldiers stood in one line. An officer walked up to them and stared them in the eye one by one: "From now on, you're soldiers of the great Chinese army! Whoever is afraid to die can go home right now! Anyone afraid to die?!" Yixin and all others shouted in unison: "No, Sir!"

Soldiers who passed saluted the officer and addressed him as Lieutenant Zhu. He stopped one of them: "Sergeant Zhao! These new soldiers will be under your command. Ten days of training for new recruits starts now!" Sergeant Zhao snapped to attention: "Yes, Sir!"

A tragedy occurred during the ten-day training. The new soldiers were all farm hands who were accustomed to physical exertion and should have had no problem with the training requirements. But for some reason, Erdan dropped to the ground during a midday run, and he didn't regain consciousness no matter what the other soldiers did. An army medic pronounced him dead. Lieutenant Zhu rushed over, throwing his cap on the ground in frustration: "God damn it! We haven't even seen one Jap and he drops dead from running a few laps! No wonder China was invaded, when it's full of softies like him!"

Embracing his childhood friend's body, Yixin was saddened by the Lieutenant's harsh words and couldn't keep from saying, "Lieutenant Zhu, this man is dead. The deceased takes precedence. He deserves some respect. Please don't criticize him like that." Lieutenant Zhu stopped and looked at Yixin. This was not the first time he'd heard the expression "the deceased takes precedence." Last time it was when he was ten and his mother had died of an infectious disease, and other people were afraid to help him bury her. The elders of his village said to the crowd: "The deceased takes precedence!" Only then did people helped the young Zhu with the funeral and the burial of his mother. Now Lieutenant Zhu was hearing this phrase again from a young soldier, and he couldn't help but ask, "Are you an educated man? How come you talk like an elderly scholar?"

Tiezi interrupted, "Lieutenant Zhu, Xu Yixin is even better than a scholar! He's not only good at reading and writing, he's also a great accountant who can rattle the hell out of an abacus! No matter how complicated an account is, he can keep it and balance it!"

"Really?" Lieutenant Zhu eyed Yixin. Then he ordered: "Sergeant Zhao, Send Erdan's body home per protocol" He then turned to Yixin: "Follow me!"

Once in his office. Zhu said, "I need a secretary and an accountant. You'll be with me. Do you want the job?" A dozen thoughts flashed through Yixin's mind: The lieutenant had asked him to do something, and there was no way he could say no. But he was determined to seek promotion in the army so his children could have a better life. The best way to gain promotion would be through combat. Would writing and accounting get him there? Then he thought – the lieutenant said he would be with him at all times. It's always good to stay close to the higher-ups, who otherwise might never know his name, even if he sacrificed his life! He should stay close to the lieutenant. So, he said in a determined voice: "I'd be honored, Sir!"

The finances and bookkeeping for the army unit were a piece of cake for Yixin. Within a matter of two weeks, everything in the account book was clear and well organized. He also provided beautiful calligraphy and expert composition for posters, brochures, notices and meeting notes. Lieutenant Zhu was very pleased with Yixin's work. About six months into his military life, Yixin ran into someone from his village who was selling fish near his army camp. Yixin asked the man to tell Lotus that he was now the secretary and accountant for his unit and he didn't need to go to combat. He wanted to make sure that Lotus didn't worry about him.

The fisherman went back to Xu Village and started bragging as soon as he sat down in Lotus's yard: "Your man is really someone! He spends all his time with an important officer. He doesn't have to fight and he lives an easy life! I think he'll be promoted to officer too!" The man said these things in hopes that Lotus would be so happy that she'd give him something good to eat. But Lotus looked concerned as she plopped down onto a stool and muttered, "What's so good about being an officer?"

Xu Pingyuan's wife had by now gone half mad. Xu Pingyuan had never come back after leaving home to join the army several years ago. There were rumors that he'd become a captain, but his wife looked nothing like a captain's wife. She still worked day and night to feed her elderly parents-in-law and her son. When at long last, two men in uniform came to her yard, she was speechless with joy, and she looked at them eagerly, hoping they had a message from her long-lost husband. They indeed had a message about her husband, but it wasn't what she'd hoped for. The message said that Colonel Xu was a great revolutionary and an outstanding military talent. He needed a wife who shared his revolutionary ideals and who could promote his military career. The message informed Xu Pingyuan's wife that he had already married someone else, a female army officer. The message said: "Let this notice be the certificate of divorce between Colonel Xu and his first wife," and it was signed by both military and government officials.

Now Lotus heard that Yixin was also becoming an officer, and it made her feel that she was losing her mind like Xu Pingyuan's wife. She was so distracted that she burned the cornbread at lunch, and in her frustration, she yelled at Daqing and Erqing when they were running around in the yard and knocking things over: "You two little imps! Will it kill you not to make trouble every five seconds?" She chased her sons with a broom.

Yixin's mother came out of her room: "What makes you curse my grandsons like that? You're their mother. You should never mention death to your own sons." Lotus froze and immediately felt remorseful toward her boys, hating herself for what she'd just said. She was worried about Yixin, hated her mother-in-law and was stressed and bitter about taking care of everyone in the family all by herself. All of her troubles hit her like a tidal wave, and she sat on the ground and bawled.

(18) THE WAIT BEGINS

Before long, it was Daffodil's third birthday. Although a girl's third birthday was not considered a special occasion in the village, lovely little Daffodil commanded more attention. Her grandma made pretty wheat buns shaped like longevity peaches, and her father Yixin came home from his army camp. The unit Yixin was with had expanded, and Lieutenant Zhu had been promoted to Captain Zhu. Yixin was now responsible for all logistics and had long been too busy to come home, but he wouldn't miss his little daughter's birthday.

Daffodil had grown into a boisterous and lively girl, and when she saw her father enter the yard, she grabbed a longevity bun and ran over to him: "Dada, this is for you!" Yixin laughed and lifted Daffodil high in the air. Daffodil said, "Dada is back so Ma won't cry anymore."

Yixin put Daffodil down and turned to look at Lotus, who was standing at the kitchen door with tears in her eyes and a smile on her face. Yixin said, "Why are you crying? Don't cry on our daughter's birthday. That's bad luck." Lotus wiped her eyes quickly and thought to herself, "It's this little girl who will tie him down to his family."

After dinner, Yixin and Lotus tucked the children in before retiring to their own bed. Yixin told Lotus, "There's something I need to tell you. Please don't tell Mother and Father yet and of course don't mention it to anyone else. Captain Zhu appreciates how I take care of things and he wants to promote me to Lieutenant. I won't be commanding any troops. It's just a title, but with much better pay."

Lotus hesitated for a long time, then said tentatively, "You work hard to make your superiors happy and it must take a lot out of you. If it's too hard, why not come home. We'll just fish and farm, which is better than living at the mercy of others. It's good to be promoted, but there's no freedom. You know you can always come home. I don't want money or power, I just want us to be together."

"I know," Yixin said, "but I finally have a future in the army. We can't be peasants for all generations to come. You're right about living at the mercy of others, but as farmers we live at the mercy of nature, which is even harder. I'm doing this to give our family a better chance. Think of the kids!"

Lotus said, "But Xu Pingyuan, he divorced his wife ......"

Yinxin pulled Lotus into his arms: "Don't think about such nonsense. I'm not Xu Pingyuan."

After being home for three days, Yixin went back to his station, and life at home returned to its usual daily routine.

One day in August, the sound of drums, gongs and brass horns sounded from the village gate. Lotus leaped to her feet: "Are the Japs here again?!" She scooped up Daffodil and ran to find her two sons: "Daqing! Erqing! Come to Mama! We need to run!" But she saw that the front gate of her yard was wide open, and Daqing, Erqing and her in-laws were nowhere to be found. Now Lotus was really worried, and she ran into the street holding her chubby, wiggly Daffodil. She felt ready to pass out from standing up so quickly and then running so fast with her little bound feet and heavy child, but she kept yelling, "Daqing! Erqing! Where are you?"

The sound of horns, gongs and drums came closer, and Lotus felt her heart thundering in her throat. From a distance, she could vaguely see a crowd of boys running towards her, and she thought she saw Daqing and Erqing among them: "The Japs surrendered! The war's over! They're gone for good! The World War is over!"

Lotus saw the crowd getting closer, but it felt as if the yelling, music and cheering were floating further and further away until she couldn't hear them anymore. Her legs gave out and she fainted.

When she woke up, she was in her own bed surrounded by Daqing, Erqing and Daffodil. While in the street, Daffodil had learned to say, "Mama, The Japs surrendered!" Daqing and Erqing both nodded. It took a long while before Lotus realized what that meant: "The war's over? No more war?"

Lotus's mother-in-law entered the room with a bowl in her hands: "How are you feeling? Have some soup. I can cook you some poached eggs too." Lotus's insides churned and she gagged with nausea. The mother-in-law looked at her and put down the bowl: "Are you pregnant again?" Lotus thought for a while. In fact, she hadn't had her period since Yixin came home three months ago.

The Japs were gone. The war was over! Lotus put her hands on her slightly bulging belly and thought to herself, "My husband can finally come home. Then I'll give birth to this new baby, and we'll have a peaceful life together."

Lotus waited day after day but there was no sign of Yixin. Yixin's father sent someone to the station to tell Yixin about Lotus's pregnancy. The man came back and said, "Your son was so busy he didn't even have time to talk. I told him about Lotus and all he did was grunt at me. It looks like he can't come home right now." Lotus was despondent. But her father-in-law said, "Of course. The Communists and the Nationalists fought side by side to drive out the Japs, but which of them is going to rule now that the country is back in our own hands? Of course he can't come home. Both sides must be on high alert right now! There may even be a civil war!"

One night, Lotus awoke to the sound of knocking. She put on a jacket and went to the front door, and when she opened it, there was Yixin! He quickly entered and closed the door behind him. Lotus was about to scream with joy but Yixin stopped her: "Don't make any noise! Don't wake up Mother and Father! I have something to tell you and then I have to leave!" Lotus said, "I'll light a candle and fix you some food." Yixin said urgently, "There's no time! I'm here to tell you that the army I'm in is the Communist army. I didn't know that when I enlisted and only realized it later. Now the Nationalists are after us. They're in control of the whole country and they'll kill any Communists they run into! I need to retreat with my troops into the northern mountains. If anyone asks, just say you don't know where I am and you don't know which army I'm with. Don't let anyone know I'm a Communist!"

"But you're innocent!" Lotus protested. "You didn't know that when you enlisted and only found out later. Can you just de-list yourself now that you know you're in the wrong army? Just de-list and come home!"

Yinxin said, "It's not that simple! It's always easier to get on a boat than to get off. I'm now a Communist Party member, and a captain too! The only thing waiting for me is immediate execution if the Nationalists find me. My only way out is to go with the Communists." He looked at Lotus's belly and said, "I'm so sorry. I may not see this child when it's born, but just wait. I'll come back for all of you!" Then he rushed out.

Lotus ran after him and stuffed food in his pockets as she sobbed and said, "Be careful! Be safe! We're all waiting for you!"

The wait began. At first, Yixin occasionally sent money, but then he disappeared without a trace. After the birth of her second daughter, Jade, Lotus spent little time recovering before going back to work. She had much to do with the livelihood her entire family depending on her. She spent her days in silence, her face expressionless as she simply worked and worked. Sometimes, she would sit by the great Baiyang Lake and think about her worry-free life as a maiden in her parents' home. But now she had Daqing, Erqing, Daffodil and her newborn daughter Jade, and she also had her old and frail in-laws to support. She was just an illiterate country woman with little bound feet. It was her inner strength and strong will that carried her through each day and helped her endure whatever came her way. She shouldered the burden of raising the four Xu offsprings and keeping her family intact.

(19) FAMINE

There wasn't a girl in the Xu family who was as sharp tonged as Daffodil. Daqing and Erqing were no match for her. She could leave them at a loss for words any time she wanted.

One day, Daffodil was feeling bored, and knowing that her mother Lotus was out, she wanted her eldest brother Daqing to take her to Baiyang Lake and teach her how to swim. Lotus had set a hard rule that nobody should ever take Daffodil to the lake, because Lotus believed that Daffodil was a reincarnation of her third son Sanqing, who had drowned in the lake. Lotus believed that the lake was a bad omen for Daffodil, and that she should stay away from that lake forever. In any case, Daqing needed to stay home to feed little Jade her lunch.

Daffodil said, "Daqing, look – if I don't know how to swim, I'll die if I ever fall in the water, so teaching me how to swim is like saving my life. Mama will reward you when she gets back!" Knowing that she was talking nonsense, Daqing replied, "We can't leave. What about little Jade?" Daffodil had a solution: "Erqing should be home any time now. He can feed Jade."

"But Mama has forbidden me to take you to the lake. Sanqing drowned in the lake. If I take you there, she'll beat me when she gets back," Daqing said.

"That's exactly the point!" Daffodil said, "Sanqing didn't know how to swim! If he'd been taught, he wouldn't have died. That's why you need to teach me!"

Daqing said, "Mama says swimming is for boys, and girls shouldn't swim."

"Can't girls drown too? Do girls just float if they fall into the lake?" Daffodil hated hearing that girls couldn't do something that boys could.

"Girls don't fish, so how will they fall in the lake?"

"Girls do laundry at the lake!"

"But that's in shallow water. You won't drown."

Daffodil lost her patience: "When I grow up I'll take a boat into the middle of the lake to do laundry! The water is cleaner there! If you don't teach me, I'll tell Mama you've been mean to me. I'll cry when she comes back!"

Daqing was worried. Crying was Daffodil's weapon. Whenever she cried, he and Erqing always got punished. But he knew he couldn't take her to the lake. In his frustration, he began shoving food into Jade's little mouth. While turning to argue with Daffodil, he accidentally put the spoon up to Jade's nose, and a peanut slipped into one of her nostrils.

Jade stared in silence for a brief second, then began wailing. Since Daqing and Daffodil had been too busy arguing, they hadn't seen the peanut go into Jade's nose and didn't know what was wrong. They tried to console Jade, but she just kept screaming!

"She never cries like this," Daffodil said. "Something's wrong!"

Daqing realized the problem when he saw Jade rubbing her nose and snorting hard. He and Daffodil laid Jade down flat on the bed and raised her face to look into her nostrils. There they saw the peanut! They tried everything they could think of, picking her nose with their pinkies, a chopstick and a thin little twig .... They held her upright and jumped up and down, hoping that would dislodge the peanut. They pushed at the top part of her nostril, hoping to squeeze the peanut out. They ran around the yard while holding Jade. Nothing worked, and in fact that peanut slid even further up into Jade's nostril! Jade was becoming hoarse from crying so loud, and Daqing and Daffodil were dumbfounded.

Just then, Erqing came home. Seeing the urgent situation, he said the only way to get the peanut out was to make Jade sneeze. He got a jar of chili pepper powder from the kitchen and put it under Jade's nose. Wailing and kicking, Jade waved her arms to push it away, and Mama's jar of chili pepper powder went smashing to the ground. Daqing, Erqing and Daffodil all started yelling out blame, complaints and new ideas. Topping all their voices was Jade's ear-piercing wailing. The yard was in complete chaos!

After coming home that evening, Lotus would have given her three older children a good beating if her parents-in-law hadn't stopped her. The three older children went to sleep with their grandparents while

Lotus held Jade in her arms. Exhausted from crying, Jade was now asleep. Lotus cried, "My poor Jadeyour father hasn't even met you! God, please don't take my Jade from me!"

That hateful peanut stayed in Jade's nose for eight whole days before finally sliding out. The whole family teared up with relief! But Jade was left with chronic sinusitis into her adulthood.

One year, there was suddenly a shortage of food. As if the great Baiyang Lake was cursed, the fishermen came home empty-handed, and children couldn't find shrimp like they used to. The abundant flocks of wild ducks, geese and other birds had all disappeared. There weren't even any frogs, and the large lotus lagoons were bare and desolate. As everyone's winter stock was nearly consumed, and nothing had yet grown from the ground, the shadow of starvation loomed over the villages like a clawed monster ready to seize lives.

All that Lotus and her four children did all day was to look for anything edible they could get their hands on. Daqing and Erqing, now big strong boys, became experts at finding edible plants in the wild. They held contests in the fields over who could find more plants to take home and make their mother smile. Eight-year-old Daffodil and four-year-old Jade also walked through the fields in search of anything that looked like food, likewise hoping to bring home something to make their mother happy. Each of the four children wished more than anything to be Mama's favorite child, to bring her happiness and receive her praise.

One day Daffodil and Jade dashed home giggling while holding something in the front of their shirts: "Mama! Mama! We found mushrooms. Big mushrooms! Red mushrooms!" They ran to their mother. Lotus looked at the mushrooms in their shirts and felt the blood drain from her body: "Did you eat any of this?! Tell me you didn't eat this! Spit it out! Spit it out, NOW!"

Daffodil and Jade were scared by their mother's yelling: "Mama, we didn't take even one bite. We were saving it all for you. Jade wanted to have just a little lick, but I didn't even let her do that." Lotus pulled her daughters into her arms and cried, "My silly girls! Those are poisonous. You'll die if you eat them! You scared me!"

For several months, they ate nothing but vegetable soup – in fact, just a big pot of wild plants boiled in plain water with a few small handfuls of cornmeal. They didn't even have any salt. All of them were reduced to skin and bones, and their clothes hung loose on their bodies. Somehow Erqing grew a big belly, which just kept getting bigger, even though he was bone thin everywhere else. The skin on his belly had a translucent look, as if it would pop with one touch. Lotus was so worried about Erqing that she packed the last little bit of wheat they had and took it to the village doctor. The doctor said, "I can't take your wheat, because I can't cure your son. Doctors treat diseases, not starvation. He needs protein. He needs meat, milk and eggs. That's the cure. But I have none of that!"

Lotus cried, "My Sanqing has already left me. If anything happens to my Erqing, I don't want to live anymore! I wish I could cut up my own body and give it to him to eat! But you know my husband has been gone for five years. I have to live on to raise my children. If not for that, I would give my body to Erqing to eat!"

Lotus's mother-in-law and father-in-law prayed to Buddha every night. They prayed for the safe return of their only son Yixin. They prayed that their grandson's big belly would shrink back to normal. Lotus was impatient whenever she heard them pray. She thought to herself, "Why don't they do something useful? They've been praying all this time and nothing has changed!"

(20) A JEEP ARRIVES

Starvation brought a pall of silence to the village. There was no sound of kids playing in the streets or women gossiping. Even the men stayed home to conserve their energy. In this dead silence, the sound of a military jeep entering the village was especially loud and disturbing. Some people were curious enough to stick their heads out for a look, and believing it had nothing to do with them, they went back inside. Others were just too hungry to care.

Lotus was preparing a lunch out of some dandelions that her sons had brought home from the field when the jeep drove up to her yard. Three men in uniform got out and walked towards Lotus, and a dozen thoughts and guesses flashed through her mind: Yixin! The army! Communists? Nationalists? Are they here to arrest Yixin? Is Yixin DEAD? Are they here to tell me he's dead? Is Yixin ALIVE? Has he been promoted like Xu Pingyuan? Xu Pingyuan! The man who divorced his wife! Is it a divorce notice?

A DIVORCE NOTICE!!!!!

Lotus stood up, her mind in a fog, and she looked like she was both smiling and crying. For a second she couldn't hear what the men were saying. She felt as if she were watching herself sleepwalking.

One of the men raised his voice a little bit: "Excuse us, Madam. Is this the Xu residence?"

Lotus murmured, "Every family is surnamed Xu in our village."

The man said, "Very well, Madam. We're looking for Colonel Xu Yixin's wife Lotus."

Lotus could almost see the divorce notice that she was convinced they were about to hand to her. Gritting her teeth, she struggled not to collapse and thought to herself: "I will keep standing! Even if my husband wants to divorce me, I need to be strong for my four children. Their mother stands tall no matter what!"

Calming herself, Lotus said in a steady tone of voice, "I'm Lotus. How can I help you?"

The three soldiers snapped to attention and saluted to Lotus in unison. Lotus was completely confused: "What is this?"

One man said, "We've been sent by Colonel Xu to hand-deliver his letter. We're also here to bring you food and to offer any help you need."

Lotus waited for a moment and then said, "Is that all? You don't have anything, like a notice, for me?"

The three soldiers looked at one another in puzzlement: "No, we weren't ordered to deliver any notice."

Lotus collapsed to the ground, and the three men hurried over and lifted her to a bench. Just then, Yixin's parents came out of their room, and the three men saluted them as well. They produced Yixin's letter.

Being the only literate person in the household, Yixin's father opened the letter and read it silently with trembling lips. Yixin's mother slapped him on the back: "What is it, you old fool? Read it out loud!"

Yixin's father said, "Yixin is going to be a government official in Beijing. He wants to take all of us to Beijing!"

Upon hearing this, Yixin's mother and Lotus both started to cry, drawing the four children running into the yard: "Daddy is a government official now. He wants to take us to Beijing!"

"What does Daddy Look like?" Jade asked. Lotus pulled Jade into her arms: "My poor girl. You're five years old and haven't met your father!"

The military officer said, "Madam, this is a happy occasion, please don't cry. Our jeep is loaded with flour, rice, pork and other food. We'll carry it into your kitchen now."

Daqing and Erqing jumped up: "We can help!"

The soldier laughed: "There's no need. Eat well and develop strong arms and legs and then you can help us."

The gloomy kitchen came to life, and Lotus felt as if she were flying. Inviting the three men to sit down at the main table, she rushed to the kitchen to make lunch. She couldn't believe her eyes when she saw the heavy bags of flour and rice and the slabs of pork on her kitchen counter. Two of the soldiers followed her into the kitchen and smiled as they said, "Madam, we're under orders from Colonel Xu to cook and serve you food. You don't have to lift a finger."

Lotus said, "No that's not proper! You're guests, and how can a hostess let her guests cook?"

The two soldiers laughed: "Madam, this is an order from Colonel Xu. We'll be punished if we don't follow it."

Lotus said, "All right, then, but I'll help you."

The two soldiers took out their army kitchen knives and cut up the pork in no time. While the pork was cooking, they made a big pot of steamed rice. The delicious smell of pork and rice was a heavenly feast to the senses, and Lotus couldn't imagine anything that would make her feel more ecstatic. The whole family was drunk from the delicious and torturing smell as they waited for the food to be ready.

As growing boys, Daqing and Erqing lived for food. While waiting for the meat to cook, they each gulped down a big bowl of rice, then ran in and out of the kitchen. Every time they passed the wok, they pulled out a piece of boiling meat and tossed it into their mouths. Lotus was afraid they'd get sick from eating undercooked meat, or from suddenly having to handle so much rich food, so she chased them out of the kitchen again and again. But nothing could stop them from going back or distract their eyes from the magnetic pull of that wok full of meat. When it was time to sit down for the meal, Lotus warned the children over and over again not to eat too much, and to leave room for water, as they would be thirsty.

Attracted by the tantalizing smell of food and the shiny jeep, villagers came to Lotus's yard to congratulate her. Lotus knew everyone was starving and that she couldn't hoard all this food to herself, so she gave a bowl of flour, a bowl of dry rice and a few pieces of meat to everyone who came by. By the time all the village families got their share, she had very little left.

After all was quiet, the three soldiers returned to the jeep and took out another load of flour, rice and eggs. They said, "Madam, we knew you'd be kind-hearted and share the food with everyone, so we saved this load just for you. Colonel Xu is being discharged from the military and he was been assigned Director of Finance in the Department of Civil Affairs in Beijing. He'll be allocated a house there and is getting everything ready. Then he'll bring all of you to Beijing. It shouldn't take more than a month." Lotus expressed her gratitude and saw the soldiers off.

Watching the jeep disappear into the distance, Lotus thought of how a person's fate can change in a day. This morning had been just an ordinary morning. But tonight, everything was different.

After the meal of pork and rice, Erqing's huge belly shrank significantly overnight. Lotus made sure he ate three eggs a day, and in a little more than a week, his belly was flat like before. Remembering how she'd complained about her parents-in-law's praying, Lotus was deeply ashamed. She knelt down to Buddha and prayed, "Powerful and merciful Buddha, I'm sorry I didn't believe in you. You saved my Erqing. You're reuniting my family. I'm forever indebted to you and will never doubt you again."

Yixin's parents refused to go to Beijing. Yixin's father said, "The world out there is dirty and dangerous. We'll keep this land and this home for Yixin. If anything happens to his career, he'll at least have this home to come back to."

Lotus asked the neighbors to look after her in-laws. She took Daqing, Erqing, Daffodil and Jade and got on a train to Beijing.

HongGe

(21) A DISPLACED BOY

After escaping the land reform bloodbath, Nanny Wu fled to Beijing with HongGe, the only remaining male descendant of Master Gao Liancai. There they found Gao Zhanxiang, the elder cousin of HongGe's father.

Gao Zhanxiang was one of the first graduates of the Beijing Union University of Medicine, and a classmate of the pioneering medical practitioners Lin Qiaozhi and Wu Jieping. After graduation, he became a resident doctor at Beijing Union Hospital and eventually a neurosurgeon. He once performed emergency brain surgery on a Communist army general, saving his life against all odds and entering the textbooks for his combination of precision, judgment and intuition. As he gained prominence among the government's top leadership, he was commonly referred to as the "First Knife" in Chinese neurosurgery.

Dr. Gao and his family lived in a house near the Summer Palace. Sighing with sympathy and sadness over the fate of their relatives in the Northeast, Dr. and Mrs. Gao had the maid prepare guest rooms for HongGe and Nanny Wu. But after they were settled, Mrs. Gao pulled Dr. Gao aside and whispered, "This is a boy from a landlord's family. Although he's only seven years old, he's still an escaped landlord! What are you going to tell the Party secretary at your hospital? How are you going to explain why we have an additional child in the house?"

The Communist Party assigned a "Party secretary" to every workplace to provide governance and leadership, including every commercial establishment, school, hospital, factory, research institution, agency, restaurant, small business and organization.... Wherever there were groups of people, there would be a Party secretary. This person had absolute authority and a direct line to the police and the Communist Party. The Party secretary and his or her team oversaw every aspect of people's personal lives, including when people got married and had children, where they lived and who was a part of their household. At the slightest suspicion, a phone call would be made to the police, and that family would see no end of trouble.

Having an escaped landlord in the house was a direct violation of Party regulations, even when the "landlord" was a seven-year-old boy. Taking in HongGe and Nanny Wu put Dr. and Mrs. Gao under considerable risk.

After thinking for a moment, Dr. Gao said, "It is in fact troublesome and risky. His family background is a blot on his prospects, but he's my cousin's son and I cannot abandon him. Let me talk with the president of the hospital and have him talk to the Party secretary. I'll tell him that since we don't have a son, I'm adopting a boy from my hometown. That will allow the boy to be properly documented to live here and go to school. But we'll need to change his name. We'll take out his middle name Peng, which links him to his generation of the Gao family, and just call him Gao Hong. That should be sufficient. After all, I command a measure of respect in the hospital, and I think the president will help me."

Mrs. Gao said, "We can say he's our adoptive son, but since he's already seven years old, he may not like to call us Mom and Dad; the best he can probably do is Aunt and Uncle."

Dr. Gao said, "That's fine, I don't mind."

Dr. and Mrs. Gao had a daughter, Gao Haitang, who was a student at the prestigious Beijing University. Since Haitang wasn't living at home, the only other people living in the Gao household were a maid named Sunyi and her husband, Laosun. Sunyi had been Mrs. Gao maid since they were both teenagers. When Mrs. Gao gave birth to Haitang, Sunyi's own son was four months old. Sunyi weaned her son from her breast milk so she could become the wet nurse for Mrs. Gao's new baby. She'd fed and helped raise Miss Haitang like her own child. Her husband Laosun was the Gao family's chauffeur and gardener.

HongGe and Nanny Wu were used to the spacious Gao compound in the Northeast; now they were confined to this two-story urban house full of things they dared not touch. The garden's flowers, shrubs and plants were so exquisitely tended and pruned that HongGe and Nanny Wu felt intimidated even to look at them. The house was filled with antiques, vases, crystals, oil paintings, flower arrangements, music boxes, huge clocks reaching from floor to ceiling, Persian rugs, a grand piano, and soft beds with lavish covers and pillows. They hardly dared to sit down for fear of breaking or soiling something.

HongGe observed that Nanny Wu was not as sharp and decisive as before and that she was somehow afraid of Mrs. Gao's maid Sunyi. Whenever she did anything, she looked at Sunyi for approval, as if Dr. and Mrs. Gao were the first-tier masters, and Sunyi the second-tier master. It seemed that HongGe and Nanny Wu had to make both tiers happy.

"Nanny Wu, don't touch that. You don't know how to use the coffee machine, and you might break it."

"Nanny Wu, I told you not to wipe the piano with a wet cloth. It will damage the wood and it leaves streaks. We're having guests this afternoon and look how bad you've made the piano look!"

"Nanny Wu, when you serve tea, you mustn't point the teapot spout at Mrs. Gao. That's very rude. Don't you know?"

"Nanny Wu, haven't we called in a tailor and made new clothes for you? Why are you still wearing your old clothes? That damages the image of the Gao family!"

"HongGe, you're a young master of the house. How come you still haven't learned how to use a knife and a fork? Didn't I show you already?"

"HongGe, I told you to brush your teeth with toothpaste. Why are you still using salt? That's why you have bad teeth! Nanny Wu should teach you better!"

"HongGe, do you really have to make so much noise when coming down the stairs? You thump around like a low-class laborer rather than stepping lightly like a young master in a decent family!"

"HongGe, why are you speaking in the Northeastern dialect again? You need to change the way you talk!"

When Dr. Gao wasn't home, Mrs. Gao let Sunyi say whatever she wanted. If Dr. Gao happened to be there, Mrs. Gao would laugh and say, "Sunyi, there's no hurry, they'll learn eventually. Nanny Wu, please don't be upset. Sunyi is trying to do the best for this family. HongGe, Sunyi is of an older generation and she instructs you because she loves you, do you understand? You should be grateful and obey Sunyi." Dr. Gao was buried in his medical journals and never noticed or cared about what was being said. As long as there was no obvious conflict at home, he thought everything was fine.

HongGe had been through a lot for a seven-year-old. The sorrow of losing his entire family, the disruption of moving to a completely new environment and the restrictions of Dr. Gao's household all drew him closer to Nanny Wu. She was the cornerstone of his life, the only person who connected his past and his present, and the only person who truly loved him. HongGe became withdrawn and spent most of the time in his room, because the moment he stepped out, he became a troublesome boy who did everything wrong.

HongGe told Nanny Wu, "I want to go back to the Gao compound."

With a sigh, Nanny Wu said, "The Gao compound doesn't belong to the Gao family anymore. It's where the county government is now. Going back there would be asking for a swift death."

HongGe said, "How about if we go back to Papa Li Ginseng in the mountains? I can go hunting and find ginseng with him and play with Tiger." Tiger was Li Ginseng's youngest son and HongGe's best friend when he lived in the mountains.

Nanny Wu replied, "That mountain has now been taken over by the government too. Thank God we left, or Qiu Jiefang would have found you."

"Can't they find me here in Beijing too?" HongGe asked with frustration.

Nanny Wu said, "The spirits of your ancestors are watching over you. We're in a good place now. Your uncle saved an important person, so no one will bother us in his house. He changed your name too, so you'll be safe. We have nowhere else to go but here."

Looking at HongGe's gloomy face, Nanny Wu embraced him: "I know. You've been through so much at such a young age. You've been through more than anyone should experience in a lifetime! But that's all the more reason for you to live a good life! You're not only living for yourself, but for all of your family. Dr. Gao says that after the New Year he'll send you to school. That's your chance to go places in life, so you need to do well!"

HongGe said: "I want to become a commander high up in the government when I grow up, and then I'll take back the Gao compound!"

Nanny Wu laughed: "Yes, become a powerful man and return to the Gao compound. But there's no one left for you to see there. Your first aunt and second aunt are still alive, but they were forced to remarry. Oh, yes! Your little cousin Lan is still alive and living with your second aunt. You could go back and see her. And maybe you could see Zhao'er and Cai Xia. They've been married for two years and must have a child by now!"

Every time Miss Haitang came home, Sunyi smiled as brightly as a blooming spring flower. She shut HongGe and Nanny Wu in their rooms so Miss Haitang wouldn't see them, but HongGe peeked at her through a crack in the door. She was so pretty and proud, and her clothes were so elegant. Mrs. Gao and Sunyi sat on either side of her, each holding one of her hands, gazing and smiling at her as if they'd go to the moon to get anything she wanted. Dr. Gao completely melted every time he saw his daughter and looked ten years younger. No matter how unreasonable Haitang's requests might seem, Dr. Gao always said yes. HongGe looked sadly at Miss Haitang: "It's wonderful to have parents. It's too bad I lost both of mine."

(22) END OF CHILDHOOD

Summer Palace Elementary School promoted new culture, so while other schools were still having a long winter break in anticipation of the upcoming Lunar New Year, the Summer Palace Elementary school was already back in session on January third.

Laosun drove HongGe to school. HongGe was wearing a new outfit and carrying a brand new school bag. Laosun told him, "Your school is not very far away, and it's easy to find. You go north on the street outside of our house, then turn west when you see the dumpling house over there. That will take you to your school. I need to drive the doctor to work every morning, so you'll need to walk to school starting tomorrow. Do you remember the way?"

His few months in Dr. Gao's house had taught HongGe how to avoid troubling anyone and how to please others, so he said in the best Mandarin he could manage, "Mr. Sun, please don't worry, I can walk by myself. I could even have walked this morning. You always care so much about me and take such good care of me." Laosun smiled.

In the distance, HongGe saw a beautiful mountain with exquisite buildings surrounding an emerald-colored lake, and he couldn't help but ask, "Mr. Sun, what is that?" "Oh! You don't know what that is? Of course, you've hardly been out in the few months you've been here. That's the Summer Palace – that's where the emperors used to spend their summers. Now it's a public garden. It's right behind your school, so you should go see it. All boys from your school go there after school."

But HongGe never had a chance to see the Summer Palace, because Nanny Wu expected him home within fifteen minutes of dismissal. If he wasn't home within fifteen minutes, Nanny Wu would lose her mind and run through the streets looking for him, so HongGe had to run home as fast as he could. Sometimes he was just a few minutes late and would bump into a worried Nanny Wu out looking for him, and he would lose his patience and say, "I'm not a three year old! I know my way! You shouldn't run around like this when I'm just a few minutes late, or all my friends will laugh at me!"

Nanny Wu said with an apologetic smile, "Yes, yes, I know my HongGe is a big boy now, and I won't go out looking for your next time. Let's go inside. You must be hungry." But the next day she would be out in the streets looking for him again. The anxious look on her face immediately changed into a relieved smile when she saw him. No matter how angry HongGe was, Nanny Wu would always run around looking for him. HongGe was so frustrated that one morning he told her, "Nanny Wu, if you go out looking for me again today, I'm REALLY going to be mad at you. I won't talk to you anymore! I hate you!" Then he walked out the door, leaving Nanny Wu standing sadly in the doorway.

At dismissal, HongGe was determined to go home late. He walked slowly and then stopped at the dumpling house to watch the cooks make dumplings. He was fascinated by how they held the dough wrapper in one hand and smeared on some filling with the other hand, then formed it into a dumpling with a quick turn of both hands. And all of the dumplings were the same shape and size! How skillful they were! HongGe stood at the window and watched for a long time before slowly walking home. He was thinking: "I'm going to make Nanny Wu run around for a really long time today so she knows she can't treat me like a baby anymore!"

When he turned into his street, there was no sign of Nanny Wu. HongGe smiled quietly – "She finally listened to me!" He walked across Dr. Gao's yard and up the front steps, but then froze as he pushed the front door open. Nanny Wu was standing in the middle of the hall weeping. Mrs. Gao and Sunyi were standing on either side of her, and her luggage was at her feet.

HongGe asked: "What's going on, Nanny Wu? Auntie, what's happening?"

Mrs. Gao put on a smile and said, "HongGe, you're home! Come have a seat and let me tell you something. It's like this: The vice president of your uncle's hospital, Dr. Yan, has asked our family for a favor. It's getting closer to the Lunar New Year and they have many chores around the house, and on top of that, their daughter-in-law went into early labor and gave birth to a new baby boy! So their house is in chaos right now. They can't find trustworthy help on such short notice. They've been to our house and have met our Nanny Wu, and they like her very much. They've asked us to lend Nanny Wu to them, just for a couple of months until they find someone more permanent. He's Uncle's boss, so we really can't say no. The good thing is that you're a big boy now, so it won't matter so much if you don't see your nanny for just a few months, will it?"

HongGe felt as if a big ball was stuck in his throat. He couldn't talk because if he did, the ball would turn into a flood of tears and shoot out of his eyes and nose. It was clear to him that Nanny Wu was never coming back.

Looking at HongGe's sad face, Nanny Wu said, "Madam, I'll go wherever you want me to go. My only wish is to say goodbye to HongGe. Please allow the two of us a little time, and I promise I'll leave right afterwards."

Mrs. Gao said, "Very well. Sunyi and I are going to the tailor, and Laosun will drive us. That will leave you and HongGe here alone. We'll be back in one hour, and then Laosun will drive you to Dr. Yan's house." With that, she and Sunyi walked out the front door.

As soon as the door was closed, HongGe yelled, "Nanny Wu!" and burst out crying.

Nanny Wu rushed over and took him into her arms. She was crying too, but she tried hard to put on a smile: "Silly boy! Don't cry. I'm just going to help out and then I'll be back. Don't worry."

HongGe shouted, "Nanny Wu! It's all my fault! I shouldn't have said I hated you. I didn't mean it! I didn't mean it at all! You're my mother! How can I hate you? It's all my fault. You can beat me. Beat me! Punish me however you want! Just don't leave me!"

Nanny Wu cried, "You silly boy! Has Nanny ever laid a finger on you? Have I ever blamed you for anything? You're a big boy going to a new-style school, and having an old country woman following you embarrasses you in front of your friends. I would be mad, too! It's all that hiding and running we did back then that left me with this non-stop worrying. I can't seem to shake it off. Please forgive me."

Nanny Wu continued, "Please don't be mad at your Auntie. She has her reasons. This is a communist country now, and anyone with a servant is an exploiter leading a bourgeois lifestyle. No one is allowed to have servants anymore. Even Sunyi, who's been with her for decades, has to leave, not to mention someone like me! It's bound to happen! Remember that your Uncle and Auntie took you in when you were running for your life. They risked a lot to raise you like their son and send you to school. You must remember how good they are to you! Don't blame them. They've already done so much for us. If not for them, you and I might already be dead!"

HongGe cried again, "Nanny Wu, when I grow up and have my own house, I'll come get you, I promise. Wait for me to grow up!"

Nanny Wu said, "I will! I will wait for you. When you have your own children, I'll help you take care of them. I'll go back to the Gao compound with you. I will wait for that day to come! You need to do well in school. Work hard. Remember, everything you do is for the honor of your entire family, through all generations, all the way back to the beginning of time!"

With Nanny Wu gone, nobody waited for HongGe after school anymore. They didn't even wait for him at dinner. If he was home before dinnertime, he would eat with Dr. and Mrs. Gao, but if he came home after dinner, he would go to the kitchen and find some leftovers to eat by himself before retreating to his room. In the morning, he got up, washed, dressed and got ready for school by himself. He grabbed a pastry or a pork bun from the breakfast table, said goodbye to Dr. and Mrs. Gao, and set off for school.

The departure of Nanny Wu brought a premature end to HongGe's childhood. He was no longer the little boy HongGe, and became Gao Hong who had to face the world by himself. But he also realized he was not alone. He had his Grandpa who had lit up his heart with his last smile. He had his Nana, who had given him her otter fur and connected him with Papa Li Ginseng. He had his birth mother, Li Meidi, who had entrusted him to Nanny Wu with her dying breath. He had his stepmother, Guan Lingzhi, who had stood bravely before the land reform soldiers to protect him. He had his father Gao Zhanren, who had entrusted him to Nanny Wu and then given his life to avenge the massacre of his family. He also had his dear Nanny Wu, Papa Li Ginseng, Zhao'er and Cai Xia, Dr. and Mrs. Gao, and all the other people who had helped him. Gao Hong would carry all of them in his heart, and live on.

(23) THE LONER

Gao Hong now had all the time he wanted to explore the Summer Palace, but he didn't go with his noisy schoolmates. They did boyish things like exploring caves, climbing trees and throwing rocks, but those things didn't interest Gao Hong. He liked to walk and think. Every day after school, he entered the Summer Palace from the North Gate and walked to the back of Wan Shou Mountain, where he found a large flat rock. He did his homework there using the rock as a desk.

School was easy for him, as he had a natural ability to absorb language and understand numbers. His unusual life experience gave him a special ability to observe, think and find deeper connections among things. His quiet, piercing eyes missed nothing. He was sensitive to his teachers' intentions and could usually predict the direction they'd be taking as soon as class started. Gao Hong also had a greater than usual tolerance for stress and frustration. While his classmates complained about the amount of homework, he quietly worked away at it and finished before the others even started. While pop quizzes left his classmates frozen with anxiety, Gao Hong would quickly analyze the teacher's objective and the reason for the quiz, and adjust his thinking and answers accordingly.

Instead of playing with his classmates in the Summer Palace, Gao Hong sat quietly outside the Tower of Buddhist Incense and gazed at Kunming Lake for long periods of time. Or he would take a long walk from the back of the mountain to the Bridge of Seventeen Arches and then to the South Island, and come back around via the West Bank. Along the way, he would gaze at the beauty of the palace and let his thoughts wander freely. He was familiar with every detail of the Marble Boat after caressing every stone on it with his eyes. He knew all the stories depicted in the paintings along the Qing Dynasty Long Corridor because he had studied them all.

Day after day, year after year, Gao Hong walked in the Summer Palace. He came to regard the beautiful park as his friend because of the endless stories behind each painting, each tree, each temple and each bridge, just as every cell of his body carried the rich history of his ancestors.

Gao Hong was different. Nobody could get close to him and he had no real friends. His teachers worried that there was something wrong with him, but they were also impressed by his obedience of all of the school rules as well as his outstanding academic performance.

Starting from seventh grade, Gao Hong became a boarding student. Aside from occasional visits to Nanny Wu, he stayed in school at all times. His relationship with Dr. and Mrs. Gao became little more than their paying his tuition and dorm fees once a year and giving him spending money each quarter. Gao Hong was allowed to stay in his dorm during holidays and school breaks, but the school cafeteria was closed, leaving him with nowhere to eat. Fortunately, the headmaster, Mr. Lu, took him home for meals during school breaks.

It was 1959, and Gao Hong was now a young man of nineteen. He had the long limbs and broad shoulders of a typical Chinese northerner, and was quiet, gentle and smart as a whip. Lower-classmen continued to discuss his amazing academic records long after he graduated. But a dark cloud always hung over him, lurking inside of his political profile and threatening him future trouble. It was the fact he had been born to a landowning family.

At that time in China, a person's family background determined everything. Having a politically "black" categorization such as "landlord" would create setbacks for a person at every turn. The days of land reform were long gone, and the nationwide massacre of wealthy people had become a thing of the past. Indeed, China no longer had wealthy people in the traditional sense. Added to that, Gao Hong enjoyed the protection of his uncle, Dr. Gao, who was well-regarded among the Communist elite. Even though it was no longer a secret that Gao Hong was a grandson of one of the biggest landowners in the northeast, and the son of the notorious vengeful landlord Gao Zhanren, he didn't have to fear for his life, but he remained a member of the political underclass. He could never escape the stigma of being a landlord's son.

Every day he looked with envy at fellow students who proudly wore badges of the Communist Youth League. How he wished he could become a member of the CYL! He'd submitted an application every six months since the age of thirteen, and he'd sought out CYL representatives and talked with them numerous times about his aspiration. They always told him, "You cannot choose your birth, but you can choose your path. You'll be allowed to join the CYL if you demonstrate good moral character, excellence in academics and community service." Gao Hong excelled in academics and was always helping his teachers and other students, and he volunteered endless hours of service to the community, but year after year, his name was left off the induction list.

After too many tries and disappointments, Gao Hong finally accepted the fact that there was an unbridgeable gap between himself and someone with a politically correct birth. It was not about how hard he tried or what he did; it was his birth that determined everything, the same as the difference between him and Miss Haitang when he was living in Dr. Gao's house. Miss Haitang didn't even need to try; her birth was enough. But no matter how hard Gao Hong tried to please them, he couldn't change the fact that he was not Dr. and Mrs. Gao's son.

This realization brought Gao Hong a sense of relief. He shouldn't be so hard on himself when everything was out of his control and was not a reflection on him. He couldn't change his own birth, after all. At the same time, the revelation saddened him greatly – if he couldn't change his situation with his own efforts, what was left to him? As an orphan, effort was all he had, and if that made no difference, what hope did he have?

All high school graduates took a week-long college entrance exam in order to be admitted to any college in the country. With his academic records, Gao Hong was confident that he could gain admission to China's crown jewel, the one and only Tsinghua University. As it turned out, his test scores were far above the admission threshold for Tsinghua University, and he should have no problem getting in, as students had been told that test scores were the only factor for admission. Nevertheless, a rejection letter came. He had been rejected!

When Gao Hong went to the college admissions center to ask about the rejection, he was told that not only would he not be admitted to Tsinghua, but he would be denied admission to any college. It was because he had been born to a landlord's family, and his father had attempted to kill a land reform team leader.

Gao Hong left the college admission center like zombie and walked back to school, where he ran into his headmaster, Mr. Lu. Mr. Lu said, "Gao Hong, I want you to come for dinner tonight" Gao Hong kept walking as if he hadn't heard him. Catching up with him, Mr. Lu said, "Gao Hong, I know how you must feel! It must be very hard. But listen to me – everything will be alright! Come to my house for dinner. I have plans for you." Gao Hong ignored him and kept walking. Mr. Lu shouted after him, "Don't do anything silly! Come for dinner!"

Gao Hong walked out of the school and into the streets. The sound of cars, buses, people, merchants .... The world was too loud and he couldn't take it anymore. He needed to run, to escape to a place where he could be alone, away from school, away from everything, including everyone who knew him. Gao Hong started to run. People looked at him quizzically, wondering why this tall young man was running through the streets of Beijing with tears streaming down his face.

His footsteps took him to Dr. and Mrs. Gao's street, to his elementary school, to the Summer Palace, to Kunming Lake and eventually to the Bridge of Seventeen Arches. Gao Hong sank down on the bridge and cried. Why? Why? What can I do? What should I do? Is it always going to be like this? Is this going to be my life?

An elderly man was passing by, and he said to Gao Hong, "Young man, please excuse me for intruding, but may I ask what is wrong? Did you break up with your girlfriend? There will always be other girls! Go back to your parents. If anything happened to you, how would your parents live with it?" He walked away shaking his head.

Watching the old man walk away, Gao Hong thought sadly: My parents? Where are they? Suddenly he heard Nanny Wu's voice in his mind: "HongGe, remember your parents are always watching you from above!" Gazing at the sky, he sat there for a long time.

Mr. Lu was setting the dinner table when he turned and saw Gao Hong walk into his house, his head hanging in dejection. Mr. Lu said, "Come in, Gao Hong, come sit down. Let me tell you – you can have a good life even without going to college! College is overrated! I know you and I know what you can do. I've talked with the department of education, and they've agreed to allow you to work at our school as a junior teacher. I know you can do it. I have the confidence to put a senior class in your hands!" Gao Hong was overcome with gratitude. With nowhere to go after graduation, staying at his high school as a junior teacher would be a heaven-sent blessing.

After graduation, Mr. Lu had Gao Hong move into the teacher's dorm and directed the school office to supply him with soap and towels. Gao Hong also received his first month's salary: $13.50. Gao Hong put the $13.50 in an envelope; since the school covered his room and board, he wanted to give his salary to Nanny Wu.

Gao Hong started preparing math lessons for twelfth-graders. He was intimately familiar with all of the math topics covered in the college entrance exam. He had achieved a perfect score on the math section of the college entrance exam, assigning him to teach twelfth grade math was an ideal arrangement.

One day, Gao Hong was buried in his math notes when Mr. Lu entered his dorm room with a smile. Handing Gao Hong an envelope, he said, "I guess you're not meant to stay here after all. This small temple cannot hold a Buddha as large as you."

Gao Hong had no idea what the headmaster was talking about. Then he looked at the envelope, which had National Institute of Metallurgical Science printed on it in golden type. Goodness! Could it be that a college had admitted him? There was a college in this world that actually wanted him? He quickly opened the envelope. Yes, he had been admitted by a college called the National Institute of Metallurgical Science, one that he had neither applied to nor heard of.

Not knowing what to say, Gao Hong looked blankly at Mr. Lu. The headmaster said, "Are you speechless with happiness? Go to college! Hurry! I think classes have already started!"

Gao Hong turned the envelope around and around in his hands without a word. Then he suddenly thought of something, and he quickly pulled open his drawer and took out the envelope with the $13.50 in it. Handing it to the headmaster, he said: "Here is my salary. I'm returning it in full. But I'm so sorry to say that I already used the towels and the soap from the school office and can't return them."

Mr. Lu burst out laughing: "What a silly boy you are! Consider this money a gift to congratulate you. Go to the school office for some new soap and towels so you can take them with you to your college dorm!"

(24) THE ZEBRA CLUB

It was the second day of classes at the National Institute of Metallurgical Science. One of the last students to move in, Gao Hong had been assigned to Dorm 3, and he'd since discovered that many new students shared his experience – they'd never heard of this college, much less applied to it, and had been admitted at the last minute after being rejected elsewhere. The new students likewise share exceptional academic records; their college entrance exam scores were among the highest in the country. All came from politically "black" families that had prospered through property ownership, business or speculation, or who had family connections overseas or ties to the ousted Nationalist government.

At that time, people with undesirable family backgrounds were referred to as "born black." Those with strong academic skills but little political capital were referred to as "white skilled." Most desirable were people with favorable political standing and strong academics, who were referred to as "red skilled."

Gao Hong and his fellow newcomers were definitely born "black" but credited "white" for their strong academic records, with no hint of red. Consequently, this "black and white" class at the NIMS was referred to as the Zebra Club.

It occurred to Gao Hong that the Party and the government recognized a strong demand for well-trained people in metallurgical science. "College applicants don't naturally gravitate to this kind of college," he mused. "We're a group of outcasts who have been summoned to fill this gap." While knowing nothing about Metallurgical Science, Gao Hong treasured this opportunity to go to college, and was determined learn all he could and excel in this field. He had no way of knowing how students of the Zebra Club would be hurled to the bottom of society during the Cultural Revolution, and then flourish as pillars of China's metallurgy industry under the subsequent era of Reform and Opening.

Dorm 3 was the most coveted accommodation in the whole school because the top three floors were occupied by the Institute's female students. Women were extremely rare at a college of this kind, and many of its departments and classes were jokingly referred to as "monk departments" or "monk classes" because of the total absence of females. Among the five dorm buildings, only Dorm 3 was half occupied by women. The female students had their own entrance, and the passageways between the female and male floors were sealed off so they wouldn't encounter each other within the building. This only added to the dorm's mystique and allure.

Gao Hong was almost twenty years old, but he'd had little contact with women or girls outside of his immediate family. He'd paid no attention to girls in elementary school, and had then attended all-boy schools in middle school and high school; even the teachers, school administrators, staff, nurses, cooks and cleaning crew had all been men. Now he found himself living in the same building as the female students, and although he never saw any of them, he couldn't keep from smiling at the thought of sharing the building with women.

Girls soon became a secondary preoccupation for Gao Hong and the other male students, however, as their attention shifted to food. It was 1960, and China was in the midst of a horrible famine. The government guaranteed the Institute's food supply, but rations were limited. The school dealt with this situation by implementing a program called Big Kitchen – Small Kitchen. In the Big Kitchen, students could eat as much as they wanted, but with no guarantee of food quality. The Small Kitchen provided a better quality of food, but in strictly rationed amounts. Each student had to choose either the Big Kitchen or Small Kitchen at the beginning of the semester, and couldn't switch to the other until the end of the semester.

The choice of kitchens was the subject of fevered debate. A student nicknamed Indy (whose family were Overseas Chinese from Indonesia and had been targeted in every political campaign since moving to China) said, "The Small Kitchen has delicious pastries, fried dough, dumplings, rice and even meat! I hear the Big Kitchen only has cornmeal buns, and those turn rock-hard ten minutes after leaving the steamer." But another student named Situ said, "The Small Kitchen is for girls! I can't imagine a man choosing the Small

Kitchen! I'm choosing the Big Kitchen!" Situ's father, a general in the Nationalist army, had been imprisoned by the Communists, so Situ had been fated for admission to this Institute, despite scoring third place in all of Beijing in the college entrance exam. He always spoke with a military certainty and manliness. Gao Hong agreed with him and also opted for the Big Kitchen.

Finally lunchtime arrived. A crowd of twenty-year-old men, having endured four periods of grueling math and physics, poured into Big Kitchen like hungry wolves, banging their chopsticks on their bowls. Four kitchen workers trudged toward the serving table with two massive baskets of cornmeal buns. Before they had a chance to put the baskets on the table, the young men dashed over, grabbed two or three buns in each hand, and started eating. After five or six buns, they were full to bursting and couldn't eat another bite. But without meat, fat or animal products of any sort, and no fruit or vegetables, the cornmeal buns weren't very sustaining. The young men would be hungry again in a couple of hours and would regret not taking a few buns with them to munch on in the afternoon. As the students headed out of the Big Kitchen dining hall, the neighboring Small Kitchen opened, and a group of young women walked in.

The Small Kitchen was separated from the Big Kitchen by glass windows, and all the young men rushed to the windows to look at the girls. Oh, how beautiful they were! And how gracefully they walked! Pretending not to notice the young men, the young women chatted and giggled as they found their seats. Each of them was presented with a small bowl of rice soup and two lovely flour dumplings with pork filling. The wrapping of the dumplings looked so white and soft, and the meat filling juicy and delicious. The grains of rice in the soup looked plump and shiny, as if they'd melt in the mouth. The young men watched the young women lift spoonsful of soup to their lovely mouths, and watched them chew the juicy dumplings with their rosy lips politely closed. The sight only made the herd of young men even more ravenous, and they remained glued to the windows, gawking at the young women for a long time.

Mixed among the young women in the Small Kitchen was one male student, and that was Indy. He made a great show of relishing his food while pulling faces at the young men behind the windows in the

Big Kitchen. Opening his palms to draw a circle motioning to the young women around him, Indy gave a laugh of utter triumph. All of the male students felt the urge to strangle Indy, but his joy was short-lived; by two o'clock in the afternoon, he looked close to tears. "How long until dinner?" He asked miserably. Situ said sarcastically, "Tang Dynasty literature is full of writings on how the beauty of women is better than any delicious food, and saying that men could literally live on the beauty of women. You were surrounded by enough beauty at lunchtime to skip meals for the next three days!"

At the next meal, the Big Kitchen students employed a new strategy. Rather than grabbing the cornmeal buns with their hands, they used their chopsticks to poke the buns like a shish kabob. By holding a chopstick in each hand and poking them into the bun basket, they both extended their reach and extended their capacity beyond what their hands could hold. Someone who was highly skilled could skewer four buns with his dominant hand, and three more with his other hand. That way, they had not only enough for dinner, but also a couple left for an evening snack.

The kitchen workers had been directed to place their baskets of buns on the counter for sanitary reasons, but now they faced a hundred chopsticks poking at them all at once and forcing them to lower the baskets to the ground. They looked around helplessly, hoping that the poking contest would end before they were spotted and scolded by their higher-ups for setting the baskets on the ground.

The Big Kitchen students had a grading system for the number of buns picked up with a pair of chopsticks. A passing grade was five buns, a B was eight, and an A was ten buns. Whoever could pick up ten would proudly hold them up like two huge kabobs and return to their seat with a hero's cheers.

The food shortage didn't affect the students' hunger for knowledge. The Zebra Club was made up of people with high academic achievement who'd lost all hope of going to any college at all. In their eyes, the Institute had paid their ransom, so they were grateful and determined to work hard.

During an evening study session, a classmate named Jiang Wannian wrote a math problem on the board, saying, "Whoever can solve this will earn my utmost admiration!" Other students in the study room began trying to solve the problem, and the soft scratching of pencils on scratch paper and the ticking clock were all that could be heard in the room. Minutes passed, then hours, but nobody could solve the problem.

Finally the other students asked Jiang Wannian, "How would you solve it?" Jiang Wannian stood up and looked at the others with a smile of satisfaction, then walked to the board, ready to impress them with his superior math skills. Instead, he found himself "hung on the board," unable to solve the problem himself! Throwing his piece of chalk at the board, he exclaimed, "I don't believe it!" He returned to his seat to try more potential solutions on his scrap paper, since the board was already full of his scribbles. The students became possessed; Gao Hong, Situ, Indy and a girl named Mai all swore they would not go back to their dorm before solving the problem, even if it took them the whole night!

Hours passed, and the students were exhausted but more determined than ever. All of a sudden, Jiang Wannian's head landed on his desk with a bang. When the others asked him with alarm if he was hurt, he looked as if about to cry as he murmured, "There's one more condition in the original problem. I just realized I left it out when I copied the problem to the board." There was dead silence for three seconds, and then the room exploded. Pencils, erasers, pieces of chalk, paper balls, hats and gloves flew at Jiang Wannian from every corner of the room. He ducked his head, saying, "I'm sorry! I'm sorry!" over and over again, then rushed to the board and wrote down the missing condition. Gao Hong and a few others immediately wrote out the solution.

Twisting Jiang Wannian's arms behind his back, the other students walked him to the campus 24-hour convenience store and demanded that he buy everyone a late-night snack as an apology. Poor Jiang Wannian dug into every one of his pockets and took out every penny he had left. It was just enough to buy two bowls of noodles, but to students living on rock-hard, tasteless cornmeal buns, noodles were a luxury. Jiang Wannian handed the store clerk his money as if giving up one of his limbs, knowing it was all he had left for the rest of the month. Under the halo of a street lamp, the two bowls of noodles were passed from one student to the next, each taking just a few strands to enjoy. The soft noodles slid down their throats without even allowing them a chance to chew.

None of these young people would have imagined at that moment that forty years later, the Zebra Club would hold a reunion in a luxurious banquet hall, and that while gazing at the spread of exquisite cuisine and rare delicacies before them, they would recall with deep nostalgia those two precious bowls of late-night noodles that they'd once shared under the street lamp outside the campus convenience store. All they would talk about was how hard up Jiang Wannian was for the rest of the month after spending all his money on those noodles. In the decades after graduation, every Zebra Club member would say, "Yes, I'll support Jiang Wannian's business no matter what, just because of those two bowls of noodles back then!"

(25) YANRUO

The dorm buildings weren't supplied with hot water, so the students had to pool their money to buy thermos bottles, which they used to fetch their day's supply of hot water from the campus water house. Each dorm room would typically buy four or five thermos bottles. One evening, it was Gao Hong's turn to fetch hot water, and as he was about to open the door to the water house, it was pushed open from inside. Gao Hong held the door open as a young woman with a thermos bottle walked out. One glance at the young woman made him freeze in place, and time seemed to proceed in slow motion as her silky hair swayed in rhythm with her soft, bouncy steps. The warm light of the water house cast a halo around her slender figure. Her head was slightly lowered, and she looked down as she passed in front of Gao Hong, but her thick lashes couldn't hide her beautiful eyes. As she floated past Gao Hong, the world disappeared into the background of her gentle glow. Gao Hong gazed at her as if in a dream.

A sudden "Boom!" followed by the young woman's scream suddenly restored him to consciousness. Releasing the door, he dashed over to the young woman and asked, "Are you all right?" Her thermos bottle had exploded, scattering a thousand silver particles all around her as she continued to grip the frame of the thermos bottle in her hand. "Are you hurt? Are you burnt?" Gao Hong asked. The young woman assured him, "I'm fine, it's just the thermos." Gao Hong looked at the ruined thermos bottle and said, "It's a good thing your thermos was enclosed on the sides and has a long handle. Most of the hot water flew downwards, and the rest didn't reach your hand. You might have been badly burned with another kind of thermos. Are you sure you're all right?" "I'm not hurt at all," the young woman said. "But I'm sorry to lose the thermos. We'd all just pitched in to buy it."

"You can take my thermos," Gao Hong offered. "We have extras in our dorm room. Remember that with vacuum flasks, you can't fill a new one with hot water right away. Pour in a little hot water first and shake it around to distribute the heat, and then you can fill it the rest of the way. Otherwise it can be very dangerous."

The young woman refused Gao Hong's offer, but he insisted with a joke: "It's perfectly fine to take things from us. Our dorm room includes the children of landlords and Nationalist officers, and people with overseas connections." The young woman laughed: "Well in that case we're worse, because we have the children of big business owners and major speculators and capitalists." They laughed together.

Gao Hong said, "Please wait here. I'll be right back." He dashed into the water house, filled his thermos with hot water and ran back out to her: "You must live in Dorm 3. I'm in that building too. Let me walk you back."

They were both silent as they walked slowly back to the dormitory. Gao Hong was so nervous that he couldn't think of anything to say. Embarrassed by the silence, he wished that they'd reached Dorm 3 already, while at the same time hoping that their walk would go on forever.

Finally he opened the women's entrance to Dorm 3 and handed her his thermos bottle: "Please take it. Hurry inside. It's chilly." He watched as she walked up a few steps, and then she turned and said, "Thank you." Gao Hong smiled and stood there looking at the empty stairs long after she was gone. Then he realized: He'd forgotten to ask her name.

The next morning at breakfast, Gao Hong had no appetite, and he stood by the window of the Small Kitchen hoping to see the girl from the night before, but she never appeared. Indy came by and patted him on the shoulder: "Stop looking that way! The girls are beautiful, the food is tempting, but neither can fill your stomach. See, I'm back with the rest of you perfecting the art of cornmeal bun kabobs!"

The Communist Youth League secretary was an important student leadership position, and the family backgrounds of members of the Zebra Club disqualified almost all of them. The exception was a student named Wu Mancang, who came from a poor peasant family. He had overcome starvation, hard labor and unspeakable hardship to barely pass the minimum admission score for college, and had ranked at the bottom of all students whose files were handed over to colleges. Given the difficulty of filling its enrollment, the National Institute of Metallurgical Science had accepted him; in any case, they needed someone with a solid political standing to lead the majority of politically tainted but academically talented students they were going to admit. Two weeks into class, Wu Mancang realized he was no match for his classmates academically, and was woefully ill-equipped to handle the coursework. With politics offering his only path forward, his appointment as CYL secretary for the Zebra Club saved the day. Wu Mancang recognized it as his avenue to success, as previous students who'd held this post had all joined the Communist Party at an early age and moved on to important jobs after graduation.

The Chinese New Year gala was Wu Mancang's first major task as the new CYL secretary. The Communist Party Committee directed that the gala should be festive but politically correct. Wu Mancang gave it all he had. He spent days arranging the program and screening performances, but ended up rejecting most of the offerings. The songs couldn't be foreign, and the dances couldn't have any non-Chinese elements. A funny skit about how to get more cornmeal buns from the Big Kitchen shed a negative light on the school. Everyone was frustrated by Wu Mancang's political correctness.

As far as Gao Hong was concerned, it didn't matter whether the Gala program was any good or not once he spotted the young woman with the exploding thermos in the audience. She was sitting just a couple rows in front of him to his left, and he couldn't take his eyes off of her. Her soft hair was pulled back behind her delicate and translucent ears, revealing her smooth, enchanting profile. Gao Hong felt lucky to be sitting behind her, where he could stare at her all he wanted without her knowing. Just as that thought crossed his mind, the young woman suddenly turned her head, and their eyes met. Her eyes glowed at him for a fraction of a second, and Gao Hong's heart stopped. He lowered his head, which seemed to be spinning in rhythm to his pounding heart. For a long time, he didn't have the courage to look up.

When he was finally overcame his dizziness and looked up again, he found that the young woman was no longer in her seat. Looking around with panicked eyes, he finally spotted her walking toward the stage with a violin in her hands. As applause filled the auditorium, Situ whispered to Gao Hong, "This is the only good performance that wasn't killed by Wu Mancang!"

The young woman stood on the stage like an angel. This was the first time Gao Hong had a good look at her in ample lighting, and he was instantly hypnotized by her soothing calmness and quiet grace. Her violin playing was as surreal and soul-touching as the voice of Guanyin Buddha from a mountaintop. Everyone in the auditorium was frozen in their seats as if spellbound, and the silence was deafening. As the young woman stepped off the stage, Gao Hong asked Situ, "Who is she?"

"You don't know her? She's Shi Yanruo, from the Department of Engineering."

Unbeknownst to Gao Hong, Shi Yanruo was already the object of longing in the hearts of many young men in the Zebra Club, and he was probably the last to discover her. He understood why the politically sensitive Wu Mancang had allowed Shi Yanruo to go on stage after killing off all the other good performances for the New Year Gala; Wu Mancang's face said it all as he stared at Shi Yanruo as if she were a goddess. Gao Hong later learned why the male students in the Zebra Club were all especially friendly toward Mai. Mai was Shi Yanruo's roommate, and therefore their prime source of information about Shi Yanruo.

Gao Hong found himself sleepless and with no appetite. All he could think of was Shi Yanruo. Weeks passed and the jasmine blossoms were in full bloom, and still he hadn't found a chance to see Shi Yanruo again. But her face and her music were always on his mind and only became fresher and more real as time went on.

Gao Hong didn't want to be like other male students, who cozied up to Mai just to get information about Shi Yanruo. He felt that wasn't fair to Mai, or a decent way to treat Yanruo. The best he could do was linger near the water house, by the women's entrance to Dorm 3, near the Department of Engineering, in hopes of seeing her. But as if she were playing hide and seek with him, Yanruo never appeared.

(26) LOVE

————————— ✶ —————————

Leaving an evening study session, Gao Hong ran into Mai, who looked anxious and distressed. "What's the matter?" Gao Hong asked.

Mai said, "I've lost my watch. It's the watch my mother left me before she died! I was wearing it just this afternoon and now it's gone! I must have dropped it somewhere."

"I have a flashlight," Gao Hong said. "I'll help you look."

The two of them walked along all the campus paths Mai had used, but still they didn't find Mai's watch. Mai started to cry: "What am I going to do? I lost my mom's watch! And tomorrow there's a test, and I haven't even begun to study!"

Gao Hong pulled a notebook out of his bag and gave it to Mai. "Here, take this and go study right now. I have all the test topics summarized here. You already have a solid grasp of the material, so just review this once and you should be good for tomorrow. I'll keep looking for your watch."

Mai suddenly remembered, "Oh! I went to Birch Yard in back of the school after dinner. Maybe I dropped it there!"

"I know Birch Yard like the back of my hand," Gao Hong assured her. "I know what your watch looks like, too. Don't worry. Go study."

Birch Yard, located at the very back of the campus, was quiet even during the day and always deserted at night. As Gao Hong carefully combed the walkways with his flashlight, the sound of soft violin playing came from the woods behind him. Gao Hong snapped to attention: "It's her!"

Worried that he might scare her, he didn't approach immediately, but stopped at a distance and scuffed the grass. Yanruo stopped playing her violin and turned to look at him. Gao Hong walked over and said, "Sorry to disturb you. I was passing by and heard you. How come you're playing here in the dark?"

Yanruo looked at him with wide, startled eyes: "And you are...? Oh, you're the boy from the water house! I'm practicing my violin, but what are you doing here?"

"Mai lost her watch," Gao Hong explained. "She thought she might have dropped it here, so I'm helping her look for it. I'm sorry to interrupt, but I wanted to make sure you were all right out here alone in the dark. Why do you practice here?"

Yanruo lowered her voice: "I don't want the others to hear me. They say playing the violin is bourgeois, so I have to go where no one can hear me."

"But it's beautiful. We were all enthralled at the Gala."

"Well, I'm done now anyway," Yanruo said. "Did you say Mai lost her watch? Her mother's watch? My Goodness! We have to help her find it." She packed her violin into its case, and Gao Hong carried it for her as they walked on the small path together.

Gao Hong introduced himself: "My name is Gao Hong, from the Department of Material Science."

Yanruo said: "And I'm ...."

"You're Shi Yanruo from the Department of Engineering. I know." Gao Hong finished her sentence for her with a smile.

And then they actually found Mai's watch, lying there beside the path. Gao Hong picked it up and handed it to Yanruo, who said joyfully, "I'll take it to her. She'll be so happy!" Then they started walking back to the dorm together.

"I want to thank you," Yanruo said, "for the watch, for helping Mai, and for the thermos bottle from last time."

"It was my pleasure!" Gao Hong assured her. "But I still don't understand why you want to hide out while practicing your violin. It's so beautiful!"

Yanruo sighed: "Someone reported me to the school, saying I'm still under the influence of my capitalist origins. My father was a major industrialist in Beijing, so I can't afford drawing attention to my background. There's no other place where I can practice in peace, so I come here at night by myself. It's kind of scary, to be honest."

Gao Hong lowered his head thoughtfully, then his face lit up: "I know a good place! Nobody would object no matter how much you practice. It's a short bus ride from our school. There's no class day after tomorrow, so I can take you there!"

"What kind of place is it?" Yanruo asked.

"You'll see. It's a place I've loved since I was a kid, and I know you'll love it too," Gao Hong assured her.

Yanruo thought for a minute. She somehow felt she could trust this honest-looking young man who had given her his thermos bottle and helped Mai find her watch. "All right," she said.

Two days later, Gao Hong took Yanruo to his beloved Summer Palace. He showed her his elementary school, and the Northern Gate that he'd walked through every day after school. He showed her the big rock he'd always sat on to do his homework. Yanruo said, "I've come to the Summer Palace a few times, but always to see the Temple and Kunming Lake. I've never been behind the hill. It's so tranquil and beautiful." Gao Hong spread his jacket on a rock so Yanruo could sit down and play her violin, then he sat on another rock and listened to her.

Every weekend from then on, they went to the Summer Palace together. When Yanruo was done playing, Gao Hong would carry her violin on his back and take her on a stroll down the Qing Dynasty Long Corridor, or they'd take a boat out on Kunming Lake. Pointing to the Qing dynasty paintings on the corridor's woodwork, he told Yanruo the stories behind them. He wished time would freeze and everything else would disappear, leaving just him and his beloved Yanruo in the Summer Palace, forever.

At first, both of them were careful not to talk about their families or their lives before college. They knew those were painful wounds that were better left untouched. Gao Hong could see a shadow of sorrow deep in Yanruo's eyes, even when she was happy. He recognized it in himself as well, and Yanruo saw it, too. It was that unspoken and untouchable sadness that bound them together, and made their hearts break for each other and yearn for each other.

Finally, Gao Hong decided to break the taboo. One evening when he took Yanruo to the Zhichun Pavilion along the lake, he asked her, "Yanruo, how are your parents doing? Are they in Beijing?" Yanruo was silent for a long time. Gao Hong said, "I'm sorry. I... I thought... We could...." He sat next to Yanruo facing the lake and said in a soft voice: "I only have my Nanny Wu. She's in Beijing. The rest of my family are no longer alive."

They both sat in silence, gazing at the soft ripples on the lake. Even in silence, they knew they were the same, that they had the same fate, the same tragedy, the same pain and the same sorrow.

After a long while, Yanruo said, "I should count my blessings. At least I still have my mother. You have it worse than I do." She slipped her hand over Gao Hong's hand. "Yanruo!" Gao Hong pulled her into his tight embrace and kissed her passionately. That first kiss on that early summer evening in the Zhichun Pavilion by the moon-lit Kunming Lake made Gao Hong feel that all the sufferings in his life now had a reason and meaning, and that all of his dreams had come true, as if the sole purpose of his twenty-one years of tragedy was to lead him to this very moment and to this very girl.

Summer Palace

The following weekend, Gao Hong took Yanruo to meet Nanny Wu. Nanny Wu had lost her position with the vice-president of Union Hospital, since no one was allowed to have servants anymore. Now she worked as a babysitter and lived in a small rented room in a courtyard near the Summer Palace. She was speechless with surprise and joy at seeing HongGe arrive with a beautiful young woman. Too flustered with happiness to know where to put her hands and feet, she mumbled incoherently, "Why didn't you tell me you were coming? This shabby little room is so messy! I'll go get some groceries...." Then she asked Yanruo, "What would you like for lunch, my beautiful angel darling? Nanny will cook you anything you'd like!"

Yanruo and Gao Hong both urged her to sit down: "Nanny, don't worry. We're not staying for lunch, we just wanted to stop in to see you. We still need to go do our homework."

"Nonsense!" Nanny Wu insisted. "No matter how much homework you have, you still need to eat! I cook fast. It won't take long." Yanruo held Nanny Wu's hands, "Nanny, we've already eaten. We're just here to see you and spend some time with you. We really don't need to eat." Nanny Wu's eyes glistened with tears as she looked at Yanruo. Turning to her cabinet, she dug around until she pulled a pair of jade bangles from an old wooden box. Slipping them over Yanruo's wrists, she said, "My darling, I hope you don't mind the old style of these bangles. They were worn by HongGe's mother, and she gave them to me before she died. They're all that she left us. I want you to have them. Such good jade is hard to find nowadays." Yanruo was about to say she couldn't accept something so valuable, but when she saw Gao Hong nodding and encouraging her to take the bangles, she said, "Thank you, Nanny. I'll treasure them always." When they left, Nanny Wu walked them to the end of her street, gripping both of their hands and repeatedly expressing her good wishes.

After saying goodbye to Nanny Wu, Gao Hong told Yanruo, "You've taken my jewelry, so now you are mine. There's no turning back." He was referring to the ancient custom that if a woman ever accepts a piece of jewelry from a man, she is his forever. Yanruo swung her little handbag at Gao Hong and chased him around as Gao Hong dodged her and ran in circles, laughing.

Yanruo also took Gao Hong to meet her mother, who lived inside a magnificent courtyard much larger than Dr. Gao's. The courtyard's three-story house was similarly imposing, made of red brick and with huge windows and grand marble pillars. Gao Hong couldn't even imagine the value of such a house in the center of Beijing. But a sign on the house stated: "Beijing Western District Government." Yanruo's mother didn't live in the house itself, but rather in a little shack in the back corner of the gigantic courtyard. Gao Hong knew what had happened without needing to ask. He thought to himself: At least in Beijing they didn't draw the names of wealthy women from a hat and give them to poor men. He was deeply relieved that Yanruo and her mother seemed to be physically safe in that small shack in the backyard of their old home.

Yanruo's mother had wide, dreamy eyes that seemed to be gazing at nothing. She murmured a brief greeting to Gao Hong from her rocking chair next to the tiny window as she rocked and looked outside. Yanruo went around the room picking up books and clothes from the floor, and she dusted the desk with a cloth. Her mother turned to her and scolded, "Yanruo, you're Miss Yanruo of the Shi house, for heaven's sake. Why are you dusting? Let the servants do it!" Gao Hong's heart ached for Yanruo as she glanced at him, embarrassed and helpless. "I will do it, Madam," he said as he walked up to Yanruo's mother.

He took the cloth from Yanruo and dusted off the desk and other pieces of furniture. Then he cleaned the kitchen, and he tightened the loose screws on the door knobs and cabinet handles. He took out the trash and mopped the floor. Yanruo followed him around begging, "That's enough. Stop. You don't need to do this. Let me do it. I can do it."

Yanruo's mother looked at her: "Yanruo, why are you following the servant around? Let him do his chores. You need to change into your evening gown. Your father has important guests coming tonight. I need to go to the dining room to make sure everything is in order."

Yanruo said sadly, "Mama, you must be tired. Why don't you lie down for a while?"

As they left the shack where Yanruo's mother lived, Gao Hong asked her, "Who looks after your mother?"

Yanruo said tearfully, "An old servant who has been with our family for decades comes to see Mama every day and brings her food. But she also has her own family to take care of, and she's old and frail. I can't wait until I graduate and can move back here to live with Mama and take care of her."

Gao Hong held Yanruo's hands: "I'll help you take care of your mother."

The news that Gao Hong and Shi Yanruo were a couple spread rapidly through the Zebra Club, and Gao Hong felt surrounded by hostility. Wu Mancang carried out a surprise "sanitary inspection" on Dorm 3, and ordered Gao Hong to clean the men's bathroom for two weeks. Gao Hong could understand how Wu Mancang must feel. After all, wouldn't he be even angrier if Yanruo was with another man? He couldn't even imagine what he would do to him.

Even his roommate and best friend Situ wasn't talking to him anymore, and turned and walked away whenever he saw Gao Hong. One day, Gao Hong grabbed his arm and stopped him: "What's wrong? Is there a problem?" Situ swung his arm free of Gao Hong's grasp and then whipped around to stare Gao Hong in the eye nose-to-nose. After a long while, Situ dropped his eyes and lowered his head. He sighed, "She must have her reasons for choosing you. Take good care of her, like that poem, 'One heart, one soul, till death.' That's what she deserves. Give her anything less and I will tear you into pieces!" He turned and marched off, leaving Gao Hong dumbfounded.

(27) A BLOOD LETTER

It was 1964 and graduation was approaching. At that time, all college graduates were assigned jobs by the Communist Party representatives stationed at their school. The students had no choice over where they would work; once they were assigned, they had to go work there, often for the rest of their careers. Where you worked determined where you lived, because it was your workplace that provided you with housing, healthcare, food rations and education for your children. The availability and the quality of these essential life resources varied greatly across the nation, with big cities like Beijing and Shanghai enjoying the largest shares. During the 1960 famine, people in Beijing at least had enough food to survive, but people outside of the big cities died en masse from starvation. Consequently, every student hoped to remain in Beijing to enjoy the country's best academic, technological, healthcare and living standards.

During those years, a Beijing residence card, which could only be obtained by being born in the city to Beijing residents, or by government assignment, was priceless. In other words, being assigned a job in Beijing meant an automatic Beijing residence card, and every student wanted that.

But in 1964, a new policy emerged: the Third Front. It was part of the government's plan for developing the vast and baren northwest region. Harsh weather, unfarmable land, primitive living conditions, areas unreachable by modern transportation, and lack of food and water all contributed to the desolation of the region.

The Communist Party was determined to revive the Northwest, and their way of doing it was by ordering businesses, schools, factories, research agencies and universities to move out of the coastal cities and establish a Northwest presence to form a unified Third Front. These institutions were also ordered to move many of their employees to the Northwest and focus their new hiring there. Unsurprisingly, very few people wanted to go to such a harsh place and lose their established residential status in Beijing or Shanghai. Once they went, they could never come back; it was nothing short of exile.

Workplaces had no choice but to assign people to the Northwest to meet the quota set by the Communist Party. Usually it was the politically tainted employees who were forced to move there. New college graduates were of course enthusiastically recruited for the Third Front.

Big posters and signs across campus read:

"Support the Third Front, Build Our Motherland!"

"The Third Front, Where the Country Needs Us The Most!"

"March to the Third Front, Serve Our Great Nation!"

Third Front was the new buzzword and the topic of discussion in every dorm and every classroom. Although the young students knew life on the Third Front must be harsh, they were tempted by the honor of serving their country, and by the praise and awards they would earn from the school.

Mai was the first graduate to volunteer to go to the Third Front, and the school played it up to the hilt, putting Mai on stage with a huge red flower on her chest. The school and department leaders took turns congratulating and praising her in front of all the graduates as Mai smiled proudly at the crowd.

Shi Yanruo took her aside and said, "Mai! Your father holds high office in the military and your mother was a martyr in the Navy. You have an impeccable family background. No one here can match it! Even if everyone else is assigned to the Third Front, it won't happen to you. Why volunteer? Do you really want to go to such a harsh place so far from home? You volunteered for this college, too, when your test scores and family background would have gotten you into Tsinghua University. What's going on?!"

Mai looked much less happy and proud now that she had left the stage. She told Yanruo tearfully, "As soon as my mother's body was in the ground, my father married a woman half his age! That woman is only a few years older than me, and she's so mean to me! I can't be around them anymore. I want nothing to do with them. I want to go as far away as possible. My father doesn't know I volunteered for the Third Front. I want him to be sorry and upset. I want to make an irreversible decision that will hurt myself and punish him! I know that once I leave Beijing there's no coming back. And that will make my father regret his betrayal of my mother for the rest of his life!"

Situ also volunteered. Gao Hong patted him on the shoulder, not knowing what to say. Finally, he said, "You're twice the man I am!" Situ gave a sad chuckle: "Remember, I'm the son of a Nationalist general. They'll assign me to the Third Front for sure, so I might as well volunteer. My father used to say that the motherland deserves all the talent of its people. I want to make the Northwest a better place for China! My father gave me valuable lessons in literature, academia and military knowledge, but the most important thing he taught me was honor. Volunteering to serve my country, that's honor. Waiting to be assigned as an exile, that's cowardice. I would not be the son of General Situ if I went to the Northwest as an exile."

Situ then lowered his voice and said sadly, "I don't want to be in Beijing anymore. You know the reason. You stay in Beijing and take good care of her. Don't ever let anything happen to her."

No matter how much promotion the school did, volunteers for the Third Front were few and far between. It looked like the school would have to assign people in order to meet the government's quota. Already a Communist Party member, Wu Mancang had direct access to information on graduation assignments, and he told everyone that assignments would be based on family background. Graduates with the "darkest" backgrounds would be assigned first. They were the ones from wealthy families that had resisted giving up their property, resulting in loss of life to themselves or others. Graduates from such families would be sent to places with the harshest conditions and would have to work the hardest to transform themselves from their bourgeois and counterrevolutionary origins.

As soon as Gao Hong heard this, he ran to the women's entrance of Dorm 3 to wait for Yanruo. He knew that Yanruo's father had been one of the biggest business owners in Beijing, and that he'd taken up arms to protect his wealth when his business empire was taken from him. While under siege by Communist troops, he'd taken his own life, leaving behind his young daughter Yanruo and his wife, who suffered a mental breakdown from the trauma. If what Wu Mancang said was true, Yanruo would be among the first assigned to the Third Front, and he himself would not be far behind. His family was one of the biggest landowners in the Northeast, and his father was shot dead while seeking revenge. He was sure to be assigned to the Third Front as well. He wanted to tell Yanruo, "Don't be afraid. Don't worry. I'll protect you. Let's take your mother and Nanny Wu along with us to the Great Northwest. We'll start a new life there. No matter how hard it is, we'll have nothing to fear as long we have each other." Gao Hong was ready to propose to Yanruo as soon as he saw her. He wanted to be with her till the end of time and to the ends of the earth.

He waited and waited, but there was no sign of Yanruo. Every time he saw someone going into the building, he would ask, "Excuse me, could you please tell Shi Yanruo in room 504 that someone is waiting for her down here?" Finally a young woman came out and looked at him curiously: "Are you still waiting for Shi Yanruo? She's in her room crying. Her door is locked and she won't open it." Gao Hong jumped up and rushed to the door, but the young woman shouted, "Don't you dare enter the girl's dorm! I'll call security!" Gao Hong had no choice but to back out. He ran to the back of the building and shouted at Yanruo's window: "Yanruo! Yanruo! Please come down! I'm waiting for you! Please!"

Yanruo silently appeared behind him: "Stop shouting. I'm here." Gao Hong turned and threw his arms around her. Holding her tight, he said urgently, "Yanruo! Let's get married! Marry me! Don't worry. I'll take care of you. I'll take care of everything. Let's get married right away! Please!"

Yanruo smiled with tears in her eyes. Pushing Gao Hong away enough that she could look him in the eye, she said, "And then what? Go to the Third Front together?"

They walked to the front of the main campus building and sat side-by-side on the front steps. Yanruo said, "I can't leave, because Mama can't leave the Shi courtyard. She's too unstable to leave her familiar surroundings. Even though we don't own the Shi courtyard anymore and she and I will be living in the shack, it's still her home, her surroundings. She can only survive there. If we try to take her to the Northwest, she might suffer a mental collapse and jump from the train! Right now she's living in the illusion that she still has her old life. I don't know what would happen if we burst her bubble. She might take her own life like my father did!"

Gao Hong nodded understandingly: "I know your mother can't leave her home. In fact, Nanny Wu shouldn't leave either. She's in very poor health and I don't know if she could survive living in the Northwest. But we may have no choice. The graduation assignments are going to be announced in a few days. I don't know what else we can do."

Yanruo started sobbing as she said, "I have something to show you." She pulled out a piece of white cloth with writing on it. The writing was in blood — a blood letter! In the olden days in China, there was a custom that a letter written in blood meant a commitment for life, but Gao Hong had never seen a blood letter in real life. He flattened the cloth, and as he read the letter line by line, he felt his head exploding, his stomach churning and his blood turning to ice.

Earlier that afternoon, Wu Mancang had come up to Yanruo and stuffed this blood letter in her hands. Yanruo screamed as soon as she saw the words written in blood. Wu Mancang wrote that he had loved Yanruo ever since setting eyes on her. He proposed to Yanruo in his letter, and he wrote that his promise was sealed in blood.

Yanruo stared at Wu Mancang in shock while holding the letter in her shaking hands. Wu Mancang had rolled up both of his sleeves and showed Yanruo his bloody arms full of knife wounds: "I love you! I would die for you! Here's proof!" Yanruo screamed.

Wu Mancang told her, "Marry me, and you can stay in Beijing. I know I've been assigned to the Ministry of Materials. The school has a policy that husband and wife will be assigned in the same location. Marry me and you can stay in Beijing. If you say no, my life has no meaning and I don't want to live anymore. I will slit my wrist and die!"

Gao Hong felt a chill run up his spine as he listened to Yanruo describe what happened that afternoon. He pleaded, "Yanruo, You are scaring me! Don't tell me you want to marry that bastard Wu Mancang! You are scaring me! Yanruo!"

Sobbing, Yanruo said, "Yes, I'm your Yanruo. But I'm also Miss Shi. Even though we've lost the luxurious life I grew up with, and live in the ruins, I'm still the same Miss Shi. How can I just run away with the man I love when things at home become tough? I won't desert my family no matter what. I won't leave Mama no matter what. And I can't take her anywhere else; it would kill her!"

Gao Hong felt as if he were losing his mind. He grabbed Yanruo by the shoulders and shook her: "What about you! Do you love him? Do you think he loves you? He doesn't even care about his own welfare, so how can he take care of you? If he can be this cruel to himself, and mutilate his own body like this, what else is he capable of? He's a monster! He doesn't love you. If he did he wouldn't threaten you with suicide! He wouldn't back you into a corner over staying in Beijing. That's not love! That's being cruel, selfish, mean, and taking advantage of you! He's an animal!"

Yanruo looked at Gao Hong through teary eyes, and caressed his face gently with cold, damp fingers: "I'm destined to be sacrificed. But thank God I met you. The time I had with you will warm my heart for the rest of my life. I have no regrets. I have my path, my responsibilities and the things I must do. Take care of yourself. Find a nice girl and forget about me." Shaking loose of Gao Hong's grasp, she dashed back into her dorm, leaving Gao Hong as frozen in place as an upright corpse.

Three days later, the graduation assignments were announced. Yanruo was assigned to the Ministry of Materials in the heart of Beijing with her fiancé, Wu Mancang. To everyone's great surprise, Gao Hong was not exiled to the Third Front, but was assigned to a factory in Beijing. It was Yanruo's doing, as part of her bargain for agreeing to marry Wu Mancang.

Gao Hong and Situ went to the Summer Palace and sat by the Kunming Lake, drinking bottle after bottle of liquor in silence. After a while, Gao Hong vomited miserably and then lay face down on the grass, sobbing loudly. Situ said nothing as he waited for Gao Hong to quiet down. Then he said, "Don't blame her. Please try to understand her. She's in more pain than any of us. And make good use of your Beijing residence card. She sacrificed herself to get that for you."

Overcome with grief, Gao Hong said, "Please stop. Let's just swim." They changed their clothes and jumped into Kunming Lake together. Gao Hong could hear nothing but the sound of his own breathing and his arms striking water. He wanted to think of nothing but his strokes through the water; that was the only way he could bear his situation right now. He didn't want to get out of the water to face the cruel world. All he wanted was to swim on and on until the end of time.

(28) THE FACTORY

The Beijing Factory of Metallurgy Machinery was located in the Beijing suburb of Dahongmen. Following the Liangshui River south, Gao Hong spotted the factory's black metal gate. The factory compound consisted of five workshops, four blocks of employee housing and an office building. Gao Hong entered the factory with his luggage and the graduation assignment letter from his college.

The first person Gao Hong needed to see was Director Chen in the human resources office. Director Chen looked like one of the retired elderly men seen in the city's back streets, wearing their standard outfit of baggy shorts, flipflops and a white sleeveless t-shirt so worn and saggy that Gao Hong could see his belly when he bent over. Director Chen was cooling himself with a round fan made out of dried plant leaves. His teeth were black and yellow, with noticeable gaps. He tapped Gao Hong's chest with his fan: "Are you that damned rich bastard, the fucking college student?"

Gao Hong said, "My name is Gao Hong. I just graduated. I'm here to report for work."

"Graduate my ass!" snorted Director Chen. "You're on my turf now, and you belong to me. Understand? If you're a fucking tiger you have to crouch. If you're a fucking dragon you have to coil. In other words, your ass is mine. Are we clear?"

Unused to so much profane language or to being addressed in such a vulgar way, Gao Hong didn't know how to respond or what to make of it, so he stood there in silence. Director Chen slurped loudly at his tea, then plopped down on his chair and took a folder from his drawer: "I've been expecting you."

The sight of the folder made Gao Hong nervous, because he knew it was his political dossier that followed him everywhere like an ugly tail. It seemed that the dreaded dossier had arrived even before him.

Director Chen didn't open the folder, but instead pushed it toward Gao Hong's face and fanned him with it a couple of times: "You know what a piece of shit you are, and you'd better mind your step here, you son of a bitch! Can you drink?"

Gao Hong was utterly dazed and confused. What did drinking have to do with anything? He mumbled, "Yeah, a little bit. I can drink some."

Director Chen tossed Gao Hong's political dossier on the desk. "Humph! You dare to tell me you can drink some? I can knock out a pussy like you three times in one sitting!" Then he thought for a minute: "Fuck it! Go to Workshop Two and find that old asshole Zhao. You can be his apprentice. And shake off that fucking whipped cream stinky scholar look of yours!"

Gao Hong walked out of the human resources office feeling completely confused, insulted and bewildered. Never in his life had he met anyone like this. He'd heard more curse words in the last ten minutes than in the entire previous twenty-four years of his life!

He found Workshop Two, a large one-story brick building with an asbestos roof. The gigantic doors were wide open, and Gao Hong could see all sorts of machines and tools, as well as welding stations and a blast furnace. The workers were all busy with their tasks, producing a deafening racket of welding, machinery, clanking metal and electric saws that echoed through the dark and messy workshop. The air was thick with a nauseating mixture of smoke, dust and all sorts of metal and machine smells. Gao Hong forced himself to take a few more steps into the workshop. Only then did he feel the heat inside the workshop; it wasn't just hot, but downright roasting.

In spite of the tragic experiences that had left him an orphan, Gao Hong had always enjoyed a fairly decent living environment. From the privileged life in the Gao compound to the luxurious home of Dr. Gao, and even when living in the mountains with Li Ginseng or in his student dorm, he had always at least felt clean and comfortable. This was his first experience with a place so filthy, messy, hot and loud.

Gao Hong walked over to one of the workers: "Excuse me. I'm looking for Zhao Shifu." Shifu was the respectful way of referring to senior workers in the factories; it was the equivalent of "teacher," and was the way that apprentices were supposed to refer to their mentors. For Gao Hong, everyone here would be a Shifu. He knew that much.

The worker ignored Gao Hong, clearly unaware that he was even talking to him. Gao Hong followed him and raised his voice: "Excuse me. Could I please ask you a question? Which one of you is Zhao Shifu?"

The worker looked up, revealing a face smeared with machine oil and beaded with sweat, and he said in a booming voice, "Are you a man? Why are you buzzing like a fucking mosquito?"

Gao Hong felt compelled to yell, "I'm looking for Zhao Shifu!"

The worker sneered, "You can't even say a fucking 'trouble you'?" Gao Hong had never heard that expression and had no idea what "trouble you" meant. Perhaps it was short for "sorry to trouble you," and was how the workers said "excuse me." He eventually learned that words like sorry, excuse me, sorry for the trouble, sorry to interrupt, pardon me, etc. were all expressed as "trouble you" among the factory workers. Nobody could say anything different, and nothing worked except "trouble you."

Gao Hong shouted again, "Trouble you, I'm looking for Zhao Shifu!"

The worker turned his head and yelled, "Zhao Shifu!" Like a sound relay, the workers turned their heads and yelled "Zhao Shifu!" one after another, their shouts reaching into the depth of the dark workshop.

In a few minutes, a short, sturdy man wearing plastic framed glasses came out: "Who's looking for me?"

Gao Hong stepped forward and bowed: "Good day, Zhao Shifu! My name is Gao Hong. The human resource office sent me to work as your apprentice."

Zhao Shifu looked up at Gao Hong and laughed, "That old bastard Chen sent you, didn't he? Oh my! Look at that height! They say the taller you are the stupider you are, because there isn't enough brain for your body!" Laughing at his own joke, he gave Gao Hong a heavy slap on the back: "I like this kid!"

Zhao Shifu led Gao Hong to a dark, damp and cluttered dorm room: "You can share this room with Xiaoma, Qiangzi and Ershun. They're my apprentices, too." He walked out, but after Gao Hong finished unpacking, Zhao Shifu returned with a paper bag: "There were just two fried dough sticks left in the dining hall. I got them for you. Eat these first. There will be dumplings at lunch time."

Zhao Shifu's kindness made Gao Hong feel much better. Just then, Xiaoma, Qiangzi and Ershun came running over: "Zhao Shifu! Isn't it enough that the three of us wait on you hand and foot? Now you've got another apprentice?"

"You three lazy asses!" Zhao Shifu yelled. "Why are you leaving your work benches again? Gao Hong is an educated man. You three have to learn from him from now on!"

"Education my ass!" scoffed Qiangzi. "He's just another dick and two legs, like us! Who's better than who....."

"Shut up!" Zhao Shifu interrupted him.

Gao Hong had never heard people talk this way, and he stood there in profound embarrassment. Director Chen's profanity had already made him shudder, but hearing Qiangzi talk made Chen sound like a schoolmarm.

Although Gao Hong was a college graduate, he could only work as an entry-level factory laborer because of his landlord background. Working beside him were guys like Qiangzi, who'd recently been released from prison, Xiaoma, who'd been expelled from his high school for brawling, and Ershun, an illiterate peasant from a remote village. Zhao Shifu himself was just barely literate. He was a peasant who'd been living temporarily with his uncle when the factory was built nearby, and a few years after joining the factory as a worker, he found himself as a mentor with several apprentices.

After starting work the next day, Gao Hong realized that nothing he'd learned in college was at all relevant to what went on in the factory. What you needed in the workshop wasn't a college degree but physical strength, endurance, sweat and blood! The workers worked like mules under unbelievably hazardous conditions. The welders wielded their torches all day long with nothing but thin, worn masks over their faces. The blast furnace had no guardrails, and a loss of footing could mean a swift and agonizing death. Workers operated dangerous machinery, moved heavy metal blocks and did all sorts of repairs with their bare hands. In Workshop Two alone, five workers had had fingers chopped off or crushed flat, and many lost their eyesight and/or hearing over time.

Gao Hong gradually came to understand why the workers were so rough and vulgar. They simply didn't have the upbringing, the knowledge, the time, the patience or the need to refine their attitude and language. All of their attention was focused on surviving from one day to the next. They smoked, they drank, they yelled and cursed, they beat their wives and children, they fought with one another.... all because of their unbelievable hardship. They had no other outlet, and no one cared about the misery and the inhumane stress they had to endure.

Gao Hong was likewise tormented by the heat, the hazardous noise level, the pollutants and the unbearable physical exertion, but he gritted his teeth and worked as hard as he could. He felt he could deal with the erosion of his physical health, but what he could not bear was his loneliness and feeling of hopelessness. The college classmates with whom he'd spent five years now seemed to belong to another life. His education was irrelevant. His Yanruo was now someone else's wife. In fact, Yanruo herself now seemed unreal to him; he even wondered if she really existed or if he'd simply dreamed her up. If she really existed in this world, and if he'd truly once held her and kissed her, how was it possible that the world in which he lived now was as far away from her as hell was from heaven? Could someone as angelic as Yanruo really exist in this same world?

Gao Hong actually felt grateful and relieved that he hadn't married Yanruo. He couldn't imagine bringing Yanruo into a life like this. How could a beautiful and delicate crystal vase be thrown into a scrapyard? How could his Yanruo live like he was living now?

(29) THE DEATH OF NANNY WU

Every two or three weeks, Gao Hong went to visit Nanny Wu. The last time he saw her, she had a bad cough, and Gao Hong wanted to take her to a doctor. Nanny Wu refused: "There's no need! I've gotten some medicine from the pharmacy. Why waste money on a doctor? See what I got? I remember seeing this in Dr. Yan's medicine cabinet when I was a servant there, so it has to be good medicine. Don't you worry, I'll be good as new in a week. Now let me cook you something nice."

After dinner, Nanny Wu urged Gao Hong to return to his factory dorm: "You have to get up early tomorrow. Go back and have a good night's sleep." Handing Gao Hong a paper bag with a large piece of ham, she pushed him out the door.

Gao Hong was worried about Nanny Wu and wanted to check up on her again, but a "productivity contest" at the factory meant that working hours were extended, and workers weren't allowed the weekends off. Every evening, Gao Hong fell into bed exhausted, but before he knew it, he'd be jumping out of bed to head to work again. After four weeks, Gao Hong felt like he was walking on clouds and that his legs might give out on him at any time. Even Xiaoma remarked at his hunched back.

During those four weeks, Gao Hong tried to reach Nanny Wu through the public phone booth on her street, begging the person who answered to get Nanny Wu for him. But the woman said harshly, "This is a public phone! I'm not getting nobody!" The factory workers lined up behind Gao Hong to use the phone were losing patience: "Get off the fucking phone already! Find another time to call your slut!" Gao Hong had no choice but to hang up.

When he was finally allowed a day off, Gao Hong rushed to Nanny Wu's little room, but she didn't come out to greet him as usual. Her door was unlocked, so Gao Hong went in. Seeing Nanny Wu lying on her bed, he hurried over and whispered, "Nanny." When she didn't respond, Gao Hong panicked and grabbed her in his arms, shouting, "Nanny!"

Nanny Wu's body was as hot as charcoal; her face was red and her eyes half closed. She whispered, "Is that my HongGe? Nanny has been waiting for you." She struggled to open her eyes to look at Gao Hong: "My HongGe is all grown up. I can go to your mother now. I've been waiting to see you one last time so I can go in peace."

Gao Hong cried, "Nanny, what are you talking about! I'm taking you to the hospital!" He wrapped Nanny Wu in a blanket and picked her up, but Nanny Wu moaned in pain: "Put me down. It hurts too much. My body aches too much." Gao Hong gently laid her back down and said: "I'll go get a car to take us to the hospital!" As he turned to leave, Nanny Wu grabbed his hand.

"Don't leave! I'm afraid I won't see you again. My time has come. My coughing and fever have been getting worse and worse, and I know I don't have much time left. It's all right." She reached under her pillow with a trembling hand and pulled out an envelope, which she then pressed into Gao Hong's palm: "Your nanny never had much, but this is what I've managed to save. It's for your wedding. That lovely girl from the Shi family, how is she? I haven't seen her for a long time. Such a sweet girl! You two should get married soon." Then she pointed to a package next to her pillow: "This is the otter fur jacket from your Papa Li Ginseng. Never forget him!"

Gao Hong broke down sobbing. "Nanny, don't say any more! I'm going to get a car and take you to the hospital!"

Nanny Wu said, "HongGe, I have one last thing to say: Live on! No matter how hard life gets, never give up. Live on!" With that, she closed her eyes.

Gao Hong laid her down and dashed to the top of her street and then to the main road, but he didn't see any taxis. All he could do was wave his arms at the passing traffic and jump up and down yelling: "Help! Help! Somebody help me!" Cars, trucks, jeeps and motorcycles zoomed past, but no one stopped for the young man who was crazily weeping, waving and shouting. Finally, an elderly man on a three wheeled scooter stopped in front of Gao Hong: "What's wrong, young man?"

By the time Gao Hong and the man with the scooter reached Nanny Wu's room, her body was already cold and stiff. The older man said solemnly, "It's not the hospital she needs to go to. It has to be somewhere else now."

Gao Hong looked at him with wild eyes: "No! No! Don't say that! We can still save her! Let's take her to the hospital! Please! I'm begging you!"

The older man put his hand on Gao Hong's shoulder and said, "Excuse my bluntness, but can you wrestle with God? Let her go in peace."

Gao Hong sat there holding Nanny Wu's body in his arms all day. Looking at her shabby little room, he couldn't imagine how his nanny must have passed her last month, and how great her love for him must have been to keep her waiting for him to finally appear. He hated himself for waiting an entire month to see her. He hated the factory and its evil "productivity contest." He hated the cruel world that devoured everything and everyone he loved. He knew that he was a true orphan from now on.

Gao Hong phoned the factory and told Zhao Shifu that he needed to take a couple of days off to take care of Nanny Wu's burial. After he returned to the factory like a walking empty shell, he was summoned by the personnel office.

As soon as Gao Hong entered the office, Director Chen yelled, "Who the fuck do you think you are, taking off of work!"

"My nanny passed away and I needed to attend to her burial. I called Zhao Shifu and asked for two days off."

"Your nanny?! Don't give me that fucking rich bastard shit! Will you take time off again if a housekeeper dies?" Director Chen barked.

Gao Hong said, "Director Chen, my mother died when I was little, and Nanny Wu raised me. She was like my mother. I promise I'll catch up on all my work, even if it means working double shifts."

"You bet you will! Who else is going to do your shit for you?" Director Chen said, "I told Zhao Shifu that you have to make up for your missed work in three days, and at night you'll stock shelves in the warehouse! For a week!"

As Gao Hong turned to walk away, Director Chen added, "What's the big deal about a nanny? Was she your old man's slut concubine?"

Blood rushed to Gao Hong's forehead, and he turned and charged at Director Chen with fists swinging. Before he could make contact, Gao Hong was grabbed by four men who had just dashed in – Zhao Shifu and his three other apprentices, Xiaoma, Qiangzi and Ershun. Gao Hong was like a raging lion, eyes bloodshot and teeth clenched. He charged at Director Chen again and again, only to be held back by Zhao Shifu and the others. Xiaoma said, "Director Chen, don't mind him, we'll punish him for you. Just think of him as a stinky fart and let him go!"

The four men dragged Gao Hong out of the personnel office with Director Chen following and cursing Gao Hong and his ancestors at the top of his lungs. Gao Hong roared like a lion and charged towards Director Chen again. Zhao Shifu yelled to his three apprentices, "Are you three good for nothing?!" The three of them grabbed Gao Hong with every bit of strength they had and dragged him back to the dorm room. They knew all too well that if Gao Hong laid a finger on Director Chen, he would end up in prison.

Gao Hong lay face down on the damp, dirty concrete floor of the small dorm room, crying and screaming, while Zhao Shifu and the three apprentices all stood around staring at him. Ershun said, "Don't be so soft! I lost my mother when I was three and I'm still alive!" Xiaoma stopped Ershun with a stare and said, "That old bastard Chen isn't really so bad, he just has a filthy mouth. All you have to do is to beat him in a drinking contest, and he'll worship you like an ancestor!" Qiangzi said, "Stop crying and act like a man! So you hate old Chen? I'll watch the door for you while you pee in his tea mug. Then you'll be even!"

"Everyone shut up!" Zhao Shifu said. "Gao Hong, come home with me!"

Zhao Shifu lived in a one-room bungalow behind the factory with his wife, a petite woman with a kind-looking face and a name to match: Li Aici, which meant love and mercy. She sighed with sympathy as she put steamed buns and pickled vegetables on the table: "Poor young man, such a hard life you've had! Let me set you up with a nice girl!"

Daffodil

(30) THE GIRL WITH AN ACCENT

Holding her sister Jade's hand, eight-year-old Daffodil followed her mother Lotus and her two brothers Daqing and Erqing to the Beijing South Train Station. The station was so big and busy that Daffodil tightened her grip on Jade's hand and her mother's sleeve. Daqing and Erqing looked all around them and then suddenly shouted, "Dad! Dad!"

Lotus turned and saw her husband Yixin, whom she hadn't seen in five years, walking towards them. Her eyes teared up as Yixin patted Daqing and Erqing on their heads: "Almost as tall as me now!" Then he bent down and looked at Daffodil: "Is this my little Daffodil?" Daffodil whispered nervously, "Daddy." She saw shiny tears in her father's eyes. Finally, Yixin lowered himself enough to put his hands on Jade's tiny shoulders: "And this is my new daughter Jade!" Lotus said tearfully, "Jade, this is your Daddy!" Yixin turned to Lotus. They looked at each other, too emotional to speak.

Blinking back his tears, Yixin said happily, "All right, everyone, we're in Beijing now! This will be our new home, and from now on we'll all speak Mandarin. Is everyone tired and hungry? Let's go home!"

Their home was a two-room bungalow in a row of similar houses at the north end of the Department of Civil Affairs campus. The front of the campus consisted of a group of grand office buildings with marble steps and pillars where Yixin worked. Behind the office buildings was the residential area where all the employees lived. The campus included a grocery store, a dining center, a theater, a childcare center and an elementary school.

With so many children, the two-room house was quite crowded. The small room held two single beds and two desks for Daqing and Erqing, while the larger room had a big bunk bed. The top bunk was for Daffodil and Jade, while the bottom bunk was for Lotus and Yixin. It also held a desk, a dining table and a few chairs. An enclosed porch served as a kitchen with a gas stove, a standalone cabinet and a pantry shelf. The ten houses in this row were all more or less the same. The row of houses was surrounded by brick walls and a wooden gate that enclosed these ten families into a small compound. All residents of the compound shared a single water faucet and drainage ditch, as well as an outhouse for bathrooms.

Once inside the house, the four children ran around excitedly: "Look! The floor is made of tiles, not mud! Such beautiful, shiny red tiles!" "The walls are so white. I've never seen such white, clean walls!" "There's electricity! You turn a switch and the light comes on!"

Lotus looked around and said, "Such a small space for the six of us? We can't even turn around in here." Indeed, compared to their large yard and six big rooms back at Baiyang Lake, this house was just too small.

Yinxin returned with two large containers of meat and vegetables and a big bag of steamed buns. "Time to eat!" he said. "The dining hall is serving stir fried celery and roast pork today. " Lotus set the table and said to her husband, "The food at the dining hall must be expensive. We should cook at home." The kids reached out to grab the buns, but Lotus stopped them: "Go wash your hands!"

Running to the faucet in the yard, the children turned on the water and started a water fight. How wonderful not to have to go to a lake or well to fetch water! They could turn on a faucet and water ran out non-stop! How marvelous!

After devouring their food, the four kids ran to the bathroom, giggling loudly as they flushed each toilet again and again. What a miracle to see water gush out every time they pushed a lever! It was just unbelievable! Lotus stopped them: "Please stop wasting the clean water."

Finally exhausted from all the traveling, excitement, food and playing, the children tumbled willy-nilly onto one of the beds. Only after carrying each child to their own bed and tucking them in tight did Yixin and Lotus finally have some time to themselves. There was so much to say after five years that they didn't know where to begin.

The row of houses where Daffodil's family lived had the street number Thirteen, and people called it Yard 13. Diagonally across the road from Yard 13 was Xiangyang Elementary School. The following week, Yixin took Daqing, Erqing and Daffodil to school to see Headmaster Feng. The headmaster asked, "Director Xu, are these your children? Are you registering them for school?"

Yixin said, "Headmaster Feng, I appreciate your help. Yes, my sons are fourteen and twelve, and they've had some schooling from a tutor. My daughter is eight and hasn't been in school at all."

While they were living by Baiyang Lake, all the village boys were sent to an elderly wise man who looked like he was a hundred years old, and who taught them to read and write. Lotus had sent her sons to him since they were very young. But Daqing couldn't sit still for more than three minutes at a time, fidgeting as if he had ants in his pants. He forgot everything the old wise man taught him and was punished almost every day for his poor performance. He had no talent for academics but had a mechanical mind and could fix almost anything better than most adults. Lotus used to say, "My oldest boy won't be a scholar, but he can certainly earn his living with his two hands!"

Erqing was a different story. He remembered everything the wise old man taught, and taught himself many other things as well. His handwriting was also beautiful. Whenever he saw Erqing, the wise old man would smile and say, "A dragon can have nine sons, and they'll be completely different in nature!"

After administering an assessment exam for the three Xu children, Headmaster Feng told Yixin, "Director Xu, your second son Erqing has amazing abilities in reading, writing and math, and he's good at abacus too. I'll put him in fourth grade. Your oldest son's tests indicate that he should be in second grade, but considering his age, I'll put him in fourth grade with his brother. Your daughter can be in first grade." Yixin thanked the headmaster and left for work.

A teacher led Daqing and Erqing away, and Daffodil followed the headmaster to a classroom. When a female teacher came out to greet them, the headmaster said, "I have a new student for you."

The teacher led Daffodil into the classroom and asked: "What is your name?"

"Daffodil. Daffodil Xu."

The whole class burst out laughing. A few boys imitated her Hebei accident: "Da – ffo – dil.... " The teacher banged on her desk: "Silence!"

In fact, Daffodil was talking too softly for the teacher to hear, and combined with her accent and laughter of the other students, the teacher didn't catch her name. But Daffodil wouldn't open her mouth again, no matter what the teacher asked, so the teacher just led her to her seat and continued with the lessons.

Daffodil's mother Lotus had made her school bag by hand out of old fabric, and she carried her pencils in a linen bag that she'd sewed herself. Compared to the other students' sophisticated-looking store-bought school bags and pencil boxes, Daffodil's items looked shabby. Her clothes and hair were also of the Hebei Province country style, and her shoes were hand-made by her mother. All this, along with her Hebei accent, made her stand out among her schoolmates. But Daffodil was no ordinary eight-year-old, and within two weeks, she showed her schoolmates what a Xu girl was made of.

Daffodil had always had an amazing way of talking and edging everyone out with her words, and she wasn't about to change now. She was determined to learn Mandarin as the first step in her getting back at the others. She'd thought it would be difficult to learn another dialect, but she had underestimated herself. After following two Yard 13 teenage girls around for a week, she became quite fluent in Mandarin. She also learned "officialese" and "politically correct talk" from them. At that point, she returned to school.

134

"Da – ffo – dil....," a few boys sneered, imitating Daffodil's accent. Daffodil turned and spoke to them clearly and crisply: "My name is Daffodil Xu. Where are you from? How come you can't say three simple syllables right? You really need to work on your Mandarin. I'm sure you'll catch on soon!"

The boys were initially silenced, but quickly regained their composure: "You're the one from the Hebei countryside. Look at your stupid bag! Is that what you use for harvesting grain?" They all roared with laughter. Daffodil walked over and looked one boy in the eye: "What kind of family are you from? What do your parents do? You seem to have a low opinion of the working class and you seem to look down on hard-working peasants."

The boy was immediately deflated, because his parents had gotten their PhDs in America and were automatically suspected of being American spies. With his family one step away from prison, he avoided any mention of birth origins.

Daffodil turned to her classmates and said, "My mother is a proud member of the working class peasantry, which is the political foundation of our beloved country. She is virtuous and hardworking and she made this school bag for me. I naturally follow in her footsteps, so I made my pencil case by hand. If anyone is interested, I can teach you how to make one." Her classmates looked at her in silence.

The teacher stepped into the classroom just then: "We should all learn from Daffodil. She's not only skilled at sewing, but is willing to share her skills with the class. Let's have an after-school sewing club, and Daffodil can be in charge. We'll start this week!"

(31) DAQING COMES OF AGE

Daffodil's amazing verbal talents were noticed by all her teachers. After mastering the Mandarin dialect in just two weeks, she was comfortable talking with faculty and students alike, and she could win any debate, even with upper-classmen. She would do anything to win a "war of words," usually starting with good tactics and reasonable arguments. If she didn't prevail that way, she'd start talking in circles to mislead her opponents, use jargon to confuse them, put words in their mouths to irritate them, asking them pointed questions to get under their skin, and projecting negative images on them without giving them a chance to recover.

During parent-teacher meetings, all the teachers told Lotus, "Your daughter can talk!"

This only worried Lotus: "That's not good for a girl. A girl with a sharp tongue will always have trouble in her marriage."

Math was a completely different story. Daffodil did fine with simple arithmetic and had little trouble memorizing the multiplication table, but anything involving logic and reasoning made her head spin. In her mind, there was no such thing as logic, and problem solving was like pulling teeth.

For math problems involving distance, speed, travel, meet, chase, percentage and fractions, Daffodil would bite her pencil and stare at the ceiling. She'd ask, "Why is the first car going at 80 kilometers an hour? What if someone in that car needs to go to the bathroom? Wouldn't they stop? Then their speed won't be 80! You're asking me, if the second car's speed is 120 kilometers per hour, when will the second car catch up with the first. How can I answer that? What if the second car stops a lot of times, like for food and for bathroom breaks? What if the first car runs out of gas? Then the second car will catch up right away. What if the second car turns over, or is pulled over by the police? Then they will never catch up!" At first, the teacher

136

would patiently explain everything to her. Then she realized that Daffodil had a completely different way of thinking and there was nothing that could change her mind, so the teacher gradually just let her be during math class.

The after-school sewing club was where Daffodil excelled. She had watched her mother Lotus sew ever since she was a baby. When she was only four years old, she picked up a shirt her mother was making and started to sew on it. When Lotus came home and saw her, she was amazed. Even though Daffodil mistakenly sewed a sleeve closed, her stitches were even and straight, and didn't look like a small child's work at all. Lotus started to teach Daffodil how to sew, and by age seven, Daffodil could sew and embroider by herself. Now at school she was founder and president of the after-school sewing club. Her embroidery work was colorful, delicate and lively, and her crocheted tablecloth more beautiful than those bought in a store. But when it came time to elect the president for the second term, Daffodil was not elected. Club members said she was bossy, picky and had very little patience for newcomers. Daffodil wept in disappointment, realizing that she didn't really have any friends at school.

One day after school, Daffodil was walking towards the playground when she saw a crowd and heard the sound of fighting. Running and squeezing into the crowd, she found her brother Daqing fighting with a group of boys! They surrounded Daqing and hit him hard while yelling: "Stupid retard! Held back! Held back for so many years that you have a mustache!" Daqing kicked, punched and elbowed the boys like an angry beast.

"Stop! Stop!" Daffodil yelled. "If you make one more move I'll go to your mothers! I know where you live!" Daffodil knew that going to the teachers wouldn't do any good and would only make people hate her and Daqing. So she yelled the boys' names one by one: "Zhao Peng! Your dad said he'd break your legs if you fight with anyone again! I'll go to your father!" "Cai Wei! If you don't stop right now, I'll never let anyone in Yard 13 lend you their bikes!" Cai Wei was from a poor family. He always came to Yard 13 to borrow a bike to take her mother to the hospital. Daffodil's yelling made the boys stop, and she grabbed Daqing and said, "Daqing! Let's go!" Just then Erqing came running: "Daqing, Daffodil, what happened?"

Daqing had tears of anger and humiliation in his eyes, and his chest heaved. After a long while he said, "I don't want to go to school anymore. Everyone laughs at my accent, my shabby clothes, my age and my poor grades! There's no point in going to school!"

Erqing said, "Daqing, I said I'd tutor you every night. It's really not that hard. You can catch up in no time."

Daffodil added, "You need to change your accent. See, both Erqing and I speak Mandarin now."

But no matter what they said, Daqing wouldn't say another word. Once they were back home, Lotus was so worried about Daqing that she begged her husband: "Our Daqing doesn't want to go to school. He's already a grown man, please help him get a job. He's so clever, he can repair anything, and he's hardworking. You have to help him!"

Yixin agreed: "We've sent him to school for two years now, and he's learned nothing but fighting with others! He is sixteen years old now. It's time for him to do something useful."

At that time in China, labor shortages in the cities resulted in the legal employment age being lowered to fourteen, and mandatory schooling ended at that age. Young people could choose to go on with middle school or to seek employment.

Through a coworker's relative, Yixin learned that an automobile repair factory near Beijing's Guang Qumen district was hiring workers. Although it was all the way on the other side of Beijing, it was a well-established factory funded by the government. All of Beijing's taxis were repaired and maintained in this factory. It would not only provide Daqing with reliable employment and a good salary, but also allow him to gain skills and experience in auto repair, a highly desirable and marketable skill. The factory also provided government employee status and a dorm.

Yixin sat down with Daqing. "You're not happy in school. Do you want to quit?" Daqing was unsure of his father's intentions and didn't want to upset him by saying he wanted to quit school, but he also didn't want to say he would stay in school, so he lowered his head and kept quiet. Yixin said, "Would you like to learn auto repair? You can go to a factory and become a worker and earn a salary."

Daqing jumped to his feet: "Really? I'll do it!"

Just like that, Daqing left home carrying the new suitcase that Lotus packed for him and the new toiletries that Yinxin had bought him. He moved to the auto repair factory's dorm and started his life as a factory worker.

Lotus said to Erqing, "You're different from your brother. You're good at school. Please work hard and become a scholar!" Erqing nodded. He was smart like his father and excelled in school. He would definitely take a different path from his brother.

Daqing now came home only on the weekends. Every time he came back, he talked nonstop about factory life – how strict the Shifus were, how fascinating the car parts were, how fat and crazy the mice were in his dorm, and how quickly he was learning. When he received his first salary, he beamed with pride. He gave Lotus all of his salary except a small amount to spend on his meals. He even rationed that small amount to save enough to buy fruit and meat every weekend for his parents and siblings. Lotus wiped her tears and said, "My Daqing is so kind. He's too hard on himself! It's not easy being the oldest!"

The siblings all looked up to Daqing. He was working now, a grown-up who helped support the family. Their mom and dad seemed to appreciate and love him so much, and they'd save the best food for the weekend, when Daqing could enjoy it. Every time Daqing came back, it was like a festival at home.

Daffodil now held her head even higher in school. Her father was a government official, her mother was of the peasant class and her brother was of the worker class. The country gave the highest political status to these three types of people, and their family had all three! What an honorable family background Daffodil had!

Daffodil also envied how Daqing seemed to attract all of their parents' attention. She even thought to herself, "Maybe starting work early is better than spending so many years in school. See how Daqing has become such a favorite, much more than Erqing, even though Erqing is an academic star! It looks like there's an advantage to quitting school and starting work early."

She didn't realize that her parents were paying so much attention to Daqing simply because he wasn't at home all the time like the other children. Once they left home, her parents would be just as worried about their other children.

(32) A BIG FAMILY

The year Daqing took up his new official position, Lotus gave birth to her sixth child, her third daughter Duoduo. Lotus' next door neighbor, whom the children all called "Auntie Li," came over to congratulate the family. "Lotus, you're like a Buddha of Fertility!" she exclaimed. "How nice to have so many children!"

Lotus said, "My oldest is already working in a factory, and now a new baby arrives."

Auntie Li said, "Oh, that's so normal! Chairman Mao says people are the first and foremost productive force of society. Chairman Mao encourages all families to have more children, and all mothers to heroically contribute more babies to society. Many women have eight or nine kids. I've heard of some women having babies even after their grandkids are born!"

Lotus laughed, "How is that possible! They would become a laughing stock."

Auntie Li turned solemn and said, "Being able to have more children is a gift from God!" Lotus looked at her and didn't know what to say.

Auntie Li and her husband, Mr. Li, had two sons, but only the second son was Auntie Li's; the first son was born to Mr. Li's first wife, who had been stricken with an infectious disease that took her life and afflicted her son with dangerously high fevers. By the time the fevers passed, the boy was left deaf and mute and mentally disabled. Mr. Li was struggling to take care of his handicapped son as best he could while keeping up with work, when someone introduced him to Auntie Li. They married and soon had another son, Li Mingshen, but Auntie Li had suffered a life-threatening postpartum hemorrhage that required a hysterectomy and could never have any more children.

Consequently, the sight of other people's new babies gave her conflicted feelings. She was so jealous, bitter and sad that she wanted never to see them again, but at the same time, she was so tortured by the desire to see the new baby that she wanted to visit them every single day. Her inner struggles not only drove Auntie Li crazy but also confused Lotus, who never knew whether Auntie Li was going to be warm and kindly or cold and angry at any given time, or how best to deal with her.

Daffodil loved her new sister. Whenever Duoduo cried, Daffodil would talk to her mother as if she knew everything: "Mama, there's no need to dress her in so many layers and wrap her in such thick blankets. Babies get hot easily."

Lotus said, "You little know-it-all! I've raised so many children, why do I need you to teach me? You're not even ten years old."

Daffodil argued, "If you don't listen to me, at least listen to a doctor. My classmate Yazhi's mom is a doctor in a huge hospital! When I went to her house, I saw her mom cover her new baby with just a thin blanket. She even left his little bare feet exposed. She said overfeeding and overheating were two common mistakes parents make with new babies."

Lotus scolded Daffodil: "Girls should behave properly and shy away from talking about childbirth or child-rearing. And talking to your mother like this is not appropriate! A proper girl should avoid such topics, but you ...."

Before Lotus could finish, Daffodil objected shrilly, "You're not treating girls equally! Men and women are equal! You have to listen to me if I'm right, even if I'm a girl!"

Hearing her daughter yelling at her like this made Lotus' hands shake with anger. She grabbed a pillow and threw it at Daffodil: "You think you're a grown up ready to spread your wings? How dare you talk to your mother like that? A sharp tongue will only hurt you when you grow up!"

Daffodil ran out of the house and sat in the yard glowering with anger and frustration. To her, communication was not about how she said something, or to whom or in what tone, or in what context and with what others present. None of these things mattered to her. She only cared about who was right and who was wrong. The person who was wrong must listen to the person who was right, and she firmly believed that she was always right.

Seeing Daffodil sitting on her own, Auntie Li walked over and said, "You look like you've seen a ghost. What's upsetting you?"

Daffodil immediately launched into a tirade about what had just happened, and Auntie Li, raising her voice loud enough for Lotus to hear her from inside the house, said sneeringly, "Someone really doesn't know how to enjoy their God-given blessing. Such a precious baby cries all day long in her own mother's hands. What a mother! Even her own daughter can't take it anymore. Some women can give birth but can't raise. God should really open his eyes!"

Daffodil leaped to her feet and stared at Auntie Li, hating what Auntie Li was saying about her mother. She was about to say something, but Auntie Li turned around and went back into her own house.

Lotus was so upset that she didn't talk to Daffodil for two days. Although she knew she was in the wrong, Daffodil didn't apologize to her mother because she still believed that what she'd said was right and should be followed. At last Lotus sighed and told her, "Please remember, what happens in our family must stay in our family. Don't say anything to anyone outside of our family. And stop thinking that you're always right. Someday you'll be married, and is that how you'll treat your husband and mother-in-law? What kind of life will you have if you do that?"

Daffodil said, "I'll listen to them if they can persuade me that they're right."

Lotus sighed, "Who on earth can persuade you of anything?"

Daffodil huffed, "I don't ever want to get married!"

Daffodil's younger sister Jade was now old enough for first grade, so Daffodil took her by the hand and walked her to school. She reassured her, "Don't worry. You're in a much better place than I was in first grade. You speak Mandarin and you have a new store-bought bag. Our family has honorable origins. If anyone tries to bully you or make fun of you, just ask what kind of family they were born into, and they'll stop right away." Jade nodded compliantly.

As it turned out, nobody bothered Jade, and she easily merged in with the rest of her first grade classmates. Daffodil was happy for her. She was happy that Jade was no different from any other first grader, and that she didn't stand out in a crowd. She didn't have to deal with a Hebei accent, a hand-sewn school bag or a homemade shirt. Jade was sharp like Erqing, and her the teachers all said, "This girl is smart like her second brother!"

Xu Erqing's name was now well known not only in the school but throughout the district. He had brought great honor to his school by winning the district math championship, and then had tested into one of the top middle schools in Beijing's prestigious Haidian District. Now he had become the unchallenged math champion there as well. Erqing had inherited his father's handsome eyes and forehead as well as Lotus's well-defined chin and fine lips. After hitting a growth spurt, he'd shot up taller than the rest of the boys in his grade, and several girls in his school were said to secretly have crushes on him.

When Erqing did his homework, Yixin would sometimes sit beside him holding a newspaper, but rather than reading, he was actually gazing at his second son. He loved Erqing for taking after him with his brains and fast learning.

Yard 13 had a vegetable garden in which each family had a patch. Whenever there were gardening chores, Yixin would find a way of getting Erqing out of them. If Lotus asked Erqing to do any other chores, Yixin would say, "He's studying. Have someone else do it." Seeing how Yixin favored Erqing over his other children, Lotus warned him, "These are all your children. Don't be unfair."

The sensitive and strong-willed Daffodil objected, "Dad plays favorites! He prefers boys to girls!"

Yixin argued, "You ungrateful girl! Haven't we spoiled you rotten? We've let you walk all over your brothers ever since you were born!"

But Daffodil didn't listen, and from then on she was convinced that her father loved Erqing more.

Daqing had reached marriageable age. When he was a little boy in Xu Village by the great Baiyang Lake, a neighbor had given birth to a baby girl, and the parents joked with Yixin and Lotus, "Our two kids should get married when they grow up."

Although it was said in a joking way, Lotus had kept an eye on that baby girl, and had noticed that she had grown up into a beautiful, kind and hardworking young lady. When Yixin mentioned that Daqing was old enough to get married, that Xu Village neighbor girl was the first person who came to Lotus's mind, and Yixin also felt that the girl was a good match. Daqing disagreed, however; he'd lived in Beijing all these years and felt that he might have little in common with a girl from the countryside. Lotus said, "City girls are smart and fashionable, but they ask a lot of you. You're very grounded and quiet. I think you'd do well with a country girl."

It turned out that Lotus was right. Like his parents, Daqing found his new wife kind, hardworking and pleasant. After the wedding, she and Daqing lived in the married employee dorm behind Daqing's factory and gave birth to a baby boy the next year, making Yixin and Lotus proud grandparents.

Being Lotus's neighbor drove Auntie Li crazy. There was one newborn baby after another in Lotus's family. Not only did Lotus give birth to her third daughter Duoduo and her fourth daughter Hong, she also had a fifth daughter, Rong, after Daqing and his wife made Lotus a grandma! Yixin and Lotus now had two sons, five daughters and one grandson. During the week, Daqing's family stayed in their own place and Erqing stayed at school, so there were just Yixin, Lotus and their five daughters at home. But every weekend, Daqing's family and Erqing would all come home, and eleven people made the two-room house seem bursting with life and laughter, in stark contrast to the quietness of Auntie Li's house. Lotus was uneasy whenever she saw Auntie Li, as if she had done something wrong and upset her.

(33) MOTHER AND DAUGHTER

Daffodil loved living in a big city like Beijing. Compared to the repetitive routines of her earlier country life, she could meet all sorts of people and learn all kinds of new ideas. What she loved the most was the movement for gender equality. Chairman Mao said, "Women hold up half the sky." Wasn't that exciting! What Daffodil hated most about country life was the inequality between men and women. In the Baiyang Lake area, girls couldn't go swimming or attend school. Girls couldn't eat at the dinner table if there were guests in the house, or they would be considered immodest and improper. What Daffodil hated most was that girls were not allowed to talk whenever they liked! But in Beijing, she could go to school with boys, and nobody said that a girl couldn't do this or that. She could do whatever she wanted, and best of all, she could say whatever she wanted! There was nothing better than this!

But at home, especially in front of Mama, the old rules still applied. Daffodil knew that Mama considered her a troublesome child. She was not only Lotus's first daughter, but also the first daughter she was raising outside of the traditional context, in the big city of Beijing, with its multitude of new ideas and complex networks of people. To make matters worse, Daffodil was starting puberty, which made here even more rebellious. Lotus's time-tested traditional values and the rules that had been kept by generation after generation of country women were no match for Daffodil's new thinking and sharp tongue.

One day after school, Daffodil ran in and grabbed a steamed bun, saying, "Mama, I'm not coming back for dinner. I have a study group."

Daffodil followed her as she headed for the door: "Study group? What do you do in a study group? Where are you going? Who are you studying with? Boys or girls? When will you be back?"

"Mama, stop!" Daffodil protested.

Lotus grabbed Daffodil by the wrist: "Wait! You cannot go to someone's house. You're a girl! Don't just go to anyone's house! It will ruin your reputation if you stay out late."

Daffodil shook off her mother impatiently: "Mama! What are you talking about? That doesn't make any sense! It will ruin my reputation if I don't go to my study group. My teacher says I'm too arrogant and need to work more collaboratively with other students."

She headed out of Yard 13, her mother right on her heels: "Come back, you disobedient girl!" Lotus yelled. "You're upsetting me to death! How did I give birth to such a ......" She swung a broom at Daffodil.

The students who were just passing through the school gate roared with laughter upon seeing Lotus chasing Daffodil. Daffodil swung around and glared at her mother. She had the hairstyle of a country woman and was wearing a handmade baggy old-style jacket and pants. She had little bound feet that made her wobble when walking, and she was swinging a broom at her daughter.

Lotus looked downright comical. No wonder everyone was laughing. None of the other students' parents or anyone else on the Department of Civil Affairs campus looked or acted like that. Daffodil was so embarrassed that she started running and never wanted to go home again!

Daffodil ran to the front of the DCA main building, which was now quiet at the end of the work day. Its white marble pillars and stairs shone with a warm golden glow in the sunset. Daffodil walked over to a set of side stairs and sat down, raising her eyes to the sky, where golden clouds formed ever-changing patterns. She loved watching the clouds. She always let her imagination run wild and forgot about all her troubles while watching the changing shapes, patterns, colors and layers of clouds. No matter how unhappy she was, she felt she was free and happy when watching the clouds.

"Daffodil!" A girl's voice came from behind her. Daffodil turned and saw her best friend, Zhang Yufang. Yufang walked over and sat next to Daffodil: "I knew you'd be here staring at the sky. You should go home. Your parents must be worried." Daffodil turned to look at the sky again: "Yufang, look at that piece of cloud. As if it's on fire! What do you think it looks like?" Yufang glanced at it and said, "It looks like fish scales. Stop daydreaming! Aren't you always proud of your mom's poor peasant working class status? Then you need to accept her as she is. You need to accept her peasant habits."

Daffodil said, "When we were living by Baiyang Lake, my Mama was more reasonable, open-minded and understanding than all the other moms there. But now everything is different. She can't deal with changes or anything new. She resists even my smallest suggestions, even if I'm absolutely right. Like the other day I suggested that we use better table manners like our neighbor Mrs. Liu's family. When they have fish, everyone takes a whole piece from the serving plate into their own bowl before picking out the fishbones, so their serving plate is always neat. But when we have fish, everyone stabs at the pieces in the serving bowl and picks out pieces of fish to eat, leaving the fish bones behind. Within a few minutes the serving plate looks like a disaster zone. I suggested that we do what Mrs. Liu's family does, but my Mama said I was too picky and hard to please. Don't you think I'm right? Why can't my family change? My Mama doesn't let me go to the study group or anywhere else after school, and she chases me with a broom! I can't take it anymore."

Zhang Yufang heard her out and said, "Let me ask you. That Mrs. Liu you are talking about – isn't that the wife of a formerly wealthy businessman? Their kids can't even go to college because of their capitalist origins. Isn't that the family you're talking about?" When Daffodil nodded, Yufang went on, "Would you rather have been born into a family like that and always be denied everything because of your birth? You can't reap the benefit of a politically honorable birth and then wish you could enjoy the lifestyle of a rich capitalist. Sugar cane can't be sweet on both ends, and you can't expect to have it both ways. You say your mother doesn't learn new things. I think it's you – you come up with new ideas too often and too fast! Nobody can keep up with you!"

This was exactly why Yufang was Daffodil's best friend. She went straight to the point and had amazingly accurate insights. She often revealed things deep in Daffodil's heart that Daffodil hadn't even realized were there. But Daffodil never liked to admit that another person was right. She argued, "Why can't I have the best from both sides? When I grow up and live on my own, I won't keep these bad manners or habits. Who says the working class has to live like this?" "Umm, then you'll have to wait until you're independent. It's not like you can quit school and start working like your older brother," Yufang said.

Daffodil's eyes lit up: "That's right! Why can't I do that? Daqing said the minimum age for his factory is only fourteen. I'll be fourteen soon! You know, my Mama and Daddy treat Daqing like he's some kind of prince. They listen to him, whatever he says! They treat him like an adult because he's working. I want to start working too!"

"You really are crazy! Just go home!" Yufang dragged her to her feet.

All of the students graduating from the Xiangyang Elementary School were designated to attend Lixin Middle School. Students who excelled academically could test for higher-ranking schools, but Daffodil didn't dare even dream of the school her brother Erqing tested into. She knew that with her grades, she'd be attending Lixin Middle School with the bulk of her classmates.

There was no city bus from Yard 13 to Lixin Middle School, and walking there took half an hour one way. The best way to get there was by bicycle, so Yixin borrowed a bike from his department and asked a neighbor girl to teach Daffodil how to ride. Yufang's father heard of this and did the same: "We'll have the two of them learn together and they can bike to school together in the fall."

Unlike her amazing linguistic gifts, Daffodil had terrible balance and coordination, which made it very difficult for her to ride a bicycle. The bike seemed to be playing tricks on her, twisting and wobbling this way and that and tossing Daffodil off, leaving her with bruises on both of her legs. Lotus complained to her husband while dabbing antiseptic ointment on Daffodil's injuries: "How can you let a girl learn such a thing! It's so dangerous and improper! Why does she have to go to middle school anyway? She has more than enough education for a girl!"

Zhang Yufang was as tough as a boy. She tied her hair behind her head into an ugly pony tail with a rubber band, and then pursed her lips, lowered her head, arched her back and wobbled back and forth on the bike. If she fell off, she got back up and continued. She didn't care who was watching or how much people were laughing at her exaggerated posture. Even Daffodil said, "Watching Yufang ride a bike is so painful!" Some students saw Yufang and laughed their heads off, but Yufang didn't care: "If they don't like how I look, they should go look at something else. I didn't beg them to watch me." Within a week, Yufang had mastered her bike and could zoom like a bullet around the DCA campus. Daffodil sighed, "It looks so easy when you do it. But I can't ride a bike to save my life! I don't think I can ride to middle school with you."

(34) DETERMINED

No matter how much Lotus protested, Yixin was adamant about Daffodil getting more education. Just as they were butting heads, an early childhood education vocational school came to distribute brochures to Daffodil's class. It was a three-year program to train early childhood educators. The entry age was fourteen, and then at age seventeen, students would graduate with a diploma in early childhood education and be assigned work in high-profile preschools and daycare centers. This seemed like a God-send to Yixin and Lotus. In particular, Lotus thought that being a preschool or daycare teacher was a proper job for a girl. Daffodil was excited because the school was a boarding school, which meant that she could finally leave home and have her own life. And she would be working in just three short years! It was like a dream come true!

Daffodil excitedly turned in her application and went for the required physical exam, then anxiously awaited her admission notice. But Zhang Yufang's admission notice from the Lixin Middle School had come two weeks before, and there was still no response from the early childhood education school for Daffodil! She was as anxious and irritated as an ant on a hot wok.

Yixin pulled some strings to find someone inside the school and got to the bottom of the problem. It turned out that Daffodil was on their rejection list because she had failed the physical exam for being nearsighted. Daffodil wept with disappointment and frustration: "How can I be nearsighted? Says who? What's wrong with being nearsighted? Lots of teachers wear classes. Why can't I? Why do they reject nearsighted students? That's so unfair!"

Worse yet, by then the Lixin Middle School was full, and Daffodil was assigned to a school she had never heard of that was even further away with no bus access! She still didn't know how to ride a bike, so how would she get to school? None of her friends or classmates had been assigned to that school. Daffodil yelled, "I'll die before I go to that stupid school!"

Daffodil cried nonstop for two days, refusing food and water. Lotus said to Yixin, "She's too stubborn. I think this is actually good for her. She has to learn how to deal with life when it doesn't go her way."

Yixin said: "I agree. But we have to help her. We can't let her just keep crying like this."

The next day was a Sunday, and Daqing arrived with his family. They tried to console the crying Daffodil. She said tearfully, "Daqing, Sis (as she called Daqing's wife), I'm the unluckiest person in this world! What should I do?"

Lotus said, "I already told you, a girl doesn't need so much schooling. You should just stay home!"

Daqing's wife agreed: "Daffodil, Mama is right. You're already well-educated. See, I don't even know how to write my own name and I'm doing fine. You shouldn't worry. You'll marry into a good family and have a great life."

Daffodil declared, "I refuse to stay home and be a housewife like you!" As Daqing's wife smiled with embarrassment, Daffodil went on, "I want to work if I can't go to school. And I'm never going to get married!"

Daqing's wife asked Daqing, "Isn't your factory looking for female workers? You can ask around for Daffodil. She can come work at the factory. I heard they're hiring the first group of female workers this year. They even built a new women's dorm."

Daffodil sat up, "Sis! Is that true?"

Daqing said, "Don't listen to your Sis! You're too young. You should go to school for a few more years."

"Why didn't you go to school for a few more years?" Daffodil protested. "Remember how you were? You didn't want to stay in school but now you want me to?"

Daqing shook his head: "It's not like that. You don't know what factories are like. It's really no place for girls. It's filthy, exhausting and dangerous. The workers there curse and fight all the time. You're so picky and spoiled, you won't even survive a day out there. I really don't think they should ever hire girls!"

That hit Daffodil's most sensitive nerve: "Daqing! You look down on girls just like Mama and Dad do! Don't you know that Chairman

Mao said women hold up half of the sky? Why can't a factory have women? Women can work smarter and with better detail. You're not better than us! I want to go to work at your factory!"

If Daffodil decided on something, nobody could change her mind. She wanted to leave home and have a life free of her parents' control. She wanted to earn money and relieve some of her parents' financial burden. She wanted to forget that stupid school that rejected her because of nearsightedness. She wanted to escape that damn school with no friends and no bus access. She wanted to prove she was all grown up. She wanted to be among the first group of proud female workers in Daqing's factory. She wanted to be like Daqing, getting so much love and attention when coming home on weekends. No matter what her parents said and how much Daqing and his wife talked to her, she was determined to become a worker at Daqing's factory.

Weeping over her daughter's refusal to eat, Lotus asked, "Are you really sure? This is a path you're picking for yourself, and there's no turning back. You have to walk this path on your own. Your Dad and I can't help you once you're at the factory. You're only fourteen! You should seriously think about leaving home at such a young age. Don't make the decision lightly!"

Daffodil said, "I've made up my mind!"

Yixin sighed, "She's as stubborn as I was when I enlisted in the army without even telling my parents. I wouldn't listen to them back then, and she won't listen to us now! But I think she has the same courageous and adventurous spirit as me. Alright! It's all destiny!" He then turned to Daqing and said, "You've been working at the factory for a few years now. Watch over your sister, and don't let anyone bully her. See if you can help her get a good assignment. She's such a young girl, try to get her to an assignment without much physical labor."

Daqing said, "I'm friends with Xiaodong in the human resources office. I got him the glass cover for his table when he got married. Let me talk to him and see if he can assign Daffodil to a good position without having to go into the workshops. But any new employee has to spend six months in a workshop. An assignment only happens after six months." Daffodil said, "I'm fine. I can go to a workshop. If you can do it, I can do it." Daqing shook his head and sighed.

Daffodil had a forward-looking nature and didn't like to dwell on the past. She felt that the only person she would miss was her best friend Zhang Yufang. Yufang asked her, "Do you really want to go to the factory? Can you bear the hard work and tough environment? We won't even see each other anymore." Daffodil said, "We can't see each other even if I don't go to the factory. We're not assigned to the same school!"

Yufang asked, "Is it possible that you'll marry a factory worker someday?" Daffodil said, "I don't know. But even if I do, I'll pick a factory worker who is well-mannered and sophisticated. Otherwise I won't marry anyone." Yufang said, "How about this? You and I will meet and check out each other's fiancés. You take a look at mine and I'll take a look at yours. We'll only get married if we both like the guy!" Daffodil laughed, "It's a deal!"

(35) FACTORY GIRLS

The Beijing Factory of Auto Repairs was located in eastern Beijing in the Chongwen District outside of the old city wall. It had always been an all-male factory, but in order to follow Chairman Mao's directive about women holding up half of the sky, the factory had decided to hire thirty female workers this year. The factory built a women's dormitory for this purpose. Daffodil was part of this first group of thirty female workers.

On the first day for the new workers, the small yard at the front of the factory was decorated with banners and posters. Some people even played drums and gongs in celebration. Each new female worker wore a big red paper flower, and the male workers all gathered to welcome (stare at) them.

The director of the factory gave a brief speech and everyone clapped. Then the director said, "All new workers should head to the women's dorm to unpack and get settled. Then go to your assigned workshop to report to your Shifus." He then turned to a group of young male trainees: "You guys help the girls with their luggage!"

With a loud cheer, the young trainees jumped up: "Yes, Director!" One even said, "Director, you're like a father to us!" They dashed over and surrounded the girls, grabbed all the luggage and walked the girls to their dorm while grinning at them and trying to make conversation.

Daffodil's luggage was grabbed by a young man who looked like a local hooligan no more than sixteen years old: "Hey, let me help you!" he said. "What's your name? Which workshop are you assigned to?" Daffodil replied, "My name is Daffodil Xu." The "hooligan" smiled broadly: "Oh no shit! You must be the sister of Xu Daqing, Xu Shifu, right? I've heard about you. The youngest one, only fourteen, right?" Daffodil kept walking without responding to him. She didn't want to admit that she was the youngest one. The "hooligan" pumped out his chest: "Xu Shifu's sister is my sister too! My name is Gong. Sis, anything you need from now on, you come to Workshop Two and find your brother Gong, all right? If anyone bothers you, just let your brother Gong know, and I will beat the crap out of the bastard for you, all right? Oh! Are you hungry? Want me to go steal a couple sugar buns for you from the dining hall?"

Daffodil was used to being the talkative one, but she couldn't keep up with this guy today, and she didn't know how to respond. Just then, Daqing walked over and grabbed Daffodil's luggage from Gong: "Get the hell out of here!" Gong laughed and said, "Oh, Xu Shifu! Hey hey hey, everybody! Look over here! This is Xu Shifu's sister. Everyone, look after her, don't let no shit happen to her, OK?" Everyone yelled, "Got it!"

The women's dorm was a red brick bungalow with a row of three large rooms, each accommodating ten girls. As Daffodil entered her dorm room, she saw that across from the door, against the back wall, was a wall-to-wall bed spanning the length of the room. The ten girls were to share this wall-to-wall bed. On the back wall were ten hooks for clothes or bags. A coal-burning stove in front of the bed had a large cast iron kettle on it that was hissing with boiling water and steam. The room had a five-level wood shelf on the left wall and another on the right wall. There were no curtains, so the girls asked the dining center for a handful of flour, which they then dissolved in a tin can full of water and put on the stove to boil. Once boiled, the flour water mixture could be used as glue, which they used to cover the windows with old newspapers. They also put newspaper on the walls around the bed so they could lean on the walls without having to worry about dust from the white lime used to paint the walls. They put away their water basins, toothbrushes and cups, lunch pails, combs and other items.

Now it was time to decide who was going to sleep where on the wall-to-wall bed. A tall girl stood up. At twenty-one, she was the oldest among the thirty girls. Her name was Zhang Ling, so the others called her Big Ling. Big Ling said, "I know a fair way. We should arrange it by age. Whoever is the youngest will sleep in the middle, where it's closer to the stove and warmer. But be careful not to bump the stove when you get out of bed, or you might get some nasty burns. Then we'll line up toward both walls according to age. The oldest will be on either side against the walls. What do you think?"

The girls all looked at one another and nodded. Then another older looking girl stepped forward and said, "I think this is a good idea.

I'm twenty years old, so I should also take a spot against the wall." Big Ling asked, "What's your name?" The girl replied, "My name is Li Aici." Aici looked at Daffodil and said, "You should take the middle spot."

Daffodil liked Aici's name, because it meant love and mercy. Someone said loudly to Daffodil, "Don't wet the bed!" Daffodil shot back, "Speak for yourself!" Everyone laughed and started putting their bedding in their designated spots. The dorm was very simple, but after ten sets of colorful bedding were spread on the wall-to-wall bed, the room looked cheery, warm and lively.

It was fall in Beijing, and the sky was a dreamy blue. A gust of wind swirled through the fallen leaves as the girls walked from their dorm to the workshops. The gloomy factory seemed to have come to life now that the girls were there.

Daffodil was assigned to Workshop Three. She wanted to be in Workshop Two with Daqing, but Daqing said it wouldn't be appropriate for a brother and sister to work in the same workshop. He also told Daffodil, "Workshop Three is the least tiring. I asked Xiaodong and that's how you got assigned there." Daffodil felt lucky that the new girl she liked, Aici, was in the same workshop with her.

Her first impression as she entered her workshop was the unbearable noise. She had never been in such a noisy place in her life! Whether it was growing up by the great Baiyang Lake, or living on the DCA campus, she'd never heard anything so loud. If it had been sheer high volume, Daffodil felt she could probably have dealt with it, but it was the unnatural quality of the noise that drove her crazy. There was the banging and scratching of metal, and the hum and screech of parts being polished, sanded and welded. The noises were not only ear-piercing but also capable of slicing into your head and stabbing your heart. Daffodil jumped out of her skin with every unexpected noise or heart-shaking vibration. She felt she couldn't last ten minutes in this kind of environment and wondered how workers survived it day after day and year after year.

Workshop Three, where Daffodil worked, was for processing parts. Daffodil and Aici's first task was to clean the sludge off of old parts. An older worker showed them how to remove the sludge and make the part shine again. He held a part in his left hand and a small, sharp knife in his right hand, and with a turn of both hands, a groove showed the part's original silver color. He smeared the knife on the back of his left hand, and the knife became clean as new. He went on to turn and smear, turn and smear again and again. After a few rounds, he rubbed the part in a cloth, and it came out shiny and clean. The whole process took him no more than five or six seconds.

Daffodil and Aici each grabbed a small knife and a cloth and sat down by the mountain of sludge-covered parts to start working. But their knives seemed to have minds of their own, and the parts seemed to be very slippery. If they applied pressure while trying to scratch the sludge off, they were afraid of the sharp knife slipping and poking their hands, but if they didn't apply enough pressure, no sludge would come off. Finally, Daffodil scraped some sludge onto her knife, but she simply couldn't bring herself to smear it on the soft, fair skin on the back of her left hand. Aici said, "Pretend it's snow white skin lotion. Then you won't mind so much smearing it on your hand!"

After two hours, Daffodil's hand was covered with black sludge, and her left hand was bleeding from being poked by the knife more than a couple of times. Her neck and back muscles ached from being held in one position so long, and the torturing noise in the workshop was driving her mad. Aici cleaned one part after another without saying a word, her face streaked with sludge. Daffodil said as loudly as she could, "Aici! You have sludge on your face! This job is horrible!" Aici replied loudly, "This is the easiest job. Look around the workshop – nobody else is sitting down like us!"

Lunch consisted of cabbage and meatball soup and steamed buns. Daffodil despised cabbage, but after working all morning, she gobbled down her lunch pail full of soup and devoured two and half steamed buns in no time. This was twice as much as she usually ate. The smell of food and the sound of people chattering in the dining hall were like being in heaven compared to the noise and smell of the workshop.

In the afternoon, one of the Shifus wanted to teach the girls something new. He showed them how to hammer the top and bottom portions of a part together. He held the part with his left hand and swung his hammer precisely. With a bang, the top and bottom portions of the part connected so perfectly that you couldn't tell they were ever apart. The Shifu said that the most important thing was to make sure not to bang on your hand and not to have your hand caught in between the pieces you were hammering together. He said that someone had gotten their flesh caught in between and fainted with the pain. Everyone grabbed a hammer and started to work, and a banging sound echoed through the workshop.

A loud scream pierced the metallic factory noises. Big Ling was jumping up and down holding a swelling finger. Shifu came over for a look and said, "It's fine, you still seem able to bend it. Last time someone banged their finger flat."

Daffodil tried to forget the deafening noise and focus on her hammer, but she suddenly felt like she wanted to cry. It was two o'clock now; what was Yufang doing? She must have finished her first afternoon class period. What was Mama doing? Was she trying to put Hong and Rong down for a nap? Did Mama know that her Daffodil was swinging a hammer? Daffodil wiped her tears away with the back of her hand, leaving a thick line of black sludge on her face.

(36) THE MOTHER-IN-LAW

After a week of sludge cleaning, hammer swinging, screw driving and parts disassembling, Daffodil could finally go home. Daqing wasn't going home that weekend, so Daffodil took the bus by herself.

Yard 13 had never seemed so warm and lovely, and Mama had never seemed so kind and beautiful. Even the screams and quarrels of Duoduo, Hong and Rong made Daffodil smile. Without the deafening noise of the workshop, Daffodil felt a little lost. She sat there and thought, "How come this room looks so small?" Lotus was in tears: "My poor daughter has become silent and gloomy after just one week. She used to talk non-stop but now all she does is look around, as if not recognizing her own home."

Daffodil said, "Mama, I'm hungry." Her booming voice startled Lotus, and her sisters also turned to stare at her. Daffodil realized she was talking much louder after a week in the workshop. She lowered her voice: "What's for dinner?"

Lotus rushed to the kitchen: "I've made roast pork, and noodles with black bean sauce." Daffodil followed her mother into the kitchen: "I'll mash some garlic to go with the noodles. There's no garlic in the factory canteen." Lotus said, "Then you should bring some from home!" With a bang, Daffodil smashed the clove of garlic into mush with just one swing of the puree stick. She said, "Oh, this garlic is really fresh – a light hit turns it into liquid!" Lotus said, "Look at the muscles you've built up in just a few days! You must have it pretty hard at the factory." Tears began running down her face. Seeing her mother cry made Daffodil want to cry, so she said, "Mama, let's eat. I'm hungry."

The next day, Daffodil got up early to go see Yufang. The two girls giggled excitedly upon seeing each other after a week. They settled on Yufang's couch while Yufang's mother put a bowl of candy on the coffee table for them. Yufang said, "Tell me! Tell me! What is the factory like? What do you do there?" Daffodil said, "You can't even imagine! It would scare you to death! It's so loud! It's deafening!"

Yufang started telling Daffodil about her new school, but for some reason Daffodil wanted to avoid the subject. "Let me tell you about my factory dorm. Ten of us share one big wall-to-wall bed. You know what happened during our first week? It was disgusting! We covered our windows with newspaper, but some guy tried to peek in through the cracks! Big Ling caught him when she went out to dump some water. He was taken to the security office, and even the police were called!" "Really?" Yufang's draw dropped: "That's unbelievable! That's disgusting!"

"Yufang," Yufang's mother stuck her head out of the kitchen: "Daffodil has to go to work early tomorrow morning. She must be very tired, and I'm sure her parents want to spend more time with her too. You shouldn't take too much of Daffodil's time. Also, don't you have a lot of homework to finish?" Daffodil said her goodbyes. On her way home she thought, "Next time I visit Yufang, I should pick a time when her mother isn't home." What Daffodil didn't realize was that a seemingly small step in life could become a mountain that separated a river into two streams that would never converge again.

Monday morning, Daffodil had to transfer buses twice and get to the factory by 7:30. Lotus made poached eggs, but Daffodil didn't have time to eat them. Lotus chased Daffodil to the gate of Yard 13 holding a bowl of eggs: "Just eat some of them! It won't take much time at all!" Daffodil said as she ran off, "Erqing can have them!"

Lotus had no choice but to go home with the eggs. Running into her second son Erqing as he rushed out to make it to his Monday morning study period, Lotus tried to give him the eggs, but he threw his jacket on and ran off: "I don't have time! You eat it!" Lotus took the bowl of eggs and chased Erqing to the gate of Yard 13 as well: "These kids! What did I ever do to deserve such treatment!"

It was actually a good thing that Daffodil hadn't eaten, otherwise the foul smell, crowdedness and swaying of the buses would have made her throw up. Finally the bus pulled up to the factory gate. Daffodil jumped off and greedily inhaled the fresh cool air. Now she was hungry, and she ran into the factory, hoping that she could still catch breakfast at the factory canteen.

As she passed the factory office building, she saw a crowd and heard two sharp female voices quarreling. Wait! One of the voices seemed to be Aici! Daffodil dashed over to the crowd.

Back then, the workplace governed not only an employee's professional life, but also their personal life. Major life events such as getting married, having a baby, getting housing and health care, and even monthly food ration tickets were controlled by the workplace. That made the leaders in every workplace responsible not only for the workplace's business, but also the daily lives of their employees. There were no professional and personal boundaries, and many personal matters were settled through the involvement of workplace leaders.

When Daffodil pushed her way to the front of the crowd, she saw the factory director standing in the middle, with a country woman in her fifties on his left, and Aici to his right. The country woman yelled, "You are promised for marriage into our family, so you have to abide by our rules. You have no business running off and joining the workforce in the city! What about your family? Come back with me or I'll beat you until your legs are broken!" Aici yelled back, "I never consented to that so-called marriage. It's illegal to force me to marry anyone! I have the freedom to work!"

The woman yelled hysterically, "Illegal my ass! You just ask around. Everyone praises my son! All the girls want to marry my son! We only agreed to take you out of respect for your deceased parents. They agreed to this marriage when they were alive, and we are decent people who keep our promises. We can't go back on our word, so you have no choice but to come back with me!"

Aici said, "It's a new society now and a new government! I'm free to work here if I want to. There's nothing you can do!"

The factory director said, "Both of you stop arguing! Come into my office and stop making a scene out here. Everyone, go have breakfast and head to your workshops! Go on!"

The workers started to walk away, and after looking at Aici, Daffodil walked away too. Gong came over to Daffodil: "Look at that stinky old bitch! Aici can't marry her son. It would be like putting a fresh rose on a pile of cow manure. Don't you agree? Oh, you haven't had breakfast, right? The dining hall's Liu Shifu treats me like a son. Let's go, and I'll ask my 'dad' to make fresh fried dough sticks for you!"

The country woman began weeping as soon as she entered the director's office: "I've been a widow since age thirty. I have nobody but my son! Now at last he's old enough to marry, but who knew we'd be cursed with such a disobedient daughter-in-law! Why is life so harsh on me? I don't want to live anymore!"

The factory director said firmly: "That's enough! Stop crying and no more nonsense!" The woman quieted down immediately.

The director said, "Li Aici is one of our first group of new female workers. The decision to hire female workers is based on Chairman Mao's directive that women hold up half the sky. This hiring is in accordance with labor laws and government policies, and we're supported by the central government. Now you've come here to make a scene and force Li Aici to go back to the countryside with you, and you've threatened to beat her up. That's nothing short of counter-revolutionary! In our socialist state, the workers are leaders of the country. Who are you to threaten them? I should send you to the security office and the police right now! Do you understand me?"

Apparently intimidated, the woman began talking in a much calmer and softer voice: "Even if all that is true, you can't stop people from getting married..."

The director said, "Of course, our factory supports our employees' personal lives, but where is your son? Tell me the details of this marriage arrangement. Was it arranged against the wills of the young people?"

"No! Of course not!" the woman protested. "Aici's parents used to be my brother's neighbors, and they promised us Aici's hand in marriage when they were alive. The two young people have met before and they had no objections. Of course it's not an arranged marriage! My son is staying with my brother right outside of Dahongmen. You can call him in to ask him if you don't believe me!"

The director turned to Aici: "Aici, don't worry. It's a new world now and everyone has freedom to marry. Tell me if you want to marry her son or not. If you don't want to marry him, I'll ask security to escort her out right now."

Aici said, "I want to work here. I don't want to go back to the countryside!"

The director asked, "Of course you'll continue to work here, but what about marriage? She says her son is living outside of Dahongmen. I know there's a new factory called Beijing Factory of Metallurgy Machinery, and the director there used to be my coworker. They're hiring factory workers, so if you'd like, I can talk to their director and have him give this woman's son a job. That way both of you will be workers in Beijing and you don't have to go back to the countryside. But of course, that is only if you want to marry him."

Before Aici could speak, the older woman leaped to her feet: "Director, you're so kind! Aici, please think of your late mother and father. They wanted you to marry my son! You can't disobey them just because they're not here anymore. That's immoral! I know you're a moral girl who honors your parents! My son is smart and hardworking, and we'll be good to you." Aici was quiet for a while, and then she nodded to the director: "All right, I can marry him, but I'm not going back to the countryside!"

The director said, "We have limited dorm space and won't be able to offer you married housing. But the other factory is newly built and has new dorms. I'll ask their director if they can assign you and the young man a bungalow to live in. That way you don't have to go back to the countryside and you can stay in Beijing. How about that?"

Two months later, Li Aici married Zhao Min. Zhao Min was hired as a worker by the Beijing Factory of Metallurgy Machinery, and they moved into the factory's married employee housing.

After her wedding, Aici still stayed in her own factory's dorm a few days a week because the commute was too long. She only went home on Wednesdays and Saturdays. She didn't seem happy like a new bride should be. She was quiet, gloomy and irritable.

One day at lunch, Daffodil sat next to her and tentatively asked, "Aici, you look like you have a lot on your mind. Are you all right? Is everything going well at home?" Aici sighed and fell silent for some time. Then she glanced around a little bit and lowered her voice to Daffodil: "Daffodil, you have to listen carefully. This may not sound nice but it's the naked truth of life. When you look for a husband, find a man without a mother! Trust me, you don't want to deal with a mother-in-law. If you happen to have a mother-in-law like mine, your life will be ruined!" Daffodil was shocked: "Is your mother-in-law mean to you?"

Aici's mother-in-law was an illiterate country woman who had become a widow at an early age. She had never remarried and focused all her attention on her only son, who was everything to her. Watching her son getting married was like having her inner organs ripped from her body. It drove her crazy to think that her son was now with another woman. The factory gave Zhao Min and Aici only a single-room bungalow, but Zhao Min's mother insisted on living with them from the very first day. That meant that Zhao Min and Aici spent their wedding night with the mother-in-law sleeping in the same small room, on the other side of a curtain that separated her bed from theirs.

Whenever Aici came home, the mother-in-law would pull open the curtain in the middle of the night without warning, saying she heard noises and was afraid that mice might be biting her son's ears in his sleep, and she had to help her son catch the mice. Zhao Min finally said, "Mother, stop opening the curtain." His mother burst out crying and yelled that she wanted to commit suicide because her son was abandoning her for another woman. Her loud cries and screams woke the neighbors, and everyone was talking about the nighttime dramas in their home. Aici was so frustrated and embarrassed that she had stopped going home, but her mother-in-law wouldn't have it: "Did my son marry you for nothing? You don't even come home! Why does my son have to live like a single man when he has a wife!" Aici had no choice but to go home and face the frustrations again.

The mother-in-law even watched how much Aici ate. She only allowed her to eat leftovers or food that she and her son didn't want. Even so, she constantly complained: "What did I ever do to deserve such a daughter-in-law! She doesn't take care of me like a daughter-in-law should, and I have to serve her food! The only thing I don't do is to kneel to her! What a life! Why doesn't God have pity on me!"

Zhao Min was a quiet man, hardworking and smart, and he treated Aici well. But his weakness was his mother, who had total control over him. Zhao Min didn't dare utter a single word against his mother, and defending Aici would set off an atomic bomb. Aici said, "How come you're like a baby who has never been weaned? As soon as you see your mother, you're not a man anymore!" Zhao Min said helplessly, "What can I do? She's my mother."

Aici always came back to her own factory dorm as this miserable and complaining woman. Daffodil was only fifteen years old and she didn't fully understand Aici's frustration or the complicated relationship between mothers-in-law and their daughters-in-law. But seeing how unhappy Aici was, Daffodil thought all mothers-in-law must be monsters. She decided that she would never get married, just so that she didn't have to deal with a mother-in-law!

(37) FIVE STEAMED BUNS

The winter of 1958 was especially cold and dry, with the crisp autumn wind that roiled the fallen leaves soon turning into icy gusts that sapped the warmth from every corner. The only source of heat in Daffodil's dorm was the coal burning stove, which was far from enough to fend off the piercing wind that snuck in through cracks along the window and door. The girls wrapped themselves in whatever they could find at night, spreading their heavy jackets on top of their blankets and sleeping in layers of clothing. Some even wore hats to bed. In spite of their best efforts, they woke up freezing every morning, their feet numb with cold even after a whole night in bed.

One way to fend off the cold was to soak their feet in warm water before going to bed. Each girl went to fetch a basin full of boiling hot water from the water house, then walked back to their dorm in the cold wind, which cooled the water to a point where they could slowly begin dipping their toes. Ten girls sat in line at the edge of the bed with ten basins of hot water in front of them, their feet red from the hot water. Once the water temperature was finally comfortable enough for them to completely immerse their feet, everyone sighed with enjoyment: "Ah..... So warm! I hope this water never turns cold." "If I could take a hot shower right now, I'd be willing to work overtime any number of days!"

But eventually the water in the basins turned cold. The girls quickly got into bed and wrapped themselves in thick blankets while their feet were still warm. The ten basins of water were left on the floor at the head of the bed; no one would go out in the cold night to dump them. The girls all avoided drinking water or soup after 5pm in order to spare themselves the long walk to the unbearably cold outhouse in the middle of the night. In the morning, they woke up to ten basins of solid ice at the head of their bed; the basins of ice wouldn't melt all day and would be waiting for them when they came back at night. The girls would take their basins of ice to the water house and pour hot water along the edges to melt the ice enough that it could be dumped out, and then they would fill the basins with hot water to soak their feet again.

Getting up every morning in this kind of weather required courage and resolve. Big Ling said, "I just want to stay in bed till I die! I don't care about anything else!" Another girl said, "But you can't die like a hungry ghost. Go eat first, and then you can die if you want." Thinking of the fried dough, soy milk, steaming congee and golden toast in the dining hall, the girls gritted their teeth and rolled out of bed. After breakfast, these fifteen- to twenty-year-old girls would have to put in ten hours of hard labor in their unheated workshops. Thank heaven, Daqing had asked Xiaodong to assign Daffodil to the warehouse so she no longer had to work in a workshop.

Even at that, Daffodil's hands were cracked with dryness and frostbite. Daqing's wife gave Daffodil some hand cream wrapped in plastic. All of the girls gathered around Daffodil: "How fragrant!" "This cream is white as snow!" "How comfortable it would feel to rub that on your hands!" "Your sister-in-law is so nice to you!" Daffodil felt ashamed to keep it all to herself, so she shared with the others.

The girls all giggled and rubbed the cream on their hands with great care and appreciation. The fragrance spread through the room as if jasmine flowers were lighting their young faces with smiles despite the hardship.

After the Lunar New Year in 1959, food was suddenly in short supply, and strict rationing was imposed. Male workers were allowed sixteen kilos of grain per month, while female workers were allowed fourteen kilos. For workers engaged in manual labor and who had no other sources of food, this ration was barely enough to keep them alive.

Long before meal time, a crowd of hungry workers gathered outside the dining hall, banging their lunch boxes with chopsticks. Daqing ran over to the dining hall and yelled to his apprentices, "You sons of bitches! Get back to work! The lunch bell hasn't run yet and you've run off already?"

Gong told Daqing, "Xu Shifu, my 'dad' Mr. Liu is serving the food today. I'm going in early with a few others to help him keep the crowd in order. That's work too! It's contributing to the factory! How about this? I'll ask my 'dad' to give me an extra half piece of cornbread for you to gnaw on in the afternoon."

"Stop that nonsense!" Daqing scowled.

Gong tried again: "Actually, I'm going in early to get a larger serving of congee for our sister Daffodil."

Daqing hated how Gong followed Daffodil around like a dog. "Get the fuck out of here! She's my sister, not yours! Get your ass back to work!"

Gong put on a sad face: "Xu Shifu, you have a wife who cooks for you and I'll bet she gives you a solid breakfast. All I get is a bowl of congee in the morning. I pee twice and it's gone. I don't have the strength to work anymore!"

Another worker said, "That's right. Xu Shifu, if you get me two solid pieces of flatbread, I can take care of all of those damn cars this afternoon!"

Everyone used hot water to carefully rinse their lunch boxes, and then drank the water so that not a bit of food was wasted. Even if all that was left in the lunchbox was a drop of soy sauce, they'd rinse it with water and then drink the water. The desire for food occupied people's minds around the clock. They even dreamed about how to find food.

Daffodil remembered how during the famine at the great Baiyang Lake, her brothers Daqing and Erqing had gone to the fields to look for edible plants like dandelions and ferns, so she led a few female workers out of the city in hopes of finding such plants in the fields on the outskirts. What she saw outside of Beijing horrified her – the famine was much worse just beyond the city borders. There were no edible plants left. The land was bare, and even the bark had been stripped from the trees by starving people. She realized that even with food rationing, she was incredibly fortunate to be living in Beijing rather than starving to death in the countryside.

At that time, China had a household registration system under which everyone was assigned a hukou (household registration) based on where they were born or where they worked. Farmers were assigned a hukou for the village where they worked their land. All food, clothing and other basic living supplies, as well as education and healthcare, were strategically rationed by the government and could only be obtained with the hukou card in one's assigned locality. People had no freedom to move to another place unless they changed their hukou. A hukou for a major city like Beijing was basically impossible to obtain except by those born to Beijing residents, or assigned to work there by the government. People would kill for a Beijing hukou because it brought life-saving benefits that were not available elsewhere. During a famine, that could mean the difference between life and death.

The factory introduced a new concept: food substitutes. Each worker was given packets of "man-made biscuits," the ingredients of which were a mystery. The biscuits were tasteless but very filling, so the workers ate them all up and enjoyed the long-awaited satisfaction of a full stomach. But their pleasure was short-lived. The biscuits were easy to eat but hard to digest, and many workers found themselves so constipated that they had to pry their stool out with their fingers.

Over time, Daffodil's face became pale, her chin pointed and her eyes large and empty from malnutrition. But she knew things were worse back home. The last time Daffodil had gone home, she saw that her mother Lotus's legs were swollen with edema because she was giving up part of her food ration to her children. When Daffodil pressed her mama's leg with her thumb, the dent didn't disappear for a long time because her flesh had lost its elasticity. Daffodil was so worried that she decided to eat less and save some of her rations for her mother. Daqing and his wife joined Daffodil's effort, and the three of them drank large amounts of water while trying to eat as little as possible. Finally, they saved up a half kilo of food rations. That was an astronomical number during a famine, enough to save the lives of an entire family. Daqing and Daffodil used the rations they'd saved up to procure five steamed buns from the dining hall. Daqing said, "You take them to Mama. If I take my family to visit her, that's three more mouths for her to feed."

Daffodil carefully placed the five steamed buns into a plastic bag, which she then wrapped with a towel. She put the towel-wrapped parcel into a duffle bag with two layers of zippers, and clutched the duffle bag to her chest with both arms as she nervously got onto the bus for home. A young girl traveling with five steamed buns during the famine was like walking around a dangerous neighborhood with a pocketful of cash in the middle of the night.

As she hurried to Yard 13 from the bus stop, Daffodil could feel her heart pounding and beads of sweat forming on her forehead. Although feeling weak and lightheaded, Daffodil thought of how hungry her mama must be, and how happy she would be to see these five buns, so she started to run. She remembered that one time when she and her sister Jade were little, they'd scared their mother half to death by bringing poisonous mushrooms home, but this time Daffodil was all grown up and was bringing home delicious steamed buns! Five of them! The thought made Daffodil giggle out loud.

"Mama!" Daffodil called out as she ran into the house. She stopped short as she saw her mother Lotus sitting there crying. Sitting next to her on a bench was a peasant man who looked familiar to Daffodil, but she couldn't remember who he was. The man was crying, too. Lotus said, "Daffodil, you're home! Look, your uncle is here. Greet your uncle!" Now Daffodil recognized the man as Mama's only brother, who lived near the great Baiyang Lake. When Daffodil was small, her mama had forbidden her to go to the lake, believing that Daffodil was an incarnation of her son Sanqing, who had drowned in Baiyang Lake. Uncle was the only person who was allowed to take Daffodil on his little boat to go fishing on the great Baiyang Lake. He wasn't afraid of Lotus, and he did whatever Daffodil wanted. Now that youthful, upbeat, free-spirited uncle was gray-haired and gloomy. How had he aged so quickly?

Uncle held Daffodil's hands and looked at her from head to toe as he said tearfully, "You've grown so much! I'm so sad that grandma and grandpa will never see you again!" Uncle and Mama both broke down in uncontrollable weeping.

Daffodil's maternal grandma and grandpa had died of starvation. People in Beijing couldn't imagine the famine experienced by people in the countryside. In Beijing's government compounds like the one where Lotus and Yixin lived, the food rations were enough to sustain everyone's life. In the city's factories, each worker could count on an allocation of fourteen kilos of grains a month. In the colleges, students could stick their chopsticks into baskets of cornmeal buns. But in the countryside, the peasants were left on their own. In Lotus's home village, every family had someone who died of starvation, mainly the elderly and young children.

Seeing the sorrow of her mother and uncle, Daffodil took out the five steamed buns: "Mama, Daqing and I got these for you."

Looking at the buns with teary eyes, Lotus yelled, "You! The two of you must be starving yourselves to death! I don't want them. You and Daqing eat them! You'll die if you eat too little and save food for me! Don't worry about me. I have enough. Take them back. You eat them! Look how thin you've become ...."

Of course Daffodil didn't take the buns back with her. But her mother and sisters didn't get to eat even a crumb of them. Uncle's two sons were about to die of hunger, and Mama had no food left to give them. Rather than watching her nephews die, she gave Daffodil's five buns to her brother to take home to save his sons.

Lotus was too crippled by the edema in her legs to travel to Hebei Province for her parents' funeral at Baiyang Lake. Likewise, she couldn't let her brother stay overnight because she had nothing to feed him. Both Lotus and Yixin skipped a meal so they could give Uncle a bowl of noodles to eat. His stomach aching with hunger, Yixin went from one office to another in his department, up and down stairs, in order to obtain an advance on his next month's salary. With that money he bought a small bag of soybeans for his brother-in-law.

Lotus didn't have the strength to walk her brother to the train station, so they said their goodbyes at the gate of Yard 13. They didn't know if they would make it through the famine or not, so this might be the last time they saw each other.

Lotus said, "I'm so sorry. I'm a bad daughter and a bad sister. I don't know what else to do. I'm so sorry!" Holding Daffodil's five steamed buns and Yixin's small bag of soybeans, Lotus's brother waved goodbye and headed to the train station.

(38) THE CURLY HEAD

————————— ✶ —————————

The famine ended in the beginning of 1962. Gradually, the food situation improved, and by mid-1962, there was an abundance of food both in the factory and at home. The two youngest girls of the family, Hong and Rong, began to grow taller. Little Hong said, "My mouth feels delicious when I eat meat. And it feels sweet when I eat candy." Everyone laughed.

It was 1963, and Daffodil was now a young lady of twenty and a seasoned warehouse manager with six years of work experience under her belt. Every year, new girls were hired by the factory, and they followed her around calling, "Daffodil! Daffodil!" and asking all kinds of questions just as she had when she was new.

Most of the girls in Daffodil's dorm had moved out once they got married, but the rule set by Big Ling that the youngest slept in the middle was still followed. Now Daffodil was next to the wall. Every move towards the wall had made her uneasy. It seemed only yesterday that she was sleeping in the middle, and the wall had seemed so far away, but now there she was! The oldest resident in the dorm! She knew the next step for girls by the wall was to get married, but she didn't want to get married. She didn't like any of the men she knew, and she was afraid of having a mother-in-law. By far the favorite topic among the factory's married women was their mothers-in-law. They enthusiastically vented about how their mothers-in-law invaded their privacy, took their money, gave them bad food, forced them to have sons, controlled their husbands, ruined their relationships and even beat them. Daffodil was determined never to have a mother-in-law, and staying single seemed to be the only way to guarantee that. She was grateful that her parents hadn't pushed her to find a boyfriend.

In the summer, the government gave each workplace a new directive: sports teams! In the spirit of strong citizens for a strong country, each workplace was to have sports teams and allow time for employees to exercise at least three times a week. Daffodil's factory decided to start with a basketball team. Soon a basketball court was built, and a pile of basketballs was supplied in a large wire cage next to the court.

Daffodil had never touched a basketball in her life. She and a few other girls each grabbed a ball and started dribbling and chasing them. They also tried to shoot at the hoops, but the hoops were so high their balls didn't even touch the rim, net or backboard. It was frustrating to spend almost all of their time chasing and retrieving their escaped basketballs. Daffodil's stubbornness kicked in: "I don't believe it! I'll try one more time, and if my ball still doesn't touch anything up there, I swear I'll give up basketball all together!" Using all the force she could muster, she threw the ball toward the hoop as hard as she could. The ball banged against the hoop, and Daffodil was about to cheer, "I hit it!" But then she saw to her horror that the ball bounced off and hit a passer-by in the head!

Daffodil ran over to the man, who was rubbing his head with one hand after catching the ball with the other: "What kind of basketball are you playing? Who taught you?" Daffodil apologized, "I'm sorry. We're new at it and we don't know how to play. Are you all right?"

The man looked at Daffodil without a word, dribbling the ball with one hand. Daffodil was amazed to see the basketball that caused her so much frustration now acting like an obedient puppy in this man's hands. It bounced steadily between the man's hand and the ground as if it had grown a spring. Daffodil said, "Since you know how to play, you have to teach us! The tryout is next week. If we make the team, we'll tell everyone that you're our coach. Wouldn't that be nice? You might even get a raise!" The other girls gathered around him, too: "That's right. You have to teach us! Then we won't bump other people in the head, and you'll save the factory paying for head injuries!"

The man walked the basketball into the court: "It looks like you've never played before. You shouldn't start with shooting. Start with basic drills like dribbling. First try dribbling while standing still and not moving either of your feet. See how many times you can dribble. Remember to start over if you move either foot. The second step is to walk the ball. Then you can see if you can run while dribbling. Now, stand and dribble and see how many you can do.”

Daffodil asked, “How many can you do?” He replied, “I can go from morning till sunset.”

“You’re bluffing!” the girls all said. They each got a ball and started to dribble, but the balls had minds of their own and wouldn’t listen to the girls, either hitting a foot or rolling away.

“Are you shooting yourselves in the foot?” the man laughed. “I told you to dribble the ball, not slap it in the face. Your palm and fingers can’t be so flat and stiff. Relax your fingers so your hand is shaped like the ball. Use your arm muscles to push the ball down, and let your hand follow the bouncing of the ball.”

Daffodil realized this was her exact problem: She was slapping the ball hard with a stiff palm, and her hand was too far from the ball. She observed that the man’s hand was close to the ball at all times. Daffodil was observant and quick to imitate, and by adjusting her movements she could soon dribble beautifully.

With a nice curve, the man tossed his basketball into the wire cage and said, “Keep on practicing. The goal is to dribble one hundred times without losing the ball, and then to walk the ball around the court twice without losing it. Then finally run the ball around the court at least once without losing it.” With that, he walked away.

Watching him walk away, Daffodil saw that he had a head of rare naturally curly hair. The girls walked over to Daffodil and said, “That curly-head is good!” A girl named Wang laughed, “Look, Daffodil’s basketball is as red as a flower ball, and it landed on a curly-head!” All the girls roared with laughter.

Wang was referring to an old Chinese custom: When a girl came of age, she would throw a red flower ball to a crowd of suitors, and whoever the ball landed on would be the one she married.

The girls all laughed hysterically and started to chant:

> Her basketball is red, Landed on a curly-head!
> Her basketball is red, Landed on a curly-head!

Daffodil was furious, but the more she yelled for them to stop the louder they chanted. Soon all of the girls in the factory began chanting whenever they saw Daffodil:

Her basketball is red, Landed on a curly-head!
Her basketball is red, Landed on a curly-head!

There was nothing Daffodil could do to stop them.

The girls practiced every day on the basketball court, and soon they were running their balls around the court like pros. On the morning of the tryout, Daffodil went to the hairdresser next to the factory and had her long hair cut short.

The factory director and an official from the department of transportation were sitting at a table by the basketball court, and many people from around the factory had gathered at the basketball court to watch the tryout. A line of men and a line of women stood at attention waiting to try out. Daffodil ran to the court and stood proudly at the head of the line of women. Suddenly someone walked up from behind and said to Daffodil, "Don't try to shoot the hoop today. Hitting the director's head, or worse the official's head, would not be a good way to become famous."

Daffodil whipped around and saw that it was that curly-head! Before Daffodil could say a word, he walked past her and approached the table where the director and the official were seated and shook hands with them. Then he addressed the crowd through a loudspeaker: "Comrades, my name is He Guanglin from Workshop Four. I'm going to run today's tryout. Now the women's team, announce your number in line!" He pointed at Daffodil, motioning for her to start.

As soon as He Guanglin pointed at Daffodil, members of the women's team started to giggle. Someone chanted in a hushed voice:
    "Her basketball is ......"
"One!" Daffodil interrupted the chanting and shouted her number. Then the girls all call out their numbers one by one.

He Guanglin ordered, "Women's team, odd numbers take one step, forward!" Daffodil and six other girls stepped forward and each of them was given a ball. He Guanglin directed them to dribble, walk and run. Daffodil was the only one who didn't lose her ball the entire time. Then He Guanglin passed a ball to each of them to see how well they could catch it. Daffodil was a little nervous when it was her turn. In a gentle upward curve, He Guanglin passed Daffodil the ball and it landed securely in her hands. Daffodil passed it back and he caught it effortlessly. After everyone had a chance to try out, ten men and ten women were picked to form the new basketball team. Of course Daffodil was one of them. When Daffodil's name was announced by He Guanglin, the women's team could barely hold back their giggles.

The transportation official gave a speech, followed by the factory director. He Guanglin was appointed the coach for the basketball team, and he announced that practice was every Monday, Wednesday and Friday at 7am. Finally he said, "Dismissed!"

The muffled giggles of the women's team turned into a roaring laughter. The girls couldn't hold back one second longer. They clapped and chanted:

> Her basketball is red, Landed on a curly-head!
> Her basketball is red, Landed on a curly-head!

There was nothing Daffodil could do but run away as fast as she could! As she dashed off, she couldn't help but give a quick glance in He Guanglin's direction. He was putting away the basketballs, shaking his head and silently laughing. As Daffodil's eyes met his, he winked with a smile. Daffodil was so embarrassed that her blood turned to fire! She wanted to vanish from the face of the earth and never come back again! Those girls have really gone too far! she thought. How am I ever going to face my coach again?

They say that whatever you're afraid of is usually the first thing you will run into. At lunchtime, Daffodil ran into He Guanglin again. Looking as if she'd seen a ghost, she turned and ran. He Guanglin called out to her, "Daffodil! Stop running!" He walked up to Daffodil and said, "Don't let the chanting bother you. The more you care, the more they'll do it. Just ignore them and they'll soon get bored with it. Be there tomorrow morning for our first practice. Don't be late." Then he walked off.

The next morning, as Daffodil was on her way to the basketball court, a bunch of girls made strange noises and giggled behind her back, and she almost wanted to quit the team. He Guanglin lined everyone up, and after warm-ups, he ordered the men's team to run laps and the women's team to start with shooting. Daffodil was puzzled: "He himself said new players should start with simple drills. How come he's asking the team to start shooting without any instructions?" She saw that He Guanglin was standing not too far from the hoop.

As the women's team shot at the hoop one by one, basketballs landed on He Guanglin's head and back more than a couple of times. One girl's basketball didn't even touch the backboard or rim before hitting He Guanglin straight on the head. Every time He Guanglin was hit, the women's team laughed hysterically. At last, He Guanglin said, "That's enough for now. Back in line. The reason I wanted you to shoot at the beginning of your first practice was to show you that shooting without basic skills is not going to work. Even if you score by luck, that's not going to help you win a game or become a good player. We need to start with the basics first. Understand?" Everyone replied in unison: "Yes!" He Guanglin said, "Very well. Five laps. Get ready, run!"

As Daffodil started running, she saw He Guanglin turning to her with a slight nod and smile. She realized that he was trying to help her. He'd allowed himself to be hit on the head and back on purpose to help her escape the embarrassing chanting. Daffodil smiled back with gratitude.

(39) FIRST KISS

Once Coach He Guanglin's curly head was hit by many basketballs thrown by many teammates, everyone lost interest in chanting, and Daffodil finally regained her peace. She was grateful for He Guanglin's kindness and the smart way he'd handled the situation. Now that the chanting had stopped, Daffodil found herself thinking of him a little more often than she cared to admit.

Workers in different workshops normally didn't see each other during work hours, but they all sat and talked together in the canteen. Daffodil normally sat with other members of the women's basketball team. One day, He Guanglin led some members of the men's team to their table and asked, "Can we sit with you?" All of the women said yes, except for Daffodil, who lowered her eyes and focused on her food. She could sense He Guanglin looking at her, and in fact she wanted him to look at her, but she would not look up.

Silence did not come naturally to Daffodil; she was usually more talkative than anyone else. But whenever He Guanglin appeared, Daffodil immediately fell silent, refusing to talk or look at him. Even so, she managed to observe him closely.

Daffodil found that He Guanglin was different from other factory workers. He was courteous and well-mannered and never used profane language, which was extremely rare in the factory. The factory culture among both male and female workers was to use profanity even in normal conversation. The three essential words were "fuck," "shit" and "bitch," and it seemed that nobody could complete a sentence without using at least one of those three words. If the situation involved feelings of frustration, anger, jealousy or even happiness, then all hell broke loose. Those three words became far from sufficient, and the conversation would begin to involve the sexual capacity, size or deformity of reproductive organs, or the malfunctioning excretory organs of people's ancestors. There seemed no other way to express strong emotions, and no one would take you seriously if you didn't talk that way. But He Guanglin never spoke this way, and unlike other workers, he was clean-shaven, well-groomed and a non-smoker. The more different he seemed from other workers, the more interested Daffodil became in him.

Daffodil's coworker Wang was especially sensitive and therefore the first to catch on. She fastened her shiny dark eyes on Daffodil, then on He Guanglin and back on Daffodil again. She pulled Daffodil aside: "What's going on between you and Curly Head? You like him, don't you?" Daffodil stopped her: "What are you talking about! You must be crazy."

"You shut up like a fucking safe when he's around, and I saw you glancing at him! I think he likes you too! During that first practice, he put his fucking head on the line to save your ass, and don't think I didn't notice. He sits with us and watches your reaction when he talks. Oh, the look! I know that look! If that sucker doesn't like you, you can write my name backwards." Daffodil just rolled her eyes, since the Chinese character for Wang looks the same written backwards or forwards. "So when did you become an expert on men's eyes?" she shot back. "Maybe you need your own eyes checked."

She could say what she wanted to Wang, but Daffodil couldn't deny to herself that her insides churned with nervousness whenever she saw him. Was she really in love? Aici finally had enough of Daffodil acting absent-minded and neurotic, and she went to Workshop Four to dig up information about He Guanglin. It turned out that He Guanglin was the son of a businessman who had owned the biggest marine goods company in Southern China. When the Communists took power, the parents happened to be in Hong Kong on business while He Guanglin was visiting his aunt and uncle in the countryside near Beijing. His parents wanted to come for him, but the borders were sealed and they had been separated from He Guanglin ever since. Because of his capitalist family background, He Guanglin wasn't allowed to go to college and was assigned to be a worker at this factory. Aici said, "He seems to be a good person, but his background is a big black mark. He'll face adversity for the rest of his life! You need to think this over carefully."

Daffodil said, "What do I have to think about? It's not like I like him or anything, he's just my coach." Aici wasn't having it: "That mouth of yours! You daydream all day long, and you turn into someone I don't know as soon as he shows up. Don't deny it to me!"

Summer soon turned into fall, and the days were becoming shorter. Another week came to an end, and the workers rushed through lunch so they could return to the workshops to finish their afternoon work and go home early. He Guanglin and a few members of the men's basketball team were sitting with the women's team as usual. One of the young women said, "It's getting dark much earlier now. It's quite scary on the bus when it's dark." Then she turned to Daffodil and said, "Daffodil, didn't you say a man was following you last weekend? What happened? Wasn't your brother with you?"

Daffodil hesitated. She didn't want to talk about the incident in front of so many people, and especially not in front of He Guanglin. Daqing was a production line leader now and constantly worked overtime. Daqing's son suffered from motion sickness, and Daqing's wife was pregnant again, so they rarely accompanied Daffodil back to her parents' house on the weekends now. Most weekends, Daffodil rode the buses by herself, and last weekend, a man on the over-crowded bus purposefully pressed himself against Daffodil. Daffodil tried to push her way through the crowd to get away from him, but he followed her all the way to the end of the bus. When Daffodil got off the bus, the man got off as well and followed her. She was so afraid that she started to run. The man maintained a distance of about five meters and followed her all the way to Yard 13, where Daffodil immediately locked the gate behind her. She didn't mention the episode to her parents for fear of making them worry, and had only told a couple of girls in her dorm. She was surprised that it had been brought up at the lunch table in front of everyone.

Casting a quick glance in He Guanglin's direction, she replied to the girl, "It was nothing. I think I was being too sensitive. That man was probably just walking in the same direction and wasn't really following me." The girl said, "Well, you sure sounded scared when you told us about it." Everyone agreed that young women should be careful, because there were all sorts of perverts on the buses. Daffodil sensed He Guanglin looking at her, and she lowered her eyes and kept quiet.

After work, Daffodil quickly packed a few things and rushed to the bus stop to head home. She was surprised to see He Guanglin at the bus stop and asked, "He Shifu, are you waiting for a bus too?" He Guanglin walked over to Daffodil and said, "Don't call me He Shifu. You can call me Guanglin. Aici told me you lived in Haidian District and I happen to be on my way to visit a friend in Haidian. We can ride the bus together." Daffodil was nervous and happy. She said, "A few buses stop here. Which one are you taking?" He Guanglin smiled and said: "I'll take whichever one you take." Daffodil lowered her head and listened to her pounding heart.

It was rush hour and the bus was packed tight. He Guanglin carried Daffodil's bag for her while holding two bars on either side of her. This kept the crowd away from Daffodil and gave her some space of her own. Daffodil stood in the space enclosed by the two bars and He Guanglin's arms, feeling much more comfortable than the usual bus rides when she was jammed so tightly between other bodies that she could scarcely breathe. People joked about the brutally packed buses of Beijing in those days. One saying was that a pregnant woman shouldn't get on a bus, or she might be squeezed into a miscarriage, but a woman who wasn't pregnant could end up pregnant from being pressed so tightly against so many men.

But now Daffodil had her own space, and she wasn't squeezed or even touched by other passengers. She couldn't imagine how much muscle strength He Guanglin had to apply to keep the crowd out of this precious little space. He Guanglin's body didn't touch Daffodil's, but they had to stand very close to each other. Daffodil could hear his breathing and smell his pleasant manly scent, and even imagined she could feel his heartbeats.

The next bus they took was not so crowded. Now Daffodil and He Guanglin could stand side by side and have a nice conversation about their factory and their basketball team. Just as they were enjoying the moment, Daffodil's face suddenly stiffened. She glanced sideways and moved closer to He Guanglin as if she were afraid of something. "What's wrong?" He Guanglin asked "Are you all right?" Daffodil said, "It's that man from last weekend. He's behind me." He Guanglin looked behind Daffodil and saw an extremely thin man with glasses staring at Daffodil and trying to push through the crowd. He Guanglin put his hand on Daffodil's shoulder and pushed her behind him. Towering over the man, he put his face next to his and demanded, "Where do you think you're going?"

The man was startled and mumbled, "I'm not going anywhere." Quick as a flash, He Guanglin pulled an ID out of the man's top jacket pocket and read out, "Beijing 46th High School. History teacher. Wang Liben. That's you, right? This isn't your first time bothering people on this bus, is it?" The man said, "You are stealing from me! I'll yell for help if you don't give it back!" He Guanglin said, "Good. Go ahead! My girlfriend and I actually want to take you to the police station right now! Or maybe we should go see the headmaster of the 46th High School tomorrow?"

Reporting misconduct at someone's workplace was like a death sentence to that person. Because people didn't have freedom to change jobs, and all of their income and housing came from their workplace, people avoid trouble at any cost. On top of that, the leader of each workplace had a direct line into the police, and misconduct such as bothering girls on a bus could bring an immediate prison sentence. At the very least, it would mean losing his job, making him a social outcast and depriving him of any means of making a living.

With a shaky voice, the man said, "Please.... I don't know you and you don't know me. Let's just go our separate ways. Please give my ID back to me. I'm getting off at the next stop." He Guanglin lifted him up by his collar and said, "You'd better get off at the next stop, because if you don't, your next stop will be the police station or the headmaster's office. And let me tell you something else: This is not a good bus line for you. Take a different bus from now on and don't ever let me see you again!" The bus pulled up to a stop, and He Guanglin threw the ID in the man's face. The man fumbled to pick the ID up from the floor and hurried off the bus.

Daffodil's eyes were big and teary, and she was shaking with fright. He Guanglin put an arm around her shoulders: "Don't worry. It's all right now. He's gone and he won't bother you again." Daffodil said, "But what if I run into him again, when I'm alone?" He Guanglin assured her, "He won't dare to bother you now that we know who he is and where he works. He can't afford to lose his anonymity. It's like we're holding the key to his grave. He'll stay away from you for sure. It'll be all right, I promise. Here, wipe your tears."

He Guanglin walked Daffodil all the way to Yard 13. Daffodil said: "This is my home. Would you like to join my family for dinner?" He Guanglin said, "That's very kind of you, but no thanks. Go on in, and once you're inside I'll leave." Daffodil remembered: "But aren't you here to visit a friend? Where does he live?"

He Guanglin smiled with embarrassment: "Oh, umm, my friend, I think he's somewhere close by. Don't worry. Go home and have dinner. You must be hungry."

The next weekend, Daffodil ran into He Guanglin at the bus stop again. She asked, "Are you going to Haidian District to see your friend again?" He Guanglin scratched the back of his head and said, "Um, something like that." One weekend after another, He Guanglin continued to accompany Daffodil home.

As their bus ran through the historic streets of Beijing, soft, warm streetlights bathed them in a golden glow. They stood close to each other feeling the tenderness and longing in their hearts. Daffodil looked up at He Guanglin's handsome and well-shaped face; he looked strong and gentle at the same time. As she stood in the warm and comfortable space that he made for her with his strong arms, her hair brushed his shoulders and she asked, "You don't have any friends in Haidian, do you?"

He Guanglin looked into Daffodil's eyes and smiled. His gaze was gentle but it made Daffodil dizzy, as if she saw a fire burning deep inside his eyes. His lips parted slightly, and he lowered his face to hers, but Daffodil turned away. He Guanglin put his face in Daffodil's hair and whispered into her ear, "I just want to be with you."

They stood like that all the rest of the way. Without a word and without moving a muscle, they listened to each other's breathing and heartbeats. Everything around them seemed to have disappeared. There was a garden on the way from the bus stop to Yard 13, and that's where they had their first kiss. The winter night was no longer cold or dark, for they held each other in their arms.

(40) COUSIN TROUBLE

The news that Daffodil and He Guanglin were a couple traveled fast. Seeing no need to be secretive about it, Daffodil smiled whenever asked. Aici and Wang both said, "What did I tell you? You had the nerve to deny it! When can we expect your wedding candies?" Daffodil said, "What wedding candies? We just started going out." Aici joked, "Daffodil, you really listened to your old sis Aici. I told you to find a man without a mother and that's what you did!" Daffodil laughed at the coincidence.

As more people came to know about them, He Guanglin told Daffodil, "We don't need to tell everyone about it. Once we get married, they'll all know."

"Who said I'm going to marry you?" Daffodil teased.

The winter nights didn't seem as cold as before. That was because He Guanglin found ten large bottles with good seals and gave them to the ten girls in Daffodil's dorm to use as hot water bottles. Each girl took one to the boiler room and filled it with hot water, then wrapped it in a towel and put it under her blanket. The bottles kept the girls warm all night, and everyone was delighted: "We really have Daffodil to thank. Curly Head wanted to look after Daffodil and gave hot water bottles to the rest of us too."

Instead of going home every weekend, Daffodil now spent her weekends with He Guanglin. Sometimes they went to Jingshan Park or Beihai Park, and other times they would buy candied haw kabobs and walk around the streets of historic Qianmen. He Guanglin tried to teach Daffodil how to ride a bicycle, but Daffodil said, "Bikes are not my friend. I can't ride a bike to save my life!" So He Guanglin put Daffodil behind him on his bike, and they zoomed laughing through the beautiful streets of Beijing.

At the Lunar New Year, Daffodil wanted to bring He Guanglin home to meet her family, but He Guanglin hesitated and said, "I need to spend the New Year with my uncle. I'll be back on the fifth day and will be very happy to pay respects to your parents then." Daffodil was disappointed that he wouldn't visit her parents on the first of the year, but when she couldn't change his mind, she said, "All right, the fifth then. But you'll need to come early that day, because it's the last day of the New Year break, and everyone has to return to work the next day. We'll make dumplings for you."

On the morning of the fifth day of the festival, Daffodil went out early to buy a fresh cut of pork and then minced it by hand. Then she mixed the ground pork with peanut oil, sesame oil, soy sauce, chopped spring onions, salt and yellow chives to make a delicious dumpling filling. Daffodil's mother Lotus cleaned the whole house and dressed her younger daughters in brand new clothes: "Your new brother-in-law is coming to meet us today. You need to be on your best behavior, and keep your new clothes clean. Don't soil them."

Yixin said, "How time flies! Now even my little Daffodil is getting married! If only this would happen to my second son. He's so dedicated to school! College after high school, and now graduate school after college. He's still not married!"

Daffodil said, "What brother-in-law? What marriage? Who says I'm going to marry him? Don't talk like that yet." But even as she said this, she felt happy and contented inside.

Morning turned into afternoon and then evening, and still He Guanglin did not appear. Daffodil was so upset that she had no appetite for dinner. Lotus said, "Don't worry. He has to take a train to Beijing, and then a bus from the train station to our house. The trip is unpredictable. The train could be running late, or maybe it was even canceled if there's a snowstorm where he is. Don't worry, he can come visit us any time. We'll make dumplings for him again!"

Daffodil barely slept. At the crack of dawn she jumped onto an early bus and rushed to the factory, then headed straight to the men's dorm. He Guanglin's roommate said that He Guanglin was still not back. When the work bell rang at eight o'clock, He Guanglin was still nowhere to be seen. Daffodil went to the switchboard office to ask if there had been any calls from He Guanglin, but the switchboard operator said he hadn't called. Now Daffodil was worried. She hoped that nothing had happened to him.

Around ten o'clock, a girl from Workshop Four ran over to the warehouse: "Daffodil, Daffodil! Curly Head's back!" Daffodil left a quick note for her fellow warehouse manager, Big Ling, and ran towards Workshop Four. From a distance, she saw He Guanglin running in her direction, so she stopped to catch her breath. Guanglin ran over and said, "I'm so sorry. Something happened at my uncle's and I couldn't come back yesterday. I took an overnight train and just got here. I'm sorry I had no way of reaching you. You must have been so worried. Please apologize to your parents for me!"

Daffodil asked, "What happened at your uncle's?" Guanglin looked sad: "I can't describe it in just a sentence or two. I'll tell you all the details later. My workshop manager is angry with me for being late. I haven't slept for the whole night and I have to get back to work." Daffodil pulled out two pieces of candy from her pocket and put them in Guanglin's hands: "You haven't had time for breakfast, right? Here, have some candy."

Guanglin looked at the pieces of candy in his palm and weighed them as if they were lead. He looked truly sad: "Daffodil, you're so good to me. I'm so sorry. I ......"

Daffodil interrupted him: "It's all right. I'm not upset, and my parents aren't either. They even said they'll make dumplings for you next time, to make up for last night. You haven't slept all night, so be very careful in the workshop so you don't get hurt. Go! Hurry! Isn't your manager angry at you already?" She pushed He Guanglin away.

At lunchtime, people from Workshop Four told Daffodil, "The manager gave Curly Head only ten minutes for lunch so he can make up for his missed work." Daffodil said, "He's crueler than a stinky capitalist!" At dinner time, Daffodil looked for He Guanglin again, but people from Workshop Four told her, "He was too tired to eat and went straight back to the dorm to get some sleep." Daffodil got him some dinner and took it to the men's dorm. He Guanglin's roommate came out and said, "He is fast asleep. I don't think even a thunder storm can wake him up. Do you want me to wake him for you?" Daffodil said: "No, let him sleep. Here's his dinner. Please give it to him when he wakes up." The roommate took the container and said, "He's lucky to have a girlfriend!"

Early next morning, Daffodil woke to the distant sound of shouting voices. Who was quarreling so early in the morning? A girl came in and said, "Daffodil, you should go and see. Curly Head's uncle is here, along with his cousin, and they're yelling in front of the office building. The director and head of personnel are there too. I don't know what's happening. You should go take a look."

Daffodil was baffled! Uncle? Cousin? Head of personnel? What was going on? She jumped out of bed and got dressed, splashed cold water on her face to wake up, put on her jacket and ran to the office building.

A crowd had already gathered there, with the director and Mr. Liao from personnel standing there in the middle. He Guanglin stood on one side of them, while on the other side was an elderly peasant and a country girl in her twenties with red, chapped cheeks. Daffodil ran over to He Guanglin: "Guanglin, are you all right? What's going on??"

Before He Guanglin could say a word, the elderly peasant shouted hysterically: "That's her, isn't it? Is it her?" He Guanglin stepped forward to stand between the man and Daffodil: "Uncle, this has nothing to do with her. Leave her out of it! Let's go to my dorm so we can talk in private. We don't have to do this in front of everybody."

The director said, "That's right! In fact, let's go to my office. It's cold here and my office is nice and warm."

"No!" the man yelled: "I want everyone to hear! The people have justice in their hearts! I can tell from how my nephew protects her that it's her! She's the slut who's stealing someone's husband!"

"Uncle! You're lying!" He Guanglin shouted.

The crowd buzzed with chatter, and Daffodil felt as if the ground were collapsing beneath her: "He Guanglin! What's going on? Tell me!" He Guanglin pleaded, "Daffodil! You have to listen to me and trust what I say. I'm single. I don't have a wife! My cousin was engaged to me when we were little. These past few days I went back to annul this stupid engagement."

The uncle leaped angrily: "No! Guanglin and his cousin were engaged when they were babies. We were a rich family back then, and my daughter was a young miss of a prominent household! It was Guanglin's grandpa who decided this marriage. Now our family is poor and my daughter is a peasant, and Guanglin has met a slut like you. Sure, you're younger and prettier than my daughter, so now he wants to cancel this engagement with his cousin. What kind of justice is that?"

He Guanglin said, "Uncle, you have to stop this nonsense! It was an arranged marriage and it's invalid. This is a new world with a new government, and everyone has freedom to marry who they want. You can't force me to marry your daughter! And anyway, cousins aren't allowed to get married – that's the law! The old custom of cousins getting married is now illegal!"

The director and Mr. Liao also said, "Sir, your nephew is right. The old arranged marriages are no longer legally binding and are invalid. People are free to marry who they want. He Guanglin and your daughter are not married. He's free to be with whoever he chooses. And he is right about cousins getting married. That's against the law now."

The uncle couldn't understand why cousins were not allowed to get married. In his mind, it was a tradition from ancient times that cousins married in order to strengthen the family. The director and Mr. Liao explained to him that blood relatives weren't allowed to get married. The uncle then asked them to define a blood relative. The director said: "See, their mothers are sisters, right? They're connected by blood, so they can't get married."

At that moment, the cousin, who had remained silent all this time, took a bottle from her pocket and said, "If he rejects me, I don't want to live anymore!" She raised the bottle to her lips, but Mr. Liao knocked it out of her hands. The bottle shattered on the cement ground, spreading the odor of DDT. The cousin cried, "You can knock over my bottle but I can still use a knife! If you won't let me die here, I can die right outside of your gate! You can't stop me! Give me my man or I will die, and it will be on your hands!"

The director and Mr. Liao were both frozen with alarm. Then the uncle recalled, "My daughter isn't a blood relative of my nephew! My daughter's mother died giving birth to her. Guanglin's aunt was my second wife and not my daughter's birth mother. So my daughter has no blood connection with Guanglin. They should be able to get married even under the new law!"

This was the first time He Guanglin heard that his cousin wasn't his aunt's daughter, and he didn't believe it: "Uncle! You're making this up! And it doesn't matter anyway. I will not marry my cousin, whether she's a blood relative or not! If she's in hardship, I can support her financially, but I cannot marry her and that's final!"

With a shrill scream, Guanglin's cousin jumped up and banged her head against a corner of the front steps of the office building. Blood gushed from her head and she fell to the ground. As the situation dissolved into chaos, the director quickly called in the staff nurse to stop the bleeding and then ordered a car to rush Guanglin's cousin and uncle to the hospital.

The director said, "He Guanglin, Daffodil Xu, come to my office! Everyone else, get back to work!"

(41) HE IS GONE

After a long talk, the director and Mr. Liao handed down the official position of the factory: The factory could not take on the liability of a suicide. If He Guanglin wanted to continue his employment at the factory, he had to guarantee that his cousin would not commit suicide, and it looked like the only way to do that was to marry her. Now that the factory leadership understood that He Guanglin and his cousin were not blood relatives, the personnel department could approve their marriage. If He Guanglin didn't want to marry his cousin, the factory was fine with that too, but in order to avoid liability, the factory would have to let He Guanglin go. That meant He Guanglin would lose his status as a worker and also his Beijing residency. No other factory was likely to want him with this kind of baggage. He would have no choice but to return to his uncle's village and live as a peasant there.

The director then said to Daffodil, "You're a victim in this matter. I've asked you to come here in hopes that you will support the factory's position."

Daffodil said mechanically, "I support the factory's position."

He Guanglin shouted, "Daffodil!"

Daffodil yelled back tearfully, "What do you want? What do you want me to do? Should I drink DDT and bang my head on a corner like her? Isn't it enough that one woman wants to die for you? Do you want me to do the same?" She ran out of the building and back to her dorm, hiding herself under her blanket and weeping.

Everyone was talking about the incident. Many people felt that the cousin and her father were completely in the wrong. Many felt it was unfair to deprive He Guanglin of his Beijing resident status if he didn't marry his cousin, which was like sentencing him to exile. But another view was expressed by the "Wife Union," and that view denounced Daffodil and He Guanglin.

The Wife Union was a nickname for the wives of factory workers. The vast majority of the factory's workers were male, and most had come to Beijing from the countryside. They'd been lucky enough to gain a Beijing residency card and bring their wives and children to live with them in Beijing. Most of the women in the Wife Union were from the countryside, illiterate and not very well adjusted to life in the city. They felt lost and scared in Beijing, and focused their lives on their husbands, their kids and the kitchen. They were completely dependent on their men financially, emotionally and in all other aspects of life. With this huge psychological disadvantage, they were often insecure and irritable. In particular, they were jealous and suspicious of the young female workers who worked, talked and laughed with their men. If there was the slightest hint that any man was going to leave his original wife from the countryside for a girl from the city, it touched the most sensitive nerve of the entire Wife Union. Their view of Daffodil was therefore harsh and censorious:

"Her father is a senior political official. Look what a spoiled brat she is! I bet her mother is a slut just like her. Otherwise how could she marry someone in such a high position?"

"Stealing men from us poor country women? We have nothing but our men. She can't steal everything we've got!"

"The old saying goes that 'A wife three years older than the husband is gold to the family'. Marriage between cousins is the best of all. If that bitch dares to destroy such a good marriage, she deserves to rot in hell."

"Just because she's a city slut doesn't mean she can take advantage of us country women. That's right! The cousin should threaten them with suicide! I would do the same! Even if I died and those two sub-humans got married, God would curse them so they never have children if they have blood on their hands! Even if she gets pregnant, she'll have no hole in her bottom to let the child out!"

"That mother-fucker should be fired if he doesn't marry his cousin! He'll become a fucking peasant and live like a dog! Then see if that slut still wants to marry him! He won't even be good enough to marry his cousin. Then he'll know what's really good for him!"

"That son of a bitch wants to throw away his wife for some city cunt? Firing him is letting him off too easy. He should be shot dead!"

The husbands of these women were also forced to express their contempt towards Daffodil and He Guanglin. Even neutral language was not tolerated by their wives. It was as if their men were more likely to toss them aside and marry city girls if they didn't condemn Daffodil and He Guanglin harshly. The men in the factory soon stopped supporting Daffodil and He Guanglin.

When the uncle and his daughter came back from the hospital, they refused to leave the factory until they were given an answer. Fearing another suicide attempt, the factory leaders found space for the uncle and his daughter in the factory dorms. Every day, the two of them went to the director's office to cry and yell. Finally the director had enough of it. He called in He Guanglin and ordered him to make a decision within one week – either to marry his cousin, or to leave the factory and go back to the countryside.

He Guanglin looked as if he'd aged ten years overnight. Whether he stayed in the factory or went back to the countryside, he had to face the cruel reality of losing Daffodil. There was no way he could stay without marrying his cousin, and there was absolutely no way a girl like Daffodil would leave Beijing and marry a peasant. And once he gave up his hard-earned Beijing residency, he could never get it back again. No other city would employ him, either, after he had been expelled from Beijing. He would live the rest of his life as a peasant. The famine a few years earlier and the many people from his home village who had died of starvation were still fresh on his mind. He had to stay in Beijing for the sake of sheer survival. But what about Daffodil, the girl he loved? He didn't even have the courage to face her now. Was he doomed to spend the rest of his life with someone he didn't love?

Call him selfish or call him weak, but under the tremendous social pressure and the need for survival, He Guanglin married his cousin Chen Tianxiang. The wedding was quick and simple, and the uncle returned to the countryside right afterwards. Chen Tianxiang and He Guanglin moved into the married employee quarters as a neighbor to Daqing.

Those were the darkest days for Daffodil. The man she loved had married another woman right in front of her eyes and was now the neighbor of her brother Daqing. Daffodil hated He Guanglin for being too cruel to even say goodbye to her. He was like a turtle retreating into his shell and never showed his face to her again. Daffodil thought to herself, "If he can't even face the woman he loves at a time like this, he's not a real man!"

To many people, He Guanglin's marriage to his cousin Chen Tianxiang only confirmed Daffodil's "scarlet letter" reputation. Women from the Wife Union stuck up their noses in triumph whenever they saw Daffodil, and Chen Tianxiang also gave Daffodil a piece of her mind: "Coming to visit her brother again? Who knows if she's really here to see her brother or to catch a peek at someone else's husband!" Daffodil stopped going to Daqing's house. Throughout the factory, only Gong and his friends were nice to Daffodil, and they did whatever they could to put a smile on Daffodil's face.

Weekends were no better as Daffodil had to face her parents' questions: "What happened to that young man you were going to bring home? When is he coming again?" Daffodil finally shouted at her mother, "Stop asking about him! He is DEAD!" Daqing stopped Lotus with a warning stare. Unable to control herself any longer, Daffodil burst out crying.

Lotus pulled Daqing and his wife aside to ask for the details. Wiping away her tears, she said, "I somehow had a bad feeling about this. I knew my eldest girl would run into trouble with men. My poor girl. Please don't feel too sad. It's all part of destiny. There will be other men. Better men." Daffodil cried, "Mama! Who on earth could be better than him?" Lotus laughed: "Well, that's silly talk! The world is full of men. Even if he's a knight, there will still be someone better than him. And what kind of a man is he, really? He's cruel and cold-hearted. He's not someone you can rely on. I'm glad you broke up!"

Daqing's wife also tried to console Daffodil: "We really can't blame He Guanglin. It's so hard to get Beijing residency. People would kill for it. So many people died during the famine in the countryside. There's no way you could go to the countryside with him. Even if he didn't marry Chen Tianxiang, you two couldn't stay together. This is the sad fact in our society, and no one can do anything about it."

Daffodil resigned from the basketball team, and she no longer talked or laughed with her friends. She kept her head down and her words at a minimum. Every day she went nowhere but the warehouse, the dining hall and her dorm, while bearing the unkind murmurs and jokes that followed her everywhere. The only two people who could comfort her were Aici and her childhood friend, Yufang.

Yufang had by now graduated from the Lixin High School. She hadn't been admitted into any college, but because of her parents' connections and her beautiful calligraphy, she was hired as a front desk receptionist in the Department of Transportation, where her mother worked. She had been working for two years now.

Yufang was tall and slender, her skin was fair and delicate, and she was always pleasant and friendly, so many young men in the DOT were attracted to her. Soon, a tall and handsome young man from Northeast China became Yufang's boyfriend. But then the daughter of the Secretary of Transportation fell in love with Yufang's boyfriend, who left Yufang for her. The Secretary of Transportation was against this relationship and told his daughter, "If he can cold-heartedly leave Yufang for you today, he can leave you for someone else tomorrow! This is not a trustworthy man. You should stay away from him!" But the daughter was stubborn and would not listen to her father. Soon they were married, and after the wedding, the man was quickly promoted and became the youngest director in the DOT.

Yufang was devastated. She said to Daffodil: "Men are so selfish! They can say they love you, but when faced with temptations like promotions and Beijing residency, they only think of themselves! They won't give up anything for you!"

Daffodil said, "Didn't we say we were going to check out each other's boyfriends? We forgot to do it! I never met your boyfriend and you never met mine. No wonder neither of them worked out. We really need to bring our men to each other for approval." Yufang said, "That's right! We have golden shiny eyes like the Monkey King, and can see through men like X-ray!"

"Our golden eyes are not that good! See what happened?"

"Golden shiny eyes like the Monkey King's only work on the men of others, not on your own men. When we look at our own men, all we see is roses and sunshine. Even if he leads us over a cliff, we'd jump happily!" Yufang replied.

Daffodil said sadly, "I will never have a boyfriend again. There's just no point."

HongGe and Daffodil

(42) THE DUMPLING DINNER

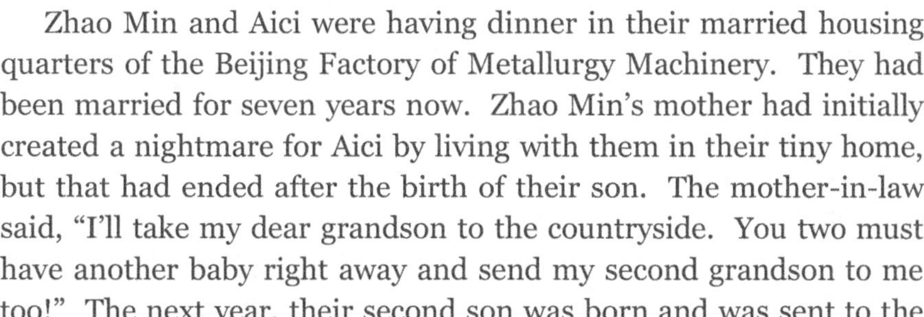

Zhao Min and Aici were having dinner in their married housing quarters of the Beijing Factory of Metallurgy Machinery. They had been married for seven years now. Zhao Min's mother had initially created a nightmare for Aici by living with them in their tiny home, but that had ended after the birth of their son. The mother-in-law said, "I'll take my dear grandson to the countryside. You two must have another baby right away and send my second grandson to me too!" The next year, their second son was born and was sent to the mother-in-law.

Aici understood her mother-in-law. She had been a widow from an early age and was emotionally dependent on her only son. She didn't really want to be crowded into that small room with Zhao Min and his new wife, but her greatest fear was to be alone, so she felt driven to invade their personal space. A woman with no psychological independence is like an emotional parasite who creates tragedies for herself and people around her. But now that her grandsons were born, the mother-in-law could become something like a mother again by raising them, so she was willing to leave Zhao Min and Aici alone.

At last, Zhao Min and Aici had their own space, their own home, and it brought them closer to each other. But missing their two young sons overshadowed their joy and became a new source of misery.

Zhao Min was now a highly skilled worker with considerable seniority and a salary to match. Even after sending money to his mother to support his two young sons, he and Aici had quite a bit left over for themselves each month, even enough to enjoy occasional delicacies like pork dumplings. Now over dinner, Aici asked Zhao Min, "How's that apprentice of yours, the tall one who's an orphan? He's such a fine young man. I want to set him up with a girl."

Zhao Min said, "Gao Hong lost his nanny a few months ago, and it's like he lost his mother! He hasn't talked much since then, and just works and works. Such a kind and honest fellow. He must be twenty-four or twenty-five by now. We really should find a girl for him!" Aici thought for a minute and then said, "Tell him we're having pork dumplings this Sunday and we want him to join us!"

Twenty-four-year-old Gao Hong had experienced more tragedy, devastation, heartache and loss than many people in their lifetimes. He'd was quiet and almost always deep in thought, his loneliness and hopelessness chewing him up inside and weighing him down. He thought of himself as two completely separate beings, one physical and one emotional. The physical Gao Hong was a prisoner of endless labor in the factory, enduring filth, heat, noise, danger, unbearable physical exertion and malnutrition. But the emotional Gao Hong suffered the even greater pain of endless loneliness and desperation, of not identifying with anything in this ridiculously cruel world, and of hating every minute of this meaningless and hopeless existence.

The death of Nanny Wu had severed Gao Hong's last emotional tie to this world. Like a kite without a string or a boat lost at sea, he floated outside of a world that had become irrelevant to him. He even thought of ending his life because he could see no meaning or hope. But Nanny Wu's dying wish stopped him: "You have to live on! No matter how hard it is, live on!"

Yes, he was the only male descendant of the Gao family. Grandpa, Grandma, Papa, Mama, Stepmother Lingzhi, Nanny Wu, Zhao'er, Cai Xia, Papa Li Ginseng, Uncle, Aunt and many others who had helped him, as well as his beloved Yanruo, they must all want him to live on.

The only blood relative he had left was his younger cousin Gao Lan, the daughter of Gao Hong's second uncle and aunt, and now the stepdaughter of a peasant since Second Uncle's death and Second Aunt's forced remarriage. Gao Hong had once written a letter to Second Aunt and Cousin Lan and enclosed a photo of himself in front of his factory. But it was like a stone thrown into the ocean, with no response.

Gao Hong numbed himself with a heavy workload that left him no time or energy to think about anything. He went to the dining hall when he was almost fainting from hunger, and he collapsed on his bed when exhausted from the day's work. The whole process started over again when he woke up the next day. This endless repetition made Gao Hong feel like he was just waiting for his death. This feeling tortured him even more when the weekend arrived and he jumped out of bed at the crack of dawn, only to realize he didn't have to go to work. He dressed slowly and ate his breakfast slowly. With his body relaxed and his stomach full, the dreadful feeling of waiting for his own death would emerge and consume his whole being, making him want to bang his head against the wall!

He occasionally received letters from his college best friend and roommate, Situ, and his classmate Mai, who had gone to the Third Front in the Northwest. Life seemed harsh out there, but Gao Hong sensed happiness in their letters. Situ and Mai were now married, and in their spare time they cultivated a garden so they could have enough to eat. They sent a picture of the two of them sitting by their vegetable field, looking just like peasants, with sun-browned skin and torn straw hats. But their smiles were so bright that Gao Hong could only feel happy for them. Sometimes he even thought: Maybe I should go to the Northwest to seek a new life. Anything is better than the shithole I'm in now. He wrote them in antient style formal Chinese:

Dear Brother Situ, Sister Mai,

I hope this letter finds you well. Please accept my warm congratulations on your wedding. You are both descendants of military heroes and the kindest and most honorable people I know. You belong together, and I wish you all happiness, peace, health and love.

The most beautiful time of my life was the five years of college that we all spent together. Every minute of those five years warms my heart. You said, "The motherland deserves every talent," and I have always been inspired by your words. I had my nanny to care for, but now she is in heaven. I would like to join you in the Northwest. What do you think?

Forever your brother, Gao Hong

Situ and Mai replied in similar classical style Chinese:

Dear Brother Gao Hong,

How we rejoiced to receive your letter! It is as if you were with us and speaking to us in person! Mai and I are honored and overjoyed to receive your kind words. It is with great sorrow that we hear the passing of your beloved Nanny. Please take good care of yourself. We are sure that your nanny's greatest wish was your well-being.

Not a day that passes without us thinking about the wonderful five years at our beloved college. What would I not give to be with our old classmates again? But please pardon my bluntness, I beg you to reconsider your wish to come to the Northwest. "The motherland deserves every talent," my father used to say. But what is our motherland? It's the people. The people constitute our motherland. You and I are a droplet in this vast ocean. Serving the motherland means serving the people, which can be done anywhere!

You have not been outside of Beijing and you may not have a perspective on China's remote areas. If you are running into difficulties in Beijing, I can guarantee that the situation is ten times harder elsewhere. It is easy to leave Beijing, but impossible to go back. Please reconsider. Please do not let Yanruo's sacrifice go to waste.

Your brother and sister, Situ, Mai

The beautiful, cultured language of their correspondence, seldom used now, was like a special code that separated them from their filthy, distasteful, profane and offensive surroundings. Gao Hong thought about Situ's letter over and over again. Situ was right. He and Mai smiled because they had happiness in their hearts. Gao Hong's heart was empty, and simply going to the Northwest would not change that. It would only put Yanruo's sacrifice to waste.

One weekend, Zhao Shifu told Gao Hong, "My wife and I want to invite you for dinner. We're making pork dumplings." Before Gao

Hong could responded, Qiangzi came out of nowhere: "Shifu! What about us?!" Zhao Min turned to Qiangzi and said, "Some other time. My wife has something to discuss with Gao Hong."

Gao Hong thanked Zhao Min and thought to himself, "Situ is right. The people are the motherland. People like Zhao Shifu, Aici and Qiangzi all have their weaknesses, but they're all good people and the core of this country."

Aici had made a point of observing Daffodil in recent days. She still seemed quiet and sad two years after her breakup with He Guanglin, changing from a carefree girl to a mature woman. Daffodil was already twenty-two years old, an age when most women were already mothers!

Aici asked Daffodil, "Daffodil, you're not going home this weekend, are you?" She knew Daffodil only went home every other weekend now. "I'm making pork dumplings tonight, so why don't you come help me and then stay for dinner?"

Daffodil said, "Aici, you are always so good to me. Pork dumplings are such a special treat, you and Zhao Shifu should enjoy them without me." But Aici wouldn't take no for an answer: "Please come! My wrist aches and I can't chop the meat. All Zhao Min cares about is his chess games. I can't make the dumplings without your help!"

Once they were on the bus, Aici said, "Daffodil, you're already twenty-two. How about if I set you up with someone nice? Just give it a try." Daffodil looked out the window without saying anything. She could still feel the warm space that He Guanglin made for her on the bus with his strong arms, and remembered his manly scent and his lips almost touching hers. That bus ride had been two years ago, but it felt like yesterday.

Aici sighed, "You have to let go! I'll introduce you to a nice guy who's not from around here, so no one will know. Just meet him once and decide if you want to see him again. I won't say another word about it. Just meet him once, please?" Feeling she could not say no, Daffodil gave a small nod. "That's wonderful!" Aici said. "I'll tell Zhao Min to have him join our dumpling dinner this evening."

Daffodil jumped: "This evening?!"

(43) A GIRL RESEMBLING YANRUO

Aici and Zhao Min's little room was hazy and warm with the steam from the pork dumplings cooking on the coal burner. Daffodil placed steamy hot dumplings onto a serving platter and was turning to lay it on the table just as Zhao Min entered with a tall young man. The gust of cold air they brought in with them made the steamy haze seem even heavier.

"Just in time!" Aici greeted them. "Gao Hong, this is Daffodil from my factory." Then she turned to Daffodil: "This is Gao Hong, Zhao Min's apprentice. He'll be joining us for dinner."

Gao Hong hadn't known there would be another guest. When he turned to look at Daffodil, his draw dropped. Standing next to the coal burner was a girl who looked almost exactly like Yanruo! Gao Hong felt his head spin, and he was frozen in place.

Embarrassed by Gao Hong's stares, Daffodil nodded slightly and turned to serve the dumplings. Zhao Min slapped Gao Hong on the back: "What's wrong with you! Let's eat!"

Gao Hong realized Aici was setting him up with a date again, as she had done several times before. Gao Hong was never interested, letting his mind drift during the date or refusing outright to meet the girl, and he'd thought that Aici might be upset enough never to help him find a girlfriend again. But today, she'd brought him a girl who looked like Yanruo!

Aici set the table so that Gao Hong and Daffodil were facing each other and gave them warm introductions: "Gao Hong, Daffodil is known in our factory for her kindness and beauty, and she's a good basketball player too!" Daffodil raised her eyes to look at Aici, who realized that she'd misspoken and put more dumplings into Daffodil's bowl: "Here, Daffodil, have some more." Then she continued, "Daffodil, Gao Hong is a college graduate! He's the best-educated man in the whole factory. It's a pity he's stuck in Zhao Min's factory, but he'll rise above it and do great things someday. And look how tall and handsome he is!" She went on, "Tomorrow is Sunday and I hear there's a lantern festival at Taoran Park. Gao Hong, why don't you take Daffodil there tomorrow?" Gao Hong smiled and nodded.

Gao Hong ate very little that evening. The brutality and hopelessness of factory life made him greatly appreciate anything and anyone that could even remotely remind him of his college life. He wasn't in a rush to find a girlfriend, but Daffodil looked so much like Yanruo. Gao Hong felt that if having a girlfriend and getting married was something he had to do in life, this girl was closer to what he'd wanted than all the other girls he'd met. Daffodil's first impression of Gao Hong was also favorable when she saw that he was tall and handsome, with perfect manners.

After dinner, Aici and Zhao Min suggested that Gao Hong should ride the bus with Daffodil and make sure she returned to her dorm safely. Daffodil said, "That's not necessary. The bus is quite safe. I can ride by myself." Gao Hong's ingrained gentlemanly nature made him say, "Absolutely not. It's already dark. I'll ride the bus with you." The room suddenly fell silent, and then Aici and Zhao Min both laughed: "That's right. Gao Hong should go with you."

In the quiet winter street, the only sound was of Gao Hong and Daffodil's footsteps on the snowy ground. Gao Hong broke the silence and asked Daffodil, "Do you usually go home on the weekends?" Daffodil said, "I go every other weekend." When he learned that Daffodil's home was in the Haidian District, Gao Hong said happily, "I lived in Haidian when I was younger, near the Summer Palace. Tell me about your family."

Daffodil said, "I have a big family: my parents, two brothers and four sisters, and my sister-in-law and nephew, eleven people in all." Gao Hong felt a wave of warmth: "That many people can't even fit around a dining table!" Daffodil said, "Whenever we're all at home, my mama makes noodles with black bean sauce. It's easy and delicious. Otherwise how can you cook for eleven people in such a short time and in a cramped kitchen?"

Gao Hong could almost see the heart-warming picture of a big family around a dinner table, each with a big bowl of noodles. How lovely! How joyful! He had vague memories of eating with his family and seemed to remember some large, round dining tables. Papa, Nana, First Uncle, Second Uncle and Dad sat on one side. The other side was First Aunt, Second Aunt and Stepmother Lingzhi. Cousin Lin, Cousin Ning, Cousin Lan, Cousin Yu, Cousin Quan and himself sat at another table. Cousin Lan was so small that her nanny had to hold her throughout the meal. The children were surrounded by nannies and maids who helped them eat their food and soup. Gao Hong couldn't remember what they ate, but the memory of being warm and full and surrounded by family and servants had left a deep impression.

Daffodil turned to look at the silent Gao Hong: "What about you? Don't you go home on the weekends?" Gao Hong sighed, "I'm a lone ghost. My family is all gone." Daffodil realized she had touched a sore point and became quiet. Gao Hong looked at her. She looked even more like Yanruo when she was quiet.

Soon they arrived at Daffodil's dorm. Daffodil said, "It's getting late. You should go before the last bus leaves." Gao Hong said, "I'll wait for you at nine o'clock tomorrow morning at the main gate of Taoran Park." Daffodil didn't answer him directly, but simply said, "Good night."

Daffodil didn't go to Taoran Park the next day. In her mind, she hadn't said yes, so Gao Hong should know she wouldn't be there. She wasn't particularly interested in Gao Hong. She thought of him as just another nice guy, not much different from many others she had met.

On Monday morning, Aici rushed over to Daffodil: "Sis! You are really too much! You should at least have let Gao Hong know that you didn't want to go out with him. He stood at the entrance to Taoran Park for two hours waiting for you in this snowy, freezing weather, and now he's sick!" Daffodil couldn't believe her ears: "What? I didn't say I'd go! He's sick from waiting for me in the cold? Oh, my!"

Then she remembered: "He told me he's a lone ghost, with no family around. Is that true?" Aici said, "That poor guy is from a landowning family, and everyone was killed. He's the only one left. He's an orphan." Daffodil's heart ached: "Who's going to take care of him while he's sick?" Growing up in a big family, Daffodil couldn't imagine being alone while sick, and her maternal instincts kicked in.

Gao Hong was a man of his word. Under his reserved and seemingly unapproachable demeanor, he was actually a kind and simple soul. It wasn't that he was in love with Daffodil, but as long as he'd nodded to Aici, and as long as Daffodil didn't say no, he would go and wait for her.

He had asked himself while waiting, "Am I here to meet Daffodil or am I here to meet a replica of Yanruo?" He didn't know the answer. All he knew was that he wouldn't have nodded to Aici and wouldn't have come to stand here in the bitter cold wind if Daffodil hadn't look so much like Yanruo. At the same time, he kept reminding himself that Daffodil was not Yanruo. They had the same eyes and looked incredibly alike, but they had nothing else in common.

Gao Hong developed a fever that evening. He skipped dinner and went to bed in hopes that he would feel well enough to face Monday's work after a good night's sleep. His roommates, Qiangzi, Ershun and Xiaoma, had all gone next door to play cards, and their yelling and the sound of cards being slammed on the table could be heard from far away. Gao Hong was desperate for a drink of water, but he remembered that all of the water bottles in the room were empty. He was half asleep when he felt a soft hand on his forehead. Opening his eyes, he saw Aici and Daffodil and struggled to sit up. Aici said, "Please don't get up. Daffodil is here to see you. I have something cooking on the stove at home, so I'll leave you now."

Daffodil opened a thermos and said, "You need to stay well hydrated during a fever. Here, I've brought wonton soup. Have some while it's hot." Gao Hong looked gratefully at Daffodil. Nanny Wu had always made a point of giving him wonton soup when he was sick.

"Look how messy and filthy your dorm is! I can't believe you guys live like this," complained Daffodil as she placed a bowl of wonton soup into Gao Hong's hands. Gao Hong smiled: "We're actually neater than a lot of others."

Gao Hong and Daffodil finally went to the lantern festival at Taoran Park. They didn't consider themselves a couple. They were just two friends who occasionally went together to a park or a movie. Months passed and they were still just friends.

(44) THE CULTURAL REVOLUTION

The willow catkins fluttering in Beijing's streets had disappeared, and new green leaves covered the trees. Summer had arrived. The temperature in the workshop shot up as fast as the tempers and shouting of the workers. One day after work, Zhao Min told his four apprentices, "Come back after dinner, all of you. There will be a meeting tonight, and you're all required to be there."

Xiaoma asked, "Shifu, will they give me a girl at the meeting? If not, I'm not coming!."

Zhao Min mimed kicking Xiaoma in the leg: "You asshole! Even if they were handing out girls they wouldn't give one to a bastard like you. You all have to be here. It's some directive from the central government. Everyone is supposed to take part in the Cultural Revolution."

Qiangzi and Ershun objected in unison: "Shifu! Have mercy! A cultural revolution? Really? We have no culture, so how are we expected to have a revolution? You always say Gao Hong has class and culture. Let him go! He should be the focus of the Cultural Revolution!"

Unfortunately, what they said was fairly close to what eventually happened.

China's leader, Mao Zedong, launched the Cultural Revolution in 1966 as a means of strengthening his grip on the Communist Party and on the entire country. Multitudes were mobilized to create chaos and seize power in every social sector. Schools replaced normal subjects with political indoctrination, and young students joined the upheaval in the name of revolution. The police force was abolished, the justice system was paralyzed, and violence filled the streets. Leading officials were forced out as Mao skillfully directed public discontent toward his political opponents. He imposed dictatorship over China at the cost of inflicting unbelievable bloodshed and injustice on the people.

At the beginning of the Cultural Revolution, gigantic posters were put up everywhere, often anonymous and full of accusations. Anyone mentioned in such a poster was automatically considered guilty, no matter how spurious the accusations, and there was no way for them to plead their innocence. People were shunned, imprisoned, beaten, tortured and even killed on the basis of the ironclad law and verdict expressed in the posters.

Each workplace, school and residential district fell under the control of a "revolutionary committee." Members of the committee were appointed by higher-level Communist Party officials, and were authorized to imprison, torture and kill anyone they deemed guilty.

Anyone could put up a poster, and removing them was strictly forbidden, so every wall in the factory was soon covered with posters. People kept their heads down as much as possible to avoid someone accusing them of something.

This hostile and unpredictable environment brought out all the worst in human nature. Anyone bearing a grudge or disliking someone could just put up a poster and accuse them of something and have them locked up in a makeshift jail. Sometimes, someone who suspected that someone else was about to put up a poster about them might seize the initiative and protect themselves by first putting up a poster about that person. Some people were accused of espionage because they'd received letters from abroad, while others were labeled counterrevolutionaries because they had complained about something. Some were accused of treason because they refused to publicly denounce family members who lived abroad, while others were accused of corruption because they seemed to live better than others. Countless people were accused of crimes after their personal diaries or private conversations were made public. Some couples ratted on each other after a quarrel and sent their spouses to prison. Friends turned on friends, brothers turned on brothers, children betrayed parents. No one was safe in this hellish campaign.

The first posters that went up criticized the factory's director and Party secretary. Both of them were immediately seized by the revolutionary committee and beaten until their bones showed through their mutilated flesh. The revolutionary committee members also shaved off half of the men's hair in what was referred to as a "yin-yang hairstyle" in order to expose them to public humiliation, after which they were forced to clean every bathroom in the factory every day. No one in the factory dared to talk to them for fear of being associated with their crimes. Overnight, they went from the leaders of the factory to complete outcasts.

Zhao Min told his four apprentices sternly: "If any of you dares to cause trouble, or post anything, or even watch those barbaric acts, I'll beat you up myself! Stay low key. Stay quiet. Stay away from crowds. I'm warning you, I have no way of getting you out if anything happens to you!"

The next person who appeared on a poster was an elderly worker from Workshop Four. His crime was believing in a foreign religion. The elderly man and his wife were forced to wear wigs made of yellow yarn to imitate foreigners, and to wear black robes like foreign missionaries. They were dragged onto a stage, and young revolutionary committee members slapped them in the face while asking, "Why do you believe in a foreign religion! Why don't you believe in Marxism!" The old man said, "God isn't foreign. Jesus is Lord and Savior of the Chinese people, too. He's not just for Westerners. He loves us all, even you!" "Shut up! The 'Ma' in Marxism is a common Chinese name, but the 'Je' in 'Jesus' is never heard in Chinese! You're spreading counterrevolutionary toxins!" Gangs of youngsters leaped onto the stage to take turns beating the elderly couple until they were finally beaten to death.

Zhao Min watched over Gao Hong and his three other apprentices like a hawk. Aware of Gao Hong's landlord's background, he smelled trouble. He told Gao Hong: "Stay indoors as much as possible. Don't talk to anyone! Just work! Stick with me at all times, inside and outside of the workshop. Don't ever be more than two steps away! Even if you need to go to the bathroom, you have to go with me! I'll walk you to your dorm every evening, and you stay there until I come get you in the morning. Understand?"

More people appeared on posters and were taken away. They were accused of being counterrevolutionaries, traitors, spies, thieves, rightists (as opposed to proper leftists) and degenerates ... Then people with bad political backgrounds started to become targets, and people from capitalist or landlord families started to appear on the posters and be tortured. Gao Hong knew his time was at hand.

One morning, Gao Hong's birthname appeared in large print on a new poster: "Expose the Escaped Landlord Gao Penghong (Gao Hong)" the poster's title read. Both names were written in distorted characters with large red X's across them. The content of the poster detailed how Gao Hong's father, Gao Zhanren, had taken revenge and then been executed. The poster even said that the Gao family still hid a valuable jade Crimson Eyed Buddha in hopes that it would bless them with restoration to their former prestige. Gao Hong was reading the poster with wild eyes when people from the revolutionary committee rushed over with weapons in their hands, yelling, "Gao Hong!"

Four people dashed out of the workshop and surrounded Gao Hong before the revolutionary committee members could grab him. They were Zhao Min and his three other apprentices, Xiaoma, Qiangzi and Ershun, who locked their arms together to form a circle around Gao Hong. The revolutionary committee members yelled, "Tie Gao Hong up! Lock him up!" Zhao Min shouted, "Fuck off! Any move you want to make will be over my dead body!"

The leader of the revolutionary committee, a man named Jiang Lige, waved the others back. "Zhao Shifu, you're hard-core working class," he said, "You're one of us, so why are you protecting an escaped landlord?" Zhao Min replied, "Chairman Mao said 'A person cannot choose his birth, but he can choose his path.' What Gao Hong's father did has nothing to do with him. He was only six years old! His adoptive father is Gao Zhanxiang. Do you even know who Gao Zhanxiang is? He saved the life of a general! How dare you lock up Gao Zhanxiang's adopted son?!"

Ershun yelled at the committee members, "Don't give me that fucking landlord shit. Have you ever seen a landlord who works and eats with us? Is your head in your ass?"

Xiaoma added, "His girlfriend is the daughter of a government official. Would a real landlord have that kind of girlfriend?"

Qiangzi's voice was louder than everyone's: "Don't waste your words on these bastards! Let me tell you something. I'm from a poor peasant family going back eight generations. You assholes want to lay one finger on Gao Hong, you'll have to do it over my dead body. Kill me! Kill me if you dare! Let's see if you dare to kill a poor peasant and a working-class brother!"

No matter what the revolutionary committee members said, Zhao Min and his three apprentices continued to yell and curse, and they wouldn't let anyone get close to Gao Hong. Finally, Xiaoma lost patience, and picking up a piece of sharp glass from the ground, he pressed it against his own neck to force the revolutionary committee members to leave. The tip of the glass pressed deeper and deeper into Xiaoma's skin, which started to bleed. Gao Hong yelled, "Xiaoma! Put that down! I'll go with them!" He knew that going with the revolutionary committee members meant being tortured and maybe even killed, but he couldn't let Xiaoma die for his sake.

The revolutionary committee members weren't afraid of loss of life, but the life of a solidly dirt-poor factory worker like Xiaoma couldn't be sacrificed lightly. Finally they turned and walked away.

As soon as the revolutionary committee members left, Zhao Min pulled down the poster about Gao Hong and tore it to shreds. Gao Hong tried to stop him: "Zhao Shifu, don't!" He knew that ripping up a public poster was punishable by death. But Zhao Min didn't care. He yelled at the crowd that had gathered around them: "Anyone who picks on Gao Hong won't have many days left to live! I guarantee it with my life! Whoever wants a swift death can try me!"

Just like that, Zhao Min, Xiaoma, Ershun and Qiangzi saved Gao Hong's life.

This incident was like a time bomb for Zhao Min and his apprentices, and could cause them endless trouble and unbelievable danger. But the next day, everyone's attention was diverted to something else: The head of the revolutionary committee, Jiang Lige, was found having sex with a female worker! They were discovered half naked at the back of Workshop Two by the factory security team patrolling with flashlights. The scandal set off an explosion throughout the factory. Many had been coveting the power of the revolutionary committee, and now was their chance. All members of

Jiang Lige's revolutionary committee were locked up, and a new group of revolutionary committee members rose to power. Jiang Lige was forced to kneel on a stage wearing a big sign that said "Rapist" while people threw rotten vegetables and eggs at him. Many who had lost loved ones because of him now jumped on stage and beat him without mercy. Soon Jiang Lige was dead.

The female worker with whom Jiang Lige was caught having sex was also taken prisoner. Back then, a woman who was exposed for having sex outside of marriage was called a "worn out, stinky shoe." The woman's arms were tied behind her back, a pair of dirty, worn-out shoes was slung around her neck, and she was paraded through the streets in a cart to humiliate her while people threw all kinds of things at her. She committed suicide after spotting her son in the crowd while her face dripped with rotten eggs and sewage.

Anything could happen to anyone on any day. No one knew who would be next, and everyone feared that one day, for reasons they could not imagine, they themselves would become a target. In this bloody and hostile world, all Gao Hong could focus on was how to stay alive.

He was now extremely grateful that he hadn't married Yanruo. Forget about giving Yanruo a happy marriage – how on earth could he have protected her in a world like this? How could he have ensured Yanruo's safety, whether in Beijing or in the Northwest? He shuddered every time he thought about it. If he had married Yanruo, it would have been the equivalent of leading her down the path to a rapid death.

One time, Gao Hong secretly went to the Ministry of Materials to ask about Yanruo. It turned out that Yanruo's husband, Wu Mancang, was doing quite well in the Ministry. He had gained a lot of political capital during the Cultural Revolution, and his solid poor peasant family background had given him enough power to protect his capitalist-origin wife. Gao Hong found himself actually grateful to Wu Mancang, knowing that if not for him, Yanruo would have been beaten to death many times over by the famously cruel revolutionary committee at the Ministry of Materials.

The Cultural Revolution profoundly changed Gao Hong. He now identified with the factory workers one hundred percent, and no longer frowned upon their profanity, poor hygiene, lack of manners, short tempers and violent outbursts. Now Gao Hong could see the kindness beneath their rough surfaces. Compared to the hypocritical intellectuals and officials, these workers were genuine human beings.

Gao Hong stowed away all of his college books, deciding never to look at them again. Let them disappear like his self-identified intellectual status!

Gao Hong no longer shaved every day, or took pains to launder his clothes. He let himself turn into a typical factory worker with stubble on his face and oil stains on his clothes. He stopped combing his hair, and wore the typical factory worker's hat that he had once hated so much. He also abandoned his table manners, learning to eat noisily and in large mouthfuls while talking and laughing.

But the cornerstone transformation that truly integrated him into the masses of factory workers was his use of profanity. The first "fuck" that came out of Gao Hong's mouth made him shudder, but triggered roars of laughter from the workers, who had never heard Gao Hong talk like that. After some practice, this new way of talking became not only acceptable but highly effective and enjoyable to Gao Hong. He felt liberated and empowered and wondered why he'd never tried it before. This was his turning point. Everything else followed naturally after that as he talked, swore and cursed as expertly as any other worker. Zhao Min laughed, "You're sounding more like my actual apprentice every day!"

Gao Hong hadn't seen Daffodil for a long time. Aside from his worries over how chaotic and unsafe things were, Gao Hong subconsciously resisted Daffodil because of her lack of education. He noticed that he couldn't talk with Daffodil the same way he'd talked with Yanruo, and that Daffodil thought very differently from him on many topics. But now, he decided to go see Daffodil. Wasn't he just an ordinary factory worker like everyone else? So what if he was a college graduate? So what if Daffodil wasn't like Yanruo? Hadn't Yanruo married someone else in any case? It was high time for him to be married, and even his obligation as the only male descendant of the Gaos. If he had to get married, and was a factory worker struggling at the bottom of the food chain, wouldn't Daffodil be his best choice?

A girl entered Daffodil's dorm room and said, "Daffodil, there's someone here to see you." Daffodil stepped out and paused for a moment before recognizing Gao Hong. She hadn't seen him for a long time and had almost forgotten about him; even Aici, who used to ask how things were going between them, had finally given up. Now, seeing Gao Hong standing there, Daffodil couldn't help feeling surprised. "I have two Beijing Opera tickets," Gao Hong said. "Do you like Beijing Opera? Let's go together. It's right at Zhushikou."

On their way, they talked about what had been happening at their factories, and Gao Hong realized the cruelty and chaos was even worse at Daffodil's factory. Fortunately, Daffodil had a politically advantageous family background, as well as benefiting from her seniority and the protection of her brother Daqing, who had become the director of his workshop. Many had died at Daffodil's factory, but Daffodil was safe. They both sighed and grew silent, their sadness, helplessness and feeling of suffocation lingering like the smell of diesel on the bus. Gao Hong said, "At least we can still go to the opera." Daffodil agreed, "Yes, what else can one hope for in a world like this?" With that, they started going out together again, bringing each other much-needed warmth in the bone-chilling cruelty of the Cultural Revolution.

Both Gao Hong and Daffodil were long past the customary age for getting married. They'd been going out off and on for three years, but somehow neither felt motivated for marriage. Aici couldn't take it anymore, and she asked Daffodil, "What on earth are you two waiting for? Are you marathon runners? You're already twenty-five. At your age, other women have toddlers. You need to hurry up!" Daffodil said, "He's never said he wanted to get married."

Aici went to Gao Hong: "You think a girl as good as Daffodil will wait for you for the rest of her life? You two have been going out for three years and you're still dragging your feet? Daffodil is beautiful, smart and has a good family background. You're already twenty-eight! Who on earth doesn't get married by that age?! You're all alone, and she has a big family. If you marry her, you'll have a family too!"

"Aici is right," Gao Hong thought as warmth washed through his heart. "I'll have a family and I won't be a lone ghost anymore." Gao Hong knew that Daffodil had the beauty of Yanruo and the kindness of Nanny Wu, and that he would never come across such a fine woman again. So what was he waiting for? Even he didn't know. Could it be that he still had reservations about Daffodil's lack of education, or that he still couldn't get over Yanruo, who was now a wife and mother?

In the silent depths of the night, everything became crystal clear to Gao Hong. It wasn't that he had reservations about Daffodil, or that he couldn't get over Yanruo. It was that he knew that marrying Daffodil would mean saying goodbye to the old Gao Hong: the Gao Hong born as a young master in a prominent family, the Gao Hong raised by China's most famous neurosurgeon, the Gao Hong with incredible intelligence and a superb education, the Gao Hong well versed in ancient Chinese literature and who loved romantic poetry.... That Gao Hong would be gone forever, and would be replaced by a Gao Hong whose only reason for existence was to do manual labor in a factory, who struggled to stay alive in the cruelty of the Cultural Revolution, who wanted nothing more than a small bed in a damp, filthy dorm room; a Gao Hong who used foul language and who earned his meager salary with his blood and sweat; a Gao Hong with no more hopes and dreams. It was the difference between the young master Gao Hong in his mind and the flesh-and-blood Gao Hong in reality.

The young master Gao Hong who lived in his mind wanted to marry Shi Yanruo, and would never have met, much less wanted to marry, someone like Daffodil. But the physical factory worker Gao Hong lived in a different world and should count his blessings if he could marry a woman as good as Daffodil. Gao Hong's tragedy was that despite his crystal clear awareness of the pitfalls in this relationship, he felt he had no better choice than to marry Daffodil. He knew that his only shot at happiness would be to say goodbye to the young master of the Gao family and never look back. Because every time he looked back, his marriage to Daffodil would suffer. Was he ready? Could he do it?

After a sleepless night, Gao Hong started writing a letter to Daffodil. He wrote about his birth and what it might mean to be with someone like him in the political underclass. He wrote what a wonderful girl Daffodil was, and that earning her hand in marriage would be the best thing that ever happened to him. He told Daffodil of his loneliness and his longing for a big family. He told Daffodil about Nanny Wu and the Gao Compound. His pen gained a life of its own and led him down a dreamy path. Then he woke up and hastily finished the letter. Standing in front of the mailbox, he held the letter over the opening and hesitated.

This would not be his first marriage proposal. Last time, it was to Shi Yanruo when they graduated. At that time, there had been no hesitation, no sleepless nights, no weighing of options; he'd just rushed to her and pulled her into his arms and said, "Marry me!" in front of all the students who were passing by. Now he and Daffodil had been going out for three years without having so much as hugged or kissed each other. He couldn't imagine that he was proposing to a girl he'd been treating as no more than a friend. He felt something was missing. He shouldn't be thinking this much, or writing or calculating or hesitating this much. Something was wrong, but he didn't know what it was. He turned the envelope over and over in his hands until it suddenly dropped into the mailbox slot of its own volition, leaving his hand frozen in mid-air.

He heard the clacking sound of the letter landing at the bottom of the mailbox. It resonated deeply in Gao Hong, reminding him of a sound from his childhood. As he stood there staring at the mailbox, Gao Hong finally remembered that it sounded like the crisp and pleasant clinking of his mother's jade bangles. Those bangles had been worn by his mother, and then by Nanny Wu for many years, and were finally given to Yanruo. "You accepted my jewelry, so now you are mine....." Gao Hong could see himself and Yanruo laughing and chasing each other in the streets. But Yanruo was not his, nor would she ever be. Gao Hong sighed and walk slowly back to his factory dorm.

It had been a few days since Daffodil received Gao Hong's letter, but she found herself feeling very neutral about it. She was not surprised, excited or uneasy, not particularly happy or unhappy, she just felt.... neutral. She knew that Gao Hong was an incredibly kind and nice man, but for some reason she couldn't find the motivation to respond to his proposal. Aici kept urging Daffodil to do something: "Let me tell you, those Wife Union bitches are still calling you a slut behind your back, and they're still spreading rumors about you. Everyone knows it's nonsense, but imagine what a mother-in-law would think! If you had a mother-in-law who heard any of this, you'd be doomed for the rest of your life, and you'd regret that you didn't marry someone like Gao Hong. As long as he's happy, his whole family is happy. If he loves you, his whole family loves you. You're young and haven't had to deal with in-laws, but let me tell you, this is an opportunity you don't want to miss!"

Daffodil saw Gao Hong as a kind, reliable, honest and hardworking man, and she actually appreciated that he had never touched her during the three years she'd known him. She considered that a sign of respect and decency. She particularly liked that Gao Hong had a lot more culture and class than any of the other factory workers she'd met, and that he was more well-mannered and sophisticated than anyone she knew. It was true that Gao Hong had picked up some of the rough mannerisms from the other factory workers in recent years, but Daffodil was confident that she could change him back to his mannerly and cultured self. She knew he had it in him, and that he could do it. What she didn't know was that Gao Hong simply didn't want to do it, as the only way he could live with himself was to forget about his past. He simply could not give Daffodil what she hoped for, and that planted a time bomb in their relationship from the very beginning.

Daffodil's reply to Gao Hong was subtle and brief: "I know you're a good man. I'd like to invite you to meet my parents this Sunday."

Carrying a box of pastries and bags of fruit in his hands, Gao Hong walked towards Yard 13 with Daffodil. He asked nervously, "Do your parents know I'm coming?" Daffodil assured him, "I called my Dad. They know."

The first person to greet them was Auntie Li from next door: "Oh, look! Daffodil's boyfriend is here! Oh, such a tall young man!" Little Hong and Rong both ran out of the house: "Big Sis, is this our new brother-in-law?" The two older girls, Jade and Duoduo, rushed over and pulled Hong and Rong aside: "Stop talking about old and new! Go play!" They smiled at Gao Hong and respectfully greeted him: "Brother-in-law!"

Gao Hong wasn't used to being surrounded by so many people, and it was disconcerting to have the four girls address him as brother-in-law. He greeted Auntie Li and passed the pastries and fruit to the four sisters. Then Daffodil led him into the house to pay respects to her parents. Lotus and Yixin received Gao Hong warmly and led him to the guest's chair, just as Daqing arrived with his wife, son and two daughters. Erqing and his newly wedded wife were home as well. The little two-room house and its corridor and small yard came alive with the swarming family members talking, laughing and greeting one another while the children went chasing each other through the crowd. All of the adults came up to introduce themselves to Gao Hong, who found himself utterly overwhelmed with bowing, shaking hands and nodding to people.

As if all this was still not enough, Daffodil had invited her childhood friend Zhang Yufang, whose only mission was to "check out" Gao Hong. She'd done nothing but stare at Gao Hong since entering the house, making him feel so embarrassed that it was as if a thousand tiny needles were poking his back inside his shirt.

The heart-warming scene he'd dreamed of was now a reality as the big family noisily gathered around a table with bowls of noodles and black bean sauce in their hands. Gao Hong ate and ate while watching and listening to everyone. He felt as if he were back in the Gao Compound's main dining hall, full and warm and surrounded by family.

Daffodil pulled Yufang aside: "What do you think?"

Yufang said, "Oh my, he's taller than the coat closet! I'd get a neck ache after looking at him for a few minutes. And he can really eat!"

"No, seriously," Daffodil said, "What do you think?"

"He seems honest and decent," Yufang said.

"He has a lot of decency. Let me tell you something, we've been going out for three years and he's never touched me, not even a small hug! Isn't that a decent man?"

Yufang eyed Daffodil carefully: "Really? But that's not right! Does he love you? It has nothing to do with decency. If a man acts like that, he doesn't love you."

"Oh stop it!" Daffodil scoffed, "That's nonsense. You think I should marry a greedy ass-pincher who's always groping me all over?" They both burst out laughing.

Just then Gao Hong came over and asked, "What's so funny?" Daffodil and Yufang turned to look at Gao Hong and both started laughing again.

After dinner, Yixin and Lotus sat down with Gao Hong and Daffodil and asked, "Have you two picked a date for the wedding?" Daffodil looked at Gao Hong, and Gao Hong said, "How about the New Year?"

(46) ALCOHOL AND CIGARETTES

At that time in China, all household resources were completely controlled by the government. The only way to obtain housing was through your workplace, and it was allocated on the basis of seniority. Although Gao Hong was three years older than Daffodil, he had only started working after graduating from college. As a result, by the time of their wedding, he had just over four years of work seniority, while Daffodil already had ten years. Daffodil's factory assigned her a one-room flat in Four Corners, a married employee housing complex right behind the factory. The complex had four rows of single-room houses, with twelve houses in each row and two houses at the end of rows one and four for a total of fifty units. Both factories approved the marriage application of Daffodil and Gao Hong, and they began preparing for the wedding.

Early in the morning on December 31, 1967, Daffodil's roommates woke up early to help her get ready. With considerable trouble, they'd obtained a piece of fragrant soap for Daffodil to wash her hands and face, and they rubbed sweet smelling lotion on her skin. One girl even brought a small piece of rouge and dabbed it on Daffodil's face and lips. Daffodil looked as pretty as a spring peach blossom! Another girl named Hao brought a small bottle of jasmine fragrance, which the girls sprayed on Daffodil's hair and clothes. They combed Daffodil's thick hair and decorated it with the only ornament they could afford: pieces of red yarn. The girls all said, "Daffodil is such a beautiful bride. Gao Hong is so lucky!"

Daffodil's mother Lotus had prepared a wedding outfit of red wool for her, since it was customary for the bride to wear red. The girls didn't have an iron, so they filled a big flat-bottomed metal mug with boiling water and "ironed" Daffodil's wedding outfit with the bottom of the mug.

It was Lotus's first time to be the mother of the bride, and she had come to stay at Daffodil's dorm to prepare for the wedding. She told Daffodil the old tradition that a bride shouldn't open her mouth on her wedding day until she reached her husband's home, and that way she would have many sons. Lotus interrupted her: "Mama! Those are the old ways. I don't believe in any of that! I can't bear to go all morning without talking, and I don't want children anyway. They're too much trouble!"

The girls all went to the dining hall for breakfast. Lotus held Daffodil's hands and said, "My dear daughter, I can't believe it's your wedding day. Mama only knows the old ways that you don't care about, but I have a few things to tell you that I've learned in life, and I hope that you'll take them to heart. You're strong-willed and sharp-tongued. Thank God you don't have a mother-in-law. I'm so relieved! But you have to be gentle to your man; don't be stubborn. Gao Hong seems to be good-tempered and low-key, but I can tell he's also strong and sensitive. Don't contradict him. Be good to him and obey him. Only then can you have a good marriage. Being sharp-tongued with your man is like sowing bitter melon seeds. All the bitterness will later come out a hundred-fold for you to chew and swallow."

Daffodil was irritated by her mother's words: "Mama! This is a modern society. Men and women are equal, but you're still teaching me that old ideology of bound-foot women. Why should women have to obey men? I hate that!"

Lotus sighed: "Bound feet or not, modern or ancient, the natural laws between men and women never change! I've seen so many families, and all of those with strong-willed and sharp-tongued wives are unhappy. You'll see for yourself, and I hope soon. Remember, a hurtful word from your mouth is like driving a nail into the wall; even if you regret it and pull the nail out, the hole remains there. Don't put nails in your new wall. Remember Mama's words."

The girls all returned with containers of food and surrounded Lotus and Daffodil to rush them through breakfast. Just then, men's voices came from outside: "The bride should please come out. The groom is here!" Gao Hong, wearing a brand new outfit, was surrounded by workers from his factory.

Daffodil walked out of her dorm with her mother by her side and her friends around her. Loud cheers and whistling erupted from the crowd outside as everyone surrounded Gao Hong and Daffodil and walked with them to their new home. Gao Hong and Daffodil stole glances at each other and smiled shyly.

The little one-room house was decorated with traditional red "double happiness" wedding posters. In accordance with tradition, Yixin and Lotus had brought large amounts of wedding candy and cigarettes, which Gao Hong and Daffodil threw to the crowd to spread happiness and receive people's well wishes.

With no room for so many people in the tiny room, two tables had been set up in the yard, with coal burners next to the tables to fend off the bitter cold. The famine had only recently ended, and the whole country was still struggling with poverty. Gao Hong and Daffodil, as well as Yixin and Lotus, had put everything they had into preparing a simple wedding banquet. The dishes included roasted peanuts, pork headcheese, tofu, sausages, fish, soybeans and vegetables, with ten dishes for each of the two tables. It wasn't enough to feed the crowd, but everyone could have a few bites to share the happiness, and a little liquor added to the cheer.

Zhao Min raised his shot glass: "Let me say something." Everyone quieted down. Zhao Min looked at Gao Hong and said, "Gao Hong has been my apprentice since he left college. In these few years we've been through a lot together, and he's become someone I would give my life for. They say a Shifu is like a father to his apprentices, and I couldn't agree more. I'm only a few years older than Gao Hong, but he's like a son to me! I'm so happy that he's getting married. Gao Hong! Three shots! Straight up!" Gao Hong felt a wave of warmth rushing to his eyes, and he blinked back his tears as he downed three glasses of liquor. Showing his empty glass to Zhao Min, he said, "Shifu!"

Traditional Chinese alcohol culture is about more than just drinking. Toasting and making the host and hostess drink as much as possible is not only expected, but is considered each guest's sole mission for the evening. Toasts are made based on social hierarchy, with many unspoken rules regarding the order of toasts and how many times each person can toast. Accepting someone's toast to the fullest and without hesitation is an act of respect and loyalty, while any refusal, hesitation or bargaining with a superior or a senior is socially unacceptable. When Zhao Min told him to drink three shots, Gao Hong drank three shots without question or hesitation.

Qiangzi, Xiaoma and Ershun leaped from their seats: "Hey, what about us?! We can't claim to be on the same level as Zhao Shifu, but how about if we each drink two shots with you?" Gao Hong smiled nervously, realizing that he wouldn't last very long drinking like this. Daffodil came to his rescue: "The three of you! Each of you wants two shots, and that's six shots total. That's twice as much as Zhao Shifu! The nerve! I say he can drink two shots total with all three of you." Lotus tugged on Daffodil's jacket to make her sit down, but Daffodil shook her mother off.

"Well, coming to your new husband's rescue already?" the three fellow apprentices said in a chorus. "So how about if you drink for him?" Other male workers all rose and crowded around the table to force Gao Hong to drink. Gao Hong was in no position to say no, but Daffodil's sharp tongue and quick wits proved effective in fending off the amount of alcohol pushed on him. The men all looked at one another and said, "Gao Hong's new wife is not someone to mess with!"

Even with Daffodil by Gao Hong's side, his factory friends wouldn't let him off easy, and he was soon woozy from drinking. Suddenly remembering that he had not yet toasted his parents-in-law, Gao Hong struggled to his feet and tried to keep his balance as he walked over to Yixin and Lotus: "Mother, Father, please accept this toast from your son-in-law. I will love you and honor you as my own parents." Yixin and Lotus both said, "Thank you! And we will love you and honor you as our own son! Thank you for toasting us. That's good enough and you don't have to drink it." Finally, all the liquor was gone, and Daffodil breathed a sigh of relief. She took out the cigarettes and passed them out to the guests.

A worker said, "Gao Hong! How come I've never seen you smoke, you bastard?" That reminded everyone: "Oh! That's right! That son of a bitch never smokes. Light one up for him! What kind of man never smokes?" Daffodil stood up: "Hey! Can't you teach him anything good? Are drinking and smoking the only things you know?!" Everyone said: "You didn't let us drink with him, and now you don't let us smoke with him. What fun is that? Let's all leave!" Gao Hong quickly said, "No, no, don't leave. I'll do it. I'll smoke."

Daffodil was about to speak again, but Lotus squeezed her daughter's arm to stop her. "Mama! What?!" Daffodil turned to stare at her mother. Zhao Min and Aici walked over to Daffodil and said, "Just relax, everyone is having a good time. It's your wedding day, so don't make a scene. Just relax." A loud cheer came from the crowd as Daqing ran back with a newly purchased bottle of liquor. Daffodil glared angrily at Daqing.

At long last, all of the guests were gone, and Yixin and Lotus had also gone home with their kids. Gao Hong was so drunk that he'd collapsed in a chair, sound asleep. Daqing and his wife helped Daffodil clean up. Daffodil complained, "He's as drunk as a dog, and he smoked so much too. Look at how he's starting our marriage with all those bad habits!" Daqing's wife consoled Daffodil: "Men are all like that. They all drink and smoke." Daqing added, "Stop being so uptight. You have to give men some freedom. If you act like that in front of his friends, people will say he's a pussy!" Daffodil stormed off to take out the trash.

Daqing and his wife helped Daffodil carry the unconscious Gao Hong over to the edge of the bed. They helped take off his jacket and lay him flat on the bed, then said their good nights and left.

Daffodil locked the door behind them and then sat on the edge of the bed and looked at Gao Hong. He was so tall that the bed didn't seem long enough for him. "He might bump his head if he moves," she thought. Gao Hong's face was flushed from the alcohol, emphasizing his thick eyebrows, arched nose, long lashes and large, deep-set eyes. Daffodil thought to herself, "He almost looks like a foreigner." Daffodil had never looked at Gao Hong this closely before, and she really enjoyed it. "This is my husband. My man for life." She felt a wave of tenderness in her heart.

She took off his gigantic shoes and then his socks, and mustering all her strength, she rolled him over to one side of the bed to make space for herself. Lying down fully clothed, she pulled a big blanket over both of them and turned off the light.

As if in a dream, Gao Hong smelled the fragrance of jasmine flowers, like the jasmine bushes that lined the campus walkway from the water house to Dorm 3. Opening his eyes slightly, Gao Hong saw beautiful moonlight pouring in the tiny window, the same moonlight

that had bathed the Zhichun Pavilion in the Summer Palace. He
wanted to swim in Kunming Lake, as if falling into the embrace of his
mother. "Oh, right," he remembered, "Didn't I just get married? I
shouldn't be alone. That's right. I'm married. Finally married." He
turned in Daffodil's direction, and seeing the beautiful shiny eyes next
to him, he pulled her into his arms and murmured, "Yanruo, Yanruo!"

Daffodil didn't know what Gao Hong was talking about, and
thought he was saying it was too hot in the room. "Too hot?" Daffodil
said. "It must be all that alcohol. It's not really hot at all." Raising
her head, she saw that Gao Hong was fast asleep.

The next morning, Gao Hong woke up extremely thirsty. At first
he didn't know where he was, but reality returned to him when he saw
Daffodil sleeping next to him. Noticing that both of them were fully
dressed, Gao Hong realized that was how they'd spent their wedding
night. He shook his head and chuckled. He got out of bed, drank a
tall glass of water and then headed out to get breakfast.

When he returned to their little room with soy milk and fried
dough sticks, Daffodil was already up and around. Dressed and with
neatly combed hair, she sat there silently. Gao Hong said, "I got
breakfast for us. Come have some food." Daffodil looked at him, then
joined him at the table without a word. Gao Hong said with
embarrassment, "I drank too much yesterday. I'm sorry, I fell asleep,
and I don't remember anything, I ....." Daffodil said, "Just Don't drink
that much again." Gao Hong said anxiously, "Of course not! I won't
do it again. It was just for the wedding. Once in a lifetime, really. I
didn't even want to drink that much, but I couldn't say no."

Gao Hong watched as Daffodil ate her breakfast without a word.
Gao Hong said, "I, I fell asleep like a dead pig and didn't even say a
word to you. Are you mad at me?" Daffodil said, "No, I'm not mad.
And you actually said something to me. You said it was too hot." Gao
Hong was puzzled: "Hot? I thought it was freezing last night."

Daffodil said, "I'm just thinking about what my mother told me.
She said it's a bad sign if a newly wedded couple isn't intimate on their
first night together." Gao Hong immediately said, "Let's make up for
it!" He jumped up to pull the curtains. Daffodil said, "Oh, stop! We
don't have to believe an old wife's tale. The neighbors will talk if we
draw the curtains during the daytime." Gao Hong pulled open the

curtains again and sat back down: "It's New Year's Day today, so how about if I take you to Zhongshan Park?" He had been intending to take Daffodil to his beloved Summer Palace, but Zhongshan Park came out of his mouth instead. He realized that the Summer Palace was full of his memories of Yanruo, and he felt he could never take another woman there.

The night of January 1, 1968, was Gao Hong and Daffodil's real wedding night. For the first time, they were one, and for the first time, they put this small home into the most treasured depth of their hearts. They felt that no matter how cold and cruel the world was, as long as they had this home of theirs, they would be happy.

(47) COUSIN LAN

Married life was sweet and exciting. Gao Hong bought a bicycle so he could commute from his factory to their little room in Four Corners every day. Daffodil and Gao Hong didn't eat in the factory dining hall very often anymore. Instead, they bought a little coal burner and cooked their own meals in order to save money and have better quality food. Gao Hong told Daffodil that as a child, he'd always loved pork belly braised with soy sauce, ginger and rock candy, so Daffodil went out and bought a big piece of pork belly that cost her a whole yuan. A whole yuan! That was a large amount out of their meager salaries! As soon as Gao Hong saw the big piece of meat, he felt stricken by the thought of spending so much money. He told Daffodil, "I actually don't like pork anymore." Daffodil gave Gao Hong a slap on his back: "You have to eat it all even if you hate it! And all in one sitting, or else!" Then she marched to the kitchen to braise the meat.

The delicious smell of braised pork made the whole yard smell heavenly, and the neighbors all asked, "What delicacy are you cooking? It smells so good!" Daffodil put the gigantic bowl of braised pork in front of Gao Hong and watched him stuff piece after piece into his mouth. Gao Hong tried to share the meat with Daffodil, and to save some for the next meal, and he tried to persuade Daffodil to pack up some of the meat for her parents to enjoy, but Daffodil was determined: "No! You eat it! Eat it all! Right now!" Throughout the decades of their marriage, Gao Hong could never forget that Daffodil had once given him the luxury of feasting on delicious braised pork, even when they couldn't really afford it.

In Beijing in those years, the Communist system allocated resources based on a well-defined class system. Zhongnanhai, where the central government and its officials were located, naturally received the country's best luxuries and resources. Close behind Zhongnanhai were the military compounds, where the officers and families of the country's armed forces were located.   Other government campuses such as the Department of Civil Affairs, where Daffodil's parents lived, were in the third tier, but they still enjoyed living standards greatly superior to those of ordinary Beijing residents. The schools their children attended, the healthcare facilities available to them and the housing and daily living supplies they had access to were all beyond what was provided to ordinary Beijingers. The next tier consisted of the universities, research institutions, art institutions, media centers and other establishments, who could provide at least apartment buildings and decent schools to their employees. As to the factory workers, they were at the bottom of the food chain, living in single-room flats that were often run-down shacks with no indoor water supply or private bathrooms. Four Corners was this kind of area with shacks inhabited by the bottom-of-society factory workers.

Lacking running water in the living units, everyone had to share an outdoor faucet to fetch water. The drain under the public faucet was the only sewer for all of the twelve families in Row One of Four Corners, and there were no natural gas pipes; each family had a coal burner for cooking and heating. Everyone used a shared outhouse during the day and a chamber pot at night. Living under such conditions meant a lot of daily chores – fetching water, dumping sewage, taking out the trash, dumping and cleaning the chamber pot each morning, storing coal, installing pipes for the coal burner.... even laundry was a significant undertaking.

Gao Hong tried to take care of as many chores as he could to spare Daffodil worrying about them. As an orphan and someone used to manual labor, Gao Hong had developed the habit of working hard, caring for others before thinking of himself, and trying not to trouble anyone at any cost. And he felt guilty toward Daffodil, knowing that he couldn't love her the same way he'd loved Yanruo. Daffodil was his life partner but not the love of his life. For that he was sorry, and he was willing to do whatever was necessary to make it up to her.

The men of Four Corners tended to be ill-tempered, exhausting themselves at the factory and then bringing their frustrations home to vent on their wives and children. The women in Four Corners gritted their teeth and endured their hardships, trying their best to make ends meet and keep their family fed. Even so, their men would often beat them when they were drunk or in a bad mood, and now and then a woman would threaten suicide. There were no peaceful families in Four Corners; yelling, cursing, crying and violence were so common that it felt almost abnormal if a family went for any amount of time without fighting.

Gao Hong and Daffodil were the only couple who didn't fight. Gao Hong was easy-going; living at the mercy of others since he was very young had left a permanent mark on him, and he avoided conflict at any cost. He would yield, retreat, hide, give in, apologize and make concessions just to keep the peace, even if it meant doing extra work or tolerating unfairness. All he wanted was peace. But Daffodil was loud and entitled. As soon as she raised her voice, Gao Hong would do whatever she wanted to keep her quiet. He had taken on almost all of the household chores, from cooking to roof repairs, from laundry to coal burner pipes. If Daffodil threw a little tantrum, Gao Hong would be extra attentive to make her happy. All of the women in Four Corners were jealous of Daffodil: "You must have done something really good in your previous life to get such a caring husband in this life! Look how he spoils you!" Daffodil replied with a proud smile, "Of course, why else do you think I married him?"

The only thing Daffodil was unhappy about was that Gao Hong had become a smoker and a drinker. His new favorite pastime after work was to talk and laugh while drinking and smoking with his fellow workers, and he would come home smelling like a chimney. Director Chen from the human resource department at Gao Hong's factory now treated Gao Hong like his own son. That was the same Director Chen who had given Gao Hong his first dose of profanity when he'd reported for work the first time, and the same Director Chen whom Gao Hong had punched for his insulting comments when Nanny Wu died. But now, their shared indulgence in alcohol had made them best buddies, and Director Chen would do anything for Gao Hong after a bottle of liquor.

Gao Hong had perfect self-control and discipline in everything but drinking and smoking. Daffodil became so angry that she smashed all of Gao Hong's bottles of liquor and burned all of his cigarettes, but Gao Hong still didn't stop, he just became more discrete. Daqing told Daffodil, "It's all right. Let him be. Every man in the factory is like that, so how can you expect him to be different? At least he rarely gets drunk, and when he is drunk he doesn't make trouble or beat you up. That's already better than most of the workers in these factories."

Sometimes on weekends, Gao Hong and Daffodil would go out to Xinjiekou to enjoy the district's historic snack stands and dumpling houses. They'd buy a delicious dinner from the hundred-year-old shops, or go to Chongwenmen for rice cakes. They ate the most mouthwatering snow-white rice cakes with layers of green and red dried fruit, topped with red bean paste and a dusting of powdered sugar. Those rice cakes made them feel full and warm throughout the night and into the next morning. One Saturday evening, they finished their rice cakes and then walked hand-in-hand to Zhushikou's Beijing Opera House to enjoy a performance. Gao Hong said, "We can afford these luxuries now that we don't have kids, but once we have kids we won't be able to spend money like this." Daffodil said, "Don't worry! Spend away!"

As they stood in line at the entrance of the opera house, Gao Hong suddenly felt as if someone was looking at him from the dark side street. He turned and he saw nobody, but when he turned back to Daffodil, he again felt that someone was looking at him. The person seemed to disappear as soon as he raised his eyes. Gao Hong lowered his head to pretend to look down, but scanned the side street with his peripheral vision. He saw someone in a heavy coat and large hat, but couldn't tell whether it was a man or a woman. When he turned to look, the person retreated into the darkness. Reluctant to alarm Daffodil, Gao Hong accompanied her into the opera house and walked her to their seats: "Why don't you sit down first. I need to go to the washroom." Daffodil said, "Hurry up, it's about to start!"

Gao Hong quickly walked out of the opera house and to the entrance of the side street. It was much quieter now, since everyone had entered the opera house, and he heard a hushed female voice calling him: "HongGe, HongGe!" The hair on the back of his neck stood up, and he felt chills go down his spine. He hadn't been called HongGe by anyone since Nanny Wu's death. Whoever called him that had to be from the Gao Compound where he was born.

Glancing around nervously, Gao Hong motioned for the woman to follow him. He entered a tea shop across from the opera house and bought two cups of tea, sitting in a quiet corner. Soon after that, the woman entered the tea shop and sat opposite Gao Hong with her back to the entrance. With her hat pulled down and her head lowered, Gao Hong couldn't see her face, but only a thin woman's chin. "Who are you?" Gao Hong asked.

The woman pushed her hat back and raised her head: "You mustn't recognize me after all these years, and I wouldn't recognize you if not for the photo you sent us. I'm your cousin, Gao Lan."

She pulled from her chest pocket a letter and a picture, and Gao Hong's jaw dropped. It was the letter he'd written years ago to Second Aunt and Cousin Lan, with the picture of himself in front of his factory gate glued to the letter. Gao Hong stared at the woman. She had large shiny eyes, fair skin, a tall and slender figure, a round face and a pointed chin, the typical features of the Gao family. Gao Hong could see Papa's sharpness and bravery in her eyes, and given that she possessed his letter and picture, there was no doubt that she was his only remaining blood relative, Cousin Lan.

"Cousin Lan!" Gao Hong's voice rose. Gao Lan put a finger to her lips to hush Gao Hong as she glanced around nervously. "What's wrong?" Gao Hong asked, "Are you all right? What brings you here? How's Second Aunt? How have you been all these years?" Gao Lan sighed and said, "My Mama died seven years ago. She suffered so much from her marriage to my stepdad, but finally she's gone. She is free. No more suffering! She endured too much. She told me about you and said you were my last blood relative and that I should come to you if I was in need."

Gao Hong asked, "How are you? Why are you in Beijing? What about your stepdad?" Gao Lan's eyes flickered with a cold sorrow: "I killed him."

"What?!" Gao Hong almost fell out of his chair.

"That old bastard. He tortured my mother for so many years and then he went after me. He jumped on me when I was sleeping. He didn't know what Gao girls are made of! I reached into my sewing box and grabbed my scissors and stabbed him in the back, and the old bastard died on top of me."

Gao Lan looked at the horror-struck Gao Hong and continued: "The police came for me and I ran into the snowy mountains. I almost died. I almost starved to death. But thank God I ran into Tiger. I went into the mountains with him."

"Tiger? Tiger Li?" Gao Hong asked.

"That's right, Tiger Li. Do you remember him? He's Li Ginseng's youngest son. He said he used to play with you when you were little and lived in the mountains," Gao Lan said.

"Of course I remember him! What about Papa Li Ginseng? How is he?" Gao Hong would never forget how Papa Li Ginseng had saved him and Nanny Wu while they lived with him in the mountains for a year. Li Ginseng had even wanted to adopt Gao Hong, and his youngest son Tiger was Gao Hong's playmate.

"Papa Li Ginseng has passed away too," Gao Lan said sadly. "Tiger and I gathered a group of brothers, and we occupied the mountain for years. We were heavily armed and nobody could touch us. Those were the good times! Now they've got Tiger! They've sentenced him to twenty years in prison for banditry! That's why I'm here to see you."

Gao Hong felt like his head was going to explode, and he was at a complete loss. "What are you going to do? How can I help you?"

Gao Lan said, "I need money! I've gathered up our mountain brothers, and we're going to break Tiger out of prison! We've already bribed a guard."

"You what?! That's punishable by death!" Gao Hong hissed.

Gao Lan gave a chilling sneer: "Death? Haven't there been enough deaths in our family already? You think they will let us live if we don't fight? Tiger will die if he stays in prison. Those sub-humans will make sure of it. They won't let him out alive! I have my stepdad's blood on my hands, and if they catch me, it's a death sentence for sure! I'm not afraid to die. What I can't bear is dying without a fight. I wouldn't be a descendant of the Gaos if I died like a coward, and Tiger wouldn't be a son of Papa Li Ginseng if he died without a fight!"

Gao Lan continued in a softer voice, "HongGe, I'm pregnant with Tiger's child. I'm his woman, dead or alive. Please give me all the money you have, and I'll get Tiger out. We'll be forever indebted to you, and Papa Li Ginseng will also bless you from up above!"

Gao Hong didn't hesitate. He rushed Gao Lan to the little room he shared with Daffodil and took out his savings from his five years of work, Daffodil's savings from her ten years of work and all the money that Nanny Wu had left him. There was 380 yuan in total, and he gave all of it to Gao Lan.

Gao Lan said, "I'm so sorry, HongGe. I wouldn't have come to you like this if it wasn't a life or death situation, and if I had anywhere else to turn. Your wife will be upset when she finds out. I'm so sorry. But I have to ask you not to tell her about the prison break. The danger is too great. It's safer if one less person knows, so I'd rather she doesn't know. I owe you an enormous debt, and I will repay you, whether in this life or the next."

Gao Lan then pulled a jade pendant from inside of her collar: "HongGe, look! Do you remember this? It's our Gao family heirloom, the jade Crimson Eyed Buddha! First Uncle slid it into First Aunt's pocket as he was taken away. She guarded it with her life for years and then gave it to my mother before she passed away. My mother gave it to me. Look, it's such a pure and translucent piece of jade, as flawless and clear as water except for the two bright crimson dots in the buddha's eyes. Do you remember it?"

Of course Gao Hong remembered the Crimson Eyed Buddha. He'd been taught about it ever since he was a baby, by his parents and by Nanny Wu, but this was the first time he'd actually seen it. It was an absolute miracle that this treasure was still in the hands of the Gao family. He held it in his palm, feeling the warmth and the smoothness of the jade. Gao Hong said, "Cousin Lan, please take it with you. You can sell it to save your life."

"I'd rather die than selling our jade Crimson Eyed Buddha!" Gao Lan said, "HongGe, you're the only man left of our family, so I should give this to you. But I still need it for now. If I ever need to send someone for you, I'll use the Crimson Eyed Buddha as a token. There's only one of them in this world, so when you see it, you'll know it's from me. Remember, if anyone comes to you in the name of me or Tiger, don't trust them unless you see the Crimson Eyed Buddha! Don't admit to anyone that you know us unless you see this token!" Gao Hong put his hands on Gao Lan's shoulders and nodded solemnly, and then Gao Lan turned and disappeared into the darkness.

Returning to the opera house, Gao Hong sat down next to Daffodil. Daffodil said, "It's almost over! Where have you been?" Gao Hong said, "I had an upset stomach."

(48) THE MONEY INCIDENT

Gao Hong stared blankly at the opera stage, worrying how on earth he was going to tell Daffodil that he'd given away the money they'd saved from a decade of back-breaking work. And he couldn't even tell her the reason! What was he going to do? Should he tell her the truth, about Gao Lan and her prison break plans? No, he realized that Daffodil wasn't someone who could keep a secret. She would bring danger to Gao Lan for sure if she knew.

While they were riding the bus home, Daffodil found Gao Hong quiet and preoccupied, but he assured Daffodil that he was fine whenever she asked. Daffodil thought, "It looks like his stomach is really bothering him. He'll need a good rest tonight."

Gao Hong lay wide awake in the moonlight. They kept their money in a deep corner of their coat closet and normally didn't touch it, so Gao Hong guessed he should have a couple of days before Daffodil discovered that the money was gone. He had to find a good way to tell her before she found out. He couldn't help but think that none of this would be a problem if Yanruo was his wife. She would understand him, support him and share his hardship. But Daffodil? Gao Hong turned to look at his slumbering wife. She looked so much like Yanruo. Maybe he was underestimating Daffodil; after all, she was his wife, so maybe she would understand and support him just like Yanruo would. That flicker of hope excited him so much that he felt the urge to wake Daffodil up and just tell her everything. But something stopped him. He remembered how Daffodil had once advised him to take the initiative to "confess" to the factory's Communist Party committee about the bad influence of his evil landlord roots, and to express his wish to be accepted by the Party. Of course, Gao Hong hadn't done that, and Daffodil didn't insist, but recalling it now made Gao Hong reluctant to take the risk. After all, one word could mean the end of Lan and Tiger's lives.

How Gao Hong wished there was a person who could understand him and be his ally in this tough situation! But who would that be? Suddenly, a figure appeared in his mind. That's right! His mother-in-law Lotus! Gao Hong had long noticed that although Lotus was an illiterate bound-foot old woman from the countryside, she was actually smart as a whip and full of wisdom. She was kind, understanding and open-minded, and had incredible emotional strength.

The next morning, Gao Hong set out on his bike as if he were going to work as normal, and Daffodil also went to work. But then Gao Hong called in sick and headed straight to Haidian District, where his in-laws lived. By the time Gao Hong arrived, his father-in-law had gone to work, and the younger girls had all gone to school, so Lotus was the only one home. She was surprised to see Gao Hong: "Why are you here? Is something wrong?"

Gao Hong said, "Mother, everything is fine and nothing is wrong, but I need to talk to you about something." Lotus led him into the house and poured him some tea, wondering if Daffodil and Gao Hong were fighting. But then it would be Daffodil coming to see her, not Gao Hong. Lotus was truly puzzled and concerned.

Gao Hong sat next to Lotus: "Mother, you know my own mother died when I was very small, and now thank God I have you. I respect and love you like my birth mother. I have a problem, a life-or-death situation, that I need to tell you about. Please give me your advice." Lotus gripped Gao Hong's hand: "Of course, my dear boy! Does Daffodil know?" Gao Hong said, "I haven't told her yet. I'm afraid that she won't be able to keep it a secret, and if this gets out, lives will be lost and I may also be in danger!"

Lotus said urgently, "Then tell me! I won't even mention it to your father-in-law. I would never say anything to harm my own son-in-law. Daffodil would never say anything to harm you either, but she's a straightforward person who can't keep a secret even if she wants to. It's good that you didn't tell her."

Gao Hong told Lotus everything, from the days of land reform, to the only other survivor in his family, Cousin Lan; from Gao Lan killing her stepfather in self-defense to her coming to Beijing; from Papa Li Ginseng to Tiger and Gao Lan's baby. The only thing he left out was the prison break. He told Lotus that Gao Lan needed money to buy another identity so she could have her baby in peace and wait for her husband Tiger to be released from prison.

"Mother, I'm so sorry that I gave all of our savings to my cousin, including Daffodil's life savings from her ten years of hard work. I haven't had the courage to tell Daffodil yet. I'm here to tell you first and ask for your advice. I promise I'll work extra hard from now on so that Daffodil never suffers any hardship!"

Lotus quietly heard Gao Hong out and then asked, "Is that it? Is there anything else?" Gao Hong replied, "That's all."

Lotus chuckled, "That's nothing! It's just a little bit of money. You have only this one cousin left and she's in need. Of course it was right for you to give her the money. I wouldn't want you as my son-in-law if you hadn't!" Gao Hong was so overcome with gratitude that he felt tears rushing to his eyes.

Lotus thought for a minute and then said, "Daffodil is an honest and simple girl. She loves you and would never say anything to harm you, but she's never kept a secret in her life. She's like a straight pipe: What goes in comes out. She's kind and thinks that everyone else is as kind as her. She never suspects anyone. I'm worried she might spill your secret without meaning to, so please don't tell her too much."

Gao Hong nodded in agreement. Lotus continued, "Just tell her that your cousin came to you, pregnant and desolate, so you helped her out. Leave out the parts about killing her stepdad and the husband in prison. Don't tell anyone; no one else should know! Otherwise you might be considered an accomplice in hiding a fugitive, and then God knows what would happen to you! I'll go home with you today, and if Daffodil makes a scene, I can help you console her."

It was soon noon time, and the younger sisters came home from school for their lunch break. Lotus gave them their lunch and sent them back to school, and then she cooked dinner and sealed it in some containers. Gao Hong wrote a note for his father-in-law to let him know that Lotus was going to Daffodil's house and would not be back for dinner. Lotus put on her scarf and jacket, and after locking the door behind them, she said, "Let's go."

With great care, Gao Hong carried his mother-in-law Lotus on the back seat of his bike while weaving through the rush hour traffic from

Haidian District to Chongwen District and then to Four Corners. By the time they arrived, it was already dinner time. As they got off the bike and walked into Four Corners, they heard loud noises in Row One, where Gao Hong and Daffodil lived.

Neighbors and coworkers were gathered in front of Gao Hong and Daffodil's little room, and Daffodil was yelling at the factory's Security Director: "I don't care if the lock is intact! You're in charge of security, so you have to solve this case! There must be a thief, otherwise where did my money go? There must be a counterrevolutionary criminal trying to harm the working class! This is something of great political importance. You can't just stand there and watch it happen!" The Security Director said, "All I'm asking is whether it's possible that your money has been misplaced and that your husband knows where it might be. I'm not saying the security department won't help you, but there's really no sign of a break-in." Daffodil's voice rose to new heights: "Are you saying I don't know where I put my own money?! What's the Security Department good for? Don't you have a direct line to the city police? I'll call the police directly if you keep asking me these ridiculous questions! I don't care if there's no sign of a break-in. You're just using that as an excuse for your negligence. You're refusing to serve the working class!" Daffodil's harsh words were like knives and could cause political problems for the security director.

Gao Hong and Lotus hurried over. Gao Hong was dizzy with panic and desperation. This was totally out of control! Even if he wanted to tell Daffodil everything, he couldn't do it in front of the neighbors and the security director! That would destroy Gao Lan, Tiger and himself all at once! Through his panic, he heard his mother-in-law Lotus's voice: "What's all this fuss?" she demanded loudly.

Daffodil turned and saw her mother: "Mama! What are you doing here?" Her eyes darted between Gao Hong and Lotus. Lotus said to the security director, "Sir, I'm so sorry. My daughter is being disrespectful and out of line. Please accept my apology!"

The security director was significantly younger than Lotus, whose age accorded her considerable respect. Accepting the apology of an elder was socially unacceptable at that time in China, and having Lotus apologize to him in front of the crowd was something he had to handle very carefully, for the sake of his public image. The security

234

director said, "Madam, there is no need to apologize at all. It's completely all right, and I understand. I'm trying my best to serve the working class." Lotus said, "And you're doing a fine job. We are grateful!"

Lotus then turned to the wide-eyed Daffodil: "You're not a teenager anymore. When will you stop being so impulsive? You shouldn't have alerted the security office before asking among your own family first! You are making a scene because the money is gone? It's because of me. I asked your dad to call Gao Hong at his workplace this morning and asked him to bring the money to me. We just got back and were about to tell you about it. You've been yelling at the poor security director for nothing, and making a scene in front of all of the neighbors!"

Grown sons and daughters were expected to support their elderly parents financially; it was considered a duty and a virtue. So Lotus's statement that Gao Hong had brought money to her was entirely believable and also a pleasing explanation for the whole situation.

The crowd breathed a collective sigh of relief: "What a good son-in-law! He's so kind and supportive of the elderly. There is no thief, so let's all go home." As the neighbors left, Lotus shook hands with the security director and respectfully sent him on his way.

Gao Hong looked at Lotus with admiration and gratitude. Although just an illiterate old woman from the countryside, her wisdom, calmness and problem-solving skills were astonishing! She had resolved Gao Hong's crisis. He couldn't imagine what he would have said to Daffodil and the security director if he hadn't brought Lotus home with him. He'd have been doomed whether he told Daffodil about Gao Lan or not.

Daffodil went inside with her mother, and Gao Hong followed them. "Mama hasn't had dinner yet," he said. "I'll go get some food from the dining hall." He grabbed three lunch boxes and ran out.

Daffodil asked, "Mama? What's going on? Is something wrong at home? Why would you ask Gao Hong to bring you so much money?"

Lotus sat down next to Daffodil: "My dear daughter, calm yourself. Remember, what happens in our family stays in our family. Always consult Gao Hong before talking with anyone outside of the family.

Never alert the security department. That's asking for trouble! You shouldn't let anyone know what goes on in our family!"

Daffodil was impatient: "What's wrong? Is someone sick and in need of money?"

Lotus said, "There's nothing wrong and no one is sick. It's just that a relative of Gao Hong's from his hometown is pregnant and in need, so Gao Hong helped her. Don't be mad at him. He did it with my approval!" Daffodil was completely baffled: "What on earth is going on? What does his hometown have to do with anything? Didn't he say he had no family and no relatives?"

Gao Hong arrived back just then: "Mother, Daffodil, let's eat. The dining hall is serving meat tonight."

Plagued with a hundred questions, Daffodil yelled, "Gao Hong!" But Lotus stopped her: "Let's eat first. Everything can be settled after dinner." With that she started eating. Lotus asked Gao Hong, "Are you two comfortable here? The pipes on your coal burner are very well built. Did you do that yourself?" Gao Hong said, "Yes, Mother, I did that. It's actually working pretty well." Lotus smiled: "What a smart son-in-law!"

Lotus talked and laughed over dinner as if nothing had happened. Apart from the coal burner pipes, she talked about the color of the curtains, and the type of wood used for the furniture. She talked about everything but what Daffodil was dying to find out. Daffodil had a hundred questions for Gao Hong, but her mother's small talk completely derailed and deflated her.

After dinner, Lotus said, "Gao Hong, now is your chance to tell Daffodil what happened. I'm here to help you two. I know my own daughter. Daffodil has a mouth as sharp as a knife, but a heart as soft as tofu. She's very reasonable."

Gao Hong said, "I know that, Mother. Daffodil is very good to me, and everyone says I've married a rare treasure." Daffodil said, "Stop buttering me up! Out with it!"

"Umm, I, uh, it's like this," Gao Hong started. "I don't have any relatives left, except one cousin, and she came to Beijing yesterday. She's pregnant and alone, so I took pity on her and gave her our money. But I'll earn it back! I'll work overtime to earn it all back!"

"Your cousin was here? When? How come I didn't see her?"

236

"She came last night when we went to the opera. I ran into her when I went to the washroom," Gao Hong said.

"So you took her home and she took the money and left?" Daffodil asked.

Gao Hong mumbled, "Something like that."

Daffodil was beside herself: "What kind of nonsense is this? Don't you know how to do anything at all? It doesn't matter how much money you give her, you just can't do that behind my back! Your cousin will think I'm a miser! Whenever we give your family money, it has to be from me, just like if I want to give money to my family, I would always have you do it. That's the sensible and polite way to do things. Don't you know anything? You're ruining my reputation by giving your family money behind my back! You need to let me do it, don't you understand?"

Gao Hong had never thought of it that way, but now he realized that Daffodil was right. But what could he have done, given Cousin Lan's situation?

"Besides," Daffodil continued, "Your cousin just took the money and left without a word, not even one word to me, her cousin-in-law. What kind of rudeness and nonsense is that?"

"My cousin said she was very grateful to you. She wants to repay us a hundred times over." Gao Hong said.

Daffodil stopped him: "I don't want her repayment! I want basic courtesy. She should at least have met me and greeted me. Disappearing without a word and without showing her face – what kind of a person is this? What kind of a family would raise such a disrespectful and senseless girl?" Gao Hong didn't know what to say.

"And you!" Daffodil poked Gao Hong on the forehead with her sharp-nailed pointer finger, "Why didn't you tell me when you came back to the opera house? Upset stomach? You just lied without even blinking! And then why didn't you tell me this morning? You have a nerve bringing my mother here! It looks like I've underestimated you. You are really something else!"

As Daffodil's voice became sharper and louder, Lotus interrupted: "That's quite enough. I wanted to come visit you. I haven't been here since your wedding." Then Lotus turned to Gao Hong: "What Daffodil said has some truth to it. No one in Daffodil's situation would be very happy about it, wouldn't you agree? Just let her talk it out. Women are like this. Once she lets everything out, what's left in her heart is her love for you. Please try to understand and don't be upset."

Lotus said to Daffodil, "I know you're upset, but he's the man of the house. He's your husband. You cannot speak so harshly to him. I think he put off telling you because he really cares about you and didn't want to upset you. He must have spent a sleepless night trying to think of a good way to tell you. He came to me for the sake of your marriage. If he had told you earlier and you had exploded at him with no one here to put out the fire, you would have both ended up getting hurt. Waiting until now to tell you is what I call a real man's sound decision. If he were like you, never able to hold in anything, what kind of marriage would you have? If you ask me, Gao Hong has done nothing wrong, so enough of your foolish temper!"

Lotus then took fifty yuan from her pocket: "Your father got a raise, and I want to share some of the money with each of my children. Here, you two take this." Gao Hong wanted to kowtow before his mother-in-law. He knew his father-in-law only made about seventy yuan a month, and that was the family's only source of income. There was no way he had gotten a raise, certainly not as much as fifty yuan. This money must have been Lotus and Yixin's savings for the entire year. He said with grateful tears, "Mother, I'm so sorry to cause you all this worry. I cannot take this money. I know you need it. I should be taking care of you and Father, but all I've ever done is cause you worry. I'm so ashamed that I can hardly face you."

Upon hearing Gao Hong say this to her mother, Daffodil's anger subsided. She said to Lotus, "Mama, please take this money back. My younger sisters need new clothes and nutritious food. Gao Hong and I have enough from our salaries. Ma, you know me, I'm not upset because he gave all of our money to his cousin, I'm upset because he did it behind my back. It's a blot on my reputation, and his cousin didn't even have the decency to pay me respect as her cousin-in-law." Tears streamed down Daffodil's face.

Lotus gave Gao Hong an encouraging nod, prompting him to console Daffodil. Then she stood up and said, "It's getting late and I should be on my way. You two need to go to work in the morning, so get a good night's sleep."

Gao Hong wanted to take Lotus home, but Lotus insisted, "I know the way! It's bus 23 and then bus 103, which drops me off right in front of the DCA." With that, she walked out and closed the door behind her.

Gao Hong held Daffodil in his arms and sweet-talked her as much as he could. Daffodil cried for a long time before quieting down. She said, "If Mother hadn't been here, I'd have gone to Aici and Zhao Shifu and told them everything and had them scold you! I've never felt so badly treated in my life!"

While saying his consoling words, Gao Hong thought sadly to himself, "I was right not to tell her everything. She's not someone who can keep things inside the family. She needs to vent and she needs emotional support, even if that means involving outsiders." Gao Hong was sorry to conceal something from his wife, but what made him even sadder was that he would have to continue to do so, not only this time, but if anything risky arose in the future. How he wished Daffodil was someone he could trust, rely on and confide in!

After the Cousin Lan incident, a distance grew between Gao Hong and Daffodil. It wasn't about money. Daffodil felt that Gao Hong wasn't with her and that his heart was somewhere else. No matter how nicely he treated her, she felt that Gao Hong was keeping another space in his life, outside of their marriage and shared life. She felt that although Gao Hong rarely went into this space, whenever he was there, he was no longer her husband and she had no influence over him. And she would never be able to get into this space, because Gao Hong wanted to keep her out.

(49) NEW PARENTS

Spring turned into summer. As the temperature rose, Daffodil found herself losing her appetite, and all she wanted to do after work was to lie down. Gao Hong was very worried, not only because he didn't want Daffodil to be sick, but because he had been trained by Daffodil to feel that he could only relax when Daffodil was happy and relaxed. Daffodil was a loud and dramatic woman. Often she sounded like she was losing her temper, but in fact all she wanted was Gao Hong's attention and affection. Growing up in a big family where her father was a workaholic and her mother was busy raising too many kids, the only way she could get attention was by loudly exaggerating her discomfort or unhappiness. That's how she had dealt with things growing up, and now it was how she dealt with Gao Hong.

Gao Hong, on the other hand, had grown up at the mercy of others, and any loud or abrasive conversations made his insides churn. In particular, anyone talking loudly at home made him feel anxious; his biggest wish was for everyone at home to be peaceful and not upset. His childhood experience had taught him that whenever there was any loud talking at home, he'd be the first to be punished, regardless of whether it had anything to do with him or not. Over the years, it had become his habit and survival instinct to console any agitated person at home at any cost, and if there was no way to calm that person, he'd run out as fast as a mouse seeing a cat.

"What's this!" Daffodil's loud, high-pitched voice made Gao Hong jump out of his skin: "It's already the end of June, and the cherries are still so small? Cherries are usually big and plump in June!"

He quickly said, "Small cherries actually taste better. The bigger ones may not be as tasty."

"I don't like small cherries! I feel like I spend all my time spitting out the seeds without getting much to eat," Daffodil pouted.

"I'll buy you some big ones tomorrow."

"But what about these little ones?" Daffodil's voice got sharper.

"I'll eat them." Gao Hong quickly took the container.

"Then what about me? You know my appetite hasn't been good. Don't you care about me?" Daffodil yelled.

In fact, she didn't want any cherries, she just wanted Gao Hong to hug her and sooth her. But Gao Hong was physically and mentally exhausted from his day's work, and all he wanted was some peace. He said, "I'll go right now and buy some big cherries." Then he got on his bike and rode away.

Gao Hong heading out was in fact the last thing Daffodil wanted. She needed his company and his affection, and didn't want him going out again after a long day of hard work. It would be a waste of money too! She was so mad at Gao Hong's failure to understand her that she refused to eat the bigger cherries he brought home. Tired and defeated, Gao Hong sat silently on the edge of the bed.

Daffodil couldn't bear his stupidity and couldn't understand why he didn't know what she wanted. She began complaining about a back ache, about being tired, about the weather being too hot, about the smell of the room giving her a headache.... Finally Gao Hong couldn't take it anymore: "What the hell do you want?"

Daffodil burst out crying: "What do you think I want? You don't care about me!" Gao Hong felt as if his head was going to explode.

They'd fight like this every few days. Gao Hong tried his best to make her happy, but he also needed a peaceful home where he could relax after long days of back-breaking work. Once when Daffodil started complaining of discomfort again, Gao Hong said, "I'm not a doctor. You should go to the infirmary."

Marching out of the house, Daffodil said through clenched teeth, "You're so mean. I hope they find I have a terminal illness so you'll regret being so cold-blooded!" Gao Hong shook his head and sighed.

Gao Hong was finally dozing off when he heard a knock on the window: "Gao Hong, Dr. Cheng from the infirmary sent me to get you. Your wife is pregnant." Gao Hong shot upright: "What? What did you say?" The girl from the infirmary said, "Your wife, Daffodil, is pregnant!"

Gao Hong jumped out of bed and began dashing out the door, but the girl laughed, "You don't have any shoes on!" Gao Hong quickly put on some shoes and started running again.

When Gao Hong reached the infirmary, Daffodil turned away from him and wouldn't take with him. Gao Hong begged and apologized. Dr. Cheng laughed, "Daffodil, that's quite enough! You told me he didn't care about you, but it looks like he treats you like a Buddha. I bet there isn't any other man in this factory who treats his wife so well. You're about to be a mother. You should stop being so childish." Dr. Cheng was pregnant herself. She answered their questions, gave them a bottle of prenatal vitamins and sent them on their way.

On the way home, Gao Hong treated Daffodil like a delicate piece of porcelain, and Daffodil finally smiled with contentment.

Ever since losing Nanny Wu, Gao Hong felt he had no more connection to the world, floating in the air like a kite without a string. Nothing tied him down, not even his marriage to Daffodil. But the new life they were bringing into being was his flesh, his descendant and the bloodline of the Gao family. No hardship could overshadow the joy of this new life. As long as their generations continued, there would always be hope.

Daffodil asked, "Do you want a boy or a girl? I know you're the only male descendant of the Gao family. Do you want a boy to carry on your family name?" Gao Hong said, "Oh, those are old customs. It's a new world now. Boys and girls are equal, and I'd be happy with either one." Daffodil smiled: "That's more like it. I can't stand those male chauvinists!" Gao Hong said, "I'd actually prefer a daughter. Mr. Guan from my factory is always showing off his two beautiful daughters at work. Ahh... how wonderful would it be to have a couple of beautiful girls following me around when I'm old!" "How do you know your girls would be beautiful?" Daffodil teased. Gao Hong replied, "Because daughters of men with heavy beards are always beautiful. Look at this face full of stubble – my daughter would be the most beautiful of all!"

Daffodil's talent for sewing and embroidery now came in handy as she made cute little onesies, hats, booties and bibs, each prettier than the next, drawing the awe and envy of her neighbors and coworkers. Lotus joined Daffodil in her sewing as well. She said, "Remember to

242

use old fabric and make sure it's already broken in. New fabric should never be used for a newborn."

Daffodil's belly grew gigantic, with stretch marks extending across the lower part of her belly. Finally her due date arrived. At a time with limited medical technology and little anesthesia available, Daffodil exhausted herself through twenty-nine hours of excruciating labor before giving birth to a chubby little girl. As soon as her daughter was born, Daffodil felt the last ounce of strength drain from her, and she fell asleep.

The night they brought their new daughter home, Daffodil and Gao Hong held the baby as if she were a delicate treasure. Her cute little fingers and toes were like little peanuts, and Daffodil and Gao Hong couldn't stop counting them again and again. They felt blessed that the baby was so quiet and was sleeping like an angel, but then all of a sudden she started to cry. Daffodil and Gao Hong didn't know what to do. They held her, walked around, patted her, rocked her and checked her diaper, but she kept on crying.

After long and frantic desperation, Daffodil and Gao Hong suddenly realized: The baby must be hungry! There was no such thing as classes for new parents at that time. They were really left on their own and had no idea that a baby needed to eat every two to three hours. It was already late at night, the stores were closed and they had no formula. Daffodil unbuttoned her shirt and pressed her nipple to the baby's mouth. The baby latched on and suckled hard. "My poor girl!" Daffodil said. "She's so hungry!" Unfortunately, Daffodil had no milk. The baby got nothing from all that suckling and began crying again.

On that winter night, Gao Hong pedaled his bike as fast as he could, knocking on the doors of one store after another. Finally, an elderly man who lived above his convenience store got out of bed and stuck his head out of the window. Upon hearing Gao Hong was in urgent need of food for a newborn, the elderly man opened his store and sold him some formula. Dashing back home, Gao Hong found Daffodil holding the baby tight and looking nearly mad with desperation.

They didn't have running water in their unit, and the water from the shared faucet in the courtyard wasn't safe to drink unless boiled. Gao Hong boiled some water, prepared a bottle of formula and then dipped the boiling hot bottle in a basin of cold water to cool it before giving it to the baby. The baby fastened her wide eyes on the bottle in her daddy's hands, as if knowing she had to wait. Gao Hong shook the bottle and dipped it into cold water, then he took it out, shook it again and dipped it into cold water again. After watching this repeated several times without getting any milk, the baby began screaming as if she were being murdered, and Gao Hong and Daffodil felt like they were having heart attacks. Finally, the bottle was at the right temperature, and they stuck the nipple into the baby's mouth. The baby chugged the milk down so fast that she choked a little on it. Daffodil and Gao Hong both had tears in their eyes: "This poor girl, born to such bad parents who let her go hungry for so long..." After a whole bottle of formula, the baby finally fell asleep. Gao Hong and Daffodil looked at each other and agreed, "We need to buy more formula."

The feeding problem was immediately followed by pooping. Daffodil had made diapers for the baby from pieces of old, worn-out blankets. But the baby seemed to have a straight pipe from her mouth to her bottom, and pooped as soon as she ate. Often she would poop as soon as she was changed. Each change of diapers required Gao Hong to mix cold water with boiled water in a basin, after which he would hold the baby over the basin of lukewarm water while Daffodil washed and cleaned the baby's bottom and applied baby powder. Then they would lay the baby on the bed to put on a new diaper, but sometimes she would poop again before they finished, and the whole process had to start over again.

With no running water or drain in their unit, Gao Hong had to run back and forth between their unit and the public faucet in an endless cycle of fetching water, bringing it home and boiling it, dumping the mess into the sewage drain, going back home to gather the soiled diapers and then take them to the faucet to wash them, and then going home to hang the diapers out to dry. Oftentimes, Gao Hong and Daffodil realized after the baby had gone to sleep that neither of them had eaten a meal all day.

(50) MAO'S BOOK

Daqing's three daughters had all been named by their grandmother Lotus. All three of the girls' names contained the character Xia, meaning colorful cloud. Lotus naturally believed that naming Daffodil's daughter would also be her job, and she'd thought of the names Hongxia, Junxia, Caixia, Meixia, Jinxia ..... Gao Hong burst out laughing when he heard the names, and Daffodil said, "Oh my goodness, Ma! Can you please stay out of it? Those sound like names for country girls!" Lotus was baffled: Xia is beautiful, why not Xia?

Gao Hong wanted to name his daughter Muyu (immersed in misty rain), since she'd been born on a misty winter's night, but Lotus didn't care for that name. She insisted that the baby should be named Jasmine, as she was pure and fragrant as a jasmine flower.

Jasmine was a charming baby with shiny eyes and a beautiful little round face. Her little nose and mouth were delicate and perfect. When Jasmine was five months old, a woman on the bus suddenly said, "Oh look! This baby has such long earlobes! I've never seen a baby like that!" Daffodil was astonished, having seen nothing but beauty and perfection in her daughter. Now she notices that Jasmine's earlobes were in fact as long as the Buddha's! They didn't look like a baby's earlobes at all and were completely out of proportion to her head and face. Daffodil was devastated. She thought to herself: Jasmine should grow her hair long to always cover up her ears. She became so worried that she could hardly sleep for several nights. But Grandma Lotus wasn't worried at all. In fact, she was gleeful: "Silly girl! Haven't you heard the story of the Buddha? Having long earlobes is a sign of good fortune and a long life. With her Buddha earlobes, Jasmine will be the most successful and prosperous member of our entire family!"

Daffodil's six months of maternity leave soon came to an end and she had to return to work. Finding a caretaker for Jasmine became the paramount priority for Daffodil and Gao Hong. The daycare center at the factory where Daffodil worked only accepted children aged two and older. The age restriction was lifted only for the employees of the daycare center. Daffodil would not qualify to send her daughter in at this early age as she didn't work there.

Normally female employees would hire someone from the Wife Union to take care of their baby until they turned two years old. But Daffodil despised the women from the Wife Union. They had decided that Daffodil was a slut, and that meant she always would be in their eyes, even though she no longer had anything to do with her old boyfriend, He Guanglin. Besides that, Daffodil couldn't bear their cursing and their vulgar behavior such as spitting on their fingers to wipe scraps of food off of their babies' faces.

Grandma Lotus wanted Daffodil to send Jasmine to her: "I'll look after her for you during the week, and you can come visit her on Sundays." Daffodil didn't want to be separated from her daughter, although it was commonplace back then for children to be raised by their grandparents so both parents could work full time.

The thousand-year tradition of men being the bread-winners and women being the caretakers for children and households was abolished overnight by the Communists. Mao's directive that "women hold up half of the sky" sent the vast majority of women into the workforce all across China. The media portrayed homemakers as lazy, poor, plain-looking, dull, uneducated, lower-class and unable to contribute to society. Some movies even showed sympathy and understanding to men who left their homemaker wives for "professional women." Homemakers were provided with no health care coverage, housing benefits or pensions from the government. They were solely dependent on their husbands, and in the case of divorce, a homemaker would be left desolate, without a livelihood or a place to live.

Under the circumstances, it was unthinkable for Daffodil to quit her job and care for Jasmine, which would degrade her into the socially disadvantaged Wife Union that she despised. She had to find child care for Jasmine no matter what. Finally, Daffodil found a nice older woman two blocks away and sent Jasmine to her while she was working. That way she could see her daughter and look after her every day after work. But Jasmine became sick every time she was sent to the granny's house, returning with a fever every two or three days. Gao Hong and Daffodil had to take turns requesting leave from work. They tried sending Jasmine to a few other babysitters, but she came back sick just as often.

Taking time off was no easy matter back then. During the Cultural Revolution, every workplace was like a jungle. Everyone was on high alert for possible danger or potential accusations, often brought by people in their trusted personal circles. It was common for people to expose or inform on someone they suspected might bring danger to them. Everyone tried to lie low and not draw attention to themselves.

For Gao Hong, his landlord background was like a bomb that could go off at any time, no matter how hard he worked. Taking time off under such circumstances was equivalent to seeking a quick death. But if Gao Hong went to work, Daffodil had to stay home to take care of Jasmine when she was sick, and that meant that Daffodil's coworker Big Ling had to cover for Daffodil.

Big Ling complained loudly: "Is that daughter of yours made of gold? Look how often you've missed work! Thank God it's not a son, or you'd quit your job and join the Wife Union." She pointed to a stack of boxes full of auto parts that had just been delivered to the warehouse: "Put these on the shelves!" Daffodil spent the whole day carrying heavy boxes.

The exhausted and frustrated Daffodil came home only to be met by a distressed-looking Gao Hong and a screaming Jasmine. Gao Hong had tried everything to console Jasmine and to bring her fever down, to no avail. He was exhausted and hungry, as he'd had no time to eat. As soon as he saw Daffodil walk through the door, he said eagerly, "Thank God you're home! Jasmine's fever is still pretty high. I think we should take her to the hospital. Can you take tomorrow off from work? I have to go back to work tomorrow no matter what."

Daffodil felt overwhelmed by her worries about Jasmine and her anger at Gao Hong: "You've been home all day. Why didn't you take her to the hospital? What were you thinking! What kind of a father

are you? And you have the nerve to ask me to take another day off!
Do you have any idea what I go through every day at work?"

Gao Hong said, "I understand. But I have to lie low at my factory.
Zhao Shifu says I have to tuck my tail between my legs. I can't afford
to draw attention. Zhao Shifu and Xiaoma risked their lives to save
me last time. With my family background, taking too much time off
puts both myself and them in danger!"

Daffodil was beside herself: "How stupid I was to marry you! Your
low birth has doomed me for life!"

Gao Hong stood there dumbfounded as if struck by lightning. He'd
never thought Daffodil would say such a thing. Daffodil yelled, "What
are you standing there for? Off to the Emergency Room!"

Gao Hong was silent on the way to the hospital. Having grown up
in a foster-parent situation, he cared deeply about what other people
said to him or thought of him; any negative signal made him jump out
of his skin, and any harsh words hurt him deeply. His sadness knew
no bounds when he heard his own wife say that it had been a mistake
to marry him because of his tainted birth. For some reason, Yanruo's
name sprang to his mind, but he didn't want to think of Yanruo at a
moment like this, because the pain was too much to bear. He sighed
and held his daughter tight.

Daffodil was a woman with a lot of harsh words but not many bad
feelings. She would say anything that came to mind when she was
upset, but then quickly forget all about it. As they entered the hospital
lobby and she saw Gao Hong so silent and sad, she became upset again.
"Why are you showing me such a long face?" she screamed. "Aren't I
worried enough that our daughter is sick, without you giving me the
silent treatment and that despicable face? What did I ever do wrong?
Tell me!"

Gao Hong glanced at the people in the lobby with embarrassment:
"Please lower your voice. People are looking at us! I'm not making a
face at you, I'm just worried about Jasmine."

Daffodil's voice was as high-pitched as ever: "Who's looking at us?
Who do you think you are? Do you think anyone has the slightest
interest in looking at you and laughing at you?"

Gao Hong said, "Let's go to Registration."

At 11pm, they finally emerged from the Emergency Room with prescription meds and went home. After giving Jasmine the medicine and putting her to bed, Gao Hong and Daffodil collapsed next to their baby and fell asleep without having dinner.

At long last, the weekend arrived. Jasmine's fever had subsided and she was playful again. Gao Hong and Daffodil both gave a sigh of relief. They put Jasmine on the bed and fenced her off with pillows and rolled-up blankets, then went to the dining hall to get food. They were back in fifteen minutes. One look at little Jasmine made the color drain from their faces. Daffodil dropped her container of food on the table, and Gao Hong ran to the windows and drew the curtains. Jasmine had somehow gotten hold of a pen and a book of Mao's quotations. Holding the pen in her chubby little fist, she was waving her chubby arm and drawing dark, heavy lines over the portrait of Mao Zedong!

During the Cultural Revolution, Chairman Mao published many books, which were treated like holy writ. There were also portraits, statues, sculptures and printed images of Mao everywhere, and damaging a Mao portrait or a Mao book was considered a serious crime. In Daffodil's factory, someone had wrapped some shrimp in an old newspaper without noticing a portrait of Mao on the back page of that newspaper, and the dampness of the shrimp stained Mao's portrait. As a result, the man was labeled a counterrevolutionary and sentenced to life in prison. Another person had respectfully and worshipfully used a wet towel to clean a plaster Mao statue, only to have the water stain the plaster. That person was beaten to death by Red Guards. With a mutilated Mao book in their hands, Daffodil and Gao Hong felt as if a bomb was going to go off at any minute and blast them into oblivion. They both stood there frozen.

Finally Gao Hong said in a hushed voice: "What if we tear this page out?" But he knew that a Mao book with a missing page would put his family in just as much danger. Daffodil whispered, "Taking out one page is no good. We have to make the whole book disappear." Gao Hong stared at Daffodil: "H-how?" Daffodil pointed to the stove.

They looked at each other with wild, scared eyes. Burning a Mao book was a crime that could cost them both of their lives! Gao Hong was deeply touched that Daffodil trusted him enough to even suggest such a thing. In the Cultural Revolution, many husbands and wives turned on each other and reported their spouses' counter-revolutionary actions, even something muttered in their sleep. Daffodil was trusting Gao Hong with her life.

Gao Hong made up his mind. He was the man of the house, so if someone had to do it, it should be him. He said to Daffodil, "Jasmine hasn't gone out for days. Why don't you take her out for some fresh air? Watch the front door."

After a moment's hesitation, Daffodil picked up Jasmine and walked out the door, closing it tightly behind her. With shaky hands, Gao Hong tore out a few pages at a time and put them into the coal-burning stove little by little. He didn't want to put too many pages in at once for fear that the neighbors might notice heavy smoke coming out of his chimney and suspect that he was burning something. And God forbid that he put too much in and a page was not burnt completely; then he would be doomed! But he didn't dare put too little in, either, because if he took too long, neighbors might wonder why he had his curtains drawn in broad daylight, and might knock on his door to see what was going on. If that happened, he and Daffodil would both be dead!

Watching the flames engulfing the Mao book page by page, Gao Hong felt a sense of release. His family had all died under the regime, and he'd been forced to live like a cockroach. That powerful regime with its iron fist was now burning, curling up and disappearing! Gao Hong focused his gaze on the flames until the last bit of paper vanished.

He opened the back window a crack to let the smoke out little by little. Then he opened the front door slightly and pulled Daffodil and Jasmine inside. Daffodil anxiously stared into Gao Hong's eyes and he gave her a small nod. Then he turned to pull the curtains wide open so the neighbors would not be suspicious.

Still holding Jasmine, Daffodil collapsed into Gao Hong's arms. Gao Hong held the two of them for a long time. Then he said, "Let's send Jasmine to your mother."

(51) GRANDMA'S HOUSE

Growing up with Grandma Lotus was the happiest memory of Jasmine's life. She was now a cute little girl giggling and running around Yard 13, her childhood heaven. The sound of stir fry and the banging of pots and pans in the crowded kitchen, the loud neighbors, Grandma Lotus's fast words in her heavy Hebei dialect, the sound of Grandpa's bike as he came home from work, and the high-pitched quarreling between Aunt Hong and Aunt Rong all came together to form a symphony of warmth and safety for Jasmine.

And there was Cousin Feifei!

Feifei was Uncle Erqing's daughter. The math genius Uncle Erqing was now an assistant professor of mathematics at Beijing University. As he was fluent in French, he was often sent by the DOE's Foreign Aid Bureau to teach math in Africa. His wife was his college classmate and was now head of the math department at one of Beijing's most prestigious high schools. Between the DOE Africa projects, Beijing University and the demanding math department at a top high school, they had no time for their daughter Feifei, so they decided to send her to Grandma Lotus. She became Jasmine's best childhood companion.

Feifei was one year younger than Jasmine, and unlike Jasmine, who inherited her father Gao Hong's towering Northeasterner's height, Feifei inherited her mother's petite stature and was a full head shorter than Jasmine. Their height contrast was matched by the difference in their characters. Jasmine was easygoing and didn't care much about what she considered to be insignificant things, but Feifei was as sensitive as a sore thumb and always had to have her way. Every time Grandma cut an apple in half for the two of them, Feifei would quickly grab the bigger and prettier half before Jasmine even noticed them on the table. Grandma decided to teach Feifei a lesson. She cut an apple into two uneven halves, with one significantly bigger than the other half, and then had Hong and Rong hold Feifei down so

Jasmine could pick first. The problem was that Jasmine couldn't tell the difference between the two halves, and she randomly picked the smaller one! Feifei immediately grabbed the bigger one and ran away. Grandma Lotus said with disappointment, "Do you only focus on growing your height? You should grow some sense, too!" Jasmine couldn't understand why it mattered. It was just two apple halves, and she didn't care if Feifei got the bigger piece.

The contrast in character and the occasional squabbles didn't stop the two cousins from becoming best friends and playmates. Running wild in the vegetable garden behind Yard 13, they saw two little green bean seedlings on the border between Grandma's garden and the neighbor's garden, so they dug them up and planted them in Grandma's garden. They spent the whole summer giggling over their little secret whenever Grandma said the two "surprise seedlings" grew the strongest of all. Jasmine and Feifei picked wild flowers and long grass and asked the neighbor girls to weave flower crowns for them. They gathered catkins and made "bird nests" in hopes that a bird family would settle there. After each rainy day, Jasmine and Feifei dashed out to splash in the puddles. Snowy days were like magical adventures for them, and they would run around in the snow until it was pitch dark.

Grandma Lotus tucked them in tight on winter nights, and fanned the mosquitos away from them on summer nights. She would tell them folk stories from Hebei in her heavy Hebei dialect. Jasmine had an amazing acumen for languages and was able to imitate Grandma's Hebei dialect since she was very small.   She could also retell Grandma's tales exactly, even using the same intonation and facial expressions. Jasmine was happy and content living with Grandma and considered Yard 13 her home. To her, Gao Hong and Daffodil were simply visitors who came to see her every two or three weeks.

Every time Daffodil visited her daughter, she was hit with a wave of emotions. More than anything, she yearned to raise her daughter herself, but she knew it was impossible. Gao Hong's family background could blow up on both of them at any moment, and in the heat of the Cultural Revolution and the unbelievable cruelty and instability of their workplaces, they had no choice but to be available for work and political meetings around the clock. Tardiness, taking time off or leaving work earlier than others could be catastrophic. They not only had no time for their daughter; they didn't even have time for themselves. They ate at the factory canteens and never cooked at home. They got up at dawn to pay "morning respects" to Mao in the factory ceremonies every day, and then after a long day of work, they had to attend "evening respects" ceremonies as well. Every night they got home after 10 pm, exhausted to the point of hardly being able to speak to each other.

Sundays were their only days off, and only if they weren't needed at work. On those rare days off, they would finally have time to do laundry, clean the house and do some much-needed shopping. But the Red Guards were everywhere. These youngsters, claiming to be catalysts for social change, were allowed to take matters into their own hands. The Red Guards claimed they were soldiers of Chairman Mao and were revolutionaries cleansing society of anyone who posed a threat to communist ideals. Gao Hong and Daffodil tried to stay behind closed doors as much as possible, as it was commonplace for Red Guards to seize people on the streets, shave their heads and even beat them to death. Of course staying home was no guarantee of safety, either. Red Guards could burst into any home at any time to ransack it and take people away. Under such circumstances, there was no way they could raise Jasmine themselves.

Daffodil hadn't worried about Gao Hong's family background when she married him. In fact, she was happy that he came from a well-educated family with good manners and a nice up-bringing. But now she hated it, and she blamed Gao Hong for not being able to raise her daughter herself. If not for him, Daffodil would be fearlessly holding her head high as the daughter of an honored revolutionary official with peasant family origins. On top of that, Gao Hong no longer had the grace and manners that Daffodil had admired back then. He smoked, he drank, he went for days without shaving, and his clothes were ragged and dirty. He tried to be just like the other workers in the factory, using profane language, spitting on the ground, talking loudly and taking pride in being short-tempered. Daffodil thought to herself, "The only thing he doesn't do is beat his wife. If he did that, there really would be no difference between him and the rest of the workers! Except, of course, for his dark birth!" Daffodil became increasingly bitter over time, especially when she saw her daughter Jasmine.

Nudged by her Grandma, Jasmine reluctantly and carefully greeted her mother: "Mama." Feeling a flood of emotions raging through her, Daffodil was at a loss for words. She frowned and murmured: "Why does Jasmine looks like she's lost weight? Her cheeks aren't as rosy as before. She doesn't look healthy!" Daffodil said to her mother Lotus, "Mom, you should give her more fruit and vegetables. Don't always fill her up with rice and buns. Look at her face. She doesn't look as healthy as before!"

Daffodil was complaining only out of love for her daughter, but hearing her mom say these things to Grandma in that accusatory tone made Jasmine feel like she was sitting on needles. To Jasmine, Mama was a woman with a loud, shrill voice who was always criticizing her and blaming poor Grandma. She felt sad that Grandma was being scolded by Mama because of her. It was all her fault for not being healthy-looking and pretty enough to please Mama. But Jasmine didn't know what she had done wrong and what she could have done differently to avoid all this.

As he watched Jasmine growing taller and more distant from them week by week, Gao Hong was also very sad. He also felt sorry and grateful toward his mother-in-law Lotus for taking on the raising of his daughter at her advanced age. He told Daffodil, "Watch your tongue. Mom works so hard to raise Jasmine. Don't blame her for anything."

Daffodil jumped like a cat whose tail had been stepped on: "I'm impressed that you know this much! Whose fault do you think it is that Mom can't enjoy peace and quiet in her old age and has to raise your daughter for you. You have the nerve pretending to be a saint! Are you trying to hide the fact it's all your fault?" Gao Hong went silent immediately.

Jasmine looked at her mother, then her father, and then at her poor Grandma. Everyone had a long, sad face, and it was all because of her. Jasmine felt her hands and feet go cold as if dipped in an ice bucket. She thought to herself, "Mama, Dad, please leave. I don't want you to come see me next weekend either. Then the two of you won't have to fight, and poor Grandma won't get scolded because of me."

Every time the weekend approached, Jasmine would become so anxious that she lost her appetite. She asked repeatedly, "Will my parents be here this weekend?" Grandma Lotus said, "You poor girl! Do you miss your parents? I'll ask Grandpa to call your Mama." This scared Jasmine so much that she vowed never to ask again. If Grandpa said, "Daffodil called me at work, she won't be here this weekend," Jasmine would immediately bolt down a big bowl of food and run out to play. If Grandpa brought home a message on Saturday evening that Daffodil was coming to see Jasmine on Sunday, Jasmine would sit there, quiet and worried, for a long time. Grandma finally figured out what she was thinking and said sadly in her heavy Hebei accent, "My poor girl, deflated as soon as she hears her parents are coming!"

To Jasmine, a peaceful household was of the utmost importance. Her biggest wish was for the people around her to be happy and calm, with no conflicts. This came from her father Gao Hong, who would gladly take on extra work or material loss for the sake of peace. Any quarreling, bickering, fighting or any hint of conflict would threaten his sense of safety and cause him emotional pain.

Grandma Lotus and Baby Jasmine

(52) FALSE IMPRISONMENT

Gradually, Gao Hong and Daffodil accustomed themselves to life without their daughter at home. Many times, they discussed how and when they should bring their daughter home, but harsh reality deterred them every time. Raising a child was like cross-country running; if you ran every day, it became routine, and on days you didn't run you'd feel that something was missing. But the longer you went without running, the more you'd be intimidated by the distance, and the less likely that you'd start running again. Before they knew it, Jasmine had turned four years old and was still living with Grandma Lotus.

One afternoon in early summer, Daffodil was at work in the warehouse when someone from the factory's revolutionary committee came in: "Daffodil Xu, the factory central office needs you. Please come with me." Daffodil's coworker Big Ling said, "Off you go. What are you waiting for?" Daffodil thought that both Big Ling and the person from the revolutionary committee were acting a bit odd, but there was nothing she could say, so she followed along, wondering what was going on.

Upon entering the factory central office, Daffodil was shocked to see the security director, the head of the Youth League, the factory's Party secretary, the head of the factory and the head of the revolutionary committee sitting in a semicircle around a wooden stool, which was clearly meant for her. It was as if she was a suspect facing interrogation. It turned out that three boxes of hardware were missing from the warehouse, and the inventory tracking logs indicated that they had gone missing during Daffodil's shift. Although the three boxes were not large, the hardware inside of them had a market value of 500 yuan, which was a huge sum of money at that time.

Dumbfounded, Daffodil repeatedly said, "It wasn't me! I didn't take them. I have no idea what happened." The head of the factory said, "Calm down and think carefully. Try to recall every detail. Don't worry, everything will be all right as long as you tell us the truth." But the security director took a different tone. He had always been a difficult and bitter person, and he still vividly remembered when Daffodil had yelled at him in front of the crowd when she thought someone had broken into her home and stolen her money. He said sternly, "We're giving you a chance to tell the truth. It's such a huge amount of money, just think about what will happen if we send you to the police! Of course, you don't have to say anything now. You can save it for the police station, but I'm not sure you'd come out alive!"

Daffodil was so angry that she burst into tears. She hated the security director for being so harsh to her, but she knew that what he said was true. During the Cultural Revolution, most of the suspects sent to the police station never came back at all.

For several days, Daffodil was locked up in a side room attached to the factory central office, and was forbidden to have any contact with anyone. She was forced to write a "confession" recounting her family origins going back three generations. She was forced to write how she came to work in the factory, and for what purpose, and what she'd been doing in the factory all these years. She had to write a "self-criticism" that included any violation of the factory rules, anything that might cause disharmony among coworkers, and any occasion when she hadn't given 100% of her effort at work. They also made her write about her past relationship with He Guanglin, as well as her husband Gao Hong's family origins, work behavior and political standing. Finally, they demanded a minute-by-minute count of everything she'd done in the past five days, and any witnesses for each item on the list.

Daffodil wrote with great care and thoughtfulness. She had to be very specific and very detailed for fear of being accused of a poor attitude. But she also had to avoid too much detail, for fear of inconsistencies or lapses of memory if she was interrogated in the future – such mistakes could prove fatal! Writing about Gao Hong's family origins was especially frustrating and terrifying as she struggled over how much to reveal. She felt that she was doomed no matter what she wrote, and she again boiled with resentment over Gao Hong's unfortunate birth. As a husband, he could not protect her and even put her in greater danger!

Every confession that Daffodil wrote was returned to her with a comment: "Not detailed enough! This shows a bad attitude! You must be straightforward with the leadership of the factory. Tell us everything in detail, or we will send you to the police!" They ignored Daffodil's desperate cries that she hadn't taken anything from the warehouse. Nobody believed her. She saw no way out.

Daffodil had to spend her nights in that side room with the door dead-bolted from the outside. One night she was lying on a pile of hay on the floor and weeping when she suddenly heard the deadbolt quietly slide back. Two dark figures came into the room. Daffodil started to scream, but one of the men dashed over and grabbed her, covering her mouth. Daffodil realized that it was her husband Gao Hong, and he was accompanied by her brother Daqing. Daffodil collapsed into Gao Hong's arms and sobbed.

"Stop crying!" Gao Hong implored her. "This is not the time to cry! Tell me everything, every detail, anything you can remember, so I can get you out!" Daqing also urged Daffodil: "Out with it! Hurry!"

Daffodil said, "Nobody believes me, but I have no idea what happened. I had an upset stomach that day and left work early, but I swear I locked the door! I double checked! Nobody could have gotten into the warehouse without a key! I don't know why the hardware was missing the next morning. And the tracking book shows it happened during my shift. I have no idea how! I swear in the name of Chairman Mao that nobody could have gotten in without a key!"

Gao Hong said to Daqing, "It has to be an insider." Daqing snorted, "Hmph! I don't trust that Big Ling one bit! I'll get to her tomorrow!" Then he turned to Daffodil and said, "Stay strong and grit your teeth. Don't admit to anything you didn't do. It looks like they haven't tortured you, but even if they do, you have to be strong. There isn't one soft bone in our entire Xu family! Don't admit to anything, no matter what!" Daffodil nodded.

Gao Hong added, "Did they ask you to write confessions? Remember to write carefully, and don't write anything that could cause problems for you later. Whatever you write is permanent and can never be erased!"

Daffodil lost all patience upon hearing this: "You have a nerve telling me this bullshit! Don't I know the danger? Do you know how hard it's been for me? If not for your damned family background and your damned cousin who put me in conflict with the security director, I wouldn't be in this situation!"

Almost passing out with shock and fear, Gao Hong quickly tried to console Daffodil: "All right, I know. We won't talk about it now." Daqing knew nothing about Gao Hong's Cousin Lan, and he asked, "A cousin? You have a cousin? Did your cousin upset the security director?" Gao Hong said, "I'll tell you later. Let's go before anyone sees us!" Gao Hong and Daqing hurried out.

The next day, Daqing confronted Big Ling, marching up to her and staring her in the face. "What do you want?" Big Ling asked, taking a step back. Daqing said, "I heard they're interrogating everyone who works in the warehouse. Maybe it'll be your turn this afternoon. I also hear they want to search your house and my sister's house. In fact, Daffodil hopes they'll do a search, because that will clear her name. If I were her, I'd ask for a search immediately!"

Big Ling said nervously, "You're crazy!" and quickly left. Daqing's apprentice Gong walked over and said, "Xu Shifu, don't worry. I'll keep an eye on that bitch! I won't let her pour dirty water on our sis!" Gong had liked Daffodil from the first time he'd met her, but Daffodil never had any interest in him. Now Daffodil had become a wife and a mother, and Gong was also married, but he still felt very protective toward Daffodil. Daqing had always hated Gong chasing Daffodil around and calling her "sis," but now he nodded without saying anything.

At dusk, He Guanglin came knocking on Daqing's door: "Gong sent me to get you and Gao Hong. You two hurry to the back of the factory. Gong is there watching them. I can't show my face, but you should go quickly!" With that, he left. Gao Hong and Daqing rushed to the back of the factory and found Big Ling and a man with the three missing boxes of hardware. Afraid of a house search, Big Ling had decided to sell the hardware she'd stolen, and now she'd been caught red-handed! Daqing, Gao Hong and Gong tied up Big Ling and the buyer and dragged them to the central office.

Big Ling ended up going to prison, but to everyone's surprise, Daffodil still lost her job at the warehouse! She was allowed to go home, but she was assigned work as a nanny at the factory day care center. The factory gave her a letter saying she was at fault for failing to protect the factory supplies effectively and giving Big Ling an opportunity. Rumor had it that this was the security director's idea.

Daffodil burst into the central office, slammed her fist on the table and cursed at the top of her lungs: "Fuck your grandmothers in their graves! You locked me up for no reason and you're not even giving me a fart of apology! You're taking away my job? You think I'm a softie? If you dare do this to me, I'll show you who you're dealing with!"

Afraid that Daffodil would get herself into unimaginable trouble, Daqing and Gao Hong came up and started to drag Daffodil away. She kicked and screamed: "Gao Hong! What kind of a man are you? They walk all over me and you can't even let out a loud fart! All you know how to do is give money to your Goddamned cousin! I hate you!"

Upon hearing Daffodil mentioning his cousin in public, Gao Hong swept her off her feet and ran back home, where he threw Daffodil on the bed and quickly bolted the door. Trying in vain to control Daffodil's wild kicking and scratching, he finally yelled, "Enough! Stop it!" Gao Hong had never shouted at Daffodil, or raised his voice to her at all. This booming yell shocked and enraged Daffodil.

"Wonderful! You've graduated to shouting at me and using force on me! I must have been blind marrying a loser like you! Why do you turn into a crazed donkey whenever I mention your cousin? What is it? Do you have something to hide? Do you think I like talking about your sub-human cousin? It's been years since she disappeared with my money, and she hasn't even sent us a letter. What kind of a human being is that? Was she born and raised by humans? Or is that your family tradition? Was everyone in your family like that? Then I think you deserved what you got! It serves you right that you were robbed and killed! Your whole family deserved to die!"

Gao Hong released Daffodil and stared at her in shock and disbelief while taking a few steps back. He couldn't imagine that these words would come from his own wife's mouth. They were like knives striking straight to his heart. He shook his head slowly, realizing what a stranger Daffodil had become to him and how distant they had grown from each other. Was this really his wife?

In fact, Daffodil instantly regretted her words upon seeing Gao Hong's reaction. She knew she'd stabbed Gao Hong in his most painful spot, and she wanted to say something to save the situation but she didn't know how. Never in her life had she ever apologized to anyone or admitted that she was wrong under any circumstances. In her marriage, she'd always done and said whatever she wanted, and Gao Hong had always gone along with her. Now that she wanted to apologize to him, she couldn't bring herself to do it.

But on further thought, Daffodil was overcome with self-pity. They'd locked her up for days and now were forcing her to work in the day care center, which was full of vulgar women from the Wife Union. Daffodil despised those women and would rather die than work with them. She couldn't raise her own daughter, but now she had to go take care of other people's children every day. What kind of a life was that! "It's all Gao Hong's fault!" Daffodil decided. "If not for his dark birth, Big Ling wouldn't have dared to do this to me, and if his cousin hadn't taken our money, I wouldn't have made an enemy of the security director. It's all his fault!"

Daffodil felt suffocated with rage and frustration. She hated how Gao Hong stood there facing the wall without coming to her, holding her and consoling her. At a time like this, Daffodil needed an excuse to talk to Gao Hong again. If he had turned around or even given Daffodil a look, Daffodil would have come to her senses and reconciled with Gao Hong. But Gao Hong could not and would not turn to her, and his silence so enraged Daffodil that she came down on him even harder: "You deserve to die too. You burned the Mao book!"

Gao Hong whipped around and grabbed Daffodil by the shoulders. Eyes red and teeth clenched, he hissed, "You crazy bitch! Yes, I burned it, because you wanted me to! Let's both go to the revolutionary committee and die together!" He really meant it. He really wanted to die.

"I'm not afraid of death! If it weren't for Jasmine, do you think I'd want to live?" Daffodil cried.

Gao Hong froze. Yes, Jasmine! His poor little Jasmine! Gao Hong released Daffodil and collapsed like a deflated balloon.

(53) LILY

————————— ✶ —————————

Gao Hong and Daffodil did not speak with each other for seven days. Their suffocating life made thirty-three-year-old Gao Hong begin developing deep wrinkles on his forehead. But no matter how hopeless the situations was, God always found a way to make him go on. Daffodil was surprised to find that she was pregnant again.

They immediately ended their cold war, and Gao Hong returned to his usual practice of trying to make Daffodil happy by meeting her every demand. Daffodil also calmed down and accepted her assignment of working in the factory day care center. After all, it had the benefit of allowing her to bring her child to work. After her second baby was born, she'd be able to take care of it rather than sending it off to live with Grandma again.

On another rainy winter night, Gao Hong and Daffodil's second daughter was born. Unlike the quiet and delicate baby Jasmine, this new baby was strong and loud, kicking her feet and waving her little arms. Her eyes were so shiny and focused that they hardly looked like the eyes of a newborn. With one look into his new daughter's eyes, Gao Hong lost his heart to that little baby, as if a ray of sunlight had shone into his otherwise dark life. He named his new daughter Lily.

The mad routine of baby cries, bottles, diapers and sleep deprivation started all over again, but this time Gao Hong and Daffodil were prepared. They had bought adequate formula and diapers in advance, and they were calm and poised when Lily cried. They knew what they needed to do and never panicked as they did with their first baby Jasmine. When they had Jasmine, neither of them ever slept when Jasmine was awake, and they both gazed at Jasmine for almost the entire time she was asleep, which wore them out in no time. But with Lily, they both slept when Lily was asleep, and they took turns sleeping when Lily was awake.

Relaxed and at ease, they were able to enjoy Lily and even to enjoy being parents of a newborn. Daffodil said, "I never imagined raising a baby could be like this. If I'd known, I wouldn't have sent my

Jasmine away! I think Lily is a tough one. Maybe she'll grow up to protect Jasmine!"

When her maternity leave ended, Daffodil took Lily with her to work at the factory day care center. Lily spent all day with her and came home with her every evening. The thought of sending Lily to Grandma never occurred to Gao Hong and Daffodil. Daffodil occasionally said, "Let's bring Jasmine home. If we can handle one baby, we can handle two. Afterall, Jasmine is five years old now!"

But it remained just an idea. Jasmine continued to live with her Grandma month after month, year after year.

The birth of Lily made Gao Hong cut down on his smoking and drinking. This was partly because Lily brought him happiness and purpose and relieved his depression, but it was also because money became so tight that Gao Hong had to reduce his expenses. Daffodil began to hope that Gao Hong would quit smoking and alcohol altogether, but that was wishful thinking.

One evening, Daffodil was required to return to the factory day care center after dinner for evening political studies. She headed home after work, walking briskly with baby Lily wrapped in a thick blanket to fend off the late winter cold wind. Just as she reached the door of their home, Gao Hong arrived at almost the same time. Daffodil said, "Let's just have something quick for dinner. I have to go back to work for political study. You stay home with Lily."

Gao Hong's eyebrows were tied in a knot and his lips clenched tight as if holding something back. Daffodil knew that whenever he looked like that, he'd a terrible day at work. Gao Hong cooked in silence, making two pieces of sweet sesame paste flatbread, and cooking a meatball and cabbage soup. For some reason, today's meatballs were not well-formed and fell apart in the broth. When he served the soup, Gao Hong gave all of the well-formed meatballs to Daffodil and put the loose bits of meat in his own bowl. It had become Gao Hong's habit to always give Daffodil the best he had, and tonight was no different.

They hurried through dinner, and then Daffodil grabbed her coat and scarf and rushed to the door. Gao Hong looked like he wanted to say something, but he didn't have time. Glancing at him, Daffodil thought he was acting rather strangely, but she rushed out without saying anything – after all, she couldn't be late for political study.

When an exhausted Daffodil came home late that night, she froze at the door, blood rushing to her head. The room was hazy and suffocating. How many cigarettes had Gao Hong smoked to fill the room with so much smoke! He was lying asleep on the bed, fully clothed and still wearing his shoes, which had soiled the bed sheet that Daffodil had devoted so much time to skillfully embroidering. What drove her absolutely insane was that Gao Hong was still holding a lit cigarette between his fingers, and it was burning a hole in the little blanket that covered the sleeping Lily!

Daffodil stared at Gao Hong with rage-filled eyes. Who on earth was this man lying in her bed with his messy hair, dirty clothes, and a face that hadn't been shaved in days! This couldn't be the same Gao Hong she'd been so fond of just a few short years ago. He looked old, worn, hateful, vulgar and completely lacking in self-control. Daffodil wondered how on earth she could have married someone like this.

"Gao –– Hong ––– !" Daffodil screamed at the top of her lungs. Gao Hong was so startled that he sat bolt upright: "What? What's wrong?"

"Look what you've done! Didn't you quit smoking? What the hell are you doing? Do you want to burn Lily to death and burn down this house? Why don't you just burn both of us to death and get it over with? I've had enough! I can't take any more of your shit!"

The drowsy Gao Hong had now been fully awakened by Daffodil's screams. He'd wanted to enjoy some cigarettes, and planned to open the windows and let the smoke out before Daffodil got home, but he'd been so tired that he fell asleep with a lit cigarette still wedged between his fingers. The black hole on Lily's blanket scared Gao Hong. "I'm so sorry," he said. "It's all my fault. I shouldn't have fallen asleep. Thank God Lily isn't hurt."

"You have the nerve to say such bullshit!" Daffodil dashed over to Gao Hong and pounded on him with her fists. "You're a piece of worthless shit! Good for nothing! You wanted to commit arson! You wanted to burn our daughter to death! You harmed her with your smoke! If you want to die I won't bat an eye, but leave my daughter alone! You piece of shit! What kind of a father are you? You're worse than a pig!" Daffodil kicked and punched Gao Hong with all her might while yelling like a mad woman. Gao Hong tried in vain to hold her down.

At last Gao Hong erupted and shouted, "That's enough! Stop it!"

Daffodil's shock silenced her for a moment. Little Lily woke up and howled at the top of her lungs, and Daffodil broke out in shrill sobs as well. She grabbed Lily and dashed to the door. Gao Hong hurried to stop her: "My Goodness, please stop! I'm begging you! Where do you think you're going with a baby on a cold night like this?"

"I'm going to die with Lily!" Daffodil shouted hysterically. Gao Hong took Lily from Daffodil and brought both of them back inside. He had no choice but to apologize, beg and curse himself repeatedly.

Finally Daffodil responded. She wanted Gao Hong to swear on his own life that he would never ever touch tobacco or alcohol again. Gao Hong almost laughed out loud, knowing that would be an empty promise, impossible for him to keep. But his only way out was to swear. He wanted to talk to Daffodil and reach a resolution that both of them could live with, but he knew Daffodil was not a person who would bend any of her rules. Anything she set her mind to had to happen no matter what. The only way for Gao Hong to survive in this marriage was to do whatever she said before there was hell to pay.

To Daffodil, her reasoning made indisputably perfect sense. Everyone knew alcohol and tobacco were detrimental to your health. They were also a waste of money and could cause fires and accidents, not to mention the effect of the smoke on others. Why couldn't Gao Hong just quit such a bad habit, since it was for the sake of his own health and the family's well-being?

Her logic certainly had its merits, but it didn't take account of Gao Hong's vulnerable mental state. He'd been scarred by the hardship and sadness of his life and his childhood traumas, and now in a hostile political environment, he had to mind every detail of his daily life in order to survive. The self-monitoring and self-suppression for the sake of survival had taken a heavy toll on his mental health, leaving him little capacity to resist the consolations of tobacco and alcohol. He knew his oath meant nothing. Daffodil had forced him to do it, so he did it, but he knew that nothing would change. But Daffodil believed him, unaware of the further heartbreaks to come.

(54) THE CRIMSON EYED BUDDHA

It had in fact been one of those days during which Gao Hong experienced extreme emotions that he couldn't discuss with anyone. While he was carrying out his morning tasks in the workshop, Qiangzi came over to him and said, "There's a little boy asking for you at the gate." Having no idea who this could be, Gao Hong went to the gate of the workshop and saw a boy of seven or eight. The boy handed Gao Hong a cornmeal bun: "Is your name Gao Hong? A man across the street told me to give you this. He said he'd give me a meat pie if I gave it to you!" With that the boy started running towards the street. Bewildered, Gao Hong chased after the boy: "Wait! Who are you? Who's the man and why did he want you to give me this?" "I don't know!" the boy ran out of the factory and crossed the street.

Continuing to follow the boy, Gao Hong saw a man in a heavy coat giving the boy a package of food. As the boy ran off happily, Gao Hong crossed the street and walked towards the man. The man in turn lowered the brim of his hat and walked towards Gao Hong. At the moment the two of them passed each other, the man quickly said, "Come at noon!" Then he disappeared.

Gao Hong made his way back to the factory and then examined the cornmeal flat bun in his hand. He was shocked to feel a hard object inside of it! He quickly went behind a tree and broke the bun open. Stuck in the hard, golden cornmeal was a piece of jade as green and translucent as a spring lake. It was the Crimson Eyed Buddha!

Gao Hong spent the rest of the morning trying to focus on his work, but in fact he was counting each passing minute. The Crimson Eyed Buddha was in his inside pocket, right over his chest, and he could almost feel gentle warmth flowing from the precious heirloom. At long last it was time for lunch, and Gao Hong hurried out and crossed the street. The man was hiding behind an electric pole, and when he saw Gao Hong, he turned and started walking. Gao Hong followed him to a shack along the street. There the man told him, "Lan and Tiger sent me."

A wave of joy and relief washed over Gao Hong: Cousin Lan and her husband Tiger were alive!

It had been six years since Cousin Lan had come to him for money to break her husband Tiger out of prison, and Gao Hong had heard nothing from them since then. How wonderful it was to hear that they were still alive! But Gao Hong remained cautious and asked, "Who's Lan? Who's Tiger? And who are you?"

The man nodded and said, "Brother, you don't know me. I understand. How about this? I'll talk and you listen. You don't have to say a word." He took out a picture and compared it with Gao Hong. Gao Hong recognized the photo of himself that he'd mailed to Cousin Lan and Second Aunt many years ago.

The man went on to relay his message. After taking Gao Hong's life savings six years ago, Cousin Lan had returned to the Northeast where her husband Tiger was imprisoned. With the money from Gao Hong, she and Tiger's mountain brothers had risked their lives and broken Tiger out of prison. But the real danger had only begun. While fleeing and in hiding, Lan had lost her baby, and the hemorrhaging nearly took her life. Tiger had no choice but to bring Lan to Cai Xia and Zhao'er, the former servants of Gao Hong's stepmother Lingzhi. They took pity on Lan and Tiger and sent them to the rural home of Cai Xia's mother. After a few months in hiding and recovery, they continued running from the police; by then, wanted posters with their pictures on them had been posted throughout the country.

Over the next few years, Tiger was captured and he escaped again, and this time they decided to head to a faraway place. They wanted to escape China! "I can't tell you where they're going," the man said. "They're risking their lives to fly high and far. Lan wanted me to give you the Crimson Eyed Buddha and this picture. She said if anything happened to her, she didn't want these two things ending up in anyone else's hands. She also wanted to give you this picture of her. It's the only one. Tiger said to tell you that he thinks of you as his flesh and blood brother. The otter fur jacket from his father connected the two of you for life. He said he'll repay you what you've done to save his life. If he can't repay the favor in this life, he'll be sure to watch over you and protect you in his next life."

The man added, "Lan wanted me to tell you to raise your children well. She can't have any children after that miscarriage, so she says the Gao bloodline now depends on you and you alone. I have to go." He put the pictures in Gao Hong's hand and turned to walk away, but Gao Hong grabbed his arm: "Brother, what's your name?" The man looked at Gao Hong and said, "That's not important. We'll meet again if fate allows."

That evening, after Daffodil rushed off for her political study session, Gao Hong took out the otter fur jacket that Papa Li Ginseng had given him. He carefully sewed the Crimson Eyed Buddha inside the padding of the jacket, and then put the jacket back deep into the storage chest. He carefully placed Cousin Lan's photo into an album. The Gao family had all but disappeared. Nanny Wu was gone, First Aunt and Second Aunt were both deceased, and now Cousin Lan and Tiger were heading to parts unknown and might never come back. He was the only member of the Gao household left in this world, and the otter jacket, Cousin Lan's photo and the jade Crimson Eyed Buddha were the only things that connected him to his origins. They were there to remind him that he was a descendent of the honorable Gao family from the great Northeast.

While Gao Hong was deep in thought, little Lily started to squirm and cry. Knowing exactly what to do, Gao Hong washed her up, patted her dry and put her in a clean diaper. Holding Lily in his arms, he felt a sense of purpose. He told her softly, "You and your sister are the only Gao offspring. The two of you have to grow up safely and grow up well. That is Daddy's life mission!"

Holding Lily, Gao Hong longed for his older daughter Jasmine. He hated himself for sending Jasmine away to her grandma. He thought to himself, "Cousin Lan is right. The Gao bloodline depends on me and me alone. What have I been doing all this time? What's more important than my daughters? Jasmine is the first Gao child of her generation and I sent her away!" Gao Hong was near tears with remorse and shame. He swore that he would bring Jasmine home and raise her with Lily and never be separated from them again!

But harsh reality continued to nag at his mind. It was already hard enough making ends meet with just one child. How could he and Daffodil take on another? But there had to be a way. Gao Hong paced back and forth, deep in thought.

Whenever he had a decision to make or needed to think through a complicated matter, Gao Hong yearned for a cigarette. Daffodil's strict control of his smoking made Gao Hong crave cigarettes even more. He thought that he might have just two cigarettes, and then he'd open the windows to let the smoke out before Daffodil got home. But after two cigarettes he'd lit another, and then he'd fallen asleep without opening the windows, resulting in the blow-up that followed.

He couldn't share his thoughts and internal struggles with Daffodil. He would certainly never dream of telling her about Cousin Lan. It was even too dangerous to tell her about the Crimson Eyed Buddha, Gao Hong decided. When they'd first gotten married and moved into their new home, Daffodil saw the otter fur jacket in Gao Hong's luggage and asked, "What is that? It smells terrible!" Gao Hong said, "It's an otter fur jacket. My Papa Li Ginseng hunted this otter, and then my Grandma had the jacket made for me."

"It's been so many years. This jacket is child-sized and you can't wear it anymore. Let's throw it away, it stinks! Oh wait, the lining is made of silk. I can cut the lining out to make something else. But we should throw the fur away!"

Gao Hong jumped up: "That's otter fur! Do you know how valuable it is?"

Daffodil said, "Then we should sell it!"

Gao Hong replied firmly, "No. This otter was caught by my Papa Li Ginseng. Otters are animals with spirits, and an otter fur doesn't just end up in the hands of any random person. They say the hunter and the receiver of the fur are connected for life. Nanny Wu went to great lengths to protect this jacket. Even when we were at the verge of starvation, we didn't sell it. She handed it to me on her deathbed and told me to take care of it. We should keep it in a safe place."

Daffodil snapped, "I wouldn't have married you if I'd known you had all these ties to the old world. With my honorable birth, I should be able to hold my head high anywhere I go, but now I have to live with my tail tucked between my legs. All because of you!"

"Well, it's too late now," said Gao Hong, trying to laugh it off.

After that, Gao Hong put the otter fur jacket into a plastic bag and added some mothballs to preserve it. Then he sealed the bag with tape and put it deep into the storage chest. Every time Daffodil opened the chest, she complained about the smell and scolded Gao Hong for putting that "bomb" in her house. She worried that if the Red Guards raided their home, the otter jack might cause them enormous trouble. She even told Gao Hong to turn the otter jacket in to the factory's revolutionary committee and eliminate the danger.

Cousin Lan, the otter fur jacket, the Crimson Eyed Buddha, the cigarettes and liquor, and Daffodil's devastatingly quick and destructive tongue all separated the two of them like a formidable valley. Gao Hong remembered that he'd never loved Daffodil in the first place, and now whatever fondness he'd felt for her was rapidly eroding in their chaotic and suffocating married life. He'd lost all patience with her, and shouting matches followed by silent treatments became a revolving routine for them.

Of course, they both loved their two daughters, regardless of what they felt for each other. When Daffodil heard that Gao Hong wanted to bring Jasmine home, she immediately said yes. No matter how much hardship it might cause, Jasmine coming home would make their family complete.

Jasmine

(55) GOING HOME

Although Gao Hong and Daffodil had resolved to bring their eldest daughter home, making their decision a reality required considerable thought and effort. As soon as they mentioned it to Grandma Lotus, the older woman's expression turned sour. Grandma had raised Jasmine since she was small, and the sudden decision to take her away caused Grandma to hold back tears, although she didn't attempt to refuse.

"You live in such a small one-room house. Where will she stay now that she is grown?" Grandma asked.

"It's no problem, Mom," Gao Hong assured her. "We'll set up a small bed for Jasmine, and Lily can keep sleeping with us in the big bed. During the day, Jasmine can go to the daycare center where Daffodil works. In a little over a year, she'll be old enough for school, and our neighborhood is just a short walk from the elementary school." Gao Hong said.

"Then why not wait until it's time for her to go to school? Your little one is still so young. Wait until the younger one can run around before you decide to raise both kids," Grandma persisted.

Daffodil turned to Jasmine and said, "Baby, would you like to go home with Mom and Dad? There's your little sister at home, and you can play with Mom at the daycare center. How about that?"

Jasmine widened her eyes in shock and asked, "For how many days?" Daffodil replied, "Oh, you're asking how many days? You'll come home to live with us, not with Grandma anymore."

Jasmine stood frozen for a few seconds, then burst into loud sobs: "I'm not going! I'm not going! I want to stay with Grandma! I want to stay with Grandma...."

Never expecting this reaction, Daffodil felt her heart turn upside down. This was her own daughter, her own flesh and blood! Why was she so detached from her mother that the idea of going home with her was so horrible? Daffodil felt heartbroken at seeing her daughter cry so miserably, but she was also determined not to indulge her too much. It seemed that Grandma had really pampered the child too much. Daffodil told her mother Lotus, "Mom, look how spoiled she's become! She'll be spoiled rotten if she doesn't come home with me!"

Then she turned to her daughter, wanting to comfort her, but Daffodil wasn't good at consoling anyone. Her way of consoling children was to express her own feelings: "Stop crying. You should have come home with Mom long ago. Grandma is exhausted from taking care of you, haven't you noticed? Don't you feel sorry for Grandma? If you come home, you can help Mom take care of your little sister. You're a grown-up girl now, you can't just play all day. It's time to do something meaningful."

This just made Jasmine cry even harder. For her, "going home" meant leaving her familiar surroundings and the loved ones she spent every day with, and going to a completely strange place. There, she would face a mother who always complained and considered her a burden to others, and often yelled and shouted. She would also be with a father who always seemed unhappy, and a little sister she barely knew, and who did nothing but cry and eat. Mom even said she'd have to help take care of her sister – how could she take care of a baby? And Mom said she was too old to play all day – did that mean she couldn't play anymore after she went home? Would she never see Grandma again? The more Jasmine thought about it, the sadder she became, and she wailed even louder.

Seeing his daughter's misery and knowing that Daffodil didn't know how to talk to her, Gao Hong hugged Jasmine and said, "Dad knows you love Grandma's house and don't want to leave Grandma and Feifei. Dad will bring you back to Grandma's house every week from now on to see Grandma and play with Feifei. You'll see them as often as you like; you'll always come back. Now you'll have two homes, okay?"

Jasmine still shook her head vigorously and continued crying, and Grandma Lotus also began to cry: "Both of you, get out! Are you even fit to be parents? You send her here and then take her away whenever you feel like it. Do you think a child is like a basket of potatoes that you can just pick up and move wherever you like? Potatoes sprout and are ruined if they're not put in the right place! Do you think you can just take a child away whenever you want?"

Lotus grabbed a broom and swished it at Daffodil and Gao Hong to drive them out. Daffodil panicked: "Mom, you keep spoiling her! If you keep this up, she won't listen to us anymore! Did you think you could keep her until she's married?"

Daffodil turned to Yixin, "Dad! Please talk some sense into her!"

Yixin was miserable himself at the thought of Jasmine being taken away. "Don't rush things. Moving takes time, let alone moving a child. You two should start by coming over every weekend and playing with Jasmine, taking her to the park and getting to know her. Once she's comfortable with you, she'll naturally want to go with you. Here you've shown up like a ferocious demon, all angry and red-faced. I wouldn't go with you if I were Jasmine."

With that said, Gao Hong and Daffodil had no choice but to leave dejectedly.

Jasmine had been sleeping in a small bed with her younger cousin Feifei, but after all this uproar, Jasmine insisted on sleeping with her grandma. She felt as if her stable little world had been turned upside down, and uncertain about the future, she clung tightly to her grandma to find a bit of security and relieve some of her fear and sadness. She couldn't understand what was happening. She'd been living so happily at Grandma's house, and now her mom and dad insisted on taking her to their home. Didn't they know how cruel this was?

Jasmine lay in Grandma's arms, her eyes wide as she gazed at the familiar window sills and the ceiling, and smelled the familiar scent of her blanket. On the wall was a line that she and Feifei had drawn mischievously with a ballpoint pen. Jasmine had touched that line many times with her little hands. Every morning when she woke up, the first thing she saw was that line. She would wake up to the sweet smell of Grandma's toasted buns, hear her aunt and uncle going to school and the neighbors cooking in the courtyard, and the squeak of neighbor Grandpa Liu opening the courtyard door. Day after day, everything was the same, making her feel safe and secure. Was all of this going to disappear now? Was she really going to a strange place?

Jasmine woke up crying several times throughout the night. Her heart aching, Lotus said, "Ah, what a pity. They should have raised their own child, but once you sent her here, don't think of taking her back. Otherwise, it's the child who suffers!"

Gao Hong and Daffodil visited Jasmine regularly over the next few weekends, but no matter how hard they tried to please the child, she clung tightly to her grandma's clothes and avoided her parents. Even when Grandma went to the bathroom, Jasmine insisted on following her every step of the way. Gao Hong and Daffodil suggested taking Jasmine to the park, but she adamantly refused. She wouldn't even speak to them.

Jasmine lived every day in immense fear that if she wasn't careful, her mom and dad would take her away. Then she'd have to live in a strange place and would never return to Grandma's house or ever see Grandma again.

Daffodil was heartbroken. "We've treated her so well, why does she regard us as enemies? Why is she like that? How did I give birth to such a child?" Gao Hong comforted her: "We think we're treating her well, but she doesn't think so. If we force her to come home, we're her enemies, no matter how good we try to be."

Jasmine hid behind Grandma, watching Gao Hong and Daffodil cautiously with her long-lashed eyes. As soon as they approached her, she began to cry. Eventually Daffodil cried too. Gao Hong said, "Maybe we should take it more slowly. Her heart is tied up in knots from all this rushing, and we'll be in trouble if we push too hard." Daffodil cried out, "What knots? What knots? I'm her mom!"

Yixin stepped forward and said, "You two should have thought about this day when you sent the child here! There's no other way now. Listen to me, leave the child here and wait until she's in first grade to take her back. A year makes a big difference. Your mom and I will talk to her so by then she'll be mentally prepared. If you're so determined to take her away now, even I won't allow it!"

Lotus quickly said to Jasmine, "Be good, your dad and mom won't take you away now, alright? Listen to Grandma." Jasmine nodded desperately. Lotus said, "Next year you'll start elementary school. Then you'll go to your mom and dad's place to attend school, and you can't make trouble like this anymore. Otherwise, I'll let your mom and dad take you away tonight."

Little Jasmine didn't really know what next year was, or when she would start elementary school. She just knew that she didn't have to go with Mom and Dad now and could continue staying at Grandma's house. She promised, "I'll go next year, I'll go to elementary school, I won't make trouble anymore."

Daffodil picked up Lily and left in a huff. From then on, Daffodil burst into tears every time she thought of Jasmine. Her own daughter – how could this be? "Thank God Lily is with me and not with anyone else," Daffodil said.

"It's not the child's fault," Gao Hong comforted her. "It would have been different if you'd raised her from the beginning. Now I regret sending Jasmine away. But luckily, she's agreed to come home next year, and next year will be here before you know it."

Gao Hong and Daffodil had a year to establish a close relationship with Jasmine before she reached school age, but in fact, they were too busy to visit Jasmine very often. On top of that, they couldn't bear to face Jasmine's rejection, anxiety, fear and estrangement. Today turned into tomorrow, this week into next week, one month into the next month, and a year passed by in a flash.

During this year, little Jasmine seemed to have grown up a lot. She knew that Grandma's house had changed from her permanent safe harbor into a home that she'd have to leave at any time. She didn't know when that terrifying "next year" would arrive, but she knew it would come one day, because Grandma and Grandpa would often remind her:

"When you go to your dad and mom's house next year, be sure not to fight with your sister. She's younger, so you have to be nice to her."

"When you go to your dad and mom's house next year, remember to stay clean. Don't eat without washing your hands, because your mom likes cleanliness!"

"When you go to your dad and mom's house next year, you'll sleep in your own bed."

"When you go to your dad and mom's house next year..."

Little Jasmine thought that if this "next year" thing never came, Grandma and Grandpa would just be talking, and that wouldn't be so bad. But then one day, Grandma suddenly said, "Next month you're going to your dad and mom's house. You should come back and see us often." Jasmine was dumbfounded: "Didn't you say next year?" Grandma Lotus said: "That's right. Next month will be next year. Your mom and dad have already filled out your registration form for elementary school."

Finally, one day, Grandma said, "Come on, Grandma will take you for a ride on a big bus!"

On the bus, Jasmine sat close to her grandma. With tears in her eyes, Grandma said, "Let's go to your dad and mom's house. Starting today, you're going home."

Jasmine didn't dare cry out loud in front of the strangers on the bus, so she just sobbed quietly, tears streaming down her face. Her heart felt as if it was sinking into an ice cellar. She'd known this day would come sooner or later, and was completely powerless to resist. What adults decided, children had no way to change. She wished she could grow up quickly so that maybe then she wouldn't have to follow adults around like a dummy.

When they arrived at the small house in Four Corners, Mom and Dad greeted Jasmine with big smiles: "Jasmine is home! Come in! We've made delicious food for you!"

Gao Hong and Daffodil put bowls of food in front of Jasmine, then carefully picked the bones out of the braised fish and put the tender fish meat into Jasmine's bowl. They saw that Jasmine's eyes were red and swollen from crying, but apart from piling her bowl with food that she couldn't eat, they didn't know how to comfort her. They didn't know that at this moment, the child didn't need food; she needed someone to hold her, to tell her they understood her feelings and to cry with her.

After dinner, Lotus got up to go home. She deliberately avoided looking at Jasmine because her own tears were flowing non-stop. When Jasmine saw that Grandma was about to leave, she lunged forward and grabbed Grandma's jacket, shouting, "Grandma!" Gao Hong and Daffodil rushed over to hold Jasmine back, prying her fingers open one by one and forcibly separating her from Grandma.

"Mom, go quickly!" Daffodil urged her mother amidst Jasmine's ear-piercing cries. Lotus quickly left the house and closed the door behind her, and then she sank to the ground outside, sobbing, "My poor child! If I'd known this would happen, I wouldn't have raised anyone's child!"

(56) A SOLITARY GIRL

Jasmine had quiet eyes and a sensitive heart. Her delicate emotions far surpassed those of most children her age. For some children, adapting to an unfamiliar environment might be easy, but for her, it created profound pain in her life. She became quiet and reserved, and her dark eyes were filled with fear and uncertainty. She did little more than quietly gaze out at this unfamiliar world.

Jasmine's first discovery was that her parents were actually deadly enemies to each other. Daffodil and Gao Hong had become used to arguing, and their normal way of communicating was simply to shout. They could shout at each other over the smallest matters, and even their calmest conversations were loud and their words sharp and abrasive. They were accustomed to the foul language of the factory, and exchanged insults freely. For Daffodil and Gao Hong, all of this was normal, but for Jasmine, who had grown up in the peaceful environment of Grandma's house, it was nightmarish.

She didn't understand what was going on, why her parents always argued so loudly and endlessly. Having just returned home, Jasmine often wondered, "Is it because of me? Are they unhappy because I came back, and that's why they fight?" Jasmine watched them anxiously all day long. At Grandma's house, everyone spoke kindly and pleasantly; there was no cruel language or insults like this. Now that sense of security was completely gone. Jasmine was eager for guests to come to their house, because she found that Dad and Mom would stop fighting and chat and laugh with their guests. But the peace was short-lived; in no time, they would start hurling insults at each other again, and Jasmine would feel like she was falling into an abyss.

One indelible scene from Jasmine's childhood memory was when the power went out one evening, and the house was lit by only a small candle, dim and flickering. Daffodil and Gao Hong suddenly started fighting for no apparent reason. Gao Hong's angry eyes were blood-shot; he grabbed Daffodil by the collar, pushed her down, and shook her violently while shouting, "What the hell do you want? Tell me! What the fuck do you want?" Daffodil replied, "What do I want? I want to fucking piss you off!" Jasmine saw her father's terrifying expression, his red eyes monstrous. Two-year-old Lily stood there and bawled, and Gao Hong went over and picked her up. Jasmine didn't dare to cry and could only plead in a shaky voice, "Mom, Dad, please stop fighting, please stop."

That night Jasmine couldn't fall asleep, as she was afraid something might happen in the darkness. The next day, she worked up the courage to ask her mom, "Why do you and Dad always fight?" In a foul mood at that moment, Daffodil shot back, "Isn't it all because of you? You're the one who makes us angry!" Jasmine's heart sank into an ice hole. It became a habit for Gao Hong and Daffodil, when they argued fiercely in front of Jasmine and Lily, to say to Jasmine, "It's all because of you! You make us so angry!"

Jasmine thought, "It's true! It's all because of me! Me! I must have done something horribly wrong to make Mom and Dad so miserable! I must be so terrible! I must be such a bad girl!" At that age, she couldn't understand the danger and cruelty that Daffodil and Gao Hong faced daily in the brutal turmoil of the Cultural Revolution. Nor could she grasp the many hardships they faced, or the misery of their marriage due to their incompatible backgrounds. Their marriage had been a mistake, resulting from society being turned upside down, but all that Jasmine knew was that they said it was because of her, that she had made them like this. She felt that she must be an extremely terrible girl to have turned her parents into such monsters! Jasmine's heart was filled with desperation, sorrow, self-loathing, confusion and inexplicable anger. All she knew was that since returning home from Grandma's house, she hadn't experienced even one brief moment of happiness.

Jasmine refused to go with Mom to her workplace. She'd rather stay home by herself. Daffodil had no choice but to lock Jasmine at home alone. Gao Hong said, "She's almost school age and she won't go anywhere, let's not lock her in."

Daffodil gave Gao Hong an annoyed look: "Do you have the memory of a dog? Don't you remember that girl Qiuling from the fourth row?" Gao Hong immediately fell silent. Four Corners hosted people from the lowest rung of society. Among the four rows of flats in Four Corners, a family living in the fourth row had an eight-year-old daughter named Qiuling who went out to play one day and never came home. She was found late that night in a deserted warehouse, raped and unconscious. Qiuling's mother was so overcome with rage and sorrow that she lost her mind. Now all she did all day was cry for her daughter.

Observing his daughter Jasmine's tall figure, beautiful eyes and delicate features, Gao Hong said, "Lock her in!"

Jasmine felt at ease being home alone. Even at a young age, she enjoyed solitude and thinking her own thoughts. She would find books on the bookshelf to flip through, already knowing how to read many Chinese characters even though she hadn't yet started school. She couldn't understand the books on the shelf, but she could more or less recognize titles that often contained characters for "metal" or "industry." Her father later told her that they were books on metallurgy, industrial ecology and metal material processing.

Jasmine also used the watercolor paints her father bought her to "put on makeup." She would color her lips and fingernails red and line her eyebrows and eyes with black, and then stand in front of the mirror admiring herself. Then she would slowly wash all the paint off. Another thing she enjoyed was collecting candy wrappers. She would press the colorful wrappers flat in a book and then stack them together, finding great enjoyment in it. She also enjoyed looking at the frost flowers on the window, slowly changing her viewing angle to let the sunlight refract through the frost in a variety of dazzling colors.

Often, it wasn't until her parents were about to return home from work that Jasmine realized that she'd forgotten to eat lunch. She would quickly take out the lunch box her parents had left and would finish the food, afraid that they'd be angry if they came back and found the food uneaten. Then Jasmine would hastily complete the tasks her parents had assigned to her that morning, such as washing socks, peeling vegetables or making the beds. Day by day, Jasmine enjoyed being home alone and living in her own little world.

The children in Four Corners seemed to be generally wild and unattended. Their parents were all incredibly busy and let the children run around the yard until dusk. The girls played jump rope, beanbag toss and hide-and-seek, while the boys played with metal hoops and wrestled and fought, all as agile as little monkeys, their skin chapped and red from the cold. Only Jasmine was always locked inside, untouched by wind or sun, keeping her face fair and tender. Daffodil applied her skill to making beautiful clothes for Jasmine, and with her knowledge of nutrition, she ensured that Jasmine had a balanced diet. Consequently, when Jasmine occasionally went outside, she looked as fair, gentle and beautiful as a young lady from a distinguished family, compared to the typical dirty, snot-nosed and malnourished kids in Four Corners.

The children in Four Corners never saw Jasmine alone. Whenever she went out, it was always with her father or mother. No other family in Four Corners kept such close watch over their child. Jasmine had no friends and could only watch other children playing outside through her window. She liked observing them. Although she'd never spoken to any of them, she knew who was good at jumping rope, who threw the beanbag the farthest, who was a good or poor loser, and who liked to play tricks behind the backs of others. Over time, Jasmine could even tell the birth orders of the kid within their families. The eldest children wore either adult clothes or well-fitting children's clothes, while the youngest often wore oversized children's clothes that had been handed down from their older siblings. Jasmine noticed that no matter how much fun the eldest children were having, they always went home when it was time, while the youngest ones disregarded curfew and were utterly unruly.

Daffodil was very worried about Jasmine. She said to Gao Hong, "That girl never talks. She just sits there staring outside and daydreaming. I wonder what she's thinking about. Is she missing her grandmother? I make so much delicious food for her and such beautiful clothes, but she doesn't seem to care!" Gao Hong said, "Don't worry. It's all right." When Gao Hong looked at Jasmine, he seemed to see his younger self sitting on Wan Shou Mountain, gazing at Kunming Lake deep in thought. Back then, he couldn't play with other children; everyone thought he was strange. Only he knew how rich his inner world was. Gao Hong knew that his elder daughter Jasmine was just like him.

Jasmine did miss her grandmother, and her heart was sad and lonely. She heard her mother say she was daydreaming, but she liked being silent and alone because anything that interrupted her thoughts was something unpleasant, like her parents arguing again or her sister crying or her mother complaining about something she hadn't done right. Rather than listen to all that, she preferred to be alone in peace.

(57) LIFE IN FOUR CORNERS

No matter how tumultuous and ever-changing the world was during the Cultural Revolution, the symphony of daily life in Four Corners never missed a beat. The lively stream of noises around important matters such as pots and pans, firewood, rice, oil and salt never ceased. At her grandmother's house, Jasmine didn't concern herself with practical matters and fully enjoyed her childhood. In Four Corners, however, she came face-to-face with reality for the first time.

One day, when Jasmine was gazing through the frost-covered window of their home, the wrinkled face of Lao Chen appeared. Raising one hand to the brim of his worn, soft hat to block the sunlight and his other hand to adjust his black-rimmed glasses, he peered into the window and asked, "Jasmine, where's your dad?"

"My dad's not home," Jasmine replied.

"The door is locked. Your parents aren't home, and they locked you inside? Alas! what if there's a fire, you won't be able to get out!" Lao Chen shook his head disapprovingly. "I brought you a key for the water faucet. From now on, you'll need it to fetch water. We've locked the water tap in our row to prevent people from the second, third and fourth rows from stealing our water. Got it? Tell your dad when he gets back, will you?"

Each of the four rows of houses in Four Corners had its own water tap, which was shared by the twelve households in that row, and the cost of the water was divided evenly among them. Two days earlier, a mischievous boy from the second row, nicknamed Limping Qiang, had been sent by his mother to fetch water from the first row tap during a quiet time in the day. That was intolerable! Lao Chen wouldn't stand for it: This essentially reduced water costs for the second row by stealing water from the first row. Lao Chen felt a strong sense of responsibility, as his house was right in front of the water tap, making it convenient for him to fetch and dispose of water, so he had voluntarily taken on the task of overseeing the tap. He had dashed out of his house and chased off Limping Qiang, who had hobbled nimbly back to the second row with his water bucket.

"Don't think I won't scold you, just because you're a cripple!" Lao Chen yelled. His wife came out too, and commented, "Imagine having a mother who sends her crippled son all that way to fetch water just to save on water costs. It's so inconsiderate, I imagine all their descendants will be crippled too!"

Lao Chen's wife's shrill voice instantly rallied several other women from the first row, who opened their back windows and started shouting insults at the second row. After the first row women had thoroughly insulted the sexual organs and abilities of the second row's ancestors for several generations, the second row women yelled back with even sharper insults, ensuring that the ancestors of first row residents would also suffer dire sexual infirmity.

"Hmph! Think you can defeat me?" sniffed Lao Chen. "I'm a seventh-level worker!" Factory workers were categorized by skill levels, and Lao Chen was quite proud of the level he'd attained. The next day, Lao Chen brought tools from the factory and installed a metal box on the first row's water tap, leaving only a small hole. Only his specially made "water key" could reach into the hole to turn on the tap.

After going door-to-door to distribute a "water key" to each of the twelve first row families Lao Chen went home proudly humming a tune.

The water key made first row residents happy for a few days, but problems soon arose. In the first incident, Aunt Li watched her son Erxiang struggle to turn on the tap with the water key. After scolding him a bit, she sent her older son Daxiang to fetch water, but he also couldn't turn on the tap. Aunt Li slapped the table so hard in frustration that she sent her two sons running off in a fright. Shortly afterward, Aunt Li could be heard shout from inside her house, "You brats! You made me so mad I forgot to put oil in the scrambled eggs, and now they're all stuck to the pan!"

Next, Ruizi's mother stood leaning on her door frame, watched Ruizi struggle with the water tap. Furious, she yelled, "You useless brat, you can't even turn on a tap! The pot's going to burn dry before you fetch a drop of water!"

Ruizi was a feisty girl, and although only seven years old she knew how to handle her mother. She shouted in a voice loud enough for the entire row to hear, "Chairman Mao said no cursing. Are you defying Chairman Mao?" Ruizi's mother's face changed immediately, and she retreated inside. She was descended from a landlord family, so anything remotely political scared her. She truly feared her daughter, who would accuse her of opposing Chairman Mao at the drop of a hat.

Ruizi's house and Aunt Li's house flanked Jasmine's house, and listening to the commotion on both sides made Jasmine aware of what a critical matter the fetching of water was for every household. When her father Gao Hong came home from work that evening, he happened to see Aunt Li's boy Daxiang carrying a bucket of water into their house, and Gao Hong laughed approvingly, "Look at this boy, helping out with the housework now!"

Hearing her father's words, Jasmine grabbed their water key and an empty water bucket, and dashed to the water tap. Before Gao Hong even realized what was happening, Jasmine was staggering home gripping a half-filled water bucket in her delicate little hands, and spilling most of it on herself in the process. When Gao Hong realized that Jasmine had gone to fetch water, he hurried over with a big smile and said, "All right, all right, let me do it, let me do it!" Jasmine was overjoyed to see her father smile at last; it made even the soreness of her arms and hands worthwhile.

By dinner time, Gao Hong had misplaced the water key and had to borrow one from a neighbor. After a few days, someone remarked, "You borrow the water key three times a day. Do you really use that much water? No wonder everyone's water bill is so high!" Gao Hong and Daffodil became the new targets of everyone's complaints.

As the result of these multiple grievances, the water key, initially meant to benefit the first row residents, was retired. As Lao Chen removed the metal box from the tap, he muttered, "I don't care anymore! Good intentions are just treated like donkey tripe!"

Although the water key was abolished, the fierce battle over water theft continued. The conflicts spread from the first and second rows to the third and fourth rows, with everyone taking turns stealing, being stolen from, guarding against theft, retaliating against theft and taking revenge. This cycle repeated year after year in the dusty and impoverished Four Corners.

All of the men in Four Corners worked at the same factory, and most of their wives also worked in the factory compound, either in the kindergarten, the warehouse, or, if they were lucky, in the factory health clinic, which made them appear knowledgeable, clean and spirited. Donghui and Minghui's mother worked in the health clinic; her hands and face were always clean, she had a calm smile, her hair was neatly combed, and she never participated in the neighborhood cursing games. All the children in the courtyard would immediately stop running and shouting when they saw her, and grubby little boys would quickly wipe their runny noses with their sleeves. Donghui's mother was a notable figure in Four Corners, and Daffodil enjoyed chatting with her, even though she usually didn't like socializing with others. Donghui and Minghui were the only children she allowed Jasmine to play with in Four Corners.

The women in Four Corners respectfully called Donghui's mother "Doctor Cheng," but they often teased her while knitting together.

"Doctor Cheng, you know everything, don't you? Can anything be hidden from you?"

"Doctor Cheng, I heard there are three sizes, large, medium and small. Who has the nerve to ask for a large or small size? Everyone probably asks for the medium size, right? Aren't the large and small ones piling up in the supply room?"

The children never understood what these "large, medium, and small" things were and didn't think it had anything to do with them until one day, they found some transparent elastic things in the dump that could be blown up into two-part balloons.

The dump was actually a big pit across the street from Four Corners. All fifty households in Four Corners dumped their trash into this pit, which over time filled to overflowing and began to emit a pungent smell. Despite this, it was a paradise for mischievous boys, who were always finding things to play with. The transparent two-part balloons were their proudest discovery.

The naughty boys were running around the courtyard chasing the balloons as their parents came home from work. Wei Liang's father arrived first, and tossing his bike aside, he grabbed Wei Liang by the collar and threw him to the ground, then took off one of his shoes and slapped Wei Liang's face with it. Next, Lao Chen came up and did the same to his son Xiao Sheng, while Uncle Li grabbed Daxiang and Erxiang like an eagle catching chicks and hauled the wailing boys home. Limping Qiang slunk away in hopes of escaping before his father showed up.

Jasmine watched this strange scene through the window, and the girls playing jump rope in the yard were also stunned. "What's going on? Why are they all hitting their sons?" Ruizi said, "Don't mind them, let's keep playing!" She continued chanting the most popular jump rope rhyme: "Ride a red horse, cross the ocean, raise three red flags, liberate Taiwan!"

That night, an unprecedented collective shouting match took place among the women in the courtyard. Each woman took to the stage as if not shouting loudly or harshly enough would imply that those "balloons" came from their own home. In their effort to prove their innocence, the women reached historic highs in both volume and vocabulary, their insults extended from ancestors to descendants, involving both sexes, and frequently referencing animal organs. It was an event that would go down in the history of Four Corners.

Daffodil and Gao Hong kept Jasmine and Lily inside and turned on the radio so the sisters could listen to music. Then they also went out to join the collective cursing in order to prove that the discarded condoms had nothing to do with them. Jasmine couldn't focus on the music, preoccupied with how different her parents' home was from her grandmother's home. It seemed that everyone here had a short fuse and was always fighting and cursing, both inside and outside their home. Every household seemed to be filled with constant rage. Jasmine thoroughly disliked this environment, and amid the noisy shouting and the weird-sounding music on the radio, she wept silently, missing her grandmother deeply.

(58) STARTING SCHOOL

Outside Four Corners lay an eternally dusty asphalt road that was perpetually jammed with trucks, cars, hand-pulled tractors, horse-drawn carts and a multitude of bicycles, all vying for space on the narrow path. Dirt mounds alongside the road served as makeshift walkways for pedestrians, and a few minutes' walk along these dirt mounds led to the back street and then to Shili Primary School, which nearly all of the Four Corners children attended.

The Four Corners children who started first grade with Jasmine included Xiao Sheng, the son of Lao Chen from first row; Ruizi from next door; Limpy Qiang from second row; Yue from the third row, who was often beaten by her stepmother; Wei Liang, a tall boy from fourth row; and Xiao Bing, the son of Big Ling, the woman who had been sent to jail after stealing from the warehouse where Daffodil had previously worked. These children were all placed in the same class.

Shili Primary School enrolled new students at the end of the year, and they started school after the Lunar New Year winter break. The wind had yet to blow all the remnants of red and green firecracker from the streets when the seven-year-olds from Four Corners donned their new shoes and jackets, shouldered their cloth school bags, and headed for school.

Parents repeatedly warned their children to walk along the dirt mounds and avoid the road, as the trucks were not mindful of pedestrians. The flat, snow-covered road was too tempting, however; children would run onto it, sprint a few steps, and then slide on their plastic-soled shoes before running and sliding again, dodging trucks, cars and bicycles and ignoring honking horns until they finally reached the school. Occasionally a child would fall, scattering the contents of their school bags and quickly scramble to snatch their pencil box and notebooks from under the wheels of passing vehicles to avoid the inevitable beating at home if any of their newly-bought school supplies were damaged.

Although the workers and their wives at Four Corners were largely illiterate, they had a near-religious dedication to their children's education. Their children's academic progress seemed to be their only hope, a ray of light in the bleakness of Four Corners.

As a university graduate from the 1960s, Gao Hong was the only educated man in Four Corners, but despite being an intellectual from a once-prominent family, he appeared no different from the other oil-stained, dusty workers. Once his children started school, however, the difference became apparent. The daughter of this educated man sat quietly in her chair, wrote neatly, understood her assignments, and consistently performed well in exams to achieve excellent grades.

One day, Jasmine was at home doing her homework when the tear-stained face of Xiao Sheng, Lao Chen's son, appeared at the window, followed by Lao Chen himself, looking fierce and brandishing a fly swatter. As Jasmine opened the door, Lao Chen kicked Xiao Sheng inside and scolded, "Get in there and ask what the homework is for today! I'm tired of always being embarrassed by you!"

Jasmine saw the bloody marks on Xiao Sheng's face, surely inflicted by the wooden handle of the fly swatter in his father's hand. It turned out that Xiao Sheng had been beaten for forgetting his homework. Holding back his tears and looking humiliated, Xiao Sheng asked Jasmine about the homework, and Jasmine quickly told him. She felt like crying, but she didn't know what to say to comfort Xiao Sheng.

As soon as Xiao Sheng stepped out of Jasmine's house, he forgot the page number Jasmine had told him and had to come back to ask again. Lao Chen followed him in and slapped him hard across the face with the wooden handle of the fly swatter: "You can't even remember after asking! Why do I have such a useless child? Why can other kids remember, but you can't?!" Jasmine quickly tore a piece of paper from her homework book, wrote down the page number, and handed it to Xiao Sheng. After hesitating for a moment, Xiao Sheng snatched the paper from Jasmine's hand and glared at her with hatred before turning to leave. "I'll deal with you, you devil face!" Lao Chen yelled as he chased after him.

Lao Chen was infamous for beating his child. Seven-year-old Xiao Sheng never smiled and rarely spoke to anyone. In class, he was always distracted, staring at the floor or out the window. Xiao Sheng took a grim pleasure in catching cicadas and dragonflies, which met a miserable fate in his hands as he dismembered them bit by bit or repeatedly submerged them in water and watched them twitch until they died. A childhood filled with oppression had twisted his heart, and torturing defenseless little creatures was his only source of temporary release.

Staring out the window, Jasmine felt sad when she saw other children being beaten. Neighbors often referred to Jasmine as a shining example, infinitely better than their own children, when scolding and beating them, and as a result, the children of Four Corners harbored a deep resentment toward her. They hated Jasmine, but afraid of confronting her, they avoided her. Jasmine thought sadly to herself: You all ignore me, thinking I'm the good child that all parents love, but I get beaten at home just as much as you do. At least you have friends to talk to and sympathize with you, but I have no one.

Daffodil and Gao Hong valued their children's education with a religious fervor. As with the other Four Corners families, their children's schooling was a lifeline and glimmer of hope in their otherwise dull and hopeless existence, the one thing that they could change and manage through their own efforts in their otherwise tightly controlled lives.

Jasmine was actually an excellent student, often scoring perfect marks in Chinese and math, and if she fell short, it was still 98 or 99. But she still never met the exacting standards of Gao Hong and Daffodil. They had strict requirements for her posture, the way she held her pen, and the distance of her eyes from the table, all of which provided reasons to beat and scold her. In particular, Daffodil's obsessive and fiery temperament was fully displayed in her discipline of Jasmine.

Often, as Jasmine sat down to do her homework, Daffodil would slap her across the face, shouting in her high-pitched voice: "Are you sitting up straight? Your back is hunched like a pot! How are you holding your pen? No wonder your handwriting is so bad! Hold the pen higher, do you hear me? Are your eyes a foot away from the book? Do you want a beating? Lift your head!"

Under her mother's reprimands, Jasmine would sit with her back straight, her pen and head held high, and her eyes straining downward to see her book, but Daffodil was never satisfied: "Look how crooked your book is! If you don't straighten it, I'll hit you!" Jasmine had to keep the edge of her book perfectly parallel with the edge of the table. Then Daffodil would say, "Read out loud as you write!" Maintaining such a posture and writing while reciting the words was like torture to Jasmine.

Daffodil didn't know that maintaining straight posture and a lifted head while doing homework was beyond the capability of even a national war hero like Dong Cunrui. Children's hand muscles aren't fully developed, so holding a pen too high makes it hard to control; holding it lower is more natural for kids. There's also a visual disparity between a person's left and right eyes that makes reading most comfortable at a slight angle rather than perfectly parallel to the table edge. But Daffodil didn't care about these things; she only knew her ways, which she believed were the absolute truth. Daffodil was uncompromising about what she decided was right, and anyone who disagreed was scolded as "stubborn as a mule," including Gao Hong, while following her instructions too slowly also drew her wrath.

Jasmine would start her homework in the required posture under Daffodil's watchful eye, always on edge, knowing that her mother's slap could land at any moment. As she shakily wrote a word, Daffodil would snatch the eraser and wipe it out: "No good! Do it again!" Jasmine didn't understand why it wasn't good or why she had to redo it, but she obediently wrote it again. Daffodil's slap landed hard: "It's like a spider crawling! If you don't do it right, I won't let you do it at all!"

How could she not do it? Jasmine wondered. Her teacher would collect the homework tomorrow. But she didn't dare say anything, so she wrote another word. This time, Daffodil said furiously, "So you CAN do it right! Don't take my kindness for weakness, you shameless brat!" Bewildered, Jasmine looked at the two words in front of her, unable to see any difference between them. Daffodil shouted, "What are you staring at? Write!" Trembling, Jasmine wrote another word, only to feel Daffodil's slap land on her back: "You're not sitting up straight again! You have the memory of a dog!"

Doing homework each day was a torment, and Daffodil's yelling and beating made it last all evening. Daffodil's punishments evolved from slaps to pinching and twisting. Once, for some unknown reason, while Jasmine was doing homework, Daffodil grabbed her left hand and beat her palm with a wooden ruler until the ruler broke. Jasmine didn't dare to dodge or cry. Her palm was so bruised and swollen that she couldn't make a fist for days, and for a long time, she had no ruler to use in class. Her mother seemed to have forgotten about the incident until Jasmine one day timidly said while they were in a store, "I need a new ruler." Daffodil asked, "What happened to your ruler?" Jasmine froze and thought to herself, "Has she forgotten? It was so agonizing for me, and she just forgot?"

Jasmine cautiously reminded her: "You broke it when you hit me." She glanced at her mother, hoping to see a trace of remorse, but there was none. Daffodil sneered coldly: "Hmph! So proud of it, aren't you? You have a nerve to mention it!" Jasmine remembered this as the first time she thought, "My mother doesn't love me," and she was only seven years old. That night, she cried secretly. She hadn't cried when her mother beat her, but that night, when she believed her mother didn't love her, she cried alone in the dark.

Gao Hong often told Daffodil not to beat Jasmine so much. "Jasmine has been home for such a short time and already feels we prefer Lily over her. If you keep beating her, she'll feel even less close to us. She can't stop thinking about her grandmother. You can't beat her like this." Hearing this made Daffodil become agitated; her greatest pain in life was that Jasmine was closer to her grandmother than to her. In Daffodil's mind, there was only one person to blame for this: Gao Hong. If his politically-disastrous landlord background hadn't forced her to live so humbly, would she have sent Jasmine away? But now he didn't help discipline the child but even made snide remarks! Thinking of this sent Daffodil into a fit of crying, screaming, scratching and hitting as she cursed Gao Hong's ancestors and made his life miserable.

(59) MOTHER'S WORDS

In the factory dining hall, Daffodil was complaining over lunch with Aici: "Aici, how did I end up with such a stubborn and incorrigible man? He smokes, drinks, ignores hygiene and has a terrible temper. He sighs all day long as if I've wronged him, but without me, he wouldn't have enough to eat! Why does he act like I owe him?"

Aici said, "You need to stop. Enough is enough. Everyone knows how good-natured Gao Hong is and how you constantly bully him. Let me tell you, with your mouth and personality, it's a good thing you don't have a mother-in-law, or she'd make your life hell! You should consider yourself lucky to have Gao Hong. He handles everything at home and outside, even emptying the chamber pot. Isn't that right? Can you say it's not? He's so good to you, and you're still not satisfied?"

Daffodil's face turned sullen, and she fell silent. Yes, to outsiders, Gao Hong seemed like the perfect husband. He took on all the chores, saved every penny he earned to buy nice things for Daffodil and the kids while skimping on himself. Shouldn't she be content? But Daffodil felt a deep, unspoken misery in her marriage. No matter how well Gao Hong treated her, he remained emotionally distant, never sharing his innermost thoughts or appreciating Daffodil's efforts for him and their children. With her skillful and meticulous handiwork, Daffodil made beautiful clothes for Gao Hong and dressed their daughters charmingly. Yet, Gao Hong seemed oblivious to the sweetness and happiness of their life together. His constant gloom and sighing infuriated Daffodil.

In terms of temperament, it was true that Gao Hong never hit his wife, unlike most other men in Four Corners. But he was no longer the gentle and patient man that he'd been when they first married. Now, he spoke harsh words casually, and even when he wasn't being outright insulting, he could still be abrasive. Daffodil felt no warmth or affection from him.

"Aici," Daffodil said, "you and Zhao Shifu have known Gao Hong since he graduated. He became Zhao Shifu's apprentice right out of school. Do you know if he ever had girlfriend before?"

"Oh, come on!" Aici replied. "Gao Hong is such an honest and decent man! He's never had a sweetheart. No woman ever came to see him in all those years!"

Daffodil lowered her gaze and said, "Aici, I'm telling you, his heart isn't with me. I swear to Chairman Mao, I'm sure about this!" She started to cry.

Aici could only respond, "Oh dear, you're overthinking this. You're a married woman with two kids, but you're acting like a teenage girl! I think you have too much time on your hands because you don't have a mother-in-law to deal with. A demanding mother-in-law and some difficult sisters-in-law would keep you too busy to worry about any of this. Stop crying and get back to work!"

But on her way home, Daffodil thought sorrowfully that she wasn't overthinking it. Gao Hong's heart truly wasn't with her.

Every weekend, Jasmine wanted to be taken to her grandmother's house. Daffodil was furious. She gave her daughter the best food and clothes, but it was always her grandmother that Jasmine wanted to see. And Daffodil's weekend time was so precious to her! Shopping, cooking, laundry, carrying coal, sewing – so many tasks awaited her on the weekends. How could she find time to take Jasmine all the way to Haidian District to visit her grandmother? But if she refused, Jasmine would sulk and lose her appetite, and then Daffodil would become so angry and frustrated that she would hit and scold Jasmine. Gao Hong observed, "The more you do that, the worse it will get!"

Unlike her sister Lily, Jasmine never requested anything that wasn't vitally necessary to her. Feisty little Lily would loudly protest anything and everything, even something like her share of fruit being smaller than her sister's. But Jasmine never stood up for herself. On one hand, she felt distant from her parents and didn't want to ask them for anything, while on the other hand, she didn't care about material things, only emotions. Jasmine envied her sister's assertiveness, not because of what she gained from it, but because it showed that she felt close enough to their parents to demand and receive things from them. Lily could make a scene and then later on cling to their parents for hugs and cuddling as if nothing had happened. Jasmine never felt physically close to her parents. They never hugged her, thinking she was too old for that, so her only physical contact with them was when they hit her.

Every week, Jasmine counted the days and hours until she could go to her grandmother's house, like a car running on empty that needed to reach the next gas station. It was her only escape. Weekends with her grandmother gave Jasmine the courage to face the cold week ahead with her parents. The worst thing for Jasmine was when her mother said they wouldn't be going to her grandmother's that weekend. It made her feel like a marathon runner who had exhausted all her strength only to be told that the finish line was still a long way off. She was filled with anger and despair.

But even this devastating news didn't draw a protest from Jasmine. She would just press her lips together and turn away so her mother couldn't see the tears streaming down her face.

Stifling her anger, Daffodil took Jasmine to Grandma Lotus's house in Yard 13. As soon as they walked in, Grandma sensed something was wrong. "Hey, what's going on here? You both look so gloomy that you could wring water out of your faces. What happened this time?" She hugged Jasmine, who buried her head in her grandmother's embrace and burst into tears. Daffodil was furious: "What are you crying about? I take care of you, feed you, clothe you, work myself to death to bring you here, and now you're crying? Am I a wicked stepmother? Even if I were, you should be grateful for how well I treat you! You're such a big girl but you still have no sense at all! How dare you cry in front of your grandmother? How shameless can you be?"

Holding the crying Jasmine, Lotus pointed at Daffodil and said, "You shut up! You're acting like a shrew! Who would want to be around you when you act like this? How can you talk to your child like that?"

Daffodil had nowhere to vent her accumulating grievances. The oppressive environment at work, the frustration and injustice she faced, the financial difficulties, the unhappiness, and hardships at home, all had become unbearable. Gao Hong's growing indifference and worsening temper added to what had become an unbearable burden for Daffodil. Now her elder daughter Jasmine seemed to hate her, and even her own mother was scolding her. After working so tirelessly for her job and her family, she felt utterly betrayed and isolated. She attempted to choke back her tears, but finally, all her pent-up resentment and sadness erupted in a wail.

Jasmine trembled in fear, not understanding how overwhelmed and aggrieved her mother was feeling. She thought it was her fault that her mother was crying so desperately, and her head spun and pounded. At that moment, she truly wished she had never been born, and that without her, all the dark clouds would disappear and her mother wouldn't have to cry like this anymore. Why couldn't she make her mother happy like her sister Lily did? What had she done wrong to make her mother so miserable?

Lotus also felt at a loss over Daffodil's distress. After the family went to bed that night, Lotus pulled Daffodil aside: "Tell me, what's bothering you?" Daffodil cried silently for a long time before saying, "I'm so good to everyone, but everyone hates me. Gao Hong doesn't care about me, and Jasmine treats me like an enemy..." She started crying again.

Lotus sighed, "You're so smart and capable, and kinder than anyone I know, but you're ruined by that mouth of yours. I've told you before, you can't be too critical of a man. If you criticize him too much, it's like planting bitter fruit that you'll have to chew on later; you only end up hurting yourself. How many times have I said this? But you always speak your mind in a fit of anger without considering the outcome. You might forget what you've said, but he won't. Not everyone is as careless and bullet-proof as you. People have feelings!"

Lotus had repeated these words countless times, but Daffodil had never wanted to hear them. Now, after eight years of marriage, Daffodil finally listened to the words that had always made her roll her eyes in boredom. "It's the same with the kids," Lotus continued. "I think Jasmine takes after her father — she's smart, quiet, reserved and sensitive. If you keep scolding and hitting her, she could grow up with a knot in her heart that she'll never be able to untangle as long as she lives! When you're old, you'll regret it. That would be the real bitter fruit of life you'll have to swallow, chewing and swallowing it bit by bit, the bitter fruit you are planting for yourself, all of it!"

"Mom, I think Gao Hong has someone else in his heart," Daffodil said..

"What? Why do you say that? What have you noticed?" Lotus asked.

"It's nothing concrete, I just know. I can feel it. All during the three years when we were dating, he was so indifferent, he didn't even hold my hand. Back then, I thought he was just shy and reserved, but now I realize he just didn't care about me that way. He put off getting married for so long, and then he was warm to me for about a year, but then he turned cold again. It's clear to me now that he's just enduring our marriage for the sake of the children. He doesn't have any feelings for me."

Lotus sighed and said, "I don't understand you young people. Your father and I didn't even meet before we got married, but we've still made a life together. People are all made of flesh and blood. Gao Hong is a good man, and if you sincerely build a life with him and bear his children, how will he not care for you? Just stop provoking him. Men are like horses; they respond better if you stroke them in the direction of their fur. If you keep rubbing him against the grain, how will he feel warm towards you? Even the warmest heart will turn cold."

Thinking of Gao Hong's Cousin Lan, Lotus added, "Let me tell you something else. You need to watch your mouth and be mindful of what you say to others. Anything between you and Gao Hong should stay within the family. Don't go around talking to outsiders. Only then will Gao Hong trust you and open up to you. If you keep going around talking about your problems, how will he feel secure enough to share his thoughts with you? And then you wonder why he's distant? It's because you scare him away!"

(60) NEW CONFLICT

On the way home, Daffodil thought over her mother's words. Lotus was an uneducated old lady from the Hebei Province's rural Baiyang Lake who had been a housewife all her life and found it hard to accept anything from the new communist era, so Daffodil had always dismissed her mother's words. But after experiencing the cold realities of her marriage over the years, Daffodil realized that her mother might actually have the wisdom to see through the complexities of life and understand the essence of relationships. Maybe she was right.

Upon returning home, Daffodil did her best to avoid provoking Gao Hong, and she spoke to him much more gently. As long as Daffodil didn't argue or make a fuss, their home was calm, and Gao Hong's attitude towards her greatly improved. Daffodil thought that maybe her mother was right. Perhaps she had been too harsh and hurtful in the past.

One day after work, Gao Hong rushed home holding a letter in his hand. He excitedly told Daffodil, "Situ and Mai are coming to Beijing!" Gao Hong explained that Situ was his best friend from his five years at the university, and Mai was also a close friend from the same period. The two of them had gone to the Northwest to support the Third Front construction, and now they finally had a chance to return to Beijing to visit their families. Hoping to mend her relationship with Gao Hong, Daffodil said enthusiastically, "Then invite them over for dinner. I'll make something good!"

On a Sunday two weeks later, two tanned, rustic-looking people who seemed years older than Gao Hong arrived at their house. Gao Hong dashed out and grabbed their hands, crying out happily, "Situ! Mai!" The three of them held hands, tears in their eyes. Situ said, "Gao Hong, my brother! You've aged!" Gao Hong smiled through his tears, "You too!"

When Daffodil came out to greet the guests, Situ and Mai eagerly shook hands with her, calling her "sister-in-law."

Captivated by the aroma of their mother's cooking, Jasmine and Lily were already sitting at the dining table and gazing at the array of delectable food: braised pork, mooshu pork with thin pancakes, sweet bean sauce, stir-fried bean sprouts with vermicelli, braised eggplant, braised fish, fried peanuts, coriander tofu, and pork headcheese! Jasmine and Lily had never seen so much delicious food. Moreover, their parents were so happy and smiling, unlike the usual gloom and arguments. Jasmine was overjoyed! If only guests could come every day, maybe her parents wouldn't argue and scold each other but would smile and chat instead. How warm and nice that would be! Jasmine even began to like her parents' home!

Gao Hong, Situ and Mai reminisced over drinks, and unable to get a word in, Daffodil busied herself at the little stove. With no gas stove and only a small coal stove, creating such a spread had truly taken a lot of effort from Daffodil, but seeing everyone so happy made her feel it was all worthwhile.

To Gao Hong's surprise and sorrow, Situ and Mai's life in the Northwest was not as he had imagined. The material deprivation was secondary; the real issue was the lawlessness and tyranny of the local factory manager, who acted like a local despot. People like Situ and Mai, who were upright and refused to curry favor, suffered immensely. Situ, in particular, had accidentally discovered the factory manager's secret: The manager had seduced a female worker with the promise of arranging for her to return to Beijing and then had raped her. He had also similarly coerced several other young female workers. To win the silence of the factory's Party secretary, the manager had forced two of these young women into the secretary's bed as well.

"You know, if these sons of bitches had been in my father's army unit back in the day, they'd have been executed! Everyone knew General Situ's reputation back then! My father would never have imagined his son witnessing such vile acts but being forced to stand by helplessly!" Situ downed a shot of liquor.

Gao Hong asked, "How is your father, General Situ?" Already slightly drunk, Sito replied, "A Nationalist officer who made great contributions during the liberation of Beijing couldn't survive the

Cultural Revolution. I didn't mention it in my letters for fear that it would cause you trouble. My father was beaten to death by Red Guards. A general of his caliber, dying under the belt-lashing of Red Guards." Speechless, Gao Hong kept refilling Situ's glass.

Mai said, "And what about my father? He was a Communist general, and wasn't he also beaten to death all the same?"

Gao Hong was shocked, "What happened? Wasn't your father a high-ranking general?"

"It was all because of that wretched wife of his! She was young and pretty and caught the eye of the head of the revolutionary committee, so they labeled my father an undercover spy and beat him to death. Then that witch ran off with the head of the revolutionary committee. At first, I felt that it served my father right. How could he marry that bitch right after my mother died? But over the past couple of years, I've been dreaming of my father. He was a hero, but he died without anyone to see him off. He'd spent his life fighting for the Party and the revolution, only to end up like that. He was my flesh-and-blood father after all!" Mai broke down in bitter tears.

Daffodil hurried over and put her arm around Mai's shoulders, "Oh, don't cry. You have to trust the Party and the system." Gao Hong stared angrily at Daffodil, who had no choice but to turn away.

Gao Hong quickly changed the subject: "I don't have much contact with our classmates anymore. Do you have any news about them?"

Most of their classmates had been sent to factories and were struggling at the bottom rung of society, and most had fallen out of touch. Situ said, "Do you remember Jiang Wannian? The guy who forgot to write a condition on the blackboard and had to buy us all noodles as an apology? He was such a good guy. After graduation, he went back to his hometown, but he was injured in the factory where he worked and lost an eye. He visited our factory in the Northwest a few years ago, but we lost contact after he returned. Our classmates have scattered and our class is broken apart."

Mai suddenly remembered, "Oh! Wu Mancang is doing well; he's a high-ranking official in the Ministry of Materials. Yanruo is safe thanks to him."

Gao Hong quickly glanced at Daffodil, who didn't seem to be paying attention to their conversation.

Gao Hong breathed a sigh of relief and hurriedly changed the subject: "So how about you two — how did you end up together? You married so quickly, as soon as you got to the Northwest! Hurry up and tell us your love story!"

Both a bit drunk, Mai and Situ laughed upon hearing Gao Hong's words. Her speech slurred, Mai said, "There were so few women there back then. As soon as I got to the Third Front, I felt like I'd fallen into a den of wolves. It was scary! Luckily, I married Situ right away." Situ shook his head with a smile and said tipsily, "Marrying her almost cost me my life! So many other guys hated me and wanted to kill me!"

Mai said, "You're just bragging!" Situ added, "Back then, they hated me and envied me, but now they see her as a wrinkled old lady, so they don't hate me anymore. They thank me for marrying her and sparing them!" The three of them laughed heartily, and Daffodil turned and laughed with them.

Suddenly, a drunken Situ blurted out, "Gao Hong, remember when you were with Shi Yanruo? The whole Zebra Club hated and envied you! Well, Wu Mancang got lucky, but with her background, Shi Yanruo could only save herself by marrying him. She couldn't have married you."

Gao Hong sobered up instantly and quickly served Situ more food, "Come on, Situ, have some more to eat. Mai, you too, don't just sit there!"

As the night fell, Gao Hong saw the drunken Situ and Mai onto their bus then headed for home, thinking about all the dishes that needed washing and how tired Daffodil must be. He started to run so he could get home sooner to help her.

As soon as he opened his front door, a flying plate hit him on the head, and blood started flowing down his temple. Before Gao Hong could react, Daffodil's piercing screams filled his ears: "Gao Hong! You son of a bitch! You bastard!"

Daffodil picked up plates and bowls and smashed them one by one on the ground as she screamed. Jasmine and Lily woke up, and seeing their father with a bleeding head and their mother screaming and smashing dishes, they began crying in confusion and fear, reducing the small house to utter chaos.

Gao Hong was stunned, and ignoring his bleeding head, he rushed over to grab Daffodil and snatched a plate out of her hands. "What are you doing? Are you crazy? What's going on? Speak calmly!" Afraid that their father was going to hit their mother, Jasmine and Lily cried out, "Don't hit Mama! Don't hit Mama!" They jumped out of bed and ran towards their parents. Gao Hong shouted, "Stop! Don't run!", afraid they'd cut their bare feet on the shards of broken dishes.

Frightened by their father's shouts, the two girls froze and cried even harder. Gao Hong rushed over, picked them up and tossed them back on top of the bed. There were streams of blood on the bottoms of their feet, but before Gao Hong could take a closer look, Daffodil came charging at him from behind.

"Say it! What the hell! You love Shi Yanruo, don't you! So why did you marry me? Did you want to ruin my life? I remember you calling her name on our wedding night! I thought you said it was too hot, and all these years I've been wondering why you said that in the middle of winter! Now I know you were fucking calling her name! You bastard! Dog shit!" Daffodil kicked and clawed at Gao Hong with all her might while yelling at the top of her lungs, and nothing Gao Hong did could stop her.

The commotion woke up the neighbors, who peeked in through their windows. Gao Hong knew all too well that Daffodil would not stop cursing, hitting and smashing things as long as he was in the house, and that the only way to stop her was for him to leave. Under the neighbors' horrified gazes, Gao Hong opened the door and walked out with blood streaming down the side of his face. More dishes flew behind him along with Daffodil's shrill screams: "If you fucking dare walk out the door I'll make sure you never set foot in here again!"

(61) SHE HAD HER FATHER'S EYES

The exhausted Daffodil sank to the floor, covered her face and wept. Auntie Li from next door pushed open Daffodil's door and came in. "Oh, what's going on so late at night?" Daffodil didn't respond but just kept crying.

Seeing the two crying children on the bed, Auntie Li went over and cleaned the shards of broken bowls from their little feet, and found some adhesive bandages to cover their cuts. She soothed them to sleep, then helped Daffodil into a chair, swept the floor and tidied up a bit. Daffodil said, "Li, don't bother yourself anymore. Go home and rest; it's so late and you have to work tomorrow."

Li sat down beside Daffodil. "What's going on? Your two girls are so sweet, and Gao Hong is so good to you, why do you still make such a fuss?"

"If you say Gao Hong is good to me one more time, I'll lose my temper again!" Daffodil shouted.

"All right, all right, I won't say it. But what is this really about?" Li asked helplessly.

Ignoring whoever else might be within hearing, Daffodil said loudly, "Li! He has someone else in his heart; he doesn't want to be with me! He deceived me!"

Li quickly responded, "Lower your voice! This isn't a joke! Aren't you worried about the kids hearing what you say? You must be overthinking it. Gao Hong wouldn't do that; he's so decent. Stop it! If others hear you, rumors will fly through the whole factory and you two will never be able to raise your heads!" She went to the door and said, "Everyone, it's nothing, just a little couple's quarrel. Everything will be fine in the morning. Go home and sleep; I'll stay with Daffodil."

After dispersing the onlookers, Li sat down again with Daffodil. At this moment, Aici rushed in. "Daffodil! What happened? What's going on this time? Gao Hong came to our house and Zhao Min is talking to him, so I came to check on you. What happened? Gao Hong's face is covered with blood!"

Daffodil threw herself into Aici's arms and wept. "Aici! I'm so miserable! Gao Hong has someone else in his heart; he doesn't want to be with me!"

Aici cautiously glanced at the door, seeming to see a shadow. After walking outside to check, she came back to Daffodil and said, "Don't talk nonsense! This isn't something to say lightly. That person at the door was Chen Tianxiang. If that woman heard what you said, who knows how far she'll spread it? Then how will you and Gao Hong hold your heads up in the factory from now on? Lower your voice!"

After a long time, Daffodil finally calmed down. Li went home, and Aici lay down in bed with Daffodil. She said, "When you two got married, one of you was twenty-five, and the other was twenty-eight, not eighteen or nineteen. Having a past relationship is no big deal. I know you may not want to hear this, but weren't you once with He Guanglin? Gao Hong having a past relationship doesn't matter either. He's married to you and lives with you. You need to be open-minded and not make trouble for no reason." Daffodil said resentfully, "Aici, it's not the same. I broke up with He Guanglin and devoted myself to Gao Hong, but he's still thinking about his old girlfriend even after getting married. He's never really accepted me!"

In the dormitory of the Metallurgical Machinery Factory, Zhao Min didn't say a word as he wrapped Gao Hong's wounds and then he poured him some liquor. Picking up the glass with trembling hands, Gao Hong looked at Zhao Min with sorrowful eyes, and after a long time, said with tearfully, "Shifu, you have no idea how much suffering I've endured."

Finally, Zhao Min helped the drunken, exhausted Gao Hong lie down. Looking at the sleeping Gao Hong, Zhao Min said, "You need to live well. The more suffering you endure, the more you need to strive for a good life!"

Early the next morning, Daffodil went off to work at the factory daycare center, her eyes still swollen with sadness and exhaustion. As soon as she entered, she ran into Chen Tianxiang, the cousin and wife of her former boyfriend, He Guanglin. After breaking up with He Guanglin, Daffodil had done her best to avoid him and Chen

Tianxiang. Their child was already in school and didn't attend the factory daycare, so what was Chen Tianxiang doing here?

Seeing Daffodil enter, Chen Tianxiang said with feigned surprise, "Oh! Sister, your eyes look like two cherries! What happened? Have you been crying? What's troubling you?" Daffodil ignored her and kept walking as Chen Tianxiang and a few other women from the Wife Union burst out laughing. "Karma! It's truly karma! She always acted so foxy, and now she's getting what she deserves, isn't she?" The women laughed uproariously.

Never one to be pushed around, Daffodil stormed over to the women and shouted, "What kind of shit is coming out of your filthy mouths!"

Chen Tianxiang walked over to her with swaying hips and said, "Oh, sister, we're just worried about you! If your man has found another woman and doesn't want you anymore, it's no big deal. You're still young and pretty; you can find someone else! Hey, there's an old bachelor in our village. Do you want me to introduce you? It's just a pity for your two girls..."

The women laughed hysterically, and an infuriated Daffodil slapped Chen Tianxiang hard across the face.

All hell broke loose. Chen Tianxiang screamed and started fighting with Daffodil, while the other women pretended to pull them apart, but actually helped Chen Tianxiang. The daycare children surrounded them, the younger ones crying in fear while the older children looked on in horror. Still traumatized from last night's ordeal at home, Lily was terrified at seeing her mother fighting again and cried uncontrollably. The daycare director rushed over, shouting for them to stop. When they ignored him, the director told Miss Ma from the kindergarten class, "Go call security!"

Miss Ma, who usually had a good relationship with Daffodil and had always been ostracized by the other women, didn't want to cause more trouble for Daffodil, so instead of calling security, she ran to the nearby workshop to find Daffodil's brother, Xu Daqing. "Director Xu! Someone's beating up your sister! Nobody can stop them, and her hair is being yanked out!"

Daqing jumped up and rushed over to the daycare center. Gong, hearing that Daffodil was being beaten, shouted to everyone, "Hey!

Director Xu's sister is in trouble, let's go!" The other workers rolled up their sleeves and headed for the daycare center to help their director's sister. Chen Tianxiang was grabbing Daffodil's hair and smashing her head into the ground, while Daffodil was elbowing Chen Tianxiang in the chest. The men rushed in and pinned Chen Tianxiang to the ground, giving Daffodil a chance to kick and stomp on her stomach. Finally, Daqing said: "Stop it! Let's go home!" He turned to Chen Tianxiang and said, "You bitch! If you ever dare to touch my sister again, I'll kick your guts out and feed them to the dogs!"

Daqing's wife was preparing breakfast for the kids when she saw Daqing supporting a disheveled Daffodil into their home. She quickly helped Daffodil to a chair, wiped her face, tended to her injuries and combed her hair while asking what happened. After hearing Daffodil's tearful account, Daqing's wife sighed, "Sis, as women, we have to be content with what we have. Your husband Gao Hong is a good man. Live a peaceful life and stop making trouble. Even if you need to vent, do it at home. Look at the embarrassment you've caused yourself."

Daqing added, "You need to mind your temper. It's lucky that I was around and the men in my workshop wouldn't stand by and watch you get bullied. Otherwise, you'd be dead. Don't make a public scene. Keep things within the family. You've given Chen Tianxiang something to use against you, and the whole factory will know in no time. What will people say then? I can't fight everyone in the factory for you. I can't seal everyone's mouth, can I?"

"I'm divorcing him!" Daffodil shouted. Both Daqing and his wife said, "Forget it. Who do you hear about getting divorced in Beijing? And why are you getting divorced anyway? What did he do to you? If you divorce, what about the kids? Look, you're already having a tough time without being divorced. If you do get divorced, how will you live? How will you show your face in this factory?"

After work, a dispirited Daffodil took Lily home. Gao Hong wasn't home. The stove was cold, and Jasmine was alone in the dark, sitting by the table with her head down and her homework in front of her. Daffodil felt a surge of anger pound through her head. How many times had she told Jasmine to do her homework with the light on and her head up to protect her eyes, but that damned child never remembered. Daffodil dashed over and slapped Jasmine across the face: "You're the same dog shit as your father! You never listen to me! You're such a fucking good daughter of your father!"

Jasmine raised her terrified eyes to look at her mother, and those eyes, with the same sparkle and sharpness as Gao Hong's, instantly enraged Daffodil. Daffodil saw no love in Jasmine's eyes, but only alienation, vigilance, suspicion and the burden and helplessness of someone stuck in this family when they wanting to be with someone else. "This damn kid is just like Gao Hong! I pour out my heart and soul for her and she just wants to leave me and be with someone else!" Daffodil went insane, using her fingers like pliers, she pinched and twisted the flesh on Jasmine's arm with all her strength.

Strangely, Jasmine did not cry. Her eyes were full of sadness and despair, but there were no tears. She was trembling from the pain but she did not cry. She just sat there dumbfounded. That God damned child! Why doesn't she cry?! Daffodil collapsed on the floor and burst into tears herself. Lily bawled too, the poor kid scared out of her wits.

(62) LOST HOPE

It wasn't that Jasmine didn't feel like crying. She was crying desperately in her heart, but the tears did not come. It was only when she was by herself and thinking of her grandma that she allowed her tears to flow. In front of others, she gritted her teeth and held back her tears, no matter what.

By now, Jasmine was eight years old. She still couldn't understand what was happening between her parents. They seemed ready to explode and assault her whenever they saw her. Even if they didn't beat her, she had to face the perpetual hostility and yelling they aimed at each other. Jasmine had no idea what was going to happen at any given moment, and she felt no love from anyone. Every night, when Mom and Dad said it was time to brush her teeth and get ready for bed, she felt a rush of relief that she had made it through another day.

In this household that was cold as ice, the only thing that belonged to her was the darkness of the night. There she was safe, and she could think in silence and without interruption. Mom and Dad's critical eyes were not on her, and they took a break from their wrath. She was finally free for a little while. But with this small freedom came unbearable pain as every memory of what had happened during the day rushed into her mind and made her yearn for her grandma. As soon as the thought of Grandma leaped into her mind, a profound sadness, yearning, grief and despair would mix together and drown her in surging tears. Many nights, Jasmine cried herself to sleep. On many mornings, the first thought that came to her mind upon waking up was whether she had the strength to face yet another day.

Jasmine's head hurt after her night of weeping and restless dreams. As she reached for her clothes, her arm ached, and she saw her upper arm covered with a mixture of black, blue, purple and gray bruises from her mother's pinching the night before. Jasmine put on a long-sleeved shirt so that no one at school would see.

Daffodil was up too, and she was furious because Gao Hong hadn't come home all night. When she saw Jasmine put on a long-sleeved shirt in the searing hot weather, she worried that the child would be overheated and pulled a short-sleeved shirt out for her. But her genuine concern was not reflected in her words: "Wear this! Are you afraid people will see? You should let people see, let your teachers and friends all see your bruised arm so they'll know what a shameless and worthless piece of shit you really are!"

Jasmine was so shocked that her mind went blank, but then rage took over. A voice rang in her head: "Mom hates me! She really does! It's not enough for her that I'm hurt and bruised. She has to make sure I'm publicly humiliated too!" No matter how badly Jasmine was beaten, she had never hated her mom, but having that short-sleeved shirt thrown in her face to expose her bruises and shame her in school made her hate her mom for the first time.

At that moment, Gao Hong came home looking gloomy and downcast. Upon seeing her father, and not knowing what was going to happen between her parents, Jasmine quickly buttoned her shirt, grabbed her backpack and ran for the door. Daffodil lunged forward and grabbed Jasmine by her bruised arm, and ignoring Jasmine's agonizing expression, she thrust into her hand a pork dumpling that she'd bought from the factory canteen the night before. As she continued toward the door, Jasmine heard her father say to her mom, "I'm taking the day off today. I'll take Lily to daycare and then let's talk when I get back."

Jasmine ran out, holding the dumpling in one hand while desperately tugging at her short sleeve with the other hand to cover her bruised arm as best she could. It was too early for school, so she lowered her head and walked slowly. Looking at the dumpling, she thought to herself, "Maybe Mom likes me a little bit after all. Why else would she give me a dumpling? She was worried I'd be hungry. Maybe I shouldn't hate her. Nobody should hate their mother. How wonderful it would be if Mom loved me, or even just liked me a little bit. Then maybe, just maybe, Mom would smile at me when I come home from school. Maybe she would come over and rub my arm and say that she only did it because she couldn't control herself and that she actually cared about me." These thoughts made tears rush to

Jasmine's eyes. If Mom said something like that, Jasmine would love her forever, no matter how badly she beat her. But she knew it was all wishful thinking. Mom would never say that she cared about her. A smile, then. Jasmine decided to settle for just a smile from Mom. That would be enough. Jasmine promised herself that if Mom gave her one faint little smile after school today, she would never ever hate Mom for anything and would always love her.

After taking Lily to daycare, Gao Hong came home. He had stayed with Zhao Shifu for two days until he believed that Daffodil had cooled down enough not to hit him and smash things anymore. He wanted to come home and talk to Daffodil. He'd hidden the fact that he loved someone else, and that was not fair to Daffodil. For that he was terribly sorry. But he'd tried his best to be a good husband and father, and he'd never seen Yanruo once since graduation. During the darkest and most violent times of the Cultural Revolution, Gao Hong was so consumed by worry that he'd tried to find out if Yanruo was safe. But he only did it through mutual friends. He and Yanruo had never contacted each other, despite the fact that they lived only about ten kilometers apart.

"Even if you hadn't come home today, I'd have taken today off," Daffodil said when Gao Hong entered the house.

Gao Hong was relieved and touched. Taking a day off from work was a serious matter in this political environment. The fact that Daffodil had taken a day off meant that she must have wanted to go looking for him. That meant she cared about him and wanted to reconcile. Gao Hong felt a surge of gratitude and opened his mouth to apologize for not coming home for two days.

But before he could utter a word, Daffodil continued: "I took the day off so I can go to the Ministry of Materials and ask to see that precious Yanruo of yours! I want to ask her in front of everyone what kind of a woman she is that my husband hasn't stopped thinking of her for all these years! Her husband's name is Wu Mancang, right? Does he know about you two? I want to ask him in front of his coworkers and superiors whether he knows his wife has had a secret admirer all these years. I want to warn him to keep an eye on her!"

Gao Hong's blood turned cold, and he was frozen in place. Yanruo came from one of the richest families in Beijing. When their wealth was confiscated by the Communists, Yanruo's father had put up an armed resistance and ended up taking his own life. All this meant that Yanruo was in grave danger during the Cultural Revolution, when a wealthy family was enough to get someone executed, not to mention a father who took up arms against the ruling Communists. The only reason Yanruo was still alive was because of the favorable political standing of her husband, Wu Mancang. If any rumors began circulating of an extra-marital affair, not even Wu Mancang would be able to save Yanruo.

Unfathomable fear, wrath and desperation turned into a raging fire that burnt Gao Hong to the core and brought his ice cold blood to a boil. A tidal wave of emotions made his head spin. With crazed and bloodshot eyes staring into Daffodil's soul, he advanced on her one step at a time, his body towering over Daffodil with ferocious and deadly resolve. Panicking, Daffodil leaned backwards: "What, what are you doing?"

Gao Hong grabbed Daffodil by the collar and pulled her face right in front of his, and then he said slowly but searingly: "You listen to me. If you dare take one step toward the Ministry of Materials, I will take my own life. I will leave a suicide note telling our daughters that their own mother killed their father, and I will make sure they hate you for the rest of their lives. Try me!"

His fierceness scared Daffodil so much that her knees buckled. Gao Hong lifted her up and threw her onto the bed. He said, "I'm going out right now to buy DDT. Half a bottle of that will end my life. You do what you want to do. And make your choice carefully!" Then he stalked out, slamming the door behind him.

Gao Hong rode his bike aimlessly through the streets of Beijing. He was not going to buy DDT. Someone from his factory had committed suicide by drinking DDT, and Gao Hong had caught a glimpse of the agony on his dead face. If Gao Hong wanted to die, he would choose a more peaceful way.

He entered a pharmacy and said in a calm voice: "I'd like five sleeping tablets please." Sleeping pills were a controlled substance because they were commonly used as a suicide agent, and people were only allowed to buy ten pills at a time. In order to not attract attention, Gao Hong bought only five at this pharmacy, but then he went to a second pharmacy and bought five more. He'd planned to buy five more in a third pharmacy, but surprised himself when the words that came out of his mouth were, "Three sleeping pills please." He was planning to go to a fourth pharmacy, but then decided not to. He put the total of thirteen pills into a paper pouch and stared at the red print on the label: "Tranquilizer."

Thirteen sleeping tablets would not be enough to take his life, but after saying three instead of five, he knew he didn't really want to die, so there was no point going to yet another pharmacy. Gao Hong couldn't forget Nanny Wu's last words. She'd told him to "live on, no matter how hard it gets." Gao Hong didn't want to leave his daughters. He didn't even want to leave Daffodil – what would she do without him? She didn't even have enough strength to carry the water bucket.

Daffodil lay on the bed staring at the ceiling. Her heart was aching. She'd only said she'd go to the Ministry of Materials to make Gao Hong upset. She wouldn't really go there. She knew only too well that her husband had been faithful, and that no matter how much he loved that Yanruo woman, he had never seen her in all these years. Daffodil was absolutely sure of it. She thought that maybe Yanruo didn't even remember Gao Hong anymore, and that Yanruo's husband Wu Mancang might know nothing about Gao Hong's love for his wife. Daffodil didn't want to blow this matter out of proportion and sour her relationship with her husband. She'd threatened to go to the Ministry of Materials for two reasons. On the one hand, she wanted to punish Gao Hong by making him worried and scared, and on the other hand, she wanted to see how much Gao Hong really cared about that Yanruo woman. To her great surprise, Gao Hong had reacted with a death threat! Daffodil was filled with bitterness and sadness to realize how much Gao Hong still cared about Yanruo.

What upset her even more was that Gao Hong didn't trust her. How could she do harm to her own husband? If she went over and destroyed that woman, Yanruo's husband would learn about Gao Hong and take revenge for his wife. With his political power and Gao Hong's problematic landlord birth, it would be easy for Yanruo's husband to take Gao Hong's life in the political climate of the Cultural Revolution. How could Daffodil let something like that happen? Oh, how blind could Gao Hong be? Why didn't he see that Daffodil was simply venting? Why couldn't he see that all Daffodil needed was to feel loved and comforted? Daffodil said to herself: "He disappeared for two days, but I can't even say a few words to vent? Why couldn't he just apologize and hug me? He even has the audacity to go out and buy something as vile as DDT!"

Daffodil let the whole day slip by without eating or even getting out of bed. Finally she got up, but anger, frustration and sadness made her restless, and all she could bring herself to do was to sit at her sewing machine and finish the curtain she was working on.

School was out, and Jasmine was walking home. The black-and-blue bruises on her arm had turned reddish purple, and she seemed well on her way to recovery in just one day. Walking into the house, Jasmine saw her mother and said cautiously, "Hi Mom." Daffodil just gave Jasmine a quick glance and turned back to her sewing machine. Jasmine sat down to do her homework, thinking, "Maybe Mom will come over and give me a smile? Or maybe she'll rub my arms?"

Minutes turned into half an hour, and Daffodil paid no attention to Jasmine. She was worried sick about her husband. Would Gao Hong do something stupid? Would he really kill himself? When would he come home? Every minute was torture. Daffodil found it hard to breathe evenly, and her heart was pounding. She couldn't sit at the sewing machine any longer. Feeling as if she were going insane, she stood up and paced around the house.

Jasmine was overjoyed to see her mom walking her way, excited to think that the smile she'd hoped for all day would finally become a reality. But her hopeful gaze was met with a storm of fierce slapping across her face and head. Jasmine would remember this scene for the rest of her life. She remembered the black-and-white shirt her mother was wearing, the wild look in her eyes, the twitching of her facial muscles and her high-pitched yelling: "Look at your posture! What the hell are you scribbling? Do you want to be slapped silly? There you go! Here's an abundant supply to keep you satisfied! You shameless piece of shit!" Then Daffodil turned her attention to Jasmine's bruised arm, and pinched Jasmine with all the force she could summon. Daffodil yelled through her clenched teeth, "I'll pinch you to death! I'll pinch you to death! Let your teachers and friends see it tomorrow! New bruises on top of old ones! You're on a roll! Let everyone see it!" Daffodil didn't stop until she'd used up all her strength and was shaking all over.

Looking at her mother's twisted face, Jasmine's last hope vanished, her last fantasy about her mother smashed to pieces. The rage and hatred that came over her swallowed her whole. She realized that this rage and hatred was not just against her mother but even more against herself. She hated herself for still having illusions about her mother and still holding a glimmer of hope for Mom's love. Why keep begging for love that had never been there in the first place? She hated herself for being soft. She hated herself for not being strong enough. She didn't want any love from her parents anymore. She said to herself that the only love left in this world was with Grandma.

In the evening, Gao Hong picked up Lily from the daycare center and came home. He put that small paper bag of sleeping pills deep into the medicine drawer and made dinner in silence. He didn't eat, nor did he talk to Daffodil or his two daughters. He went straight to bed.

Despite this ordeal, life went on. Gao Hong and Daffodil launched a Cold War in which neither of them talked to the other. If there was something that had to be said, they would have a shouting match and communicate the bare minimum of what was necessary through their yelling. After a while, they forgot how to talk to each other; all that was left was yelling and cursing, and their accumulated rage and frustration was vented at Jasmine and Lily. Of course Jasmine, being five years older than Lily, bore the brunt of the hurt. Jasmine no longer cared whether Mom and Dad were fighting. In fact, she hoped for them to fight, because that meant they had no time to beat her up. When she was beaten or insulted, she would not cry. She quietly endured everything while staring into the air with her big, empty eyes. She had decided that Mom and Dad did not love her, and she had given up all hope for parental love.

(63) A NEW ERA FOR FOUR CORNERS

Time flew by, and Jasmine entered third grade. The children of Four Corners had all grown much taller. Since the "balloon" incident, the adults in Four Corners seemed to realize that their children were growing up, and they tried to be more discreet. However, they couldn't escape the reality of living in single room homes, where everything from eating and drinking to sleeping had to be done in one small space. This situation became particularly strained when relatives came to visit.

Fen's Nana and Papa came from the countryside to live with them in Four Corners. Fen's mom had always been close to Limping Qiang's mom, and because there were so many people in her own house, she often went to Limping Qiang's house to sit and chat. But Limping Qiang's family also had only that one small room filled with adults and children, men and women. When the visits became too frequent, Limping Qiang's mom couldn't stand it anymore. As soon as Fen's mom left, she would jump up and shout, "Her butt is heavier than a millstone! She sits there for ages without moving! She's tired of staying at home and wants to freeload elsewhere now? She's got her eye on someone else's man?" Her shouts were meant for Fen's mom to hear.

Soon after that, chaos erupted in Fen's house with the sound of banging and clanging.

"I can't live like this anymore!" Fen's mom yelled. "Even a rat has its own den, but I don't have enough fucking space to even turn around!" Kitchen spatulas and a rolling pin flew towards Fen's dad's head, landing in the yard with a loud banging sound.

"You bitch! Want a good beating?" Fen's dad swung a broom, which hit the door frame with a loud smack as Fen's mom dodged it.

"Come on and hit me! I don't care anymore! I have to change my clothes in front of my in-laws, and when I use the chamber pot at night, I have to listen to my father-in-law's snores while peeing. What kind of a life is this? What kind of a man did I marry?" Fen's mom dumped a dustpan of coal ash into her husband's lap.

"I'm the only son of my mom and dad, and they'll stay here until they die. There's nothing you can do about it!" Fen's dad grabbed the dustpan and smashed it hard on the ground.

"You'll make me die before they do! Go ahead and take my life, I don't want it anymore! Then your children will have no mother!" Fen's mom threw herself at Fen's dad: "Kill me! Kill me now! I can't live this way anymore!"

Fen's Nana and Papa went back to the countryside, and Fen's family returned to normal. Fen's mom cooked for her husband every day to make it up to him, but he always looked miserable and angry.

Ruizi's mom came from a landowning family. Before Land Reform, when the Communists had stripped all landowners of their wealth and killed off most of their families, Ruizi's mom had been a young miss in a prominent household. Her mother was a concubine of the master of the family and had given birth to two daughters, Ruizi's mother and Ruizi's aunt. Soon the land reform team took all their land and wealth and killed all the male members of their family. The concubine was brutally tortured so she'd tell the communists where the "hidden gold" was buried. "You are the Master's concubine. His wife is dead, so you must know where they buried their gold! If you don't spill your guts, I'll let the poor peasants come in and spend some time with you.... Hahaha...." The land reform team leader gave an obscene and evil laugh. Unable to bear the torture and humiliation, the concubine had found a way to escape and drowned herself in the river. Ruizi's mother and aunt, both young girls at the time, were adopted by a kind elderly maid of the family, who raised the two girls to adulthood.

A distant relative introduced Ruizi's father, a city worker, to her mother. During the Land Reform era, the daughter of a landlord was a social outcast, and marrying a worker, the top class in the country, was like ascending to heaven. Before she left for Beijing, her teenage sister held her hand and said, "Sis, come and get me as soon as you're settled in the big city. I want to go with you! Hurry and come get me! Our adoptive mother won't live much longer and then I'll be all alone and the village's impoverished bachelors will devour me alive. You have to come and get me!"

On their wedding night, Ruizi's mother refused to yield to her husband's burning desire until he promised to bring her sister to the city and find her a husband. Soon, little Ruizi was born, but there was still no match for her mother's sister. The years passed, and the kindly maid who had raised the sisters passed away. Ruizi's mother insisted that she couldn't leave her sister alone in the village, so, the sister packed a small bundle and came to Four Corners.

One child of a landlord wasn't enough; now there was another. The authorities treated the sister as a serious threat. The neighborhood committee questioned the family, and the factory Party branch carried out an investigation, but Ruizi's father, a model worker with a revolutionary background, defended the sisters. The Party branch asked, "Have you, a distinguished worker, been corrupted by a landlord's daughter? Why won't you cooperate with our investigation?"

Ruizi's father slammed his eight-fingered hands on the Party branch table: "I did this for the revolution! When I was injured for the revolution, where were you? And now you come to investigate my relatives? No fucking way!"

The Party leaders were stumped. After all, Ruizi's father was a decorated worker who'd been recognized with merit awards, and his reputation was unimpeachable. The matter was dropped, and Ruizi's aunt stayed in Four Corners.

The factory no longer objected, but neighbors in Four Corners were less forgiving. "How do they fit in one room, men and women all together?" "I hear the three of them sleep in one bed, one sister on each side!" "Her mother was a concubine; she'll become one too." "That guy with two wives, isn't he afraid the police will get him?"

Ruizi despised her aunt, knowing that her presence invited gossip and slander. One day, while angrily peeling potatoes, Ruizi muttered, "A landlord's daughter brings us nothing but trouble! One day I'll report her as a counterrevolutionary. I'll tell people she burned Chairman Mao's books! Ha! That will get her out of our house!"

Suddenly, there was a thud behind her that startled Ruizi so much that she cut her finger. Turning around, she saw her mother kneeling on the floor and crying. "Ruizi, I'm begging you."

"Mom, what are you doing?" Ruizi jumped up.

"Do you want to drive me to death? Haven't I suffered enough? Ruizi! I know you're upset, but she's your aunt, and I'm your mother. If you get us into trouble, who will care for you, Ruizi?"

Ruizi dropped the potatoes and knife, sat down on the floor by her mother, and cried, "I won't report her. I just hate her! My classmates call her a tramp and say that I'll be one too when I grow up. I just hate her!"

Ruizi's mother pleaded, "Just bear with it, please. I'll talk to your father about building a small room for your aunt. Ruizi, don't harm your aunt or your mother. If we go to jail, you'll be branded the child of a traitor and will be cursed forever. Your father is protecting me and your aunt for your sake, so you can have a decent life."

Between each row of houses in Four Corners was a space about ten steps wide. Ruizi's father, along with Lao Chen, Fen's father and Wei Liang's father, lobbied the factory leaders for permission to build additional rooms in front of their existing ones, creating a two-room layout. The factory agreed, on the condition that they use only discarded materials from the factory and that they only work on their projects during their free time.

This news was like a spring breeze wafting over a calm pool. Four Corners experienced unprecedented unity and joy. There were no more street brawls or disputes over stolen water or condom balloons. The men collaborated, gathering up various building materials and mixing clay with straw to make bricks. If someone managed to get real bricks, everyone cheered. They collected cement, tar paper, asbestos sheets, wood, glass and even nails.

Lit by lanterns at night, the men built walls, plastered them with lime, installed windows and doors, and painted roofs. The women brewed tea, cooked noodles and cleaned. There was laughter, banter and occasional risqué jokes. Infected by the excitement, the children ran around joyfully, stealing eggs or pancakes and quickly stuffing them into their mouths before fleeing as their parents shouted, "You little rascal, that's for the workers!"

Soon, the gaps between the rows in Four Corners disappeared. Every family not only extended their rooms but also built small yards in front of their new rooms. The space between the rows was now barely wide enough for two people to pass side-by-side.

Ruizi's aunt moved to the outer room. Fen's Nana and Papa returned to Four Corners, living with the children in their outer room, and Fen's mother no longer raised a fuss. Families without outsiders placed their children in the inner room, while the parent couples moved to the outer room, ushering in a new era for Four Corners.

(64) THE SIGNATURE INCIDENT

The excitement of building an extension seemed to have temporarily improved the relationship between Gao Hong and Daffodil. However, they still quarreled frequently, with minor arguments every three days and major ones every five days. Whatever happened outside their home, or whatever pressures and grievances they faced, they had nowhere to vent but at home. This home, and these two children, became their outlets.

A child is a child, after all. No matter how disappointed Jasmine was with her parents' love, and no matter how much she vowed not to seek their affection, she still desperately longed for it. She tried to do more housework to make her parents happy. Once, she swept the floor, wiped the table, made the bed and tidied up the room before her parents came home. Gao Hong walked in and smiled, saying, "The place looks so clean! Good! Tonight I'll take you all to Uncle Zhao's house to play!" Jasmine was overjoyed! Uncle Zhao, Gao Hong's Shifu, lived nearby and had two sons and one daughter. Visiting his family was the only entertainment for Jasmine's family at that time.

The next day, Jasmine eagerly cleaned the house again, just as thoroughly as the day before, and waited excitedly for her parents to come home. But Gao Hong came home frowning that day, and ignoring the clean house, he said, "You're so grown up and still so irresponsible! You didn't wash the socks soaking in the basin, or take out the trash in the yard. What have you been doing all day?" Just then, Daffodil walked in and saw Gao Hong scolding Jasmine, and Jasmine standing there with a miserable face. Exhausted from a long day at work, Daffodil immediately glared angrily at Jasmine and said, "What is it this time? Just seeing you makes me furious! You're nothing but a demon!"

Jasmine couldn't understand why doing the same thing one day made her good and the next day made her a demon. Why were her parents happy one day and angry the next? What she didn't understand was that it had nothing to do with what she did. It was what her parents encountered outside the home, whether they were happy at work or not, that determined their mood for the day. When they were happy, they could be nice to Jasmine, but when they were not, they would scold her harshly. She was powerless to control anything or to improve the stifling atmosphere at home with her own efforts. Jasmine had no way of knowing that she and her sister Lily, whom her parents cursed and hurt every day, were also her parents' only hope and the only things her parents really cared about in their suffocating lives.

The city-wide entrance exam for middle schools was reinstated, and from then on, students had to take an exam to determine whether they would attend a good middle school or a bad one. The news put tremendous pressure on parents of children in grades one to five. The teachers at Shili Primary School instantly increased the amount of homework assigned.

For Gao Hong and Daffodil, this was naturally a top priority. Jasmine performed well in school, and although only in third grade, she seemed to have a good chance of getting into a top middle school. However, what made Gao Hong and Daffodil uneasy was that the exam was a city-wide standardized test, followed by district rankings. Although Jasmine was outstanding in her primary school, who knew how she would rank in the entire district? Gao Hong and Daffodil felt compelled to closely monitor Jasmine's studies every day, becoming extremely anxious at the slightest sign of trouble.

Gao Hong and Daffodil would go berserk if Jasmine got a homework question wrong. If Gao Hong and Daffodil saw a teacher's red X in Jasmine's homework book, they'd curse her with the vilest possible words. If they saw two, or God-forbid even more, red X's, their fists, kicks and slaps landed on Jasmine like a rainstorm.

Jasmine dreaded those bloody red X's. One day, when she got one, she was nauseous with worry for the entire day. She knew she didn't dare take out her homework book at home, but how could she do today's homework without taking the book out? The homework would be due tomorrow, and there would be hell to pay if she couldn't turn it in. She became oblivious to anything the teachers were saying in class, staring blankly at nothing until dismissal and then dragging herself home with dread in each step. Upon arriving home and seeing her angry-looking parents, she had no choice but to lie that she had no math homework that day. She felt as if on the verge of fainting as she heard the lie come out of her own mouth.

Jasmine endured the evening second by second amid the usual chorus of cursing, humiliation, sarcasm and criticism. The next morning she left home early to look for a place by the side of the road to do her math homework. As she was rushing through the arithmetic as quickly as she could, a neighbor auntie saw her and asked, "Oh isn't that Jasmine? Why are you doing homework out here in the cold wind?" Jasmine was scared to death! This auntie knew Mom and Dad well and might mention seeing her, and Jasmine would be dead if Mom and Dad found out she'd done her homework on the way to school. She said, "I just thought of a correction that I wanted to make in my homework before I get to school." With that, she finished the rest of the problems at lightning speed and dashed off to school.

Disaster hit immediately. It turned out that in the process of rushing through the eight arithmetic problems in the cold wind while keeping an eye out for anyone who knew her, Jasmine had gotten all of them wrong! The teacher mercilessly put eight gigantic red X's, and a big red D on that homework page! Jasmine always got A's, and on her worst days an A minus. She'd never gotten even a B, and now the sight of that D froze her with shock. Then, the teacher said something that made her soul shoot out of her skull: "Go home during lunch and have your Mom or Dad sign this page."

Asking for a parent's signature on a particularly noteworthy, usually disastrous, page in a homework book was a common way for teachers to communicate with parents. The signature basically meant, "I, as the parent of so and so, am aware of the poor performance of my child. I take full responsibility and will do whatever I can to mend the situation." It was a way to scold and shame the parents, as the teachers in Chinese schools had the full authority to do. Parents said things like, "I had to put four signatures in my son's homework book this year!", and then everybody knew how bad a son he had, and how frustrated and humiliated he must be.

Jasmine felt the room spinning and her head getting ready to explode. An internal voice shouted, "I'm going insane! I'm going insane! A signature! A signature!" Her school day became a fog of daydreaming. "Fairies in faraway lands, please take me away. Even if the sea monsters come to take me, I'm willing to go with them. Take me away! Take me away! I want to leave this world, and go anywhere! Grandma, Grandma, save me! I know only you can save me!"

At recess, Jasmine sat alone and stared at her classmates who were running wild on the playground: "How can they still laugh? Many of them do worse than me in school, and some are always getting parent signatures. Some even get into fights, and their parents have to go sit in the principal's office. How are they still fed, clothed and alive? Shouldn't they be beaten to death or driven out of the house?" Those were questions that puzzled Jasmine for many years to come. She hadn't had any happiness for as long as she could remember, but kids who did worse than her in school were laughing and playing happily. Why did their parents tolerate them? How were they happy?

The lunch break she had been dreading all morning inevitably arrived like a time bomb. The ringing bell was the scariest sound Jasmine had heard in her ten years of life. She thought, "Maybe I should die. If I'm dead, everything will be over." For the rest of her life, Jasmine remembered that this was the moment when she first thought of death. "But Grandma! My Grandma! I haven't seen her for such a long time. How can I die without seeing Grandma one last time! And I have no idea how to die anyway..."

With incoherent thoughts and cold limbs, Jasmine walked home. At that time in China, elementary school students went home for lunch and took a nap before walking back to school for the afternoon session. Workplaces all released their employees midday so they could take care of their kids during lunch time and return to work in the afternoon. Today Gao Hong was home to make Jasmine's lunch.

Gao Hong didn't beat Jasmine very often, and sometimes he was even patient and smiled at her. But Jasmine was still very cautious with her father, because he veered between being happy and depressed. Sometimes he'd be so sweet and smiling toward Jasmine and Lily that it was almost surreal. But Jasmine knew she couldn't let her guard down, because any tiny matter could push Dad into an angry state in which he'd knot his eyebrows, sigh nonstop, bang everything he touched, and curse everything that came into his sight.

Whenever he went into that state, Jasmine saw a dad who was destitute, who hated everything, who had lost interest and hope in everything, and who was overwhelmed by the rage bottled up inside him. As a result, Jasmine didn't feel close to Dad when he was "good" and didn't believe him when he showed love and caring. She knew it was all temporary and that he would change into the "bad" state at the drop of a hat, for reasons she could not understand.

Ten-year-old Jasmine had no way of understanding her father's suffering. His actual mental state was downright bipolar. Under the desperate situations in his workplace, his marriage and in the social and political turmoil, he was depressed beyond description. But he loved his two daughters and would summon all his strength to suppress the pain in his heart and try to be upbeat and gentle with them. Of course he couldn't manage this for very long and would have to sink into a manic stage before becoming nice and sweet again. Dad's bipolar behavior robbed Jasmine of any sense of security. She formed the habit of assessing her father and reading whether he was "good" or "bad" every time she entered the house.

Today, with a "D" in her backpack, Jasmine hoped with all her strength that her father was having a "good" moment, but she froze as soon as she entered the house. Something bad must have happened at work, because Jasmine had never seen a bigger knot in her dad's eyebrows, or a cloudier expression on his face. His lips were clamped tight, and he looked as if he was holding back violent sobs. His sighs were the most terrifying sound Jasmine had ever heard. Even in adulthood, she could not shake off the horror of hearing her father's long, low and heartrending sighs. Jasmine was so afraid to hear Dad's sighs that each one made her jump out of her skin.

Gao Hong banged a plate and a bowl in front of Jasmine and hissed, "Eat!" Jasmine felt like she was going to throw up, but she didn't dare contradict her father. She stuffed food in her mouth mechanically while Dad sat in a chair with his arms wound around his chest and his head hanging low, sighing over and over again. The sound of his sighing tore Jasmine's insides into pieces. Dad looked so old, but he was only thirty-nine.

Without a word, Gao Hong stood up and started to leave for work. Jasmine jumped up and took out her homework book to ask her dad for a signature. One look at the homework book, and Gao Hong roared: "What are you doing in school! What the hell are you doing in school! Daddy's heart is broken into pieces already. Can't you just do one thing right? Can't you?! Why is my name so worthless that it has to go on something this shameful?"

Gao Hong's face was so frightening that Jasmine was sure her dad would kill her. He really would! Gao Hong signed his name with so much force that the paper ripped. He yelled, "Go take your nap! I don't want to live anymore!"

Jasmine quickly went and lay down facing the wall. Her heart pounded at hearing that Dad didn't want to live. She had just thought about death that morning, and now Dad was talking about it too. That meant she wasn't alone. That meant that thinking about death was actually all right.

"Will Dad die? Is he going to die?" Jasmine's mind raced as she heard Dad cleaning off the coal stove with loud bangs. She lay there frozen, half expecting Dad to hit her with the fire tongs, killing her and then maybe killing himself. She told herself, "It's all right. Everybody dies eventually. I have nothing in this world that I'll miss except Grandma." She closed her eyes and called to her grandma in her heart, waiting for Dad to beat her to death. But nothing happened. Dad left. Jasmine lost all her strength and collapsed on the bed.

This was a special day. Jasmine had not only thought of death for the first time, but also heard that her father also wanted to die. It was the first time she realized that death was actually an option.

Jasmine generally didn't play with her schoolmates or join the study groups at her friends' houses after school, but had to go straight home. She also didn't dare get her beautifully made clothes dirty for fear of angering her mother; in any case, the other girls were jealous of her pretty, colorful clothes and retaliated by not including Jasmine in their games. Over time, Jasmine fell behind in the girls' games of jump rope and bean bag toss. Increasingly seeing her as a drag or an inconvenience, the other girls excluded her from their play altogether. As a result, Jasmine would sit alone during the ten-minute recess between classes, and when the other students gathered to play boisterously in front of the school gate every morning before school opened, Jasmine would quietly watch from the sidelines.

The green metal gate of Shili Primary School was tightly shut every morning until 8:15. Children gathered in the open area outside the gate, making the most of their time before school opened to play games on the dirt ground. Dressed in hand-me-downs from their older siblings and wearing shoes that lasted them for years, they looked poor but were full of energy.

The boys squatted in enthusiastic play with cigarette wrappers, which they all collected through various means and carefully folded into hard little rectangles that displayed the brands. They would place the folded cigarette wrapper rectangles on the ground like betting stakes and then try to flip them over by slapping the ground hard next to the wrappers. Those who succeeded in flipping wrappers could keep them as their own. The boys were indescribably obsessed with collecting and playing with cigarette wrappers, the value of which varied greatly. The most common wrappers were of the Zhanzheng, Nongfeng, and Hengda brands, which most boys could get from their dads or from scrounging through the neighborhood trash piles. Occasionally, someone would draw the envy of the other boys by taking out a Lihua, Xiangshan or Daqianmen wrapper. It took three Zhanzhengs to win a Lihua, and five Nongfengs to win a Daqianmen.

One morning, a third-grader named Meng Guangqi brought a Zhonghua cigarette box. The boys swarmed around him in a tight circle, and Meng Guangqi quickly gripped his schoolbag and shouted, "I'm not playing, I'm not playing, I'm just showing you!"

The boys wouldn't let him off: "Five Daqianmens, okay? Fair enough? Come on, if I lose, all five Daqianmens are yours!" "I'll bet eight Lihuas, eight to one – you can win with your eyes closed!" "Get lost! Do you even have eight Lihuas? Don't listen to him, play with me instead." The school bell rang just in time to save Meng Guangqi.

There were occasional incidents of boys cracking each other's heads open with bricks over cigarette wrappers. The school generally ignored these matters until one day, Xiao Bing from Four Corners brought a Panda cigarette wrapper.

Panda cigarettes were specially made and supplied to central government officials and senior military officers. There was a general perception that only Chairman Mao smoked Panda cigarettes, so the appearance of a Panda cigarette wrapper caused a brief silence to descend over the schoolyard. Sensing danger from the bulging eyes staring at him, Xiao Bing quickly tucked the wrapper into his pocket and held it tight as he turned to leave. The sound of hurried footsteps followed, and before Xiao Bing could turn around, his collar was grabbed from behind.

"Did you steal that from Zhongnanhai? Where did you get it?" Zhongnanhai was where Chairman Mao and the country's other top leaders lived and worked.

Xiao Bing was the son of Big Ling and Lao Xiao, the factory boiler worker. Big Ling had only recently been released from prison after being caught stealing parts from the factory warehouse, and the harsh years spent without his mother's care had made Xiao Bing more mature than his peers; although he was only in third grade, he was tall and confident. Seeing that the other boys meant trouble, he knew there was no way to settle the matter except with his fists, so he punched the leading boy in the face. A group of boys rushed at him, knocking Xiao Bing to the ground and kicking him. Xiao Bing protected his head and face with one hand while guarding the Panda cigarette wrapper in his pocket with the other and kicking at the others with his legs.

When the school bell rang, Xiao Bing walked proudly into the school with his bleeding face and obviously sprained ankle. Jasmine, Ruizi, Yue and other girls from Four Corners stared at him as he limped by them. After he passed, Ruizi said, "He's got guts! He does Four Corners proud!"

Within the hour, Xiao Bing's homeroom teacher took him to the principal's office. "Xiao Bing, tell me, where did you get that Panda cigarette wrapper?"

"My dad gave it to me," Xiao Bing replied calmly.

"Your dad?" the principal said. "I know your dad. He's the factory's boiler worker. Where would he get Panda cigarettes?"

"Mr. Principal," the homeroom teacher said, "I think this is a new development in class struggle. We should immediately report this to the factory's revolutionary committee." The revolution committees held supreme power and could easily destroy someone and their family by arbitrarily labeling them as a "counterrevolutionary."

Xiao Bing glared at the homeroom teacher and said, "How is my dad involved in class struggle? How dare you slander the working class and slander a revolutionary veteran? What's your background? What are your hidden motives? What class do you belong to? You should be the one reported to the revolutionary committee!"

The homeroom teacher's voice trembled as she shouted, "How dare you speak to your teacher like that? Are you rebelling?" She knew that her background as a member of the "stinking intellectual" class with overseas connections was a sensitive political issue, and that she should keep her distance from the revolutionary committee as far as possible. Xiao Bing had hit her vulnerable spot.

"Enough," the principal said, waving his hand. "I'll call Lao Xiao and get to the bottom of this myself."

It turned out that when Xiao Bing's father Lao Xiao was a soldier in the army, he had served as a colonel's horseman when the troops entered Beijing. After his discharge from the military, he never sought to ingratiate himself with high-ranking officers and quietly became a boiler worker. He later heard that the old colonel had been promoted to a military commissar, but more recently had been dismissed and imprisoned. Without hesitation, Xiao Bing's father took his son to visit the old colonel. On their way back from the military compound, Xiao Bing's father saw an old Panda cigarette wrapper on the ground and he picked it up and gave it to his son.

"Lao Xiao, your son dared to question the teacher's background. Impressive!" the principal said.

After school, Xiao Bing was surrounded by the tall boys as soon as he stepped out of the gate.

"What do you want?" Xiao Bing said calmly.

"Nothing much. Just let us borrow that Panda cigarette wrapper for a couple of days, and we'll return it," said the leader of the pack, his face so close to Xiao Bing's that their noses almost touched.

"No," said Xiao Bing, staring into the leader's eyes.

"You're tired of living, aren't you? Your skin is itching for a beating." The leader poked Xiao Bing's shoulder provocatively. "Guys, turn out his pockets!"

"Just try!" Xiao Bing jumped out of the circle of boys and pulled a large beer bottle from his bag, gripped the neck, and smashed the bottom against a brick. Shards of glass flew everywhere, turning the bottle into a sharp-edged weapon. He pointed the jagged edge at the leader's face. "You punk! You got lucky this morning. If you want to fight to the death, come on! If you're half the man you pretend to be, fight me one-on-one!"

With his eyes fixed on the leader and the bottle clenched tight in his grip, Xiao Bing addressed the others: "Do you think he'll let you have the Panda wrapper if you steal it from me? No! You're the ones who will get hurt, and he'll keep it for himself. Is it worth fighting for him? Anyone who's my buddy can hold onto the Panda wrapper for a day, and we'll all beat up anyone who keeps it for a second longer! But if you don't want to be my buddy, my bottle won't be your friend either!"

The boys looked at the leader and then at Xiao Bing. Humiliated and enraged, the leader lunged at Xiao Bing like a hungry tiger, but Xiao Bing swiftly and fiercely brandished his broken bottle, forcing the leader back into a corner step by step. Xiao Bing had raised his leg to kick the boy hard in the crotch when he suddenly heard his father shout, "Bing!"

Xiao Bing's father had appeared out of nowhere. Xiao Bing's kick shifted direction, landing on the boy's thigh instead. As the other boys scattered like birds and the leader limped away, Xiao Bing's father took the bottle from his son's hand and said, "You dare to curse at your teacher, fight with a broken bottle and kick someone in the crotch. My God, you're only ten years old!"

That night, Xiao Bing's father bought a bottle of hard liquor and a pound of sausage. He sat down with his son and said, "Son, let's have a drink!"

"Are you crazy? He's just a child!" Xiao Bing's mother Big Ling snatched the glass away from Xiao Bing.

"What do you know?" Xiao Bing's father placed the glass firmly in front of Xiao Bing again. "My son is only ten years old but is as strong and daring as thirty! Today I saw it clearly – this son of mine will be a force to be reckoned with!"

"Dad, I'll drink it!" Xiao Bing downed a mouthful of liquor, coughing violently as his insides burned.

That day marked Xiao Bing's coming of age. For the first time, he felt capable of protecting his family and what he loved. Xiao Bing felt like a man. From then on, the girls from Four Corners looked at him with newfound respect.

Jasmine could never understand why the boys at school always bullied her. At recess, they would catch caterpillars and put them in her pencil case just to hear her scream when she opened it. They deliberately spilled ink on her pretty dresses, laughing as she got upset. They poured soapy water into her water cup and waited to see her reaction when she drank it, or kicked dust in her eyes during school cleaning. They also did it to the other girls to some extent, but the particularly enjoyed playing their tricks on Jasmine. Jasmine despised those dirty, snot-nosed brats!

But Xiao Bing never bullied Jasmine. On the contrary, he would stop the other boys from pulling pranks on her.

(66) YUE

Jasmine was not the only child who was targeted at school. A group of kids, including Xiao Sheng and Ruizi, often bullied Yue from the third row of Four Corners. Yue, Xiao Sheng, Jasmine, Wei Liang, Ruizi, Xiao Bing and Limpy Qiang were all classmates who lived in Four Corners, but unlike the others, Yue lived with her stepmother. No one knew what had happened to Yue's biological mother – whether she divorced Yue's father, passed away or something else. Yue's father raised his two daughters Qinqin and Yue on his own before marrying a woman who already had two sons and a daughter. The blended family of seven shared that small house in the third row of Four Corners.

Yue's stepmother was a scary woman. The older stepdaughter, Qinqin, was already in high school. She was quiet, sensible, diligent in housework and an outstanding student, and became the first child in the history of Four Corners to get into a prestigious high school. The stepmother was cautious and decent to Qinqin, partly because she couldn't find much to scold her about, and partly because she thought Qinqin might be successful in the future, and she didn't want to burn her bridges. This also allowed her to present herself as a good stepmother: "See, I'm not bad to my stepdaughters, it's just that the other one is too hopeless and frustrating!"

The younger stepdaughter, Yue, was at an awkward age and didn't know how to please her stepmother, so she was often beaten and mistreated. Her clothes were tattered, and her hair was always chopped short and raggedly because her stepmother insisted on cutting Yue's hair herself in order to save money. Cutting Yue's hair very short saved the stepmother the bother of cutting it again for a while. Yue always timidly hid in a corner, and she went around with her head slightly lowered, mouth slightly open, and eyes staring widely at others. Terrified of making mistakes or attracting attention, Yue didn't dare to play and laugh like her classmates. If the teacher called her parents for any reason at all, she would be in big trouble.

Among her classmates were tough girls and naughty boys who were often roughly treated by their parents and bullied by their older siblings, and they preyed on Yue to vent their frustrations. In the first week of first grade, someone in the class called Yue a "retard" and said, "We don't want to be in the same class as a retard!" Children who initially had no prejudice against Yue didn't dare to play with her either, and joined in calling her a retard.

During one recess, when Yue wanted to go to the restroom, Ruizi led a group of girls who pushed Yue aside and rushed into the restroom first and took up all the stalls. If another girl came into the restroom, the group would give a stall to her and then quickly occupy it again after she left. Finally, Yue said, "It's my turn." Ruizi replied, "What do you mean it's your turn? We were here first and we're not finished yet. That one who just came was our friend, so we made room for her. Now that she's done, it's our turn again." Yue didn't dare to say anything, and none of the other girls spoke up for her. When the class bell rang, the girls occupying the stalls ran back to the classroom. Yue quickly grabbed a stall to pee, but didn't have time to properly belt her pants before rushing back to class. Yue's mother hadn't bought her a proper belt, and only gave her a long piece of worn-out cloth, and when Yue ran back into the classroom, the ragged cloth was still hanging around her neck. The whole class burst into laughter and jeering. The teacher angrily rapped on the podium: "Stop laughing! What's so funny? Wang Yue! Why didn't you tie your pants properly before coming in? Go stand outside the classroom as punishment!" Yue had to stand at the classroom door for an entire period.

When the students began learning calligraphy in third grade, the teacher required each student to bring a fountain pen. Although the parents in Four Corners were poor, they never skimped on their children's education supplies, and immediately bought fountain pens. But Yue didn't bring a fountain pen to class. The teacher scolded her: "Didn't I tell everyone to bring a fountain pen starting today? Where's your fountain pen?" Yue whispered, "My mom didn't buy one for me." Someone shouted, "Her mom isn't her real mother, she doesn't even give Yue enough food!" Another child said, "No wonder she's so stupid!" Everyone laughed.

The teacher reprimanded the class, "Quiet, all of you! Anyone who speaks another word will be punished!" The teacher looked at the teary-eyed Yue, wrote a note and handed it to her, saying, "Give this to your mother." A few days later, Yue brought a brand-new fountain pen to class, and she cherished it dearly.

After school, children from different neighborhoods lined up to walk home, with the kids from each neighborhood walking together in a neat line. In the Four Corners line, Yue walked behind Jasmine and Ruizi, followed by the boys Xiao Sheng, Wei Liang and Limpy Qiang. Xiao Bing was not there that day, so there were only six kids walking home together. Yue's backpack was old and tattered, and she didn't have a pencil box, so the cherished fountain pen that had probably cause her no end of trouble lay loose in her backpack. As they walked along, her fountain pen slipped out of a hole in her backpack and fell onto the asphalt road. Yue didn't realize it immediately, but the quick-eyed Xiao Sheng picked it up and shouted, "Whose pen is this?"

Yue turned around, her face turning pale, and said hurriedly, "It's mine, it's mine! Please give it to me!"

Xiao Sheng held the pen high above his head: "How can you prove it's yours? Does it answer when you call it by name?"

"It's mine! Please give it to me!" Yue was almost in tears.

Jasmine knew the pen belonged to Yue, but Ruizi glared at her sternly to stop her from saying anything, and she was also afraid of Xiao Sheng, so she didn't dare speak up for Yue. Xiao Sheng said, "Since this pen has no owner, I'll just break it!"

Dodging Yue's mad attempts to jump at him and grab the pen, Xiao Sheng quickly unscrewed the pen cap, pointed the nib down and jabbed it into the asphalt road. The nib split in two, and ink dripped out, ruining the pen. As Xiao Sheng walked away triumphantly, Jasmine tearfully picked up the destroyed pen and put it into Yue's trembling hands. The excited onlooker Ruizi became silent as well. She hadn't known that Xiao Sheng could do something so wicked.

What Jasmine got from those boys at school were naughty tricks and pranks, but what Yue got was downright bullying. Enduring this kind of childhood twisted the psyches of many of the children as they held in their stress and frustration day in and day out. Having no way to escape or resist, some of them found that their only outlet was to "rule over" someone weaker, or to torture defenseless little creatures.

Since they were the only students who didn't join in the games during recess, Jasmine grew closer to Yue. They made an interesting pair: one in ragged clothes and the other the best dressed girl in the entire school; one failing every class and the other the top student in every subject. But the pain they suffered at home brought them together, and they became friends.

Yue would tell Jasmine stories about her stepmother. Once Yue's stepmother made a stack of mouth-watering sugar pancakes. She deliberately put the biggest ones at the bottom of the stack, and the smallest ones at the top of the stack. Making sure Yue's father could hear her, she said: "Yue is the youngest in our family, so we should all take good care of her and let her pick her share first. Yue, why don't you go ahead and pick the biggest and juiciest pancake. Your brothers and sisters will choose theirs after you." The stepmother's three biological kids started to protest, but she stopped them with a glance. Yue cautiously took the smallest pancake from the top of the pile, and her sister Qinqin took the second smallest piece. The stepmother's three kids then took the biggest pieces. Yue's father appreciated how well his wife treated his own two daughters, and the stepmother smiled contentedly.

"Why didn't you pick the bigger one from the bottom of the stack?"

"Only a girl who lives with her real mother would ask that," Yue said. "Do you think she really wanted me to pick first? If I dared to pick anything other than the smallest one, she'd make me pay it back a hundredfold! I'd be the devil girl who took advantage of her brothers and sisters, who took the most and did the least, who was selfish and shameless... You have no idea how she'd make me pay for that little sugar pancake!"

Hearing this made Jasmine sad, because she felt she could relate even though Mom was her real mother. Jasmine always felt that Mom and Dad loved Lily and hated her. It had been a source of such profound sadness for so long that she felt it becoming a hard, solid piece inside of her that caused her pain every moment.

Gao Hong and Daffodil actually loved both of their daughters very much. But they were very poor at expressing affection. There's a saying in Chinese: "Nobody can hold a bowl of water completely level." And no parents can be completely fair to all of their children. Just as a person will love every one of their fingers, each finger still has a different length and receives different levels of attention.

Five years younger than Jasmine, Lily was spirited and adorable and had never lived apart from her parents. She could be coquettish and affectionate, pleasing and willful. One moment she might shout and scream over a slight upset, and the next she would cling to her parents like sticky candy. Lily was the only joy and only source of laughter in Daffodil and Gao Hong's gloomy lives. The sight of Lily always brought a smile to their faces, and they indulged her every whim. Even Grandma Lotus said, "Look how happy Gao Hong gets when he sees his younger daughter. Even his bottom is smiling."

Jasmine, on the other hand, had been separated from Gao Hong and Daffodil at a young age, and after being away for so long, there was some estrangement upon her return. Unlike her sister, Jasmine never threw tantrums or asked her parents for anything. She always kept her distance. When her parents scolded her, she just stubbornly stared back, provoking Daffodil and Gao Hong even more. Lily chattered and gamboled around her parents all the time, and she cried loudly at the slightest parental threat, making it impossible for Daffodil and Gao Hong to hit her. Jasmine avoided her parents, trying to talk to them as little as possible. She preferred to gaze out the window, thinking God-knows-what.

Gao Hong and Daffodil didn't know how to deal with Jasmine. No matter what delicious food or pretty clothes they gave her, she was never happy, and no matter how much they scolded or beat her, she was quiet and tearless. What kind of a child was this? She was like an unresponsive wooden little person with no emotions. Gao Hong and Daffodil became so frustrated and enraged that they scolded her every time they saw her. This only established a vicious cycle that made Jasmine even more distant and estranged from them, which in turn upset Gao Hong and Daffodil even more.

Moreover, Daffodil and Gao Hong firmly believed that older children should accommodate, yield to and take care of younger ones, and that an older sibling should take responsibility for what happened to their younger siblings. Whenever the sisters had a conflict, Daffodil and Gao Hong scolded Jasmine without hesitation, and lectured Jasmine to always yield to her sister's needs. Cunning little Lily quickly learned to go crying to her parents whenever Jasmine didn't do exactly what she wanted, ensuring that Jasmine would get punished every time. The iron clad rule of "Lily cries, Jasmine dies" hurt Jasmine so much that it not only deepened the rift between her and her parents, but also made her start to resent her sister.

To make matters worse, Jasmine was held responsible for all of Lily's actions. If Lily broke something, Jasmine was scolded. If Lily fell and hurt herself, Jasmine was punished. If Lily played in a mud puddle and got her clothes dirty, Jasmine was blamed and made to wash them. Jasmine was just a child herself, and expecting her to take responsibility for another child over whom she had no control was simply too unreasonable. Not even an adult can fully control all his or her children's actions, so how on earth could a child do it?

All this pressure robbed Jasmine of any semblance of a childhood. She was perpetually anxious, tense and angry. She didn't run out to play with her friends for fear that Lily would follow and hurt herself. She didn't dare win when playing cards with Lily for fear that Lily would cry if she lost. She was careful not to take too much of anything from the dinner platters for fear of upsetting someone. Jasmine always looked downcast. Her only goal and biggest wish was to keep everyone happy and avoid any trouble, even at her own expense.

One day, when Gao Hong was doing laundry, he happened to look up to fetch something just as Jasmine turned her head, and their eyes met. Gao Hong was taken aback by the look on Jasmine's face. It was a face full of worry and weariness. The knotted eyebrows and empty stare were all too familiar. Where had he seen them? After he thought about it for a long time, he realized that this was his own face when he was her age! He had been living a privileged life in Dr. Gao's house back then, but he wasn't happy. Once when he was walking past the wall mirror in the dining hall, he caught a glimpse of himself. The emptiness in his eyes and the knot in his eyebrows, why did he see them on Jasmine's face now?

(67) SUICIDE

Just as Gao Hong never considered Dr. Gao's house his home, Jasmine never felt at home in her parents' house either. Her safe haven was Grandma's house. At that time, Jasmine had no happiness and no laughter. She lived a precarious existence amidst a daily chorus of scolding, beatings, sarcasm, suspicion and accusations. Even when nobody took notice of her, she had to witness the daily and constant mutual destruction between her parents.

Jasmine asked herself, "Would Mom or Dad ever abandon this family and run away?" She hated this home, but she didn't want it to fall apart. In fact, at the same time that she hated it, she loved it deeply as well, just as she deeply loved her parents. The two conflicting forces of love and hate tore her apart and made her feel crazy.

Decades later, when Daffodil came to America to visit Jasmine, she brought along some pictures of Jasmine when she was ten years old. In every picture, Jasmine looked miserable. Her eyes were big, empty and lifeless, looking aimlessly into oblivion. The adult Jasmine clutched the pictures to her chest and wept out loud. She was holding her ten-year-old self, hugging that poor little girl who had walked alone in darkness and despair! She was holding her tight and caressing her, telling her how beautiful the world actually was, how much love there was and how much love she was going to receive someday. She was telling her that her parents actually loved her, even if they didn't know how to show it.

But at that time, nobody told little Jasmine anything of the sort, and she had no way of knowing it. She was alone in the darkness, and the only thing she could look forward to in her life was the summer break, when she could finally go to her Grandma's house.

Every day was a countdown. As summer approached day by day, Jasmine felt that she could endure any misery and hardship. After all, she was about to spend an entire summer at Grandma's house, so what did anything else matter? She believed that she was not born to live in the present but to hope for the future. She felt that she would have reached her limit if not for the beautiful summer, which made her willing to grit her teeth and hang on with all her might. She was eleven years old and could hang on for Grandma, for that beacon of light that sustained her through all those dark nights.

"Your middle school entrance exam is six months away! You shouldn't waste your time at Grandma's house this summer. You should stay home so I can oversee your studies every day." Daffodil's words hung in the air, taking their time to land on Jasmine as if moving in slow motion. It took a while for Jasmine to realize what her mother had just said. What? No Grandma's house? Was she talking to me? Me? The summer? The summer I've been counting the days for? Really? It can't be true! Jasmine felt she was being executed with slow bullets, each taking out a piece of her body while the other parts watched in shock, not believing what was actually gone.

After speaking those dreadful words, Daffodil left the house, leaving Jasmine home alone. Jasmine's mind raced. She knew Mom never discussed anything with her. She just made decisions that everyone had to follow. But it was the summer, the only thing she looked forward to! The only hope left in her eleven-year-old heart! How could Mom just take that away without a second thought?

Jasmine slapped on her own head, hoping to wake up from this nightmare. Tears streamed down her face as she repeated, "No! No!" She desperately thought, "Staying in this suffocating house twenty-four hours a day, seven days a week, without even school to break up the dread of Mom 'overseeing' me every day..... No, I'd rather die. I'd rather die! Oh.... Yes! That's it! I'll die! I'll make them sorry! I'll make them cry! I'll make them regret treating me so badly! Grandma will kill them with her wrath! That's right! I'll die!"

Jasmine paced in circles like a little beast while sobbing violently, imagining how Mom and Dad would react upon finding her dead body. A rush of vengeful pleasure washed over her. She trembled with adrenaline, fear, sadness and determination. Clenching her teeth, she muttered, "All right, you don't love me! I'll leave you! I've had enough!"

Ever since the last time she'd thought about death, Jasmine had taken special note of related information. She'd heard of cutting the throat as a way to die, but she heard a neighbor auntie say that the windpipe was on one side of the neck, and the food pipe on the other side, and you had to cut the windpipe because cutting the food pipe wouldn't kill you. The neighbors usually sat together in the yard to gossip and chat about anything and everything. Nobody paid attention to what the kids overheard, or whether their conversations were suitable for young ears. Being observant and sensitive, Jasmine heard everything, and she believed what she heard because that auntie sounded so sure.

Tearfully taking out a long kitchen knife, Jasmine tried to determine which side of her neck held the windpipe. She applied pressure to one side of her neck to see if that stopped her breathing, and when it didn't, she tried the other side. But no matter how much pressure she applied on either side, she could still breathe, so this wasn't going to get her anywhere. After crying for a while longer, she thought of something. She fetched a dipper full of water and then took a big gulp, trying to feel which side of the neck it went down. She thought the water had to go down the food pipe, so if she could find out where the water went down, the opposite side must be where the windpipe was. She took several gulps, each one larger than the one before, but still couldn't tell which side of her neck it went down.

Years later in adulthood, Jasmine relived this scene in her nightmares. An eleven-year-old girl, determined to take her own life, was holding a water dipper in one hand and a long kitchen knife in the other. With tears streaming down her face, she was swallowing gulp after gulp of cold water. And in those days in China, nobody could help poor Jasmine.

Frustrated by not being able to locate her windpipe, Jasmine tossed away the dipper and sank onto a chair and cried. Then she remembered someone saying that sleeping pills could kill you. She threw the kitchen knife onto the bed and went to the medicine drawer to look for sleeping pills. She couldn't find any, but deep in the medicine drawer was a small paper bag with the word "tranquilizer" written in red. Jasmine poured out its contents and counted the little white pills, thirteen in all. These were the thirteen pills Gao Hong had gotten a few years ago when he'd threatened suicide to stop Daffodil from destroying the love of his life, Yanruo. Jasmine wondered if a "tranquilizer" was what people commonly referred to as a "sleeping pill," and whether thirteen of them were enough to take her from this world. She looked up the word "tranquilizer" in a dictionary, but found no indication of whether it was the same as sleeping pills. What should she do?

Jasmine realized that she should leave her parents a note so they would know why she'd died. Wiping her tears, she sat down and wrote: "I decided to kill myself because you scold me and hit me so much, I can't take it anymore ..." As she was writing, Jasmine suddenly saw her Dad walking towards her. Dad had come home, but she was so focused on her note that she hadn't noticed him!

"What's going on?" Gao Hong asked. "Why are you crying? What are you writing? Let me see." Jasmine clutched her notebook desperately and refused to let her dad see it, no matter what! She thought, "Even if I want to die, I'll do it myself. I don't want to die from Mom and Dad's beatings when they find out what's in my note. They will surely beat me to death if they see it!" Gao Hong didn't insist on seeing the note.

Gao Hong would never know how overwhelmingly grateful Jasmine was to him for that moment when he didn't insist on reading the note. He gave her the privacy and respect she wanted, and for that, Jasmine would be grateful for the rest of her life!

Gao Hong didn't know what to say. Looking around, he noticed the knife on the bed and picked it up: "How come there's a knife on the bed? I know, you can use it to cut fruit for yourself as an afternoon snack." He put the knife back in the drawer and left.

As soon as Dad went out the door, Jasmine tore her note into pieces. Her suicide attempt had been derailed, and she'd lost the courage to kill herself. She sat there doing nothing until evening came. That evening was the darkest in Jasmine's life, the time when she completely broke away from her mother and from her family of origin.

Daffodil was furious, forbidding Jasmine from eating dinner and ordering her to stand in front of her: "What did you write? What did you write in that note? This won't end unless you tell me everything!" Jasmine didn't want to tell her, so she stood there without saying a word. "Out with it!" Daffodil roared.

Then Daffodil turned to Gao Hong: "You're so useless, not reading it just because she said no! If that had been me, I'd have broken her fingers one by one with my bare hands so I could read that note!" Jasmine's heart felt as dead as cold ash. She thought to herself: "Listen, listen, these are my mother's words. I have a mother like this!"

At long last, feeling that she had no choice, Jasmine said, "I wrote that I wanted to kill myself because …"

Before she could continue, Daffodil screamed in Jasmine' face at an even higher pitch: "Suicide! Fucking suicide! You think you can scare me with a fucking suicide? Go ahead, die! Why don't you die! How shameful! Do you know how people would jeer and belittle you? Don't you have any shame? How can you ever show your face to anyone?!"

Each word was like a knife that stabbed Jasmine in the heart. She had hoped her mother might feel some remorse over how she treated her; she wanted to torture her mom's conscience. But no, it didn't work. She seemed to feel none of the emotions Jasmine wanted her to feel. All she felt was shame, the shame of having a daughter like her! But Jasmine had no idea the harshest blow was yet to come.

After a slight pause, Daffodil went on in a calm voice: "You think your death will upset anyone? If you die, I might cry, but let me tell you, I'll be crying for the thousands of yuan I spent on you over the years! What makes you think I'd shed a tear for YOU?"

Jasmine felt as if she'd been struck by a bolt from above. "Did my mother just say that? Really? Is she my real mother?" Jasmine felt that even if all the world's pain and suffering were inflicted on her, it would be more bearable than hearing this cold-blooded sentence from her own mother! Those words continued to torture Jasmine for decades like a bloody knife that she couldn't remove from her heart. She lived with that knife in her heart well into adulthood. Many times, she was determined to forget what her mother had said and never think about it again. But the words gained a life of their own, returning in her nightmares and reducing her to screams and tears in the depths of many nights, even when she was over 40 years old.

Jasmine stood there like a mummy. She mentally blocked out everything else that happened that night. She could no longer hear her mother's screaming, or taste anything when her father gave her food. The next thing she knew, all was quiet, and she was lying in bed in the darkness of the night.

Jasmine thought to herself, "I'm nothing to Mom but a few thousand yuan. Even if I died, she'd feel no remorse or sorrow, or change for the better. This family will suck the life out of me. Even going to Grandma's house is just a temporary escape, and even this temporary refuge can be taken away from me at any time. What's my way out? Maybe the only way out is for me to grow up and leave this house. Yes, I can grow up and leave! I'll go someplace far away and never turn back and never, ever see them again!" As soon as this idea leaped into her mind, Jasmine stared intently into the darkness: "How silly I was! I forgot that I can grow up! Then I can leave all of this behind forever and ever! I'll never look back! Why do I need to die? I want to live! I want to live to see the day I can leave it all behind!"

After the suicide attempt, Gao Hong and Daffodil allowed Jasmine to spend the summer at her Grandma's house. But her happiness was limited by her knowledge that she'd had to earn that summer with a life worth just "thousands of yuan." Now she had bigger hopes and dreams – to leave home and seek a life of her own!

Gao Hong and Daffodil never mentioned the suicide attempt again. Decades passed and Jasmine still didn't know whether her suicide attempt actually shocked her mother, or what her parents actually thought about it.

The adult Jasmine actually saw some benefit in her mother's cruel words. By reducing Jasmine's death to "a few thousand yuan," Daffodil defeated the purpose of Jasmine's suicide attempt and shattered Jasmine's idea of making her parents suffer remorse over her death. As a result, it completely removed the idea of suicide from her head.

(68) GRANDMA GOES TO HEAVEN

Gray-haired and stooped, Yixin had long passed retirement age, but he persisted in exercising daily and never missed a day of work, come rain or shine. His wife, Lotus, objected, "You should have retired long ago! The department would function just fine without you. I've never seen someone so eager to work themselves to death!" Yixin glared and said, "Now is the best time! The Gang of Four has been ousted, the Cultural Revolution is over, and the era of reform is here! How could I possibly quit now?"

Indeed, Yixin felt it was a great time to be alive. His children were all grown, and even his youngest daughter, Rong, had gone off to university. With his health still relatively good, Yixin wanted to work a few more years. Lotus also felt much more at ease, as her grandchildren were old enough not to need her personal care. Of their seven children, six were in Beijing, with only their second daughter, Jade, remaining in Shaanxi Province, where she'd been sent during the Cultural Revolution as part of the movement to have millions of urban young people "remolded" through manual labor in the countryside. Thinking of Jade so far away always made Lotus tearful, and her heart ached with longing.

One day, Lotus noticed blood in her stool. At first she ignored it, but the blood continued to appear for several weeks. "It seems that old age brings all sorts of ailments," Lotus sighed. When her youngest daughter Rong, who was a student in medical school, came home for the weekend, Lotus jokingly said as she served her hot dumplings, "My youngest girl, now studying to be a doctor, tell me, is blood in the stool a serious matter?" Rong looked up sharply at her. "Who are you talking about? Is it you, Mom?"

Lotus was admitted to the hospital and diagnosed with colorectal cancer. The time from diagnosis to surgery to the cancer spreading and treatment being abandoned passed in just a couple of months — it all happened so suddenly!

Much weakened, Lotus lay in bed, drifting in and out of consciousness. Covered by a quilt with only her graying hair and aged face visible, she seemed to see the endless expanse of Baiyang Lake, feel the cool lake water, and hear the calls of wild ducks and geese along with the celebratory horns and the creaking of the flower palanquin. Lotus felt as if she had become that bride again, obediently remaining speechless and waiting eagerly for the time when she could finally eat. Daqing, Erqing and Sanqing were born one after another – oh, poor Sanqing, Mama's poor child! Daffodil and Jade were running around everywhere, and the Japanese came! The famine struck! The jeep brought life-saving grain and news of Yixin. Their home in Beijing where three daughters were born in succession, then daughters-in-law arriving in their home for the first time, then the first son-in-law, and their grandchildren, Jasmine, Feifei.... Every so often, Lotus thought, "I'm so tired. I can't do anything anymore."

In her drowsiness, she heard a small, timid voice: "Grandma." Lotus opened her eyes; it was her Jasmine, her sweet little Jasmine! Lotus managed a faint smile: "I heard you got into the best middle school! That's great! If Grandma dies, I won't get to see you anymore." Saying this, Grandma extended her wrinkly hand to grip Jasmine's hand.

Jasmine held back her tears, tucked her grandmother's hand back under the quilt, covered her up, and then ran out of the room. In the yard, Jasmine let her tears flow freely. Grandma, please get better! Grandma, you must live to see me grow up! I'll buy lots of delicious food for you and bring you to live in my own home! Jasmine was crying her heart out when her eldest aunt came over. "Stop crying, come in and eat." Jasmine's eldest uncle, Xu Daqing, now lived in two spacious apartments and had brought Grandma over to take care of her.

After quickly eating in her aunt's kitchen, Jasmine went to see her grandma again, but Grandma had already fallen asleep. Jasmine had no choice but to leave reluctantly with Daffodil. That departure turned out to be her last farewell to Grandma.

Two days later, Jasmine returned home from school and saw her dad Gao Hong head out wearing a formal woolen suit. Jasmine stared at her father in confusion, and Gao Hong said, "Hurry and eat, I'm leaving. Your grandma has passed away." Jasmine was silent, unable to react for a long time. Gao Hong left without looking at her again. Jasmine collapsed into a chair. "Grandma is gone, Grandma is gone!" – the one who loved her most in the world, the only person who truly loved her, was gone!

Daffodil and her siblings cried themselves to sleep every night. The daughters-in-law and sons-in-law were exhausting themselves arranging for the cremation, the farewell ceremony and various related affairs. No one considered the feelings or grief of the children, or thought of how while they had lost their mother, the children had lost the grandmother who had raised them. Jasmine didn't remember how she got through the following days, staring blankly at her books. Her parents didn't have time to care or ask about her, and no one comforted her or even mentioned Grandma's death. They didn't let Jasmine attend the funeral, nor did anyone tell her when it was. The greatest and saddest event in Jasmine's life was left for her to endure alone.

Every time she sat in a daze, Jasmine thought of how Grandma's love protected her. If Grandma had passed away a little earlier, it would have been during Jasmine's suicide attempt. Dear Grandma seemed to have known that she needed to see Jasmine through this most dangerous period of her young life, and she left only after Jasmine had found hope and affirmed her resolve for life.

The initial pain wasn't the worst – the real agony came from reflecting on the pain afterwards. Jasmine never recovered from hearing the news of Grandma's death. Even in adulthood, any mention of Grandma still hurt so much. She was never able to think of Grandma calmly, as every thought engulfed her in immense sorrow that instantly turned her back into that lonely, helpless teenage girl. Gao Hong and Daffodil never offered Jasmine any comfort or acknowledgment of her immense grief over losing Grandma.

Sometimes Jasmine wondered about Feifei. They'd grew up together at Grandma's house, and Feifei returned to her parents when she was in third grade. Did she go through similar struggles? Did she also miss the grandmother who'd raised her? But Jasmine never saw Feifei or heard any news of her.

One day, while Jasmine was sitting on a small stool in her yard and staring at the clouds, a face appeared through the gap in the front gate, and a voice called, "Jasmine." It was a low, unfamiliar male voice that made Jasmine jump up in surprise. Looking through the gate, she saw her elementary school classmate, Xiao Bing, from the fourth row. All of the Four Corner kids who'd been Jasmine's classmates at Shili Primary school were in middle school now. Jasmine had been admitted to a prestigious middle school, while Xiao Bing, with poorer grades, entered an ordinary school, so Jasmine hadn't seen Xiao Bing since middle school started. The once tough kid who used a glass bottle to fight older boys for a cigarette wrapper had now grown tall and had the deep voice of an adult man. Through the gate gap, Jasmine saw that Xiao Bing even had a little mustache; she almost didn't recognize him!

"What are you doing here?" Jasmine asked. Xiao Bing pushed at the locked gate and then spoke through it, "I heard about your situation. My mom told me. I just wanted to say, I thought about suicide too. That year when my mom was arrested, everyone called me a thief's son and bullied me pretty bad. I thought about dying. If it weren't for my grandma, I would have killed myself. I spent all night walking by the moat; my dad almost went crazy looking for me. I'm telling you, I know now that living, no matter how hard, is better than dying. We have to endure, grow up and do something big. You have to wait for the day when you're grown up. Just hang in there and wait for that day!"

Jasmine stood there, shocked to hear that Xiao Bing's thoughts had mirrored her own. No one had ever said such things to her. The pitiful Yue had been Jasmine's only friend, and she hadn't seen Yue since graduating from elementary school. With her poor grades, Yue had been placed in a bottom-tier school known for fights, crime and teen pregnancy. Yue's stepmother refused to let her continue studying: "Look at yourself! Are you trying to be a phoenix? Just start working and earn some money." Yue's father had no choice but to find her a job as a bus conductor at the age of fourteen. Daffodil forbade Jasmine from seeing Yue after that, fearing that she would be led astray. Without Yue, Jasmine had no friends.

Xiao Bing's words touched Jasmine. She nodded and asked, "How's your grandma?" Xiao Bing replied, "She passed away last year. I heard your grandma is gone too." Jasmine looked down in silence and Xiao Bing also fell silent. After a while, he said, "I'm leaving. Goodbye." Then turned and walked away.

Jasmine sat back down on her stool, and as she stared at the clouds, she realized that Xiao Bing was the only person who had mentioned Grandma to her since Grandma's passing, and the only one who had talked to her about suicide since her attempt. As she pondered this, Jasmine heard her neighbor Ruizi run out and call, "Xiao Bing, Xiao Bing! What's the math homework today? Hey, don't go!" Jasmine remembered that Ruizi and Xiao Bing had gotten into the same middle school.

(69) BOOKS AND OPERA

Gao Hong and Daffodil were so consumed by the grief and the endless chores after losing Lotus that they had no time to look after Jasmine. School work was easy for Jasmine, who would finish it quickly after returning home from school, and then find herself bored, with nothing else to do. Jasmine's middle school had issued a library card to each student, so Jasmine started borrowing books from the school library to read.

The first book she borrowed was Reader's Digest for Teens. After flipping through it, she found it uninteresting and returned it to the library the next day. As she was leaving the library, she noticed an old book on a table with two words printed on it: "Jane Eyre." Jasmine picked it up and handed her library card to the librarian, who wrote the book's title on the back of the card, stamped it, and gave it back to Jasmine.

The book Jane Eyre opened a window to the world of literature for Jasmine. Over the next few days, Jasmine no longer lived in her own world. She couldn't pay attention in school and was oblivious to everything around her at home. She was living in the world of Jane Eyre! She felt Jane's sorrow of losing her parents at a young age and living as a dependent in her uncle's house. She cried over Jane's mistreatment in her uncle's home and at the orphanage, feeling as if Jane was her own shadow. But then Jane eventually broke free and found her true love, despite Rochester's injuries and disabilities. The story of finding true love and a life partner warmed Jasmine's heart deeply. British manor life and the exotic culture were so unknown and mysterious to her. Jane Eyre's life was so full of hardship and yet so beautiful that it mesmerized Jasmine, who constantly thought, "Jane Eyre suffered more than I did, which means a girl like me can also have hope and happiness in the future, right? Is it possible?"

The second book Jasmine read was The Count of Monte Cristo. The thrilling escape from death and journey of revenge left Jasmine intoxicated. She couldn't believe that such an exciting story had existed all this time! Once she started reading, Jasmine couldn't stop! She quickly read Death on the Nile, How the Steel Was Tempered, Les Misérables, David Copperfield and Points and Lines...

With each book, Jasmine immersed herself in the stories and breathed in sync with the characters, and the reality of her own daily life became distant and irrelevant. She didn't care about her parents' arguments or their scolding and beatings. It was almost as if any injustice, suffering or difficulty had nothing to do with her. These books pulled Jasmine out of the dark abyss of losing her grandmother and brought her back to the surface, where she could see the sunlight. For the first time Jasmine realized there was such a vast world out there, and her heart could be so free. The future held endless possibilities. Jasmine was ecstatic!

Next, Jasmine borrowed a four-volume set of Dream of the Red Chamber. By now, the librarian knew Jasmine, and as she handed her the books, she said, "Borrowing four books at once? Can you finish them? Dream of the Red Chamber isn't easy to read." Jasmine replied, "I can finish them."

Indeed, she could, because once she started reading, she did nothing else. She didn't pay attention in classes, do homework, play with classmates or talk to anyone. She couldn't allow any thoughts unrelated to the books to enter her mind, and she immersed herself completely in the story, even dreaming about it at night. She first devoured the four volumes quickly, then went back to carefully savor them. She repeatedly pondered the poems in Dream of the Red Chamber. She delighted in the imagery of "Willows borrow a green hue from the dike, flowers share their fragrance across the bank," and felt sorrow over the desolation of "Cranes' shadows crossing the cold pond, the cold moon burying the flowers' soul." She thought that from the perspective of balanced tone, the word "crossing" could be better replaced with "flying," making the tone more harmonious and the image more dynamic. She lightly penciled in the change: "Cranes' shadows flying across the cold pond, the cold moon burying the flowers' soul."

This obsession with books led to a drastic decline in Jasmine's academic performance. In the second year of middle school, she, who had always scored above ninety in all subjects, saw her first score of eighty-four. Then, scores in the seventies and sixties began to appear. By eighth grade, Jasmine was at the bottom of her class. Yet she had no choice but to seek refuge in the world of novels, as it was the only thing that kept her sane in her grief over her grandmother's death.

Daffodil and Gao Hong found it hard to remain sane, however. Their elder daughter seemed to be daydreaming all the time, forgetting to eat or not feeling hungry or just eating mechanically when given a bowl of food, and showing no reaction to scolding or beatings. Her grades were a disaster, and Daffodil and Gao Hong were furious at Jasmine's lack of motivation or interest in anything.

Daffodil cursed Jasmine daily with the most venomous words: "You shameless wretch! You're the black sheep of our family! Filthy scum! You're not even worth a strand of your sister's hair. What did I ever do to deserve a shameless thing like you! If you don't improve your grades, get lost! I'm not supporting you anymore, so just quit school and go live like a tramp! I don't care if you live or die!"

But Jasmine seemed impervious, enduring her beatings with a mute expression, as if her parents were hitting someone else. Exasperated, Daffodil devised new punishments: She stopped making pretty clothes for Jasmine and dressed her in ragged old clothes, regardless of whether they were for boys or girls, with missing buttons, faded colors or worn-out shoes. Jasmine wore the tattered garments to school every day without complaining.

Finally, Daffodil discovered The Water Margin and Romance of the Three Kingdoms in Jasmine's bag and realized that these were the "useless books" responsible for her poor grades. Daffodil angrily tore up the books despite Jasmine's desperate attempts to stop her. Jasmine broke down crying: "They're the school's books!"

"Why do you borrow books from the school? You want a beating? School books are for good students, not for scum like you! With your grades, you still have the nerve to borrow useless books? Everyone knows you're hopeless scum! How do you have the audacity to borrow books!" Daffodil yelled as she dumped Jasmine's bag onto the bed, searching every book and paper until she found the library card.

The card was filled with the names of various novels, each with a stamp next to it. Daffodil shouted, "Look at you! Reading all these useless books! Is it even worth sending you to school anymore? Quit if you want! You think you deserve to read these books? Can a failing student understand them? You think the librarian isn't laughing at you for borrowing them? Aren't you ashamed? If I were you, I'd hang myself rather than live in such disgrace! You still have the nerve to borrow books!" Daffodil tore up the library card and stormed out.

Holding back her tears, Jasmine carefully repaired the torn books. Her mother's cruelty, humiliation, and relentless belittling were like knives stabbing her in the heart. But what hurt her the most was that the books that had been her only refuge after her grandmother's death would now be banned.

Fortunately, the librarian was kind enough not to pursue the damage to the books Jasmine returned, and even offered to issue a new library card. Jasmine stared at the librarian in a daze, slowly shaking her head. During recess, while her classmates all went outside, Jasmine stayed inside in her ragged clothes and laid her head down on her desk. One of her classmates, a girl named Xing Xiaowen, approached her and asked, "Are your parents not letting you read novels? Don't worry, don't be sad. You can use my library card to borrow whatever you want. You can keep the books at my house, I live right behind the school."

The first time Jasmine visited Xing Xiaowen's home, she fell in love with it. Xiaowen's father played the jinghu, the main string instrument for Beijing Opera, while Xiaowen's mother sang opera to his accompaniment, the two of them exchanging smiles full of appreciation and joy. Jasmine was mesmerized. Xiaowen said, "Don't mind my parents; all they do is sing opera!" Jasmine was shocked and terrified – how could someone speak to their parents like that? Her parents must be furious and give Xiaowen a beating!

Xiaowen's father laughed, "Hey, what's wrong with that? Our opera supports you and feeds you, so why don't you appreciate it?" Xiaowen's mother also laughed: "Your father is a jinghu master; show some respect for your old man!" Xiaowen's father nodded and winked at his wife, and Xiaowen responded, "Whatever!" The family laughed together, making Jasmine laugh too. She couldn't believe such a harmonious and happy family existed – was it real?

Xiaowen's mother took Jasmine's hand and said, "This girl is tall, has a round face, beautiful features and slender hands – a perfect candidate for Qingyi (a young female role in opera). Would you like to learn Beijing Opera, girl?"

Before Jasmine could answer, Xiaowen pulled her away, "Mom, stop bothering my friend! You ask everyone if they want to sing opera! Not everyone is like you!" She dragged Jasmine into another room. There, Jasmine was captivated by the many photos on the walls: "Xiaowen, are these all photos of your mother on stage?"

Jasmine saw an unimaginable beauty unfold before her eyes. All her life, she had only seen women dressed in blue and gray, with short hair or black braids, their faces sallow and their manners rough, struggling to cope with life. But the characters in these photos wore splendid costumes adorned with sparkling jewels, their bright eyes and expressive faces conveying emotions accompanied by elegant gestures and poised stances. It was the first time Jasmine had seen such lovely women. Her longing for beauty was instantly awakened.

Whenever she had the chance, Jasmine would go to Xiaowen's house to listen to Xiaowen's parents sing opera. Both of them worked in a theater troupe and didn't have regular office hours, often practicing at home. They enjoyed teaching Jasmine about Beijing Opera, explaining the different roles, rules, singing styles and movements. Jasmine borrowed a massive Beijing Opera compendium from them and read through each play. She discovered that the lyrics were beautifully written, with wisdom and depth, and full of historical significance and poetic imagery. Jasmine copied down large portions of these lyrics, reciting and meditating on them repeatedly. She also tuned into radio stations that broadcasted operas, and even watched a performance of The Unicorn Purse by Maestro Li Shiji on a neighbor's television.

At her young age, most would find the slow, melodic rhythm of Beijing Opera unbearable, but Jasmine was instantly hooked. After the novels, Beijing Opera provided her with another escape from reality. Its abstract expression, subtlety and imaginative props and backdrops were particularly appealing to Jasmine. Her dislike and disappointment for reality drove her to seek rest for her soul in abstract things, and Beijing Opera became the joy of her life.

(70) A HANDSOME BOY

Gao Hong and Daffodil's harsh opposition didn't make Jasmine give up reading, and she certainly wouldn't give up listening to and learning about opera. She just needed to be more discreet now. She made up her mind to keep her parents from finding out. Jasmine continued borrowing all kinds of books using Xiaowen's library card, and she read them in class, during recess and staying late after school. As a result, her grades deteriorated further and further.

Jasmine got into the habit of lying to her parents. At first, she almost fainted while telling lies, but eventually, she was able to lie fluently with a calm expression. All her lies were for the sake of staying late after school, inventing excuses such as self-study, extracurricular activities, study groups, volleyball, or required school clean-ups. In reality, she stayed at school to read novels or went to Xiaowen's house to listen to her parents perform opera.

One time, the teacher suddenly announced that there would be no classes in the afternoon, and the students would be dismissed early. Jasmine was thrilled. Xiaowen said, "Why don't we go to the theater troupe to see my parents? It's only four bus stops from the school." Jasmine couldn't believe her ears! How could such a wonderful thing happen to her?

The two girls excitedly rushed to the theater troupe. Xiaowen's mother allowed them sit down and watch the rehearsal of the sword dance from the opera Farewell My Concubine. As the percussion rhythm of "Cang-Qi-Tai-Qi, Cang-Qi-Tai-Qi, Cang-Qi-Tai-Qi-Tai-Cang! Da-Da-Da-Tai, Cang – Ling-Tai-Yi-Tai-Cang! Da-Pu-Tai, Cang!" rang out, five dancers in long rehearsal skirts holding wooden practice swords entered the stage, circled around, turned, held their swords behind their backs, and arranged themselves into their beautiful poses. Jasmine and Xiaowen applauded vigorously! Then they visited the makeup room, admiring the exquisite costumes, the glittering phoenix crowns, shiny pompons, beaded ear decorations, bright oil face paints, silk flowers, headbands, silk sleeves, hair pieces... They admired everything as excitely as mice in a candy shop.

Seeing a row of chairs in an empty rehearsal hall, Jasmine randomly sat in one. An old man came in and shouted, "Where do you think you're sitting?!" Jasmine jumped up in fright and hid in a corner. The old man walked over and said, "That's our drummer's seat!"

Xiaowen's mother came in and told Jasmine, "There are rules in the theater troupe. You can't sit just anywhere. The drummer's seat is only for the drummer and the young painted-face character. No one else can sit there." Jasmine asked, "Why is the painted-face character allowed to sit there?" Xiaowen's mother laughed, "Because once a crown prince played the painted-face character. Since then, that character has been allowed to do anything he wants in any opera troupe! Oh, there are many rules. I'll tell you more later."

Jasmine asked Xiaowen's mother, "Auntie, can I join your theater troupe?" Auntie smiled, "This girl really loves opera! Go ask your parents, and if they give permission, you can come for two hours every day after school. We have a class here for kids around your age. You can learn the rules and basics — how to stand, look and stretch. Even if you're just playing a minor role, every cell from the tips of your fingers to the ends of your hair must embody the spirit of opera. If you can learn well in that class and pass the teacher's test, we'll talk about next steps, all right?" Jasmine nodded enthusiastically. Xiaowen's mom smiled and said, "Think it over carefully. The teacher may scold you and hit you with a stick when he's mad. Are you afraid of that?" Jasmine assured her, "I'm not afraid!"

Jasmine was more sure of this than anything in her life. Aside from wanting to visit her grandmother's house when she was little, training for the theater troupe was the only thing she truly wanted to do. Jasmine knew her parents would never agree, as going to university was the most glorified path for any student, and joining an opera troupe was only for those who couldn't make it in school. But Jasmine didn't care about society's rules. She was so determined that she decided not to back down, no matter how much her parents scold or beat her.

At dinner, Jasmine's heart was pounding as she finally mustered the courage to blurt out to her parents in one breath: "My classmate Xing Xiaowen's mom is in a Beijing Opera troupe. She said I could learn to be an opera performer. Today, Xing Xiaowen took me to the troupe to see her mom, and her mom said I could go there to practice for two hours every day after school. If I get good enough, I can join their Beijing Opera troupe." Jasmine sneaked a glance at her parents, who were staring at her, and in a small voice, she added, "I want to go. I like Beijing Opera."

After saying this, Jasmine lowered her head, wondering whether her mother's slap or her father's chopsticks would hit her first. But nothing happened. Daffodil and Gao Hong didn't say anything. Jasmine waited with her heart in her throat, but still there was no response from her parents. Unable to bear the suspense, she said, "I need to use the bathroom," and ran off.

Daffodil continued eating. Gao Hong said, "Our Jasmine is tall and pretty. She might really get noticed if she visits a troupe." Daffodil said, "She can't go!" Gao Hong agreed, "I know she can't go. Learning opera is too tough. We can't let her go through that insane training. Let's talk to her nicely, without getting angry." Just then, Jasmine returned, washed her hands, and sat back down at the table. She couldn't believe that her parents hadn't scolded or hit her yet. What was going on?

Gao Hong finally said, "Daughter, you can't go to learn opera. It would be an unbearable hardship for you. It's not only vocals but also martial arts and vigorous dancing. Out of a hundred people who start, only one might succeed, and those who don't succeed end up with lifelong injuries. Do you know why, in the old days, only the poorest families sent their kids to learn opera? Because anyone who had enough food to eat would never let their kids experience the cruelty of an opera troupe. Your mom and I care about you and don't want you to suffer."

Jasmine had never heard such words from her parents! Her father actually said that he cared about her. Tears welled up in Jasmine's eyes. Daffodil noticed that Jasmine had grown up into a young lady without them realizing it. A wave of softness rose in her heart, and she said, "Is it because you're struggling with school and want to take a different path? But you don't need to. Your dad graduated from college. Look around, who else here has a college degree? Who else is as smart as your dad? You're his daughter. You would never be bad at school. I know it! You can go to college and achieve great things if you focus on your studies. That's much better than singing opera. Besides, they only said you could join the study class, not the troupe. Even if you study there, most kids don't make it into the troupe, and their schoolwork suffers. They are hopeless in school and have nothing to lose, but you're different. You can get into college!"

Jasmine's mind was buzzing. She couldn't believe her mother was saying these things. Did her mother really think she wasn't that bad? Hadn't her mother given up on her in disappointment long ago? Hadn't she regretted giving birth to such a disgraceful daughter? How could she say that Jasmine could go to college?

Daffodil and Gao Hong's words gave Jasmine their first affirmation and vote of confidence, and showed their love for the first time. Jasmine had never cried in front of her parents when beaten or scolded, but now tears streamed down her face. Gao Hong and Daffodil thought she was crying because they weren't allowing her to join the theater troupe, but Jasmine said, "Dad, Mom, I won't go."

Those few words from Gao Hong and Daffodil completely changed Jasmine. She still loved reading novels but no longer read them in class or neglected her homework. She still loved Beijing Opera but no longer used the time meant for studying to memorize opera scripts, or snuck out of school to go to the nearby opera house. She learned to limit her reading time and opera time to about an hour a day, dedicating the rest of her time to her studies. Her extensive reading and the cultural and literary nourishment she gained from opera helped her excel in literature and history courses. Her linguistic talent, inherited from Daffodil, made learning English a breeze. Her logical thinking, inherited from Gao Hong, made her stand out in math and physics. Soon, Jasmine was once again at the top of her class.

When it came time for the high school entrance exams, Jasmine had no trouble testing into the senior high section of her prestigious school. Unfortunately, her best friend Xing Xiaowen was eliminated in the tests and had to transfer to a different school.

On the first day of the new school year in September, Jasmine heard a voice calling her from behind: "Jasmine." She turned around quickly and saw a tall boy standing behind her. It was Xiao Bing from Four Corners! Jasmine hadn't seen Xiao Bing since he'd came to visit her and talked with her outside her gate when her grandmother passed away in eighth grade. Now he had grown so tall, almost like an adult!

"Xiao Bing? What are you doing at my school?" Jasmine asked.

"I got in. We're in the same class. We're the only two from Four Corners here. Yue's sister, Qinqin, used to be here, but she graduated and is now at Beijing University of Technology," Xiao Bing said.

"Oh." Jasmine nodded.

Entering her high school classroom, Jasmine saw that half the students were her old classmates from middle school, while the other half were new students from other schools who had earned admission with their test scores. Xiao Bing was one of the new students, and his assigned seat was just behind hers. Jasmine was also overjoyed to see that her new desk mate was an old middle school friend, Wang Weiwei. The two girls were so happy to see each other that they hugged each other, giggling. Some girls in the front rows were whispering and giggling while glancing at a boy sitting in the middle of the classroom. Jasmine followed their gaze and was almost blinded by the sight of that boy, who stood out dramatically from the rest of the boys in their worn, grayish clothes and tattered shoes.

This boy was almost surreally handsome, with a clean, refined appearance that combined the looks of a scholar and an athlete. His thick hair framed a perfect face, his fair and rosy skin hinting at a southern heritage. He wore a well-fitting light blue jacket and straight black pants, with a pair of rarely-seen shiny black leather shoes. The hands resting on his desk were fair and slender, and adorned with a stylish watch.

Jasmine had never seen such a boy before. To her, boys were usually dirty, smelly, mischievous and annoying, constantly bullying girls and swearing. The handsome heroes in Beijing Opera and the charming young characters in novels never seemed to exist in real life. But today, seeing this boy, sixteen-year-old Jasmine realized that characters from operas and books could indeed step into the real world and appear before her. Later, Jasmine learned that this boy's name was Lu Qiao, and that he was a new student from a school that hosted children of Chinese families from overseas.

Suddenly, one of the girls in the front row said, "My mom's here!" All the girls quickly sat up straight. Jasmine was puzzled until a teacher walked in. "I'm Mrs. Qi, your homeroom teacher," she said. Wang Weiwei whispered to Jasmine, "The girl in the front row is Mrs. Qi's daughter, Dong Xiaoxia. She's my neighbor, and her dad works with my dad." Jasmine joked, "That should make it easy to find a backdoor to our homeroom teacher." Wang Weiwei laughed, but they quickly stopped talking as Mrs. Qi tapped the podium.

(71) PUPPY LOVE GONE WRONG

A new trend developed among the girls of reading romance novels by a writer named Qiong Yao. Jasmine was swept off her feet by these books. In just two short weeks she finished Outside My Window, Clouds in My Heart, Sunset, By the Waters, Moonlight Mist, Togetherness and Separation and The Forest Swallow.

The girl students were so deeply immersed in the tragic and beautiful worlds woven by Qiong Yao that nobody listened to what their teachers were saying in class. One day, Jasmine was gazing out the window, her eyes misty and her chin resting on her hand, lost in thought about the ill-fated lovers Li Mengzhu and He Mutian in the Qiong Yao novel she'd just finished. Suddenly, she heard the teacher call out, "Jasmine!"

Startled, Jasmine shot to her feet, as was expected from students when teachers called on them randomly. The teacher asked, "Have you figured it out? What's the length of this lever?"

Jasmine was completely stumped. What lever? Was this physics class? What was the teacher asking for? She heard a faint voice behind her: "4.25 meters."

It was Xiao Bing, the class physics whizz, trying to help Jasmine out. Trusting completely in Xiao Bing's physics skills, she told the teacher, "4.25 meters."

The teacher snorted, "Clever girl! You can multitask! Now, explain how you got your answer."

Jasmine broke out in a cold sweat. But before she could speak, Xiao Bing spoke loudly from his seat, "It's just substituting the numbers into the second formula on the left side of the blackboard." Nobody was supposed to speak without being called on, so Xiao Bing was taking a huge risk.

"I didn't ask you!" the teacher snapped angrily. "Who told you to speak without raising your hand and being called on? Go stand in the

360

corner!" Xiao Bing slowly stood up, purposefully knocked over his chair and then slowly righted it, and finally made his way to the corner. Jasmine used the delay to quickly read the problem and check the formula on the blackboard, and then she explained it to the teacher according to Xiao Bing's hint. The teacher had no choice but to say, "You may sit down, but no more daydreaming in class!"

Jasmine sat down slowly and secretly glanced at Xiao Bing in the corner. He was looking at her with a cheerful smile.

Whenever Jasmine read Qiong Yao's novels, for some reason, the male lead in the book always appeared in her mind as that new student, Lu Qiao. Every love story she read, every encounter, every heartbreak, every confession, all brought Lu Qiao's image to her mind. Perhaps it was because she didn't know anyone else to connect with the people and events in the books. Only this boy Lu Qiao, whom she had never spoken to and who was handsome to the point of being unreal, seemed to vaguely resemble the protagonists in the novels, and was able to connect the literary world and the real world for Jasmine.

All the girls in Jasmine's home room were in the same situation as her. Qiong Yao's novels had awakened the yearning for romance in their sixteen-year-old hearts while they sat in a room with an exceptionally handsome and elegant boy. Every single girl harbored fantasies of Lu Qiao, especially the home room teacher's daughter, Dong Xiaoxia, who spent every class period staring at Lu Qiao instead of looking at the blackboard. But Lu Qiao seemed completely oblivious to the girls' glances and giggles. Jasmine thought, Maybe a guy like him is used to attention from girls.

One day on her way home, Jasmine was passing by Ruizi's house when Ruizi suddenly rushed out and pushed Jasmine against the wall. As Jasmine steadied herself, Ruizi shouldered her again and made her stagger. "Ruizi, what are you doing?" Jasmine demanded.

Poking her finger at Jasmine's shoulder, Ruizi said, "What do you think I'm doing? What do you think I'm doing?"

Jasmine turned to leave. She and Ruizi had nothing in common, and that girl was notorious for cursing, fighting and causing trouble. Even her own mother was afraid of her, so Jasmine certainly didn't want to deal with her. But Ruizi blocked her way: "Where do you think you're going? Are you chicken? Feeling guilty? Aren't you up to it? Aren't you up to going out with Xiao Bing? Now what? You're chickening out?"

Jasmine was furious. "What are you talking about? I'm not going out with anyone! What nonsense are you spouting? Huh, I know, you have a crush on Xiao Bing! Well, let me tell you, I don't care who you like, and Xiao Bing has nothing to do with me, so don't pick a fight with me!"

That was like stirring up a hornet's nest. Ruizi jumped at her, swearing and spewing vulgarities that didn't sound at all like something a sixteen-year-old girl would say. Jasmine went inside her home and shut all the doors and windows, letting her curse away. But soon after that Daffodil came home, and Ruizi's mother also returned. Seeing Ruizi cursing at Jasmine, Daffodil asked Ruizi's mother, "Hey, what's going on? My daughter is quiet and good tempered, you can't bully her like this." Ruizi's mother quickly dragged Ruizi home.

Daffodil had become more patient and tolerant with Jasmine, reasoning that her daughter was getting too old to be constantly beaten and scolded. But hearing Ruizi's cursing made Daffodil's temper flare up again. The older her daughter got, the more serious the issues became, and she couldn't afford to be lax! Daffodil kicked open the door, grabbed Jasmine by her ear, and pulled her out of her chair. "You shameless little slut! What did you do to make someone curse you like that? Aren't you embarrassed? What have you done?"

Jasmine shouted angrily, "Nothing, I've done absolutely nothing! If she wants to curse, how can I stop her? Everyone knows that Ruizi has always liked Xiao Bing. So what? What does that have to do with me? I really don't know why she's cursing me!"

Daffodil said, "I'd almost forgotten about that kid! Did Xiao Bing get into your school? Is he in your class? Don't you know who his mother is? His mother is a thief who went to jail! With a mother like that, what good could he be? His mother almost ruined my life, almost got me thrown in jail, you know that? Let me tell you, a fly only bites a cracked egg. You must have been talking to Xiao Bing! If you dare to have anything to do with Xiao Bing, you're putting your mother's life on the line!"

Jasmine said, "Mom! I haven't! We're just classmates, we hardly talk to each other."

Daffodil said, "From now on, you're not allowed to say a single word to him, do you hear me? Even if he talks to you, you can't respond! If you refuse to respond, he'll stop talking to you. Do you hear me? If you dare talk to him, just try it! I'll beat you to death!"

Jasmine had no choice but to agree. She really had nothing with Xiao Bing anyway; he was just a classmate. But Jasmine thought about how Xiao Bing never bullied her like the other boys in elementary school, and how he came to comfort her when he heard about her attempted suicide and her grandmother's death. He even helped her out in class and smiled at her cheerfully while being punished. Now her mother was forbidding her to speak even a word to Xiao Bing, and that was really unfair to him.

Over the next few days, Jasmine tried to avoid Xiao Bing. When he came over to talk to her, she lowered her head in silence, which thoroughly confused him. In her heart, Jasmine said, "I'm sorry, I have no choice."

The days passed, and Jasmine found her mind completely scrambled with her mother's interrogations and vigilance, Xiao Bing's puzzled eyes, Ruizi, Ruizi's mother, the constant presence of Lu Qiao, Dong Xiaoxia and the other girls whispering around him, her deskmate Wang Weiwei's curious eyes, and the endless stories in Qiong Yao's novels. All these things swirled in Jasmine's mind, creating chaos.

The way that Jasmine dealt with mental chaos was to write, to think with a pen. Reading so many literary works, combined with her natural sensitivity and the long-term anguish of having no outlet for her delicate thoughts, Jasmine had a strong desire to write. She fantasized about having a beautiful fine-lined journal in which she could write beautiful chapters in elegant penmanship, pouring out the stories in her heart. But Jasmine knew this was impossible. She couldn't keep the journal at school, but she couldn't bring it home, either. She had no private space at home. Her mother regularly checked her drawers and inspected her school bag, so there was nowhere to hide a journal.

On Jasmine's birthday, Wang Weiwei mysteriously pulled out a wrapped package and handed it to her. Jasmine opened it and was delighted to find a beautiful new journal with a sublime light yellow cover and fine sky-blue lines, exactly like the one she had dreamed of. Jasmine and Wang Weiwei hugged each other joyfully!

That evening, Jasmine looked around the small room she shared with her sister, trying to find a place to hide the journal. She convinced herself that she might be able to hide it behind the row of books on the shelf. Once ignited, Jasmine's desire to write was unstoppable. She wanted to write so badly that she persuaded herself to accept the ridiculous idea of such an ineffective hiding place.

Jasmine wrote tirelessly, pouring everything she needed to express into the journal like a flood breaking through a dam. And Lu Qiao, the handsome boy who linked her literary fantasies and real life, naturally appeared in her journal. This journal became a sanctuary where she could freely express her emotions, thoughts and dreams without fear of judgment or intrusion. But then her journal exploded in her face like a bomb.

One day, when Jasmine reached for her journal in the back of the bookshelf, it was nowhere to be found. The back of the bookshelf was empty! Jasmine's head began buzzing so loudly that it made her dizzy. Mom and Dad must have found her journal! She quickly went through the content of her journal in her head, wincing time and again at the prospect of how her parents would react. She finally became so unsteady that she had to sit down.

But then, the word "Whatever" came to her mind. Jasmine thought: "That's right! Whatever! Their punishment, yelling, scolding, slapping, making me kneel down, or making me go hungry, haven't I experienced it all? There's nothing new, and I'm not afraid of any of it!" Jasmine never considered Mom and Dad's house her home; she was simply someone who would grow up and leave this place. As someone merely passing through, she was no longer saddened by her parents' punishments, and this thought allowed her to calm down.

Two days came and went, and Jasmine was very surprised that her mom and dad said nothing. They went out every evening without telling Jasmine where they were going. Jasmine had no idea what was going on.

On the third day, when she went to school, Jasmine knew something was terribly wrong. Everyone was acting strangely and giving her funny looks. The home room teacher's daughter, Dong Xiaoxia, whispered to a few girls, and they all covered their mouths and giggled at Jasmine. Xiao Bing also looked at Jasmine with concerned and saddened eyes.

Jasmine asked her friend Wang Weiwei, "What's going on? Why is everybody acting weird?"

With a miserable look on her face, Wang Weiwei replied, "Did your parents read your journal?"

"How do you know?!" Jasmine was dumbfounded!

Wang Weiwei sighed: "My mom was at Mrs. Qi's house when your parents came with your journal. They showed it to Mrs. Qi, and...... somehow..... her daughter..... Dong Xiaoxia read it ......"

Jasmine gripped her desk to steady herself as her vision started to turn black. Dong Xiaoxia! She loved nothing more than gossiping, and this would give her enough juicy material for the entire school year! No wonder everyone was acting strange. She must have told the whole world!

Jasmine realized that she had underestimated her parents. It wasn't as simple as enduring their usual punishments. How could she have been so stupid? She should have known how creative her parents were and how mercilessly they would hurt her in the worst possible way in any situation. When she was little they sent her away to Grandma's house. Then they forced her to leave her Grandma and come back to that shithole home. They gave her not even one word of comfort when Grandma passed away. When she finally found some light and hope in novels, they tore her library card into pieces. When she finally found a good friend, Xing Xiaowen, who showed her the beauty of Beijing Opera, Mom forced her to cut ties with Xing Xiaowen for fear that she would lead Jasmine astray. When she found joy and happiness in Beijing Opera, Mom tore up and burnt the opera scripts she'd spent months to collect, then told her that she had neither the voice nor looks for opera and that people would laugh at her if they ever heard her sing. When she had the first yearning for feminine beauty in her teenage years, they made her go to school in Dad's old clothes and big, worn-out shoes. When Xiao Bing gave her the only words of consolation during the unbearable pain of her suicide attempt and losing her Grandma, Mom forced her to never talk with Xiao Bing again...

Every time there was a flicker of light in her life, her parents quickly snuffed it out with their bare hands. Why would it be different this time? Just as Jasmine wrapped her heart in deeper layers of cocoon, thinking that her parents couldn't hurt her any longer, they always found a sharper knife and pierced the self-protection that she'd so painstakingly woven in ways she could not imagine.

Jasmine raised her eyes to look at Lu Qiao, the boy who was as perfect as a poem, the boy she had never exchanged a word with. Wasn't he the new flicker of light in Jasmine's life? What reasons did she have to expect her parents sparing this new flicker? How could she hope the merciless hands that nipped all the flames in her life might be just a little bit softer this time? A sad sneer as cold as ice rose from deep inside Jasmine's chest.

Mrs. Qi took Jasmine to her office for a talk. Jasmine blocked out what she was saying and remained silent and expressionless, trying hard to restrain her anger over Mrs. Qi letting her daughter see her journal.

But what really threw Jasmine into despair was that Lu Qiao, whom Jasmine had never even spoken to, was also taken to Mrs. Qi's office for a "talk"! When he came back to class, he gave Jasmine a quick look of annoyance and resentment. Everything in Jasmine's vision turned black. She wished she was dead already!

After dismissal, Jasmine mechanically put one foot in front of the other towards Four Corners. Xiao Bing rode his bike slowly about twenty yards behind her. Jasmine stopped and waited for him to come closer, then asked, "Why are you following me?" Xiao Bing lowered his head and then mumbled, "I, I'm worried about you." Jasmine said, "I won't kill myself, if that's what you are worried about!"

For days, Xiao Bing watched Jasmine closely. Every morning when Jasmine came out of her house, Xiao Bing was waiting at the top of the street on his bike, and he followed Jasmine to school. During recess, Xiao Bing did nothing but watch Jasmine. Even if she went to the bathroom, Xiao Bing would wait right outside for her and then follow her back to her seat. At every dismissal, he followed Jasmine home and watched her go into her house.

In the days that followed, Jasmine paid no attention to all the yelling, cursing, beating and humiliation from Gao Hong and Daffodil. As if those punishments were happening in another space and to someone else, Jasmine felt no sadness and no pain. She had nothing in her heart but anger, hatred and despair. She no longer cared what her parents did, or about any of her suffering. Her only thought was to leave everything behind as soon as she could, and to never, ever look back!

(72) REFORM TIME

Daffodil and Gao Hong were particularly worried about Jasmine. She was sixteen and had grown up to be tall, slender and beautiful. Having such a pretty daughter could bring a lot of trouble. Anything could happen! So they treated any hint of a problem as a major threat. First there was Ruizi cursing at Jasmine and claiming that she was involved with Xiao Bing. Then, Daffodil and Gao Hong became furious about the boy described in Jasmine's journal. They wondered if this was why Jasmine's grades had declined. They really wanted to put a stop to it, especially because the national college entrance exams were fast approaching. They decided to establish close contact with Jasmine's homeroom teacher, Mrs. Qi, to keep track of everything Jasmine did.

Jasmine had no idea what crimes her friends had committed. In her parents' eyes, her friends had suddenly become worthless pieces of garbage. Jasmine had a good relationship with a few girls, especially Wang Weiwei. Jasmine admired her quick wit and calmness, which was likely related to Wang Weiwei's family situation. Her father was a leader in aviation manufacturing and was often away, while her mother, also a key employee in the Department of Aviation, frequently worked overtime. Wang Weiwei had to manage not only her studies but also her home, buying groceries, cooking, cleaning and taking care of her younger sister.

When Daffodil asked Mrs. Qi who Jasmine usually hung out with, Mrs. Qi mentioned Wang Weiwei, and Daffodil immediately asked if Wang Weiwei was a good child. Mrs. Qi's husband worked with Wang Weiwei's father and had many conflicts with him at work, so Mrs. Qi said irritably, "This child is petty beyond her years. She doesn't act her age. She drives hard bargains in the market and tries to save money on groceries by nickeling and diming those poor vegetable farmers. She spends more time playing with her sister than reviewing her lessons." Daffodil concluded that Jasmine had made bad friends, and labeled all of Jasmine's friends as bad influences.

Jasmine dreaded her friends saying, "Whose house should we go to for homework today? Hey, we haven't been to your house yet!" Jasmine never dared invite friends to her home, but constantly making excuses wasn't a solution either. One day, Jasmine worked out that her parents wouldn't be home and agreed to have a few classmates over. But as soon as they sat down, Daffodil came marching in the door looking as furious as a scorned character in a drama.

Her classmates quickly said, "We have to go." Jasmine didn't even dare to see them off, merely opening the door and nodding for them to leave. Daffodil asked, "Who were those kids? Write down all their names for me. I'm going to talk to your teacher tomorrow! Why did you invite them over? Isn't it enough to hang out at school? What time do you get home every day? Do you go to their houses too? Aren't you afraid their parents will get annoyed? Everyone knows you're all a bunch of bad students. How shameless can you be?"

Daffodil decided to take matters into her own hands and choose Jasmine's friends for her. She asked Mrs. Qi for the names of several good students and then asked Jasmine, "Do you get along with these girls?" Jasmine saw that one was a tattletale, another was an aloof top student, and the third was someone she'd never spoken to. She said, "I haven't had anything to do with them."

Daffodil sneered, "Hmph! I guess these good kids don't want to talk to a bad student like you! From now on, you're only allowed to talk to these three students. If I find out you're talking to anyone else, I'll pull you out of school! You're not doing well anyway!" Before Jasmine could react, Daffodil added, "I'll make a logbook. Every day, one of these three has to write about your behavior in school, and you'll bring it home for me to see." She took out a notebook and wrote, "Dear Liu Jinhong, my daughter is misbehaving. Both Mrs. Qi and I trust you, Liang Tao, and Pan Hong. Please write a few lines about her behavior in school every day."

Jasmine was stunned, unable to fathom what her mother was suggesting. How could she show her face in school? She decided that she wouldn't let anyone write in a logbook about her, no matter what!

When Daffodil saw that Jasmine hadn't used the logbook for two days, she furiously insisted that Jasmine invite Liu Jinhong, Liang Tao and Pan Hong over while she was home so she could talk to them herself.

Jasmine reluctantly asked Pan Hong, whom she had never spoken to, "Hey, want to hang out? Would you like to come to my house after school?" Pan Hong gladly agreed. To the suck-up Liu Jinhong and the top student Liang Tao, Jasmine said, "My mom wants to see you. Can you come over after school?" They were puzzled: "How does your mom know us? Why does she want to see us?" Jasmine replied, "Mrs. Qi mentioned you to my mom. I'm not sure why she wants to see you. You can come over and find out."

They all came to Jasmine's house. Jasmine sat silently as Daffodil grilled them about school and then said, "My daughter really wants to be friends with you, but she doesn't know how to approach you." They quickly responded, "Oh! We want to be friends with her too! She's so good in many subjects, especially English and Chinese, and she's good at editing the class newspapers. We thought she was too busy to talk to us or maybe that we weren't good enough for her." Daffodil was pleased and never mentioned the logbook again. Jasmine didn't become friends with any of those three girls. Perhaps they could have been good friends, but Jasmine didn't want friends chosen by her mother.

Another of Daffodil's ways to protect her daughter was to dress her plainly to obscure her beauty. Daffodil picked out Jasmine's outfit every day and insisted on cutting Jasmine's hair herself. At sixteen, Jasmine often went to school in old clothes that her mother collected from God-knows-where, with hair chopped off unevenly like a tomboy's. Jasmine could never ask for new clothes; even mentioning that her clothes were old would result in a scolding: "All you care about is your appearance! Try to care about your grades or how you can contribute to the family! Don't you know how hard your parents work? Does money grow on trees? I bet none of the good students act like you! You're just like your shameless friends! How can you learn anything good from them? One day, I'll show up at your school and announce to your teachers and your whole class what a bad girl you are, so everyone knows you're a piece of shit!" Jasmine had no choice but to remain silent.

Now in her forties, Daffodil often felt anxious and short-tempered, and her stubborn and extreme personality became even more unreasonable. She couldn't control her words or emotions, constantly saying whatever made her feel better at the moment, regardless of the audience or how it made her look. She had also gained a lot of weight. At work, Daffodil's sharp tongue had offended everyone. She had no friends, and even her siblings kept their distance.

Gao Hong had long been fed up with Daffodil after her years of irrational and harsh words. Whenever Daffodil spoke, he either lashed back or left the room, which only made her temper worse. She became even more resentful and unreasonable, looking for any outlet to vent her anger, and Jasmine was often the target.

In the 1980s, prices began to soar, but Daffodil and Gao Hong's fixed salaries hardly increased. Financial strain weighed heavily on them, and grocery shopping became a source of daily conflict. Daffodil assigned Jasmine to handle the grocery shopping, demanding that she maximize every penny. Jasmine would bike to the market, bargain with vendors, and come back with bags of groceries hanging from the front and back racks of her bike.

Upon Jasmine's return, Daffodil would interrogate her: "How much did you pay for the eggplants? Thirty cents per pound? I saw some for twenty-five cents yesterday, and they were fresher! Are you stupid? Why didn't you shop around? How much for the tomatoes? So cheap? Why didn't you buy more? You're good for nothing, just like your father! Didn't I tell you to buy more when it's cheap? How much for the cucumbers? Two yuan and change? How much change? Three pounds? Does this look like three pounds to you? This is definitely not three pounds! Go back to the vendor and demand more! If you can't get it right, you'll have to pay for it!" Jasmine also had to account for every cent of change, and any discrepancy would lead to scolding and slaps in the face.

Gao Hong had worked in various workshops at the Metallurgical Machinery Factory, then spent several years as a technician, and was now an engineer. Deng Xiaoping rose to power in China and reformists took over the Communist government. The Cultural Revolution was over and Gao Hong's landlord's birth was no longer a problem. His years of experience and solid knowledge finally paid off, making him a key figure in the factory's technical department. However, no matter how hard he worked, his salary remained stagnant. Gao Hong envied others who could afford to buy televisions, refrigerators, stereos and washing machines. He felt frustrated that his family couldn't afford any kind of appliances and seemed to still live in the Stone Age.

At that time in China, there were people who worked within the system and people who ventured outside of the system. Within the system you were given a fixed low salary, just enough to buy food and daily necessities, but you were guaranteed healthcare, housing and education for your kids, including college and graduate school expenses, as well as lifetime retirement benefits. Some people left the system and started businesses of their own. Those people could earn magnitudes more money than was possible within the system, but they had no healthcare, no retirement and no guaranteed housing, and their kids couldn't go to any school for free.

There was a joke that street vendors who sold roasted sweet potatoes earned more cash than people who designed nuclear reactors. Roasted sweet potatoes were a popular snack during Beijing winters, and the vendors needed nothing but a coal burner and sweet potatoes to start with, so they typically earned a lot of money compared to Gao Hong and Daffodil's meager incomes. At one point, Gao Hong sat down with an elderly vendor and asked him about his coal burner and his business. The older man said, "Are you interested? I'm retiring after the New Year. I could sell you all my equipment at a good price and show you the ropes. You'd be making a profit immediately." Gao Hong smiled at the old man and didn't respond. He knew all too well that the system didn't allow for side hustles, and if his workplace found out, he'd be kicked out of the system and lose all his benefits. Besides that, people generally looked down upon street vendors as uneducated and vulgar. But Gao Hong needed money and he needed it badly!

When he mentioned it to Daffodil, she screamed, "How can you be so shameless? You have no skills and now you have no dignity! I can't afford to be embarrassed like this!" Gao Hong had no choice but to abandon his idea of selling sweet potatoes.

(73) REUNION

In the setting sun, Gao Hong was walking his bicycle towards the factory exit with a group of other workers finishing their shift. He honestly didn't want to go home. Home meant arguments, shouting, and Jasmine's sorrowful, distant face, which genuinely scared Gao Hong. But whenever he thought of his youngest daughter Lily, Gao Hong couldn't wait to step into his house. No matter how gloomy life was, Lily always managed to cheer him up and give him hope.

"Gao Hong!" Someone was shouting to him at the factory gate. Gao Hong saw a tall man with a black eye patch covering one eye, the other eye gleaming with excitement as he waved vigorously. Gao Hong walked over, racking his brain to recognize this familiar-looking man. The man suddenly punched Gao Hong on the shoulder and said, "Don't recognize me? Jiang Wannian!"

Oh my god, it was his college classmate! Gao Hong excitedly punched Jiang Wannian on the shoulder and said, "You asshole! Where did you come from? Let's go! Come to my place!" Jiang Wannian said, "Let's go out for a drink. Call your family and let them know." Recalling the big argument that ensued after Situ and Mai came to his home last time, Gao Hong was in fact a bit hesitant to bring Jiang Wannian home. He called Daffodil at her work, telling her that a classmate had arrived and he would be home late. He hung up the phone before Daffodil could say anything.

"Let's go!" Gao Hong said. "I know a nice little pub!" Jiang Wannian insisted, "No, no, no, follow me. My treat!" Gao Hong said, "Of course! You think you can get away with just those two sorry bowls of noodles back then?" The two laughed heartily together.

Jiang Wannian took Gao Hong to the Lido Hotel. "What are we doing here?" Gao Hong asked. Jiang Wannian pulled Gao Hong inside: "Come on!"

The luxurious decor, exquisite dishes and superior service made Gao Hong feel out of place all evening. He hadn't seen such a grand and elegant place since leaving the Gao family mansion as a child. Having been transformed from a pampered young master to a coarse, callous worker, returning to such a luxurious environment felt like a cruel joke.

Jiang Wannian asked, "How are things at your job? Want to try something new?"

It turned out that after graduation, Jiang Wannian was assigned to a factory in his hometown in Jiangxi, where he'd lost an eye due to a work injury. He endured much suffering in various factories there, but over the years, he'd honed his skills, mastering several metal refining techniques that were unprecedented in China. Now, while serving as a technical consultant for several companies, he'd also started his own business, thriving in the process.

"Damn it, I didn't lose an eye for nothing! Those years were hell, but I've got it made now!" Jiang Wannian said as he poured Gao Hong a glass of Maotai. "Times are good and there are opportunities everywhere. It's time to make a move!"

Jiang Wannian continued, "What do you see at every turn now? Village-run enterprises! Anyone with a little capital wants to start a business, open a factory. Those bumpkins wearing suits with straw hats, and shirts and ties with shorts and slippers, they want to run factories? They don't even know which way their factory gate should face! They don't know what to do even when they set up workshops. They lack the technical know-how!"

Gao Hong said, "When it comes to technology, I haven't missed much over all these years. I know every detail in the factory, every problem, big or small. Take a cold-formed steel production line, for example. I can handle every part of it and lead any project. Cold-formed steel products can be used for vegetable greenhouses produced locally and sold locally. This is a good fit for village-run enterprises!"

Jiang Wannian slapped the table: "Exactly! A lot of factories are still doing that fucking hot-rolled steel after all these damn years! Cold-formed steel is the trend! Come out and work with me. What's the point of staying in the factory? We're all in our forties, pushing fifty. We have the skills and the energy. Don't hold back. How much is your monthly salary? Three or four hundred at most, right? I'm telling you, come with me, and if you don't make three thousand a month, you can screw my head off my neck and kick it around like a soccer ball."

Gao Hong said, "You're just bullshitting!" But his heart was thundering.

Under the early evening street lights, Jiang Wannian said, "Let's organize a class reunion. It's been more than twenty years since we graduated and we've never had one. I'll call you!"

When Gao Hong returned home, Daffodil was already tired from cooking and taking care of the girls. "Where have you been?" she demanded irritably. Gao Hong said, "A college classmate invited me to dinner."

"A college classmate? Was it Shi Yanruo?" Daffodil snorted.

"Of course not! It was someone named Jiang Wannian. You don't know him."

Daffodil sneered, "Hmph, right. Why would Shi Yanruo come looking for you? Her husband is a big shot in the Ministry of Materials. They must be living in a nice big house and eating all kinds of fancy food. Why would she come looking for a loser like you?"

"Shut your filthy mouth!" Gao Hong roared.

"Why do you get so worked up whenever your college friends are mentioned? Feeling guilty? Why would you get worked up if you're not guilty? I come home from work and cook and take care of the kids, and you go out drinking and then come home and throw a fit at me. Am I your slave?" Daffodil's voice rose by an octave.

Gao Hong ignored Daffodil and went to bed. Daffodil was full of resentment. Gao Hong hadn't given her so much as a proper look for years. How could she have such a husband! What Daffodil didn't consider was that she hadn't given Gao Hong a proper look for years, either.

The next day, Gao Hong told Daffodil about Jiang Wannian's suggestion. In fact, Gao Hong knew that quitting his job and leaving the system would mean losing the security and insurance commonly referred to as the "iron rice bowl," and it would be extremely hard, if not impossible, to return if things didn't go well. He couldn't take this step lightly. But Jiang Wannian's words, "We're all in our forties, pushing fifty..." really struck a chord with him. Was he really going to live out his life like this, struggling every day just to get by? The frustration of seeing no way forward made Gao Hong extremely restless.

But Daffodil screamed when she heard Jiang Wannian's suggestion: "Are you crazy? Quit your job? You think you're up to it? Stupid and dumb, with no cunning. If someone gives you a stick, you think it's a big needle. Do you think you can make money? Who do you think you are? They use you while they need you, flatter you a bit, and then you forget who you are? You forget that you've been a loser all your life, stepped on by everyone? Dog's memory! You can't recognize the stink of your own shit! A lifetime without even a roof over your head and still living in this house assigned to me by my factory, and you still have the nerve to talk big! If you bring up this nonsense again, get the fuck out. Pack up and find your own place! Your classmates are no good either. What are they up to? Oh, they want you to quit and make money for them, and then if you fail, they can laugh at you? Stop associating with such people! I'm telling you! If you fail after quitting, you won't be able to go back to your old job. Then what are you going to do? Go begging? Where's your dignity? How did I end up with such a loser like you!"

Gao Hong threw his bowl down with a bang and left the house, slamming the door behind him. After he was gone, Daffodil continued to curse for half an hour, but since Gao Hong wasn't there, she turned her anger on her two daughters: "Look at your loser father! How did I end up with a husband like him..." Already used to it, Jasmine and Lily went about their business as if nothing was happening, just letting their mother vent.

The class reunion was set at the rooftop restaurant of the Western Hotel in Haidian District. Jiang Wannian arrived early with Gao Hong, and as they turned around, they saw Situ and Mai walk in. After the Cultural Revolution, many in the older generation had their reputations restored. Mai's father had been given an honorary position as army general, and although he had passed away, his influence remained. Situ and Mai had been transferred back to Beijing from the remote Northwest and now worked at the Ministry of Materials. They looked significantly older than Gao Hong and Jiang Wannian, the harsh environment in the Northwest having aged them prematurely. With tears in their eyes, they held Jiang Wannian's and Gao Hong's hands, nodding repeatedly, at loss for words.

Soon, classmates started arriving one by one, some spirited, some with graying hair, some dressed smartly, some looking shabby, some lively, some quiet, some recognizable and some unrecognizable. Everyone gathered together, shaking hands, identifying themselves, chatting and sighing. This generation had suffered so much in their youth, and now they were stepping into their twilight years.

Suddenly, someone slapped Gao Hong and Situ on the back. They turned and froze for a moment, then shouted together, "Indy!" It was indeed the classmate who had eaten in the college small kitchen and then went hungry when his ration tickets were stolen! The group laughed and yelled until tears streamed down their faces.

Indy had suffered immensely over the years. His overseas connections had made him a target of persecution whenever a political campaign was launched. In those years of agony, his wife committed suicide. It was a miracle that Indy himself had survived. However, now he had inherited his family's business in Indonesia and had married a beautiful wife twenty years younger than him. Gao Hong and Situ joked, "Such a young wife and you as short and thin as a yardstick? Man, take it easy!"

Amidst the excitement, joy and nostalgia, Gao Hong and Situ often glanced towards the entrance. Occasionally, their eyes met, and they both quickly looked away, knowing all too well that they were both waiting for the same person.

(74) SEEING YANRUO AGAIN

A middle-aged man with a plump belly and a round head appeared at the entrance of the restaurant and then walked in, smiling and smoothing his thinning hair. Following him was a woman in a white dress with short, ear-length hair, a calm face and deep eyes – it was Shi Yanruo!

Gao Hong and Situ gripped their wine glasses, mouths open, frozen in their seats. The portly middle-aged man walked over and said, "Hey! Old classmates! Don't you recognize me? I'm Wu Mancang! Haha, none of you have changed a bit! How come I'm the only one who looks old? Hahaha..." Wu Mancang laughed and patted the shoulders of Gao Hong and the others.

Gao Hong and his classmates shook hands with Wu Mancang and exchanged a few words. Indy said, "Hey? Shi Yanruo is here too? She hasn't changed a bit!" Wu Mancang said, "Well, she graduated in engineering, so she shouldn't be here, but she insisted on coming." Yanruo smiled and greeted everyone.

Gao Hong looked down at his wine glass, but followed Yanruo's every move. Yanruo was here, sitting right in front of him, after twenty-four years. She was as elegant, poised and beautiful as ever; she even wore the same hairstyle she had as a student. Time seemed to have forgotten her, as if she had walked through a twenty-four-year time tunnel from the front steps of the university's main building directly to Gao Hong today.

Even so, she was also different from his beloved Yanruo. The Yanruo before him now had a touch of maturity and heaviness in her eyes that showed Gao Hong the hardships she had endured. Gao Hong didn't look directly at Yanruo, but he was watching her and sensing her intently with his heart.

"Hey, Gao Hong!" Wu Mancang raised his wine glass across the table. "Come on, we have to drink!" Gao Hong perfunctorily raised his glass.

Wu Mancang drank his liquor down all in one gulp, then slammed the glass on the table and said loudly, "I knew I had to have a drink with you today! How are you doing? Still at the metallurgical machinery factory, right? Director Hao from your factory attended a meeting at the ministry last month, and I saw him at a distance. He said he wanted to give me a report on your factory's performance, but there are too many factories under my department. I was surrounded by a whole big room full of factory directors, so I didn't have time for a word with your Director Hao." As he spoke, Wu Mancang watched Gao Hong's face and drank another glass of liquor, while Yanruo lowered her eyes and remained silent.

Several classmates came over from the neighboring table. "Minister Wu, would you sit with us for a while?" Wu Mancang said, "Hey, hey, hey, what's with the minister stuff? Today we're all classmates! You can call me Minister Wu outside this door, but now just call me Wu Mancang!" The classmates said, "Alright, Minister Wu, we know you're modest!" As they pulled Wu Mancang away, he gave Yanruo a stern look. Yanruo silently stood up with a lowered head and followed Wu Mancang to the next table.

Standing up with a livid face, Gao Hong left the dining room, dragging Situ and Mai along with him. The three of them sat on the sofa in the lobby. Gao Hong said, "Do you have a cigarette?" He took the cigarette Situ handed him, but he had to strike three matches with his shaky hands had before he finally managed to light it.

Situ said, "Don't mind Wu Mancang. Belittling your factory director in front of you was just to put you down. Don't mind him, the classmates are all watching, and no one respects an arrogant ass like him."

Gao Hong raised his head: "I don't care about that scumbag Wu Mancang! He can say whatever he wants about me. He can walk all over me. I don't care! But you two are hiding something from me! What's with Yanruo? Why is she acting like Wu Mancang's slave?!"

Mai and Situ exchanged glances, and then Mai said, "Well, everyone has a destiny. What can you do? Knowing will only add to your worries." Situ said, "When we came back to the ministry from the Northwest, we heard that Yanruo had been having a tough time all these years."

Shi Yanruo, daughter of one of the richest old money families in Beijing, had been forced to abandon her true love Gao Hong and hastily marry her pursuer, Wu Mancang, at the critical moment of university graduation assignments in order to stay in Beijing to take care of her mentally ill mother. Through Wu Mancang's influence, Yanruo was assigned to the Ministry of Materials in Beijing after graduation, and avoided the fate of being exiled to the Northeast like Situ. She and Wu Mancang received housing from the department and brought Yanruo's mother to live with them.

Although she didn't love Wu Mancang, Yanruo was grateful to him and was determined to be a good wife. During the early years of their marriage, Wu Mancang was a tolerable husband, despite being a bit chauvinistic, and Yanruo worked hard to diligently manage the household. After Yanruo's mother passed away during the third year of their marriage, the Cultural Revolution became very brutal, and given her family background and her father's history of bearing arms against the Communists, Yanruo could only survive through Wu Mancang's protection.

Over time, Wu Mancang progressed from verbally abusing Yanruo over small matters to physically abusing her, and then regularly torturing her, driving her to the brink of suicide. When Yanruo was physically unwell following the birth of their daughter and refused Wu Mancang's endless sexual demands, Wu Mancang dragged her out of bed and kicked and beat her while cursing, "Are you still thinking about that man? That Gao guy? I'm telling you, with his landlord background, I can end his life with one phone call to the Cultural Revolution Committee! Killing him is like crushing a bug. Don't try me! If you dare to try me I'll call his factory tomorrow!"

Yanruo wept herself unconscious and then had to kneel and beg Wu Mancang when she woke up. From then on, Yanruo obeyed Wu Mancang in everything, letting him torture her however he wanted. But the more she complied, the more Wu Mancang felt that Yanruo hadn't forgotten Gao Hong, and he tortured her even more. Yanruo often went to work with obvious injuries. Everyone at work knew that Minister Wu beat his wife, but no one dared to say anything.

Sometimes, Yanruo wondered if her decision to leave Gao Hong and marry Wu Mancang had been correct. If she'd stayed with Gao

Hong, even if life in the Northwest was hard, they would have been happy together. But then she wouldn't have been able to care for her mother in her old age. Yanruo's mother, born to a prominent family and married in luxury, had lost her husband and everything else and had gone insane. Her one stroke of good fortune was her daughter's companionship and care in the last three years of her life. But she would never know the price her daughter paid for those three years in a lifetime of suffering.

Wu Mancang had brought Yanruo along with him to show Gao Hong that Yanruo was firmly in his grasp, and that even Gao Hong himself was a bird in his cage, a fish in his pond!

Mai and Situ took Gao Hong back to the dining hall. Gao Hong wished he could rush over and kill Wu Mancang in that instant! Wu Mancang had fallen asleep at the table, already drunk from classmates trying to curry favor with him. Yanruo stood alone by the floor-to-ceiling window, gazing at the Beijing skyline. Gao Hong quietly walked to her side and said, "Yanruo."

Yanruo turned to look at Gao Hong like a frightened deer, then quickly glanced at Wu Mancang. His heart aching, Gao Hong asked, "Are you okay?" Yanruo lowered her head without speaking, then smiled and said, "I'm fine, how about you?" Gao Hong said, "I'm fine too."

They stood side-by-side in front of the window for a long time. Finally, Yanruo said, "Then all is well," and she turned and walked away.

Gao Hong rushed into the bathroom and splashed his head and face with cold water over and over again. He hated Wu Mancang, hated himself, hated this society, hated everything. And what he hated most was his powerlessness in the face of all this. What could he do? What could he do? Could he divorce Daffodil and marry Yanruo? That would not only destroy his own family and his daughters but also ruin Yanruo's daughter. And Wu Mancang's inevitable revenge would surely destroy both him and Yanruo. So was his only choice to pull his head back into his shell like a turtle? To do nothing? To be a coward? Gao Hong's head pounded. Apart from getting drunk, he knew no other way to muster the courage to go on living.

Gao Hong had gotten used to not expecting anything good from life, especially love and being with the one he loved. Gao Hong never felt he was entitled to such beautiful things. It was as if life offered him only the bare minimum. Like an animal, he was supposed to go through life seeking food, fighting for survival, mating, reproducing and then dying. Thinking that this might be his fate, Gao Hong had numbly accepted it for a long time, but seeing Yanruo today had cast him back into a deep abyss of pain. Regardless of his fate, how could he cause pain to Yanruo? How could he bring Yanruo harm and danger just by his sheer existence?

When Gao Hong was brought home stone drunk by Situ and Mai, it was already past eleven at night. Daffodil was still awake, restless with the knowledge that Gao Hong would inevitably see Shi Yanruo at the class reunion, and she was determined to wait for him and find out how everything went. When she saw the drunken Gao Hong, her anger flared up instantly. "That wretch! How come he's this drunk again!"

Mai said, "Sis, can you come here for a moment? I need to talk to you." She pulled Daffodil into another room, sat her down, and said, "Sis, I know you feel terribly wronged, and I understand. Everyone knew about Gao Hong and Yanruo in college. You must be so upset; we're both women, and I'd feel the same."

Daffodil immediately broke down in tears. How long had it been since anyone had spoken so comfortingly to her? Was there anyone who could understand her, even just a little bit? She gripped Mai's hand, sobbing uncontrollably.

Mai continued, "Let me be honest with you. My Situ, for all these years and even now, has had Yanruo in his heart and never let go."

Daffodil looked up in astonishment. "Really? But you...?"

"I was angry. I fought with him and yelled at him. But not anymore. Think about it: They've both held onto feelings for Yanruo, someone they haven't seen or contacted in over twenty years. What does that tell you? It tells you we married the right men, Sister! It means we married men who are romantic, loving and loyal. They hold someone else in their hearts, but they're still the best husbands they can be for us, working hard to support the family and being faithful. We should be grateful. Listen to me – as women, we need to look at the bigger picture and not get stuck on trivial matters. The more he loves someone else, the more you need to win his heart. If you keep opposing him, won't he miss Yanruo even more? Honestly, Sister, a large part of this is on you."

Daffodil rarely took others' advice, but today she found herself convinced by Mai's words. She said, "But I feel so suffocated."

"Who doesn't? Is there anyone in this world who isn't? Chairman Mao had the Gang of Four scheming against him, and Deng Xiaoping was ousted several times. Don't think you're the only one suffering. Think about Gao Hong's hardships; he's endured so much. Don't fight with him anymore; it won't do any good. I'm telling you, the more you fight, the worse you'll feel. Just try it and see."

The next morning, Gao Hong woke up groggy and with a pounding headache and saw Daffodil sitting at the bedside, looking at him. She said, "You drank too much last night. I made some porridge to settle your stomach. I've sent the kids off already. Get up and wash your face; I've prepared the water for you. After you wash up, have some porridge."

Gao Hong looked at Daffodil in bewilderment, unable to believe that she was speaking so calmly and nicely. Daffodil said, "What are you staring at? Don't you recognize me?" After hesitating for a long time, Gao Hong went to the bathroom and washed his face and hands, then sat down at the table for breakfast.

(75) TAKING THE SAFE PATH

After breakfast, Gao Hong was putting on his jacket to go to work when he noticed a wad of paper in his pocket. Unfolding it, he found pages of engineering diagrams, along with a list of names and phone numbers. After thinking very hard, he recalled Jiang Wannian grabbing him last night as he drank glass after glass of liquor at the Western Hotel. Jiang Wannian wouldn't stop babbling about technical issues and consultations, and before they left, he had stuffed a wad of paper into Gao Hong's pocket, saying, "Take a good look at this, think it over, and get back to me!"

Gao Hong couldn't remember what Jiang Wannian had wanted with these papers, so when he got to work, he called Jiang Wannian's mobile. Jiang Wannian asked, "Have you made up your mind? Will you do it?" Gao Hong replied, "You have to tell me clearly what this is about! If it's anything illegal, don't get me involved."

"Did I waste my breath last night?" Jiang Wannian was furious.

It turned out that Jiang Wannian had been contacted by two village-run enterprises who were facing technical problems that happened to fall within Gao Hong's area of expertise, and Jiang Wannian wanted Gao Hong to look at the documents and draw up diagrams for the enterprises. "There are 6 blueprints, and they'll pay you 500 yuan each, 3,000 yuan in total. I know you, this is a two-day job for you. Just work on it over the weekend and you'll be done. What do you say?"

Three thousand yuan was nearly half a year's income for Gao Hong. Moreover, looking at the questions and diagrams, he instantly knew what the problems were, and felt a strong urge to provide solutions, even if there was no money to be earned.

Saturdays were work days back then, and people had only Sundays off. Gao Hong took a sick day that Saturday and spent the whole day working on the engineering diagrams. He spent Sunday the same way, buried in work. Early Monday morning, Gao Hong called Jiang Wannian: "The six blueprints are done. Come and get them."

"You finished too quickly! No, hold off for two weeks! You can't take 3,000 yuan after just two days! They'll think it's too easy for you. Hold onto the blueprints, and I'll tell them it's a huge problem, almost unsolvable, and that you're working day and night on it. You're too simple-minded!" Jiang Wannian hung up the phone.

Two weeks later, Jiang Wannian collected the blueprints. A few days after that, several heavily tanned, rustic-looking men came to Gao Hong's house. They wore suits, but with worn-out sweaters underneath and dirty peasant caps on their heads. The elderly man leading the group grabbed Gao Hong's hands tightly, and with tears in his eyes, he said in an unfamiliar dialect, "Engineer Gao! Our entire village sent me to thank you! You're our savior!"

Gao Hong was taken aback, "May I ask who you are?"

The man said his factory's name, and Gao Hong recalled it was the one written on Jiang Wannian's papers. He quickly invited them inside. The factory director, still in tears, explained that the factory had been built with the life savings of every family in the entire village, but there was no one with engineering knowledge. They had initially hired an engineer, but he left due to the low pay.

"Ten days ago, Manager Jiang told us the problem was unsolvable, that there was no hope. Engineer Gao, you have no idea what we went through during those ten days. Every family thought their life savings were gone, and four or five household heads even considered hanging themselves! I had to go door to door, swearing in the name of Chairman Mao and putting my own neck on the line to tell them we'd pull through this! Our village is so poor, and this factory is our only hope. We have to succeed, or I would repay the villagers with my life. But now, thanks to you, our problem is solved! You're the savior of our entire village!" The old factory director was again in tears.

With that, he took out 3,500 yuan and offered it to Gao Hong. "This isn't much, but it's what every family saved up little by little by limiting their own food. Please accept it as a token of our gratitude."

Gao Hong was so ashamed and regretful that he firmly pushed the money back into the old director's hands, "Director, I'm so sorry! I should have solved the problem sooner, and I'm very sorry! I can't take your money; please use it where it's most needed."

The old director was so distressed that veins bulged out on his forehead. He insisted, "If you don't take it, it means you think it's too little! It means that you don't want to help us anymore! It means you look down on us!"

Seeing the old man's flushed, anxious face, Gao Hong reluctantly agreed, "Alright, alright, I'll take 3,000. Didn't we agree on 3,000? This is too much!"

"No, it's not! Is 3,500 yuan worth more than the lives of our entire village? I know the value and the importance of your expertise. Engineer Gao, I just ask that we can come to you if we have problems again. Rest assured, we'll pay you whatever we can. If you come to our village for a visit, we'll make sure to give you a grand reception with a big feast, and the villagers will perform a local opera for you!"

The next morning, Gao Hong rushed to the phone in his office and called Jiang Wannian, yelling, "Don't ever involve me in such a heartless business again! People nearly died because of the delay! I solved it in two days, and you made them wait two weeks. How cruel can you be?"

Jiang Wannian laughed, "You're too naive! I've dealt with a lot of village enterprises. Do you think you're the only one who can solve problems fast? I once quickly resolved a fatal issue for a village-run enterprise in Jiangxi. They were already shut down. I came in, and in just four hours I got their machines running again. But do you know what the villagers said? They claimed I wasn't worth the money, called me a cheat, and said I created the problems so I could make money fixing them. In their minds, no real problem could be solved in four hours, so I was too quick to be credible. To this day, everyone in the village still spits at me when they see me. I'm telling you, don't be a martyr. I know them better than you do!"

"You're such an asshole!" Gao Hong cursed again, but not as loud as before.

Holding the 3,500 yuan in her hands, Daffodil couldn't believe her eyes! What could they buy with this amount of money? A refrigerator, a TV, a stereo, all of that! But then she thought, Gao Hong saved their entire village, and what's 3,500 yuan compared to that? The more

Daffodil thought about it, the more she felt they'd been shortchanged. She said to Gao Hong, "You solved such a big problem for them and saved their lives, and they only gave you this small amount of money? I think they're just taking advantage of you and think you're a soft touch. Don't work for them again; don't stoop so low!"

Through Jiang Wannian's introduction, Gao Hong established connections with several other village-run enterprises. As he dealt more with these people, Gao Hong realized that Jiang Wannian's ways, although despicable, were rooted in reality. Operating on the villagers' life savings, these enterprises had highly limited visions and very emotional leadership. There was no way they could deal with any uncertainty or suspense, because too much was at stake for them. Anything good was met with intense gratitude, but any risk, uncertainty or waiting brought suspicion, blame and verbal abuse. Gao Hong had initially thought that providing technical consultation to village-run enterprises would be ten times more profitable than working in a state-owned factory, but now he saw that it was no free lunch.

Rumors soon spread in his factory that Gao Hong was making a fortune by providing technical consultation outside. Even Factory Director Hao hinted at it, saying, "You're not working as diligently these days. I think you're distracted! Pay attention! You can't serve two masters!"

Promotion time arrived in Gao Hong's factory. At a time when state-run workplaces provided life necessities such as housing, health care and education for their employees, a higher ranking meant better benefits and resources. Each year, promotion time was the most contentious time in the factory, as it determined the size of housing allocations and salaries. Gao Hong was confident that he could be promoted to senior engineer this time. He was unquestionably the factory's chief engineer and its technical backbone, but it wasn't possible to jump from regular engineer to chief engineer in one go; being promoted to senior engineer was a reasonable expectation.

To his surprise, Gao Hong's name wasn't on the final list of promoted engineers. Even younger colleagues who often came to him for technical advice were promoted to the senior level, but not him.

The entire factory was buzzing with gossip about Gao Hong, and every day, he felt like he was walking on pins and needles.

Director Chen from the human resource department was about to retire. He was the one who had given Gao Hong a hard time when he first reported to work, and the one who humiliated Gao Hong when he took time off for Nanny Wu's funeral. But by now Director Chen treated him like a son, because they had become drinking buddies. Confused about what had happened during the promotion process, Gao Hong invited Director Chen for a drink. Half-drunk, Director Chen slurred, "Did you offend someone in the Ministry of Materials? There's a Minister Wu, what's his deal? You were initially on the list, but he had you removed!"

Gao Hong felt the blood rush to his head. Dammit, it was that God-damned Wu Mancang! A sharp pain stabbed him in the heart as he realized that as long as he worked at the Metallurgical Machinery Factory, he would be under Wu Mancang's control and unable to escape his grasp. Gao Hong was furious. The thought of always being under Wu Mancang's thumb made him nauseous. Wu might still be using him to manipulate Yanruo, and he'd never know what kind of suffering Yanruo was enduring because of him.

On the way home, Gao Hong thought, dammit, I'll quit! The world is big enough that there must be a place for me somewhere. If he left the Metallurgical Machinery Factory and abandoned the system, Wu Mancang wouldn't be able to use him to threaten Yanruo anymore.

But when Daffodil heard that Gao Hong wanted to quit and go do consulting on his own, she immediately cried and made a scene, threatening to kill herself: "I've suffered with you all my life, and now you won't let me enjoy a peaceful old age! If you quit, you'll have no healthcare, no pension, nothing in your retirement. What will you do when you're old and can't work? What if you end up bedridden? Who will take care of you? Who will pay your medical bills? The kids aren't even in college yet. Are you trying to kill us all? Once you quit, you can never go back. You'll end up a beggar! I swear, if you resign, I'll die right in front of you!"

Daffodil's hysteria was so intense that her blood pressure spiked, and one morning she had to be rushed to the emergency room. Under pressure from her, Gao Hong reluctantly chose his stable but soul-crushing job at the state-run factory. But he felt like a lifeless old man, increasingly consoling himself with alcohol and becoming more impatient with his daughters. He was especially rough toward Jasmine, frequently yelling and berating her.

To Jasmine, Gao Hong was no longer the father who yoyoed between kindness and anger. Now he was always angry and had stopped trying to control his temper. He was always sighing, gloomy or shouting. Jasmine had to find a way to survive in the cracks between her parents.

(76) THE LOST PHOTO

Even in a household where the daily norm was hostility, Jasmine felt more tension in the air than usual when she came home from school one day. Something terrible must have happened.

Daffodil was half-reclined on the bed, facing the wall and wiping her tears. Gao Hong was frantically searching for something, opening all the drawers, cabinets and boxes in the house. If her mother had been hysterically sobbing and shouting, Jasmine would have found that normal, but seeing her silently weeping meant something serious had happened. If her father had been sitting there with a sullen and brooding face, Jasmine would have thought that was typical of him, but seeing him restless and frantically rummaging through everything meant something was seriously wrong.

Jasmine asked, "Dad, what are you looking for?"

"Why aren't you studying?!" Gao Hong roared. "The college entrance exams are coming up. Don't you care?!"

Jasmine hurried to the small room she shared with her sister. She could hear her dad slamming the door to her parents' room, followed by the sound of them arguing, but she couldn't make out the words.

Jasmine pressed her ear to the wall, trying to catch bits and pieces of their conversation.

"What have I ever done wrong?…"

"You've been angry with my cousin from the beginning, and this is your revenge!…"

"… I didn't throw it away… How many times do I have to say it?"

"I don't believe you! If it wasn't you, who else could it be? I know you too well!"

"… You ungrateful and despicable asshole! Don't you know how good I've been to you all these years?…"

Suddenly, her father's footsteps approached the wall, and Jasmine clearly heard, "Fine, let's get a divorce. I'll take Lily with me. Jasmine is taking the college entrance exams and will be in college after this summer, so she can stay with you."

Jasmine's legs went weak, and she sank to the ground amid her mother's sobs. What? Are Dad and Mom getting a divorce? They're really getting a divorce? And... Jasmine felt a rush of tears... Dad doesn't want me!

That night, Lily and Jasmine huddled in their small room, crying, worrying, eavesdropping and talking. Are Mom and Dad really getting a divorce? Even though they both knew their parents' marriage was a torture chamber, a veritable meat grinder that crushed everyone inside, the prospect of their parents' divorce still filled them with immense anxiety.

It turned out that Gao Hong had noticed that the photo of his cousin Gao Lan, which he had kept for years, was missing, and he'd been searching for it for two days. Gao Lan was Gao Hong's only remaining blood relative, and she'd gone on the run and her fate was unknown. Gao Hong had treasured the photo that she'd had someone deliver to him before she disappeared, and now it was gone!

Daffodil had resented Gao Lan ever since Gao Hong had given her all of their money without informing Daffodil. Since Gao Hong couldn't disclose Gao Lan's whereabouts, Daffodil believed that Gao Lan had taken all their savings and disappeared without even bothering to keep in touch. Even so, Daffodil knew that Gao Lan was Gao Hong's only remaining relative, and she wouldn't have thrown away the only photo Gao Lan left behind.

What broke Daffodil's heart was Gao Hong's deep suspicion and lack of trust, his malicious assumptions about her. It was true that Daffodil had done many things that inadvertently hurt Gao Hong, but it wasn't her actual intention! Daffodil had threatened divorce many times, but no matter how she raged, Gao Hong had never said the word divorce. But when he said it, he meant it.

That night, lying in the dark, Jasmine thought: Dad and Mom are divorcing, and Dad doesn't want me. I need to make plans. I need to become independent. I can't live alone with Mom; I'd go crazy! The college entrance exams were four months away, but that year, for the first time, teacher training colleges were allowing early admissions in May. Jasmine hadn't considered applying to a teacher training college before, but now she saw it as a way to finish the exams early and secure admission sooner. Teacher training colleges also provided a monthly stipend, which would be enough for her to live independently.

The next day, Jasmine registered for the teacher training college entrance exams in May.

After a few days of turmoil at home, Gao Hong and Daffodil returned to a state of cold war. Jasmine knew this meant things were improving and that they wouldn't divorce, but she had already applied to Beijing Normal College, also known as Beijing Teacher's College, and now she had to take the exam.

Mrs. Qi handed the admission notice from Beijing Normal College to Jasmine while she was in class with the other students. Everyone had received their high school diplomas and was preparing for the college entrance exams. Until the early May exam results came in, those who took the early exams continued preparing for the July exams in case they didn't get into any college in May. But when the red-lettered admission notice from Beijing Normal College arrived, high school was over for Jasmine. She had been admitted to a college and no longer needed to sit in the classroom with everyone else.

Holding the envelope and sensing the gazes of her classmates, Jasmine suddenly felt empty and confused. Mrs. Qi said, "You don't need to attend lessons anymore. If you want, you can go home." Jasmine didn't want to go home, but she didn't want to stay in the classroom either. She packed her bag, took the admission notice and bid Mrs. Qi farewell. As Mrs. Qi turned away, Jasmine heard a soft voice behind her: "Jasmine." She turned to see Xiao Bing.

Xiao Bing whispered, "Where are you going?"

"I don't know," Jasmine replied.

"Can you wait for me at the school gate? I'll come out in a few minutes. I have something to ask you," Xiao Bing whispered, glancing at the teacher as she walked towards the front of the classroom.

After waiting for a few minutes outside, Jasmine saw Xiao Bing appear on his bicycle. "Aren't you going to class?" Jasmine asked.

"I told Mrs. Qi I had a stomach ache." Xiao Bing laughed.

"What did you want to ask me about?"

"Oh, nothing much, I just wanted to ask where you were going."

Jasmine didn't answer and started walking home slowly. Xiao Bing silently followed her. After a while, Xiao Bing asked, "Will you come back to school?"

"No," Jasmine replied. Indeed, that school held too many painful memories. She had become a girl with a scarlet letter on her back after the journal incident. She wanted to forget it all, the gossip, her unspoken crush on Lu Qiao, the so-called friends assigned to her by her parents, and the teacher who had exposed her journal. Everything made her unwilling to return. She wished everyone at school would forget her, forget the girl whose journal was exposed, the girl with the uneven tomboy haircut and the old, oversized clothes and shoes.

Xiao Bing said, "How about if I take you to Beijing Normal College so you can see your future school? It's just a short bike ride away."

"Really? That would be great!" Jasmine was overjoyed. Yes, she was about to become a student there; why not visit her future college?

Xiao Bing smiled happily and told Jasmine to sit on the back rack of his bike. "Hold on to me," he said. Shy about holding onto him, Jasmine said, "It's okay, I won't fall."

Xiao Bing rode fast and steady. Feeling the summer wind on her face, Jasmine was ecstatic about having a day without school and without having to go home – a day to visit her future college.

The leafy campus was beautiful, with lush sycamore and ginkgo trees lining the paths. College students with school badges pinned to their chests moved between the dorms, cafeteria and lecture halls. The girls had lovely shoulder-length hair and wore pretty clothes. Jasmine loved everything about it! She couldn't wait for school to start and to move from her home to this beautiful campus.

Xiao Bing silently walked beside Jasmine as she excitedly commented on everything: "Look at the main building, it's so beautiful! And those pine trees in front of it. I love pine trees! The smells coming from the cafeteria are amazing. I wonder what they're eating? Is this a dorm? I wonder how many people share a room? Everyone is carrying a thermos, so they must be getting hot water from the boiler room. Wow, look at that huge sports field! There's even a grandstand!" Xiao Bing just smiled and walked with Jasmine until the sun dropped low in the northwestern sky.

"Oh no, I have to get home!" Jasmine said. Xiao Bing replied, "Don't worry, I'll get you home quickly on my bike."

Jasmine asked, "Where do you want to go to college?" As Xiao Bing pedaled his bike, he pointed across the street and said, "See the Beijing Institute of Computer Science? I'm aiming for that school. We could be across-the-street classmates."

Jasmine laughed, "Great, then I'll call you my across-the-street classmate, ASC, how about that?"

Xiao Bing said, "Sure, but there's just one thing: Beijing Institute of Computer Science has lots of students, but I'll be your only ASC, okay?"

Jasmine laughed heartily. Being with Xiao Bing made her feel good. She could say and do whatever she wanted without worrying about whether he liked it or not. Xiao Bing always seemed to listen and cheer her up. Jasmine felt Xiao Bing was a true and loyal friend.

As summer arrived, Jasmine was relieved of her college entrance exam burden. Gao Hong and Daffodil were less stressed about Jasmine's future, and everyone relaxed. Looking at her eighteen-year-old daughter who was about to leave for college, Daffodil felt a wave of softness and affection. She told herself she'd treat Jasmine gently and lovingly from then on. She promised herself that she would never raise her hand to Jasmine again. Daffodil also threw away Jasmine's old clothes and made beautiful dresses for her. She allowed Jasmine to grow her hair out and even bought her shiny hair clips. Daffodil's temper had improved considerably as she had passed through menopause, had stopped worrying about whether Jasmine would go to college, and had seen the financial situation of her family improve.

The college results came out for the students who took the July national exam. When Jasmine opened the mailbox one day, she saw a note:

Admitted by Beijing Institute of Computer Science

ASC

Daffodil had bought a bundle of cheap chives that were a bit stale, but which should still be perfectly edible with some careful picking and removal of the rotten leaves. Daffodil called Jasmine to help her spread the chives on the ground, and they started picking and removing the bad parts one by one. With chive leaves all over the place, the chive odor filling the room, and chive juice staining their hands, they heard a knock at the door.

Jasmine wiped her hands and opened the door. A policeman and two strangers were standing there. The policeman said, "I'm Officer Tang. Does Gao Hong live here?" Jasmine replied, "Gao Hong is my dad. He's not home. What do you want to see him for?"

Just then, Gao Hong returned. Seeing a policeman and two strangers at the door and his daughter Jasmine standing there, he hurried over and asked, "Who are you looking for?"

Officer Tang said, "Are you Gao Hong? I'm not looking for you, but these two are. Now that they've found you, I'll leave you to it. I'm needed elsewhere. Goodbye!" With that, Officer Tang turned and left.

Gao Hong and Jasmine looked at the two people. They were wearing sunglasses and fashionable clothes, and the woman had light makeup on her face. Gao Hong didn't recognize them at all. He asked, "Are you looking for me? Please come in."

The two entered without saying anything. Daffodil looked up and said, "Oh, who is it?" Jasmine cleared the chives from the floor.

The woman took off her sunglasses and said to Gao Hong, "Don't you recognize me, HongGe?"

Gao Hong was stunned. His eyes widened and he instinctively took two steps back, gripping the edge of the table behind him. Raising a hand to point at the woman, he stammered, "You are... you are... you two..."

The woman's eyes reddened with tears as she said, "HongGe! I'm your Cousin Lan! And this is your brother-in-law, Tiger!"

Gao Hong rushed over in two steps and grabbed the hands of Lan and Tiger. Then he turned and said in a hushed but urgent voice, "Jasmine! Pull the curtains tight!"

Smiling through her tears, Gao Lan said, "No need, no need! We're fine now. Didn't you see that a policeman helped us find you? Everything is fine now. There's nothing to worry about..." With that, Gao Lan covered her face and started crying.

Tiger patted Gao Lan's shoulder and said, "Hey, we finally found our cousin here. Why are you crying? Brother, I'm Tiger. My father, Li Ginseng, took you as his son back in the day, which means that we're brothers. I'm both your brother and your brother-in-law. Isn't that something?" Tiger also had tears in his eyes.

Utterly confused, Daffodil said, "Hey, what's going on?"

Gao Lan and Tiger took Daffodil by the hands and led her to sit on the sofa. Then both of them knelt in front of Daffodil and paid their respects: "Sister-in-law!"

Daffodil jumped up in fright. "Hey, you two! Get up, get up! What are you doing? What's going on?"

"Sister, you and HongGe are our saviors. Back then, poor as you were, HongGe secretly gave me 380 yuan so I could break Tiger out of prison. All these years, we were on the run and took false names, not daring to come see you. Today, please accept our deepest gratitude!" Daffodil quickly pulled them up from their knees.

That night, Gao Hong, Daffodil, Gao Lan and Tiger stayed up late into the night, crying and laughing, talking and sighing as they shared stories of the past twenty years.

The last Gao Hong had heard of Cousin Lan, she had miscarried, and she and Tiger were preparing to flee abroad. She'd had someone bring him the Crimson-eyed Buddha, a photo of herself and a photo of Gao Hong. At that time, they didn't know if they would ever see each other again.

"The Crimson-eyed Buddha blessed us. Tiger and I escaped to Hong Kong. We had to hide and live under false names until we could flee to the southernmost part of Guangzhou, across a narrow straight from Hong Kong. Thanks to the money our mountain brothers raised for us, we bought some pork buns to fill our stomachs, and then bought two basketballs and two knit bags. We put the basketballs in the knit bags, tied them in front of our chests, and gave all our remaining money to a boatman, who took us across the sea as far as he could at night. We planned to swim the rest of the way to Hong Kong waters using the basketballs as flotation devices, and then we would float and wait for dawn, hoping the Hong Kong Coast Guard would find us and take us to a refugee camp."

Gao Hong and Daffodil listened as if hearing a grizzly passage in a fairy tale. "Can basketballs keep you afloat in the ocean?"

"What else could we use? So many people wanted to cross the waters to Hong Kong and it was considered a crime of treason! All floating devices were controlled, and nobody could buy life preservers or life jackets without official papers! If we tried to buy one, we'd be certain to attract the notice of the police!"

"What would happen if you got caught in the sea?"

"Getting caught meant death. We could die in so many ways — drowning, exhaustion, hypothermia, sharks or being shot! The Chinese coastal police patrolled back and forth with search lights. Anything moving got a magazine of bullets! Just as we were about to reach Hong Kong waters, a searchlight scanned over us! Police horns started to blow and the light fixed on us. Other police boats were rushing over and bullets were flying over our heads and hitting the water around us! I was struck in the arm, but Tiger swam and pulled me along with all his strength. Luckily, a Hong Kong Coast Guard boat was right across the line. They couldn't come over to the Chinese side to get us, but they threw us two life preservers on long ropes and pulled us over. That's how we narrowly escaped death and made it to Hong Kong."

"What happened then? How did you survive in Hong Kong?"

Tiger said, "First, we were sent to the hospital to take care of our injuries, and then we were sent to the refugee camp. The refugee camp was full of people who had fled from the mainland at the risk of death, and everyone with a jaw-dropping story. The camp provided three meals a day, tents to sleep in, and help getting IDs and finding jobs."

"How could a capitalist society be so kind?" Daffodil wondered incredulously. "We've always been told that all capitalists are evil and that none of us would survive a day in capitalism!"

"They're extremely charitable and very humane!" Tiger said. "I first found work doing hard labor as a porter at the loading docks. Your cousin Lan started by washing dishes in a restaurant. Even with such hard work, we were so happy! We had enough food and there was no more running or hiding. We didn't have to watch over our shoulders anymore, we had a tent to sleep in at night, and we were earning money! We felt so blessed! We'd have been perfectly happy to live like that for the rest of our lives. Later, we saved enough money to rent a small room in a cheap neighborhood and moved out of the refugee camp. We both worked in restaurants; I did hard labor, and your cousin Lan washed dishes. Gradually, we learned Cantonese and started serving tables. Working twelve hours a day felt like nothing. We were full of energy and so grateful!"

"Do you still work in restaurants now?" Gao Hong asked.

"Later, we saved enough to start a small business selling household items, but it wasn't profitable, so we went back to the restaurants. This time, we didn't serve tables but did waste management. This dirty, hard work gave us an idea! One day, your cousin Lan said, 'These leftovers and food scraps make great fertilizer.' I remembered making compost into organic fertilizer on the mountain with my father, so I made this into a business. I began by collecting organic waste from the streets and selling it to compost factories. Later, I opened my own factory, and the business grew. Now, most of Southeast Asia's organic fertilizers are produced by our company. We're one of the top companies in Hong Kong!"

Gao Hong and Daffodil smiled happily, "That's incredible! How wonderful for you after all you've been through!"

Gao Hong asked, "Aren't you afraid of being persecuted? Another round of killing the rich and robbing them of their wealth?"

"Hong Kong is a safe society governed by the rule of law. Private property is protected by law. The wealthier you are, the better. No one kills the rich," Tiger said. "Not only are we safe in Hong Kong, but when we return to the mainland, we're classified as overseas compatriots. Officials greet us with smiles and nods, hoping we'll invest money here! We're no longer fugitives but honored guests! What a world!"

Gao Lan sneered, "Damn them! They killed and robbed our family, and now they act as if nothing happened! Invest? If I invest, it will be to rebuild the Gao family's ancestral home and shrine! I'll make them kneel and kowtow to our ancestors! I'll reclaim Tiger's mountain! Damn it, the Gao family isn't extinct yet, and even if only a woman is left, she'll fight those bastards to the end!"

"Keep your voice down!" Gao Hong said nervously. Daffodil also looked very uncomfortable.

"HongGe, come back to the Northeast with us. Let's visit the Gao family's ancestral home!" Gao Lan said.

"Yes, let's go back to see the mountain my father left me! We should visit their graves. It's really the Gao family's land!" Tiger said.

Gao Hong said, "I've dreamed of going back. I want to take Nanny Wu's ashes back and bury her in our family cemetery."

They took out Gao Hong's childhood otter fur coat and the Crimson Eyed Buddha that had been kept at the bottom of the chest all those years. Tiger said, "Brother, this otter fur coat is our lifetime pledge. It's the bond that my father set between us!" Gao Lan gently touched the crystal-clear Crimson-eyed Buddha and said, "I thought I'd never see it again. Our eldest uncle slipped it into auntie's pocket as he was dragged away to be executed. Auntie gave it to my mother before she died. My mother guarded it with her life! She handed it to me on her deathbed. As long as the Crimson Eyed Buddha is with us, the Gao family will never fall."

Gao Hong said, "Unfortunately, the old photo you gave me is lost." He glanced at Daffodil as he said this.

Gao Lan said, "A lost photo is OK. I'm here now, aren't I? I think the Crimson Eyed Buddha took the photo away so I could come to you in its place. Loss brings gain, departure brings return, it's all true!" Hearing this, Gao Hong finally felt at peace with the lost photo.

It was late at night, and Gao Hong, Daffodil, Tiger and Gao Lan were all exhausted. They lay down together, fully dressed, on Gao Hong and Daffodil's bed as there was no guest space in the house. Gao Hong fell into a deep sleep, feeling a profound sense of peace and satisfaction, knowing that the people he had been worried about for years were safe and right beside him, snoring lightly.

Daffodil, however, lay awake. The night felt like a dizzying dream. She finally understood why Gao Hong treasured that otter fur coat so much, why he'd given their entire savings to his cousin behind her back, why he'd never mentioned his cousin's whereabouts, why there had never been a letter from his cousin all these years, and why Gao Hong would get furious whenever she brought up his cousin in public. Daffodil regretted the trouble she'd caused Gao Hong over the years because of Gao Lan, and she felt sad that Gao Hong had never told her all of this, leaving her heartbroken for so long. How much can men keep inside? she thought sadly. Why couldn't he let me share his burdens?

At that moment, Daffodil especially missed her mother, whose words came back to her one by one. Was it really as her mother had said, that she'd brought trouble on herself by not knowing her place and speaking carelessly, causing Gao Hong not to trust her and leading to all this hurt and distress?

(78) BACK AT THE GAO COMPOUND

Through the oval-shaped window of the airplane, Gao Hong looked out on the vast plains and mountains of Northeastern China. This journey home was something he'd been yearning for. "Dear ancestors and my dear home, do you know that your boy and girl are about to return? Papa, Nana, First Uncle, First Aunt, Second Uncle, Second Aunt, Father, Mother, Mother Lingzhi, Cousin Quan, Cousin Yu, Cousin Lin, Cousin Ning, Nanny Wu, do you know that your HongGe and Lan are coming back?"

In Gao Hong's hands was the urn containing Nanny Wu's ashes. That saintly woman had tenaciously raised the only remaining male descendant of the Gao family and had been a mother to Gao Hong throughout those years of poverty-ridden political hostility. Gao Hong was determined to bury her as one would a mother and put her to rest in his ancestral cemetery. "Nanny Wu, HongGe is bringing you back to the Gao compound. Are you happy?"

Sitting next to Gao Hong was his elder daughter, Jasmine, whom he'd decided to bring along on this trip home. He wanted the ancestors to see the fourth generation of the Gao family, and for eighteen-year-old Jasmine to know her father's roots and see the home of her ancestors.

The pain that had been untouchable, the family history once too dangerous to mention, the longing that had once made him wake up crying deep in the night, and the all-but-forgotten grandeur of the Gao compound were all about to reappear, to be revisited, experienced and unveiled. Turning to Jasmine beside him, Gao Hong said, "Jasmine, let me tell you the story of your grandfather...."

When they got off the plane, two cars from the city's Overseas Chinese Affairs Office were waiting to pick them up. At that time, China was hot on economic reform, and government officials were rated by how much economic progress they brought to their districts. Attracting overseas capitalists to invest in their districts was the quickest way to boost the local economy and please their higher-ups. Local officials all jumped at anyone coming from outside of China, especially someone with the kind of money Tiger and Gao Lan had. Upon hearing that Tiger and Gao Lan were coming home to visit, local officials took care of everything to ensure they have a good experience.

The cars took Gao Hong, Jasmine, Tiger and Gao Lan to the city's most luxurious hotel. Early the next morning, someone from the Overseas Chinese Affairs office came over and said, "Ms. Gao, Mr. Li, do you have plans for today? If not, our city leaders would like to take you to visit our special economic zone. We hope you can give us some suggestions and opinions on the reconstruction of your hometown!"

Gao Lan hated these people who were so greedy and eager to attract investment for their own political gain. She said, "There's no rush for the tour. We came back to contribute to the construction of our hometown. Tell your city leaders that we're planning to invest heavily in this city, but it's not because we can't invest elsewhere. We chose this city because our ancestors are here. If you show respect to our ancestors, everything will be easy. Let's see if your city leaders take our ancestors seriously. We want to hold a formal ceremony at our ancestral cemetery."

The Overseas Chinese Affairs Office staff quickly jumped into action. Before long, three brand-new cars arrived at the hotel, and several official-looking people got out. They quickly walked up to Gao Lan and Gao Hong and shook hands, and even bowed to Jasmine. They introduced themselves: One was the deputy mayor in charge of the economy, another was the municipal Party secretary, the third was the director of the Overseas Chinese Affairs Office, and another was the director of the economic development zone. They brought incense, offerings, candles and other items needed for the ancestor worship ceremony. "The cars and supplies are ready, and we've informed the local government in Gao Village to assist in any way they can with your ancestor worship. This is an honor for Gao Village and our city!" they said with beaming faces.

The group first went to the ancestral cemetery behind the Gao compound, where the worship ceremony had already been set up, complete with incense tables and candles. Gao Hong, Gao Lan, Tiger and Jasmine solemnly knelt down and paid respects to their ancestors.

Then Gao Lan turned and said, "Since municipal officials are here, shouldn't you also pay tribute to the ancestors of the people to show that you take this seriously?"

Gao Lan expected the officials to make excuses not to participate, but to her surprise, they agreed immediately and knelt down to kowtow to the Gao ancestors. Gao Lan and Gao Hong exchanged glances, both sneering silently.

"These spineless wretches!" They thought, "They're not humans but just a pack of animals wagging their tails to their master. At the master's command, they could massacre an entire family, and with another command, they could kneel and kowtow to the same family they massacred." Gao Lan and Gao Hong turned her heads away in disgust and walked towards the Gao family compound.

The mottled walls and faded tiles showed the passage of time, but the stately, solemn and dignified glory of the Gao family compound remained undiminished. The wood burning stove in the gatekeeper's room looked as if it had just brewed tea for guests. The corridor leading to the inner courtyard seemed to echo with the laughter of maids chasing each other. The grand hall in the main courtyard seemed to still carry the scent from Papa and Nana's pipes, and the gate of the third courtyard seemed to have just been smashed open by Qiu Jiefang and his armed men...Gao Hong walked along, telling Jasmine, "This was my home when I was a child, the home of your ancestors."

Gao Lan turned to the city officials and said, "I've decided. My first investment project will be the restoration of the Gao compound! The Gao compound is a precious cultural heritage with significant cultural and tourism value. After restoring it to its former glory, the Gao family compound can be opened as a museum for visitors from all over. This is an excellent tourism project." Gao Lan's words drew enthusiastic applause and cheers from all the officials.

In the afternoon, Gao Lan and Tiger suggested visiting the mountain behind Gao Village. Gao Lan decided to take over the mountain for multiple projects such as ginseng harvesting, mountain produce collection and a tourism resort. "But let me be clear, once we take over this mountain, it's ours. We decide how it's managed and who gets access to it." The officials readily agreed.

In the following days, with the assistance of the local government, Nanny Wu was buried in the Gao family ancestral cemetery. New graves were also built for the Gao family patriarch Gao Liancai, the matriarch Mrs. Gao, the eldest son Gao Zhanwen, second son Gao Zhanwu, third son Gao Zhanren, the wives of the three sons, and the deceased children – Quan, Yu, Lin and Ning.

With the assistance of the local government, Gao Hong also found Zhao'er and Cai Xia, the servant and maid who had saved his life and helped him escape the bloodbath when he was six years old. They were now very old and living in a small farmhouse. When Gao Hong, Tiger, Gao Lan and Jasmine walked in and introduced themselves, Zhao'er and Cai Xia cried out, "HongGe! It's HongGe! And Miss Lan! Mr. Tiger! You're still alive?!"

Gao Hong and Gao Lan quickly helped Zhao'er and Cai Xia to their seats and brought Jasmine over to meet them.

Cai Xia held Jasmine's hand and said, "This girl is so pretty! And she's a college student? That's wonderful! Master Gao and Mistress Gao would be so proud! I always thought HongGe should have a son to carry on the family line, but this girl brings honor to the Gao ancestors just the same!"

Zhao'er and Cai Xia's two sons, Zhao Guodong and Zhao Guoliang, also came over to greet the visitors. The two sons were preparing to start a township enterprise. Gao Lan said, "Perfect timing. You can manage my two projects: The Gao family compound restoration can be managed by Guodong, and the mountain resort can be managed by Guoliang. You two elders can be consultants for the Gao family compound. Make sure it's rebuilt as it was!"

Cai Xia said, "See, girls can glorify their families just as boys can!"

Most of the old residents of the Gao compound had passed away. Even Mr. Ge from Ciji House was dead and gone. Wolf Hair Xu had flourished for a while after land reform and became a county official, but he'd been beaten to death during the Cultural Revolution. Qiu Jiefang was also overthrown during the Cultural Revolution and committed suicide in despair. His uncle Qiu Erguo's family now lived in poverty. Their children had gone to seek opportunities in the city, leaving only Qiu Erguo and his wife, who were bedridden.

Back at the hotel, Gao Hong, Jasmine, Gao Lan and Tiger sat down for dinner together. Gao Hong said, "You two are investing a lot of money here. Why don't you come back and settle here?"

Tiger said, "I'll rebuild the graves of my father, mother and brother, and I'll come back to visit and pay respects, but we won't live here."

Gao Lan said, "HongGe, don't be naive. Look at these sons of bitches. They used to wield knives against us. Why? Money! Now they flatter us. Why? Money! For the same reason, they can change sides again. Can you trust these bastards? We won't stay here, and you shouldn't either!"

Gao Hong said, "That's right, we won't stay here. We live in Beijing, and it's good there." "You still don't get it," Gao Lan said. "I'm talking about leaving mainland China!"

"What? Where can we go? You're talking nonsense." Gao Hong shook his head.

Gao Lan looked at Jasmine and said, "I've been observing her over the past few days. My niece is a smart girl and has a lot of potential. If you trust me, I'll find a way to send her to study in the United States. When your second daughter grows up, she can go too. When both girls succeed in the US, you two can move over and live there."

Gao Hong laughed, "Sure! Why don't you send her to the moon or Mars instead? Wouldn't that be even better? Hahaha..."

"I'm serious! Don't treat it like a joke," Gao Lan said. "I know it's not easy to go a foreign land. It takes a lot of motivation and hard work. As her aunt, I won't take on everything. That would be spoiling the child. I'll help build the bridge, but Jasmine has to apply to schools and scholarships by herself. If the scholarship isn't enough, she has to work part-time. I'll only step in if she's in a life-or-death situation. That way, she'll grow independent and have a promising future. I won't cripple her growth by providing everything for her. Jasmine, do you want to study in the United States?"

Jasmine had never thought about it before, but she felt a tidal wave of excitement washing over her and said, "I do!"

"Good. Auntie will buy you some books from Hong Kong and send you some English study tapes. Study hard and take the TOEFL exam. Let Auntie see how you score. If you do well, let me know, and we'll discuss the next step," Gao Lan said.

Jasmine couldn't immediately process everything, but she suddenly felt a surge of excitement, joy, hope and energy! Going to the United States to study, to travel far away, to start a new life, to experience a foreign land and exotic culture she had read about in literature, to explore the world, and to fly on her own wings – wasn't that what she had always dreamed of? She said, "Auntie, I'll take the test!"

A week later, TOEFL study materials arrived from Hong Kong. Jasmine had never heard of the TOEFL exam before and had no idea that it was the test that all foreign applicants needed to take in order to apply to American colleges. At that time, the perfect score for TOEFL was 660. Three months later, Jasmine took the test and scored an astonishing 644!

(79) CLOSURE

While waiting for the results of her applications to American universities, Jasmine started her studies at Beijing Normal College. She joyfully moved into the dormitory on the first day of school like a bird flying out of a cage. The feeling of leaving home was so wonderful! Jasmine felt that the sky was bright, and everything was fresh and full of vitality. She simply couldn't understand why other girls in the dormitory were homesick. She was so happy that she wouldn't go home unless she absolutely had to, even though her home was only thirty minutes by bike from the college.

Gao Hong and Daffodil had been afraid that Jasmine would have boy trouble, so they always tried to make her think she wasn't beautiful. "Scarily tall " and "skinny stick" were terms they often used to describe her. If neighbors or colleagues said, "Your daughter is beautiful," Gao Hong and Daffodil would quickly respond, "What? No! She's silly and awkward!" They even told Jasmine, "Remember, you are ugly. No matter what you wear, you won't look good!" Growing up, Jasmine always felt incredibly unattractive and was ashamed of her tall and slender body. Especially during puberty, when she developed earlier and more maturely than other girls, she always want to hide behind a tree, and she walked around with her head down, chest in and back hunched, wishing she could shrink away and disappear. However, during her senior summer and after starting college, eighteen-year-old Jasmine gradually realized from the compliments of her peers and the looks from boys that she was actually pretty.

Jasmine's departure thoroughly triggered Daffodil's maternal instincts, and instead of being hysterical or indifferent as usual, she became a nagging, overly protective mother. The first night Jasmine spend in the dormitory, Daffodil cried all night. She worried that Jasmine might be cold and wouldn't know to put on more clothes. She worried that Jasmine might not like the school food, that she might get up too late in the morning and miss breakfast. She worried that Jasmine might fall off the top bunk at night, or kick off her blanket in her sleep and catch a cold. The next morning, Daffodil had Gao Hong ride a bike to deliver food to Jasmine and find out what she had eaten the previous day.

When Gao Hong arrived at the school and found Jasmine, he handed her the food Daffodil had prepared and asked, "What did you eat all day yesterday?" This question made Jasmine recall that she'd eaten breakfast at home, then moved in to the dormitory, had some candies at noon, and then completely forgot about dinner. But she couldn't tell her father that, so she vaguely replied, "Uh, some, celery."

Gao Hong asked, "Was it stir-fried celery? Was there any meat? Did you have it with rice? What else did you eat?"

Jasmine quickly grabbed the food container and ran off, saying, "I'm late! Gotta go!"

When Gao Hong got home and told Daffodil, she cried even more, "Just some lousy celery! Not even any meat!"

But Jasmine didn't care about food at all. She was enjoying the freedom and happiness of living independently, so much so that even if she had nothing to eat, she was still happy! On the third day after school started, she heard someone call her name outside her window. She opened the window and asked, "Who is it?" A voice from outside replied, "ASC."

Jasmine chuckled. It was Xiao Bing, the nutcase she hadn't seen all summer. Jasmine had just come back from taking a shower, and her hair was still wet. She quickly towel-dried it and thought, "It's OK if my hair isn't done. It's just Xiao Bing, no big deal." So she went downstairs without bothering to fix her hair.

In the orange glow of the streetlight, Jasmine appeared in a floral dress, her damp hair draped over her shoulders and the light from behind forming a golden halo around her. Xiao Bing stood still, mesmerized. Was this beautiful girl with flowing long hair and a swaying dress really Jasmine? Gone were the uneven short hair, baggy pants and worn-out clothes; even the big shabby shoes had been replaced by pretty sandals. At this magical moment, the image of Jasmine imprinted itself in Xiao Bing's mind for decades to come.

Finally, Jasmine saw Xiao Bing and walked over with a smile, "Hey, ASC, what are you staring at? Don't you recognize me?"

Xiao Bing smiled awkwardly. Other girls were usually a bit shy, flustered and incoherent around Xiao Bing, but Jasmine was completely relaxed and entirely herself. When she was happy, she would talk non-stop, and when she wasn't, she wouldn't speak at all, or if she did, her sentences were straight and to the point. Xiao Bing remembered that time in high school when he was worried about Jasmine and followed her from a distance, and she turned around and said, "I won't kill myself, if that's what you are worried about." Xiao Bing felt he'd never met a girl like her.

"Crossing the street has really made a difference; you're so pretty." Xiao Bing said tentatively. Any other girl would have been flustered upon hearing Xiao Bing say this, but Jasmine said with feigned outrage, "Oh, Xiao Bing! How dare you! Are you saying I wasn't pretty before?!"

Xiao Bing quickly said, "No, no, I meant you're even prettier now." Jasmine laughed happily. Xiao Bing thought, "I'm really no match for her."

They walked slowly along the school's tree-lined paths, chatting comfortably. Suddenly, Jasmine told Xiao Bing, "I won't be here for long. I'll be going to the United States soon."

Xiao Bing almost fell down with the bike he was pushing along. "What? Really? Why? When are you leaving?"

Jasmine said, "I don't know exactly when yet. I want to go far away, to a new place where no one knows me, and start over. My aunt helped me with schools, but I'm not going to the ones she helped me get into. I'm going to a school I got into by myself. I also don't want my aunt's money; I'll earn my own. I want to be completely independent and manage on my own two feet!"

Xiao Bing lowered his head and didn't speak. Jasmine said, "Oh, I just remembered, I have dorm duty. I need to be upstairs! Got to go, bye!" With that, Jasmine ran off.

Xiao Bing stood there for a long time: "Is she deliberately ignoring me? Or has it never occurred to her that I care deeply about her?"

A few days later, Jasmine was reading a novel in the dormitory when a girl came in and said, "Jasmine, there's a guy out front looking for you." Jasmine closed the book and thought, "Is Xiao Bing here again? What does he want?"

Jasmine went downstairs and looked around, but there was no sign of Xiao Bing. She lowered her head and thought for a moment, then looked around again. That Xiao Bing! Is he playing hide-and-seek with me? Suddenly, a boy standing right in front of her said, "Jasmine."

Jasmine jumped out of her skin! When she looked closely, she couldn't believe her eyes – it was Lu Qiao, the incredibly handsome boy she'd a crush on and who'd hated her after the journal incident in high school! Jasmine was completely dazed.

"You, you, are, Lu, Lu, Qiao?" Jasmine cursed herself under her breath! After such a long, deep crush, the first words she spoke to him were so stuttering and stupid!

Lu Qiao said, "I'm going to Guangzhou for college. Our school starts late, so I'm leaving tomorrow. I came to say goodbye."

"Say, say, goodbye? To, to, me?" Jasmine cursed herself even harder! Why was she still stuttering and talking like an idiot?!

Lu Qiao took a neatly folded piece of paper from his pocket and said, "I wrote you a letter, but I thought it would be better to give it to you in person. Here, take it. I'm leaving."

Jasmine held the paper and stood there frozen, watching Lu Qiao ride away on his bicycle until he disappeared down the campus path. Then she remembered the paper in her hand and quickly opened it:

Hello, Jasmine,

I'm very sorry that I didn't have much interaction with you during high school. I know you are a very smart and kind person. We were all so young in high school and sometimes did things we regretted later. Don't take the gossip of classmates to heart, and don't worry about what the teachers said. When Mrs. Qi talked to me, she actually didn't say much, and I didn't really care about what she said. I apologize for resenting you at the time. It was very wrong of me. I regret it very much. I'm sorry for the psychological strain I must have caused you in high school. I hope you can accept my apologies and forgive me.

410

We are all eighteen now, with a vast world of possibilities ahead of us. I hope you can forget any unpleasantness, let go of the past, and embrace youth and the future. I hope we can be friends.

Sincerely,
Lu Qiao

Jasmine leaned against the wall, overcome by the immense relief Lu Qiao's letter brought her. She felt as if a heavy burden had been lifted from her shoulders. She suddenly felt that maybe she could be a normal girl after all, just like any other. Maybe she could really have a new start and be happy. Jasmine's four-year crush on Lu Qiao ended at that moment, replaced by respect and gratitude toward him.

Thinking of her imminent departure for the United States, Jasmine felt a sense of liberation. Holding Lu Qiao's note, she sat alone on a campus bench, thinking that perhaps she could leave behind all the pain, stress, loneliness and awkwardness of high school. Perhaps she could forgive her parents for their roughness and mishandling of things. Only by letting go and forgiving could she free herself from that painful period, come out of her cocoon, transform into a butterfly, and fly high in a greater, wider sky.

(80) FLY HIGH

During the process of applying to American universities, Jasmine met many young people who were on the same path, just like the lyrics from a song: "There will be a day, there will be a day, we will fly to the skies beyond the skies..." In the early 1990s, many young people in Beijing aimed to soar beyond the skies they knew, to reach higher and farther horizons and to see a bigger world.

As the day of departure approached, Jasmine went alone to her grandmother's grave. Her beloved Grandma was one of the many ordinary yet extraordinary women of North China. She was illiterate all her life, and the trajectory of her life extended only from the great Baiyang Lake to Beijing. She experienced wars, famines, turmoil and hardship, raising seven children and numerous grandchildren with her loving and diligent hands. Grandma had been Jasmine's safe haven during her childhood and teenage years, and the source of her love for life. Jasmine placed flowers on her grandmother's grave and softly said, "Grandma, I've grown up and I'm leaving. Don't worry, I'll be fine and I won't disappoint you. I'll come back to see you!"

Her grandfather, Yixin, now a retired old man, sat alone at home, dozing in his thick down jacket. When Jasmine walked in, he opened his eyes and said, "Jasmine? I heard you're going to America!" Jasmine replied, "Yes, Grandpa, I'm leaving."

Yixin asked, "When will you come back?"

Jasmine held back her tears and said, "Grandpa, I'll be back in two years." She knew this was unlikely, but what else could she say to him?

"Grandpa will be waiting for you." Yixin shed his tears. He understood that one plane ticket would cost most of the family's savings, and he'd never heard of anyone coming back after just two years after going to America. He knew he'd never see Jasmine again.

Preparing for the trip and saying goodbye to classmates and friends kept Jasmine constantly busy, and she was seldom home except at nighttime. Daffodil felt anxious. Her daughter was going so far away for God-knew-how-long. Her departure was imminent and she wasn't home much, leaving Daffodil no chance for proper conversation and advice. Daffodil recalled how Jasmine had been sent to her grandmother's home as a baby and grew up there until she was seven. After she returned, they hadn't been close. Daffodil remembered the years of internal and external troubles, the constant fights with Gao Hong and her harsh treatment of Jasmine. She thought sorrowfully, "No wonder this child isn't close to me, not even sitting with me for a few minutes before leaving home." Daffodil often cried, waiting at home for Jasmine to return.

As soon as Jasmine came back, Daffodil jumped to her feet. Unable to control her sharp tongue, Daffodil snapped, "Why are you back so late? Where have you been? You're never home! Busy with what? Your wings aren't even fully grown, and you already don't want your parents?" Daffodil's harsh words concealed her deep love, always coming out as complaints and sarcasm.

Jasmine was so annoyed that she wished she could leave for America right this minute. "Oh, Mom! I still need to buy a few books. Bye." Daffodil was exasperated. She had prepared a big meal, hoping that Jasmine would eat well before going to America, but her heartless daughter had left without even glancing at it! How frustrating!

Daqing was at Daffodil's house at the time. He sat down and said, "If she doesn't eat it, I will!" He picked up a pair of chopsticks and started eating. "Don't be mad. Think about when you insisted on quitting school and going to the factory at fourteen. Did you listen to anyone? How much did you upset Mom back then? Anyway, Jasmine is an adult now. She should go out and explore. Each generation moves forward, and that's how we progress."

Although Daffodil knew her brother was right, she still said, "Hmph! It's easy for you to talk since it's not your own child!"

Daqing pointed his chopsticks at Daffodil. "You're ruining your life with that mouth of yours." Gao Hong heard this, put down his chopsticks, poured Daqing a drink and said, "Brother, drink up!"

Gao Hong wasn't feeling very happy, either. As Jasmine prepared to leave home, he increasingly saw himself in her – those melancholy eyes, that solemn face, an exact replica. But why should she have the pain he'd had? He had worked hard, endured humiliation and preserved a difficult marriage for the sake of Jasmine and Lily. Yet Jasmine always had a pained expression, like his own in childhood. Gao Hong deeply regretted not keeping Jasmine with him when she was small, and not treating her better. Thinking of his harsh words and beatings over the years, he felt a deep pain. He hoped Jasmine would eventually understand that despite his flaws, he always tried his best to be a good father to her.

Gao Hong borrowed a minivan from work to load Jasmine's two pieces of checked luggage and one carry-on bag. Jasmine eagerly jumped into the front passenger seat beside the driver, her face full of excitement. Daffodil, looking near tears, sat in the back.

On the way to the airport, Daffodil kept saying, "Call us when you get there, don't worry about the cost. If you miss home, call us." Jasmine smiled, thinking, I won't miss home. Daffodil tried to give Jasmine a newly knitted vest, but Jasmine refused. "It's too heavy. I can't carry it. And it's so flashy, I don't want it." Daffodil wanted to say more, but seeing Jasmine looking out the window, lost in thought, she held back her words and quietly wiped her tears.

The Beijing Capital Airport was bustling with large screens, announcements and countless service counters, and Daffodil felt overwhelmed. She'd never been to an airport before. Jasmine, eyes wide with excitement, looked for her flight on the big screen. Once she found it, she pushed her luggage cart and ran while calling out, "Mom, Dad, I'm going!"

She ran to the service desk and handed over her ticket and passport to the staff. Then she realized that only passengers could enter, and her parents had already been left behind. Jasmine wanted to turn back to find them, but the staff handed her the boarding pass and directed her to check her luggage. After handling everything, the staff pointed to the left and said, "Please go to Gate 32." Jasmine headed in that direction. Looking back, she could no longer see her parents.

Years later, Daffodil was still deeply saddened, "That heartless child, such a cruel child! She ran off with the cart without even looking back at me!"

Following the signs, Jasmine walked toward Gate 32. In the distance, she saw a tall, familiar figure. "How? Why is he here?" Xiao Bing stood there with his hands in his pockets, watching Jasmine approach. Jasmine asked, "What are you doing here?"

Xiao Bing replied, "My classmate's mom works here and let me in. I came to see you off."

Jasmine laughed loudly, "Oh, you're always so meddlesome! No need! You came all this way..." Xiao Bing's gaze made her swallow her words.

Xiao Bing looked intently at Jasmine. She went quiet, avoiding his gaze, and smiled awkwardly. Xiao Bing felt a surge of tenderness: "She's finally shy in front of me for the first time, not just treating me like a buddy. But this precious first time is happening just as she's leaving."

Jasmine said, "I... I have to board now. Goodbye."

Xiao Bing smiled and said, "We were once classmates across desks, then across the street, and now we'll be classmates across the Pacific. I can't keep up with you."

Jasmine laughed, "I didn't ask you to keep up."

Xiao Bing said, "Who knows what the future holds. We will meet again. Maybe one day, you'll have to keep up with me. Go ahead and board now, or the overhead bins will be full." Xiao Bing checked Jasmine's seat number, then asked a few passengers who were waiting to board. Finally, he patted a young man's shoulder and said, "Hey brother, my friend's seat is near yours. Could you help her lift her luggage into the overhead bin? I'm afraid her thin arms won't manage it. Thanks, man!"

Jasmine muttered, "There's no need! Really! I don't even know him!" But Xiao Bing gestured for her to stay quiet. He looked at her for a long time and said, "Take care!" Then he watched her walk away.

Just as her father, Gao Hong, was the first in the family to leave the Northeast, Jasmine was the first to head to America. Her ancestors went from prosperity and wealth to being plundered and killed. Her father, once a talented and ambitious young man, was struck down to a life of hardship as a struggling laborer. Jasmine herself had a painful childhood and youth and once contemplating suicide, but she had rebuilt her dreams and was now flying towards a land full of possibilities.

As the plane soared into the blue sky, Jasmine looked at the vast land beneath her. For generations since the beginning of time, this sky was their sky, this land was their land. The northern plains of China was where her ancestors were buried and her family lived. Running in her blood was the grandeur of the Gao compound, the beauty of the great Baiyang Lake, her Papa's courage, her Grandma's love, her father's intelligence and her mother's fierceness. All of this was her treasured inheritance and her eternal wealth.

She placed her hand on her chest, feeling a cool smoothness against her skin. She was wearing the family heirloom, the Crimson Eyed Buddha jade pendant, which her father had put around her neck. This ancestral treasure had witnessed her family going from wealth and prosperity to plundering and massacre. It had seen her father's struggles and his resilience to survive. Now it would accompany Jasmine to new horizons, and it would continue to witness the new chapters of life in the next generation of the Gao family.

Jasmine's departure

Jessica Zhang is an award-winning author whose realistic fiction captures the beauty, struggle, and resilience of ordinary lives. Her work has been honored with multiple literary awards, including the Taiwan Overseas Chinese Federation's Outstanding Fiction Award and the Chinese American Librarians Association's Best Book Award.

A member of several international writers' associations, Jessica has shared her stories and insights at events hosted by the Harvard University Chinese Culture Forum, Boston Public Library, and Queens Library in New York.

Her life bridges China and the United States, a journey that shapes her writing with cultural richness and emotional depth. In addition to her novels, Jessica is an avid visual artist who illustrates her own books. She resides in the United States with her husband and continues to write stories that inspire readers worldwide.

Her works include *The Crimson Eyed Buddha* (2017), *The Land of Sorrow* (2020), and *Northern Maple* (2018), which are held in the collections of leading libraries such as Columbia, Harvard, the University of Pennsylvania, and Princeton.

EDITOR'S NOTE

Stacy Mosher

As soon as I started reading Jessica Zhang's novel, Silent Inheritance, I knew it was something special. Here the history of China during the twentieth century is laid out in the story of several generations of a Chinese family, starting with subsistence-level farmers on one side, and wealthy landowners on the other side.

The two families eventually come together through the marriage of Gao Hong and Daffodil, but this is no fairy tale ending. At this point, each of the original families has experienced war, revolution and inhuman slaughter, and further hardship lies ahead as the newlyweds face the chaos, violence and mental oppression of the Cultural Revolution launched by Mao Zedong.

Born in this time of constant threat and struggle, Gao Hong and Daffodil's daughter Jasmine navigates the tortured relationship between her parents to eventually forge her own future in the promise and hope of post-Mao China and beyond.

This is a lot to cover in one novel, but Jessica's skill is displayed in her use of vignettes to illustrate the challenges of these decades through the experiences and feelings of her characters. Informed by actual events and personal knowledge, Jessica employs nuance, realism and sympathy in depicting how shattered dreams can warp the heart, but also how human kindness can shine through in the midst of brutality. Often coming close to succumbing to despair, her characters summon the courage to emerge from their trauma, battered and bruised but ready to face the future under whatever terms are available to them.

In this respect, Silent Inheritance is not just a story of China, but of human resilience, and of locating the source of security and strength that makes survival possible – the love and loyalty of those around us. It is a story that can inspire all of us in the uncertainty of the times we live in.